Die by Proxy

Benjamin Oneal

Benjamin Oneal

© 2020 Benjamin Oneal All Rights Reserved.

No part of this publication may be reproduced, stored in a retrieval system, or transmitted, in any form or by any means, electronic, mechanical, photocopying, recording, or otherwise, without the written permission of the author.

First published by Dog Ear Publishing

This book is printed on acid-free paper.

First Published in 2018

Published by Benjamin Oneal, Anderson, IN

Second Printing, 2020

ISBN: 978-1-7346368-4-0

Library of Congress Control Number: 2020904941

This book is a work of fiction. Places, events, and situations in this book are purely fictional and any resemblance to actual persons, living or dead, is coincidental.

Printed in the United States of America

Die by Proxy

I want to thank my wife Huong, for putting up with my long hours at the computer, my children, Lucas, Kimberly, Stacy, and Justin for being often reluctant sounding boards to help me work out problems with my stories, and my three wonderful grandchildren, Aria, Merrick, and Hannah who are responsible for keeping me young.

Special thanks to Autumn J. Conley, who worked her magic, and made me realize how important a good editor can be in bringing a story to life.

Other books by Benjamin Oneal

The Benjamin Kroh Series:

Die Laughing

Science Fiction:

The Serpent's Gift

PART ONE

Dangling the Carrot

Chapter 1

The first day of summer was still a few weeks away, but the early morning breeze that blew across Interstate 69, just a few miles west of Port Huron Michigan, was warm indeed. The crickets played their chirping symphony as the other creatures of the night joined them in serenade. Clouds shrouded the moon and stars, creating an almost unspoiled darkness, save for a few stubborn fireflies that insisted on shining brightly against the hazy canopy.

Perfect, he thought as he gazed up at the cosmos, before returning his attention to the child predator at his feet. "Eric Conrad, you are the worst kind of cancer." After a pause and a shake of his head, he continued, "No, to call you a cancer is to do that disease a great injustice. It sickens me to imagine the depths of your depravity." Mr. Smith pulled his hood off and squatted, till he was eye level with Mr. Conrad, the child predator, entirely naked, gagged with his own filthy sock, and tied to a fencepost. He was so close that the smell of Conrad's terror sweat overshadowed the scent of the wildflowers beyond the fence.

"Eric Conrad," Smith continued, "I frankly have no idea why any fair and just God would allow parasites like you to exist. It is entirely unfathomable to me to think that you or someone like you could possibly harm my children. Why? Why are you still here, still taking up space on this planet, using up oxygen you don't deserve to breathe? Don't get me wrong. I do not wish to act as the hand of God, nor to deny His sovereignty and wisdom, but for what you have done, you must die. Justice will be served here and now."

Mr. Smith knew that his speech was a little wordy and over the top, but he had worked on it for a week and was proud of his creation. He felt that the occasion needed some ceremony. At that moment, he decided that he would make this same speech at each of the coming child predator deaths.

There was very little traffic at two in the morning, when he first parked adjacent to the sign that read "Wadhams Road – 1 Mile," along the westbound lane. He made quick work of setting up the blind that effectively camouflaged him and kept him out of view of any nosy passersby. It was easy enough to pull the unconscious Conrad from the trunk and carry his limp, blanket-wrapped body the seventy feet, to the place where the man would spend the last moments of his perverted existence. Only after he had tied Conrad to the metal post, securely binding his arms by his side, did he use the smelling salts to wake the highly respected educator. The ammonia triggered the inhalation reflex, and the irritating gas that rushed into his nostrils jolted him awake abruptly; wide-eyed and foggy-brained, he did his best to determine answers to questions that were far beyond his knowing.

"Mr. Conrad, I hate to leave you, but I'm afraid it's time." Mr. Smith reached back and grabbed the heavy-duty loppers he'd retrieved from his trunk.

Conrad watched in horror as his capturer positioned the high-quality pruners around his wrist, just an inch above his hand, and then slowly tightened them to the point of being very uncomfortable.

"It makes me nauseous to think what these hands have touched, you sick motherfucker. How could you destroy their innocence, and force the little ones to see and know the darkest of humanity? How dare you corrupt them? Oh, what those poor little children must have experienced at your merciless, perverted hand," Smith said, shaking his head in disgust.

As Conrad's right hand separated from his arm, Conrad screamed into the fetid sock.

Crack!

Die by Proxy

The sound of breaking bones surprised Mr. Smith, and his repulsion over the act of cutting the man's hands off threatened to hijack his resolve. He wanted to run away, to just forget that any of it ever happened. Then the pain he'd dealt with for the past year pushed into his thoughts. His wife had left him and taken his children with her. His dreams of a bright future and a successful career were dashed by an unexpected, unwarranted demotion. Then, the most important person in his life, his father, died, putting the finishing touches on his miserable loneliness. It was those circumstances beyond his control that led him to that day, to the beginning of his mission. With all that agony on his mind, he forced himself to swallow the bile that rose in his throat and pushed back any thoughts of stopping. "One down, one to go," he said without a shred of doubt, then moved the loppers to the other arm.

Conrad struggled violently as the blades tightened on his wrist. Mr. Smith removed his left hand without a bit of mercy or care. As Conrad's blood drained from his arms, the pain became part of him, and his mind drifted to unconsciousness once again, in an effort to help him flee it.

When Smith realized his captive was dying faster than anticipated, he quickly held up a sandwich bag that contained a flash drive and smirked.

The dying man's eyes opened, redder and wider than before, and he stared at the plastic bag. All thoughts of pain and of his impending death left, and real fear and fury overtook his mind. Eric screamed into his gag, pleading for mercy; he did not ask to live but begged with his incomprehensible cries for the man to keep that evidence to himself.

Smith leaned closer, to whisper into Conrad's ear, "That's right, Eric. Everyone will know it all. Your co-workers, friends, and family will finally know who you truly were, and all the evil you inflicted. I believe your parents are still alive, aren't they? Won't Mommy and Daddy be pleased? Ellie, your beautiful wife, will cringe to know she's been intimate with such a monster. For the rest of her life, the poor woman will be left to wonder if you were thinking of those pre*adolescence* girls while you made love to her. Were you? Were you, you sick fuck?"

For an answer, Conrad only lowered his gaze.

"You know, sweet little Nicholas is only 8, far too young to understand, but I'm sure his classmates will remind him that his daddy liked to play nasty with the girls in his class. Kristin, on the other hand... Surely, she's had those special health classes in junior high already. She'll be a lamb to the slaughter, left with nowhere to hide. All her peers will mock and bully her, till her self-worth is forever sacrificed. Ah, the beauty of social media! Daddy's little girl will soon be a social *pariah, unable to look anyone in the eye for fear of the judgment she'll find there. I won't* be surprised if she turns to drugs or attempts suicide to escape the pain *you* caused."

Conrad took in every word, every harsh syllable, every threat, and he clearly felt the weight of their truth. Nothing would ever make up for what he had done to those innocent children, but Smith had to do something. Conrad's last thoughts would be of the pain and devastation he had caused, the torment that would forever linger for his loved ones he was about to leave behind. As Conrad thought on those macabre truths, the man's frightened eyes took on a blank stare of nothingness.

I must work fast, Smith told himself, realizing the coming of the impending dawn and the discovery of Conrad's death. In the silence, he could hear the blood dripping from the stumps and splattering into the puddles that were already on the ground. He placed Conrad's neatly folded clothes on his lap, with his wallet on top, and then placed the bagged flash drive in Conrad's severed right hand. In the dismembered left hand, he placed another bag, one that contained a written confession, typed on the dead man's computer and printed in the dead man's office. He set both hands atop the folded clothes, one on either side of the wallet, then leaned back to look at his display.

Pleased, he stuck his head out of the blind and saw no cars traversing I-69. Satisfied that he could make an unseen escape, he gathered up the camouflage blind and his loppers and headed toward his car. He quickly stowed his tools in the trunk, jumped in his car, and headed home.

Die by Proxy

* * *

How easy it was to place the cameras. The night before, after everyone left the school building, he broke into the school through a side door. He was a bit surprised that, in the world of today with school shootings becoming commonplace, the educational facility wasn't more secure. Mr. Smith felt a little unclean in Conrad's office, even though the place was spotless and carried the faint smell of pine. *I wonder if the nasty bastard ever does his dirty business, inside these walls, on one of these desks?* This thought made him grimace. *I suppose we'll find out now.*

He needed to watch the guy for a while, to determine his daily routine, so he positioned cameras to capture every angle of Conrad's office, and then casually left the way he came. The very next day, sitting just fifty yards away on the street next to the school parking lot, he witnessed far more than he ever wanted to.

As Smith stared at his laptop in his car, the handsome 50-year-old Conrad walked into his office and locked the door. First, he called his wife to let Ellie know he would be home in about an hour. "Yes, dear, I'll remember to pick up dog food." After that, he shuffled through some paperwork, finished his coffee, and turned on his computer.

Smith watched as Conrad logged on to his school computer and visited a few hardcore sites. He winced as he downloaded a particularly nasty selection of child porn. Finally, the teacher accessed a recording of himself with a young Asian girl who couldn't have been more than 8 or 9. Smith had to turn away as Conrad masturbated, watching what he forced that poor child to do. *Enough is enough,* thought Mr. Smith.

An hour later, Conrad was fully clothed again, like a respected member of society. He headed out the door, fully intent on stopping at the store for a bag of kibble for the family pet, but when the pervert neared his car, Mr. Smith exited his 2010 Ford van and made his move. Before Conrad knew what hit him, he had been Tasered, right after he pressed the key fob to unlock his car. The educator lay on the ground, confused and convulsing.

Mr. Smith was glad no one was within earshot, because the electric ticking of the Taser's electric pulses that had left Conrad shaking even more uncontrollably were louder than he expected. Once he was sure the noise would not attract any unwanted attention, since there was no one nearby, he continued to shock Conrad in short bursts, until he was sure his victim was in no condition to fight back.

Smith pulled the teacher into the van, secured his hands with plastic zip-ties, and then followed suit with his ankles. He zapped him once more and gave him enough Rohypnol to keep him unconscious for a while. Since it was his first effort at embarking on such a mission, he marked the time so he would have some idea of how long it took for the drug to take effect and how long the deviant remained unconscious. "I hope he's out at least long enough for us to get there," he muttered under his breath, and ultimately, he was.

Back in the present, Smith realized he still had some cleanup to do to ensure that no trail could lead to him. He smiled, basking in the glory of his perfect plan and how wonderfully it was going. He excelled at the details; that was after all, his forte. *I'll show them. They tried to break me, but they failed. In the end, I'll show them all!*

The Requiter? he considered as a moniker for himself, imagining it in print and recalling the definition he'd read: *"to avenge an insult or wrongdoing."* He was indeed an avenger; someone had to look out for the children. Not only that, but the name gave him power, as if he was a superhero, which he considered himself to be, whether the law thought so or not. *If nothing else, it is a chance to teach the world a new word. Nothing wrong with expanding their vocabulary, is there?* he thought with a chuckle. When it came down to it, he settled on simply Mr. Smith, the most common name in the U.S. In Mexico he would have been Martinez, and Nguyen would have suited him in 'Nam, but in the States, it had to be Smith. *I wonder if I could pass as Vietnamese.* He laughed and decided to get some rest as he waited for the show to begin.

Chapter 2

Jerry Benson, a retired postal worker, was ready to enjoy a very beautiful day, out on a drive with his wife Joanna, headed to Lansing to spend time with their grandkids. As they were about to pass the one-mile marker before Wadhams Road, Jerry squinted in concern at something alongside the road, something that caught him off guard. "What the...?" he muttered before he applied the brakes and pulled over as quickly and safely as he could. Then, he slowly backed his car along the shoulder, careful to stay as far away from the usually busy interstate as possible.

"What is it, Jerry?" Joanna asked, looking over at him wondering why he had done something so out of the ordinary. "Surely you can hold it till we find the next gas—"

"No, it's not that," he interrupted. "Just stay put. I want to check something out," he said.

Once he was even with the Wadhams Road sign, he stopped, opened his door, and stepped out. With one foot still in the car, he peered over the top of the car. He barely noticed moving his other leg from the car and standing on both feet. At first, he was sure it was an animal, but now he saw that it was a man.

"Jerry, what's going on?" Joanna demanded, moving her hand to open her door.

"Nothing!" he said hoping not to alarm his wife of thirty years. "Stay in the car...and lock the door," he cautioned his wife before he walked around to take a closer look. Once he reached the second metal post that held up the road sign, he could see that the stranger was covered in blood. "Call 911!" he shouted to his wife, careful not to touch anything. Jerry was an Investigation Discovery junkie, and he'd seen enough shows on the Justice Network to know he had to be very careful around a crime scene.

He followed his footsteps back to the car, so as not to disturb any other lingering prints or tire tracks. To other drivers along Interstate 69, he must have looked pretty silly, trying to keep his balance while tracing his path back to his car. He peeked in the passenger window and noticed that his wife was having quite a bit of trouble operating their new smartphone. He feigned disappointment, knocked on the window, and held his hand out for the gadget when she rolled the window down.

"I'm sorry," she said. "I just—"

"It's not that difficult, Joanna. Just give it," Jerry said. Then after a roll of his eyes, he turned to hide his own struggle in operating the modern device. He finally managed to pull up the buttons to dial a number and used the touchscreen to call for help.

Joanna listened as Jerry reported his findings, but not once did she look toward the gory scene where the dead man sat.

"Hi. This is Jerry Benson, and I, uh... Well, I was just heading to Lansing to see my grandkids, and I found a dead man. We're just out here along I-69. Yeah, there's blood everywhere, and I'm pretty sure it wasn't a car accident. I'm parked next to that sign that says, wait a minute." He moved to the back of the car where he could read the sign. "Yeah, it's the one mile to Wadhams Road sign, on westbound I-69, 'bout two miles outside Port Huron. Okay, I will."

He was told by the dispatcher to stay on the line until someone arrived to take his statement. A few minutes later, sirens could be heard, and flashing lights followed. Officer Chuck Davies of the Port Huron police was the first on the scene. After a brief conversation with Mr. Benson, he examined the body, very careful to not compromise the area. He was about to put fingers on the man's throat to check for a pulse he was sure was nonexistent when he noticed that the man's hands were no longer attached to his arms. Davies had served in Afghanistan, so the sight of dismembered limbs was not new to him, but this was different. There was no war here, nothing that could possibly justify the grotesque scene before him. *This guy wasn't just at the wrong place at the wrong time, not just a victim of our average psycho,* he reasoned. *No, this was...planned.* He backed away, tracing his own steps, fully aware that he was at a crime scene, the site of first-degree murder and not just some haphazard hit-and-run or a suicide.

Officer Aaron Lake was the next to arrive, and he kept the traffic rolling along as Davies began taping off the crime scene. Within a half-hour, they were joined by a State Police unit, two St. Clair County Sheriff's units, and two detectives from the Port Huron Police Department Major Crimes Unit.

Although the crime scene was technically within the jurisdiction of the State Police, they gladly passed the reins to the PHPD Major Crimes Unit. Lt. Archie Pembrook, a fit, forty-something widower, performed a quick once-over. Since he had to wait for the medical examiner, he used that time to speak with Mr. Benson, and then passed him over to another detective who took down his statement. After that, they sent him on his way.

Lt. Pembrook had seen some pretty gruesome things in his twenty years, but the severed hands setting in the victim's lap turned even his hardened stomach. He ordered his men to erect a barrier to keep the travelers from slowing and taking pictures, and he knew he had to get a handle on the crime scene before those vultures in the press captured any of it. Unfortunately, no matter how diligent his officers were at ordering the traffic to move along, it was quickly starting to pile up with curious onlookers, some even trying to snap pictures with their cell phones as they practiced the time honored art of rubbernecking.

Twenty minutes later, St. Clair County Medical Examiner James Post arrived, a balding, pudgy guy who liked to get right down to business. While his assistant took pictures, Post examined the body. "You might need this," he said, handing the bagged wallet to Pembrook. He then turned over the hand containing the confession, waited for it to be photographed, and put the baggie in an evidence bag. He repeated the process with the hand containing the flash drive, and once everything was photographed, bagged, and tagged, the body itself was photographed, bagged, and moved to his vehicle. Once the M.E. removed the body, the crime scene techs scoured the area for anything that might be connected to the murder.

While the medical examiner performed his duties, Lt. Pembrook carefully examined the wallet. Certain that the man on the fencepost was the same man who was smiling in the driver's license photo, he pulled out his phone and took a picture of the victim and the license for his own reference. "Eric Conrad, huh?" he muttered, certain he'd heard the name before. Then, suddenly, it hit him: The man worked at the school his grandson attended. In fact, he had just received an award as Educator of the Year or something like that. *So, what are you doing here?* He asked himself. *Why would anyone want to hurt a highly respected educator?*

Two hours later, Pembrook was at his desk, waiting to hear from the medical examiner. Detectives had already been sent to inform the family and question them about possible motives. Others had been sent to the school. When Pembrook's phone rang, he quickly picked it up, listened for a moment, and then blurted, "I'll be right there. Don't move."

When the lieutenant walked into the M.E.'s office, his friend of twenty years looked at him with a very distraught expression and motioned him to a chair. "You're going to want to have a seat," he said.

"What's going on, Jim?" Pembrook asked. "I mean, it was a pretty nasty crime scene, so I understand if you're bothered by—"

"Archie, you know I've got a thick skin for that sort of thing by now. It's not the crime scene. It's...something else," Post said as he got up to shut the door and lock it.

"What else?" Pembrook asked, puzzled by all the drama.

"First, his hands were cut off *while he was still alive*, but as bad as that is, it's not the real problem. It's what they were holding. We found this in the first baggie," he said, handing

Pembrook a copy of the note.

Pembrook's hand began to tremble with the thought of what it might feel like to lose one's hand. A second later, his mind drifted back to the note, which he read aloud: "I, Eric Stuart Conrad, am guilty of unspeakable crimes against children. For this, I must be punished. I will not ask for forgiveness, for I deserve none. To my wife Ellie, my daughter Kristen, and my son Nicholas, I am deeply sorry." Pembrook then set the copy of the letter on the desk, his face etched with deep concern as he tried to wrap his head around the confession he'd read.

It wasn't long before Post broke into his thoughts with another macabre announcement. "What we found in the second baggie is...the most disturbing, I'm afraid," he said, glancing back to make sure that the door was locked before he shoved the flash drive into the USB port on his laptop. He then sat back in his chair and cast his eyes up at the ceiling, as if he couldn't bear to look at the images again.

Pembrook opened some of the JPEGs and started one of the video files. There was no doubt that the man on the computer screen was Conrad, but it only took seconds for Pembrook to see more than he ever wanted to see.

"See? I warned you," Post said as Pembrook closed the files and shook his head.

"Yeah, my grandson goes to the school where he taught," Pembrook said, nervously strumming his fingers through his graying brown hair.

After a few minutes in thought, Pembrook called his boss, Chief Toby Vincent, to fill him in on the coroner's discoveries. Vincent promptly called the St. Clair County Sheriff's Department and the Michigan State Police to schedule a meeting for the following day. "This has the potential to become very ugly, gentlemen," he said. "The best thing for everyone involved is to get ahead of this, especially before the media hounds start their feeding frenzy. We need to follow procedure, right down to the letter."

Chapter 3

Curtis Meyer sat among the computers in various states of repair in the back room of the Tech Master Computer Repair Shop in Flint, Michigan. As horrible as it was that there was a constant generation of new viruses, it meant job security for him. *Just a few more minutes on this rush job, and then it's quittin' time,* he told himself gleefully, looking up at the clock. He was more than ready to dig into his takeout.

At one minute after six, the bell on the front door sounded.

Damn, he thought as he dutifully got up to answer it. *I shoulda locked the fucking door.*

"Sorry, we're closed," he said. Then he saw who was standing just inside the door. "Oh! It's you, Mr. Smith." Curtis had mixed feeling about the man. On one hand, Smith owed him money, and he was a paying customer, but there was something about the guy that just made his skin crawl. He set his dinner on the counter as he watched Mr. Smith lock the door, turn the sign around to "Closed," and pull the blinds shut.

It was only then that Mr. Smith removed the hat that obscured his face and finally spoke. "Hello, Curtis," Smith said with an off-putting smile that gave Curtis the feeling he might very well stab him in the back. "I've got your money."

"Cool!" Curtis said, feeling just a bit better, albeit not fully at ease. A bead of fear-spawned perspiration coursed down his chubby cheek. Even though his bulky six-one frame outsized Mr. Smith by a good three inches, he was sure

Smith could rip him apart without breaking a sweat. After all, in spite of Curtis's lanky height, sitting in front of a computer all day did not lend itself to the physique of an MMA fighter.

"I applaud your efforts on our trial run. You came through on Eric Conrad, but have you been able to obtain another name for me to review?"

"Yeah. As a matter of fact, I did. A man lives close to the area you asked about, in Lansing. He brought his computer in here hoping the distance would ensure his anonymity, but when I saw what was on there, I had to dig a bit deeper. Turns out he's a youth minister with an, um...with *special interest* in the young boys in his care, and there's nothing holy about it. Also, there's also a guy near the Indiana border with similar taste. As far as I can tell, these two aren't opposed to tag-teaming occasionally," the techie said with a look of genuine disgust on his face. "Man, I don't know why you want with this stuff, but it makes me sick seeing what these guys are up to. The way I see it, they don't deserve to live." With that, Curtis handed Mr. Smith a thirty-two-GB flash drive containing the young minister's depravity, but he was careful not to touch the hand of the man who gave him such a bad case of the creeps. As he turned to put the fat envelope of money into his bag, he felt Smith move closer behind him, but just as he turned to see why, darkness overtook him as he was knocked out cold.

Curtis had served Smith well in finding Eric Conrad and the youth minister. He had also given him the tools and the know-how to post their evils on the internet without those posts ever being traced to the source. That part was particularly important, because he could not bear for their crimes against humanity to remain hidden, yet he had to protect himself by remaining untraceable, a vital part of his plan. Anonymous as he had to remain, since the twisted justice system would lock him up for doing the job they couldn't or wouldn't, he knew that once word of his deeds became known to the world, popular opinion would be on his side. Although the law would dictate his being stopped, he was sure the general public, including many of the men and women in law enforcement would root for his continued success.

Before Mr. Smith went about staging the crime scene, he needed to make sure Curtis had not sneakily recorded him on audio or visual media in any way. He quickly found the geek's video surveillance equipment and realized all those recordings were sent, in real time, to Curtis's main computer. Armed with the tech knowhow Curtis himself had taught him, Smith easily removed the hard drive and replaced it with the one he brought, simply repeating the process he'd performed earlier that day with Meyer's home computer. Finally, he emptied the register, and left the drawer open.

Now, it was time for the part of his plan that he most dreaded. Smith looked down at the unconscious Curtis and felt an inward surge of conscience, a mental conflict that needed to be resolved. He certainly wished he could avoid the collateral damage, that he wouldn't have to kill an innocent, but he could not afford to leave any trace that he'd ever been there. *Besides, how innocent can he be? He violated the customer's trust and privacy.* As soon as that inner turmoil was resolved, he reached in his pocket and pulled out a knife he had recently acquired.

Mr. Smith suddenly stopped, wondering about the telling blood spatter that might result from a stab to the heart. *I can't walk out of here covered in it, can I?* He stood there for a moment, lost in the possibilities, till something caught his eye. Curtis's neglected dinner was on a Styrofoam plate. *Shit. It's worth a try,* he thought. Smith quickly grabbed the plate, scraped the food into the trash, and pushed the knife through the center of the Styrofoam, creating a makeshift blood shield. Then, with only a moment's hesitation he placed the knife at Meyer's heart. With one hand on the hilt, and the palm of his other hand on the top of the knife, he pushed down hard.

Meyer's eyes opened briefly, full of pain and fear. He barely had time to comprehend his fate before he was gone. The plate stopped most of the spurting blood that erupted from the man's chest, much to Smith's relief, but he ultimately decided he should inflict multiple stab wounds, if only to confuse the prying police a little. It might even look like a crime of passion by a spurned lover or a drug deal gone wrong. Even though it was not a time to be smiling, one thought brought one on. *Like this geek has a girl friend.*

Curtis Meyer, once an open end, was now closed. It still pained Smith a great deal that the young man had to die, but he had to protect himself and his mission. He pushed the feelings of remorse from his mind and focused his thoughts on the future. *Indiana*, he thought, *I shall see to you soon!*

* * *

By morning, news of the body found along I-69 was all over the papers and the top stories on various TV newscasts. Someone driving along the interstate used a camera with a telephoto lens to snatch some pretty graphic images, and those were quickly posted to the internet. By evening, the media and the general public had a name to go along with the body, and the child-molesting teacher was painted as a respected educator and a loving husband and father. Everyone was in shock, and few could believe a man like that had been so brutally murdered. His church even planned a prayer and memorial service for the Educator of the Year, and his wife and children wept on camera about how much he would be missed.

While the general public mourned the loss of a respected teacher, the police quietly followed a much more disturbing path. At one p.m., with warrants in hand, the department descended on Conrad's home, his vehicles, and his office, all the while doing their best to keep the reason of their searches under wraps, following procedures to the letter, as Chief Vincent had wisely stressed.

Just one day after the discovery of Conrad's body, at five in the evening, the Port Huron community was blindsided, hit by a tsunami of emotion as they were still trying to ride out the tidal wave of sadness over the tragic homicide. Pornographic pictures and videos of Conrad and his victims appeared on the internet. One good thing was that someone had the decency to at least protect the identities of Conrad's victims, making sure not to show any of the children's faces. The damage to Conrad's reputation was done in one fell click of a mouse.

To make matters worse, the authorities were stumped.

There were no eyewitness accounts, and they had no other clues to follow, so the investigation was quickly going nowhere. Forensics could find nothing to indicate who the executioner was; the only fingerprints they found on his computer and the baggies that contained his confession and his depravity were his own. There was no handwriting to analyze, since that confession was typed, and it appeared, for all intents and purposes, that he had typed and printed it himself. If not for the fact that they found him bound and handless, it could have easily been argued that the man finally realized the evils of his ways and offed himself for the good of mankind.

In the days that followed, what had started as shock and grief over the loss of a good citizen changed to anger, fear, disgust, and hatred for a monster. Parents had to ask their children unthinkable questions, and students looked at their teachers with mistrust. The prevailing opinion was that Mr. Conrad probably deserved what happened to him, but that did little to ease anyone's mind.

Strangely enough, while news of Conrad's murder broke, another story was reported by Channel 12 in Flint, the tale of a local computer repairman being murdered in his shop near Flint. The nerd murder paled in comparison to the shock-and-awe sensationalism of the teacher's fall from grace, was relegated to a side story on the television news, and a small column on the inside of the Times Herald in Port Huron, so poor Curtis's demise was really lost to everyone but the authorities.

Chapter 4

Almost two weeks after the discovery of Conrad's body, Mr. Smith watched from his seat at a McDonald's on the northeast side of Lansing. Pearly Gates Christian Church Youth Minister Randy Jarrett was laughing and joking with two young men at a table across the room. Although he was 20, he could have easily pulled off 17. Mr. Smith's stomach turned as he watched his prey touch the boys, as often as he could. The older would-be victim almost imperceptibly shied away, but Mr. Smith noticed it instantly.

On top of looking young for his age, Jarrett looked every bit the part of a God-fearing youth minister in dress and manner. His white t-shirt with the name of his church screen-printed on the back was his disguise; he was the proverbial wolf in sheep's clothing. *How can people so easily be fooled by Jarrett and his kind?* Mr. Smith wondered with a subtle shake of his head.

The hatred he felt toward the minister boiled inside him. He had watched some of the footage on the flash drive, those recordings of secret encounters at Jarrett's house, of youth group camping trips, and what he saw almost made him physically ill. Watching him now brought those wretched visions to the center of his thoughts, and the half-eaten Big Mac stirred in his stomach. *Soon. So very soon,* he silently vowed.

Mr. Smith's attention never left the trio, though he certainly wasn't obvious about it. He knew how to blend in and observe. Those who knew him would have laughed at the no-tion, but he knew he could have been a master spy, had his life worked out differently. *Fuck them!* He cursed in his head. What the naysayers thought had once ruled his life, but that was not the case anymore.

When he saw that they were preparing to leave, he made his way to the trash, the door, and to his car. Soon, the young minister and the young men, whose parents had gladly, yet foolishly given him a temporary custody, made their way to a silver Pontiac Sunfire. The younger of the two was still laughing, seemingly without a care in the world, but the other boy walked dutifully without much mirth.

Mr. Smith understood why there was such a noticeable difference in the gait of the young men. While the youngest had not been molested yet, that vile ship had sailed long ago for the older boy. From what he gathered from the deviant's diary he'd pulled up from the flash drive, Mark, the older one, would soon be replaced by the youthful Sam, and it didn't appear that poor Sam had any idea of his cruel fate.

"And he never will, if I can help it." Mr. Smith swore as he followed them. Sam was dropped off first, and then Jarrett continued on to his home with Mark. The Sunfire pulled into the garage, and the garage door closed behind them. A sense of urgency was not a factor for Mark, since his life had already been destroyed, but Mr. Smith would not allow the perverted bastard, a monster protected by the church, to enjoy the innocence of Sam.

Around eight thirty that evening, Jarrett's garage door opened so Mark could be escorted home to his unsuspecting family. It was hard to believe none of Mark's loved ones would notice the changes in the boy's behavior, but they seemed clueless. In fact, the weekend before, Mr. Smith peeked in on a family picnic, and Jarrett was among the guests enjoying hotdogs, hamburgers, and cake, welcomed by the very parents of the boy he was molesting.

It was fortunate that Jarrett's property was bordered on one side by another property and at the back by woods. After the pedophile's car was out of sight, Mr. Smith drove to a little bare patch among the copse of trees. He parked there and made his way toward Jarrett's house. He had been there just two days prior, on a dry run, so he had a good idea of the layout. While he waited for Jarrett's return, he used the computer to write the note that would be found with his body. He also found the fuse box in the garage and turned off the breaker for the kitchen lights.

A half-hour later he felt a buzz no alcohol could give him when he heard the grinding sound of the garage door opening. There was a squeal as the car came to a stop, and a moment later, Jarrett waltzed into the kitchen and flipped the light switch. "Damnation! What the fuck?" he said with a growl when the darkness did not cease.

"What kind of language is that for a youth minister to use?" someone spoke from the blackness before he could even fully turn to go out and flip the fuses.

Jarrett almost jumped out of his skin and jerked his head around to see who had spoken to him, only to be knocked near unconscious.

Mr. Smith let the pervert fall to the floor, not at all concerned that he might hurt himself. He quickly gave Jarrett a dose of Rohypnol. The molester would be out for a while, so he also administered an injection of concentrated liquid aspirin. It was another thing he had learned from Conrad, meant to prevent any chance of the blood clotting, since it was possible that the man could survive both hands being cut off otherwise; a chance Mr. Smith was not willing to take. With only a slight groan, he heaved Jarrett up over his shoulder and headed for the door.

Once he was sure no one was watching, he made his way across the back yard, through the woods, and to his car. He was very glad Jarrett was thin, because he was already breathing hard by the time he got to the car. He used zipties to bind him, just as he did with Conrad. After placing his diseased cargo in the hidden trunk compartment directly behind the back seat, he pulled out and made his way out of the neighborhood. The hidden compartment made his trunk quite a bit smaller, but no one would ever notice unless they were specifically looking for it. He headed for a Starbucks he'd seen on his way to Jarrett's house. It was still early after he ordered his Caramel Macchiato, so he sat in a Walmart parking lot to drink it, until it was time to head for the dumpsite.

At three thirty in the morning, Mr. Smith pulled off westbound I-69 at the Webster Road exit a few miles east of Lansing. He immediately made his way down the on-ramp, but near the end of that ramp, he pulled off the road and stopped. When he was sure no one was around, he pulled the camouflage blind out of the trunk and headed for Jarrett's final resting place.

Directly adjacent to the ninety-two-mile marker on the westbound lane, he set up the blind, then went back to the car to fetch his drugged deviant. Careful to avoid the light bath from passing cars, he mentally prepared himself for the pervert's light weight, and he carried Jarrett's body the 400 feet to the blind and tied him to a tree. Once Jarrett's arms were secured to his sides, Mr. Smith cracked open the smelling salts under his nose.

Jarrett woke with a start. He tried to speak, but something in his mouth prevented it. He was naked, and he shivered in the cool early morning air. He looked into the eyes of the man in front of him and questioned his reality. *Where the hell am I? Who the fuck is this stranger, and what in God's name does he want?*

"Randy Jarrett, I frankly have no idea why any fair and just God would allow parasites like you to exist. It is entirely unfathomable to me to think that you or someone like you could possibly harm my children. Why? Why are you still here, still taking up space on this planet, using up oxygen you don't deserve to breathe? Don't get me wrong. I do not wish to act as the hand of God, nor to deny His sovereignty and wisdom, but for what you have done, you must die. Justice will be served here and now."

One thing that he had learned from killing Conrad was that it was best to save the hand dismemberment till the end, as Conrad almost fell into shock before Smith had a chance to torture his mind with exposure to the world. He pulled out the loppers and held them in front of Jarrett's eyes, then leaned in close and whispered into the pervert's ear.

Jarrett's eyes widened, and he struggled against his

restraints. He screamed into the sweaty sock stuffed in his mouth, pleading with the stranger to spare his life.

Mr. Smith held up a flash drive. "After you take your last undeserved breath, I will share your diary, these pictures, and these horrendous videos with all your friends, your minister, and your family. Can you imagine what they will think?"

Jarrett closed his eyes, as if he couldn't bear the thought.

"Although your parents have probably come to terms with the possibility that their son is gay, I sincerely doubt that this aspect of your life will bring them any kind of pleasure. I see only pain for them, and I can only imagine how your poor mother and father will feel when everyone they know witness the pictures and videos of what you did to those young boys. I wonder if their friends will look at them differently, if they will judge them and ask, 'How could you raise such a monster?' Will their candy shop lose business because of your taste for sweet young things? They will probably never be able to look anyone in the eye again; for fear that they will see condemnation in their stares. And what about your ever-proud Granny B? Didn't she just get out of the hospital? When she sees the pictures, as I will make sure she does, her heart will probably fail her again, but she will leave this Earth with your sins on her mind."

Tears flowed from Jarrett's eyes, and his body rocked with the regret of his choices. He didn't even open his eyes when the cold steel blades of the loppers were placed around his right wrist; only when his hand was removed and he realized what had happened, did his eyes snap open. He looked down at his hand lying on the ground, as he let out an ear-piercing scream against the dirty sock. Mr. Smith quickly moved to the left hand and repeated the process. Before the hypovolemic shock hit, Jarrett's judge, jury, and executioner held the pictures of his parents and Granny B in front of his weakening gaze. His head shook, and he screamed a weak and muffled, "Nooo!" When the relief of shock overtook him, his body slumped against the ropes that held him in place.

As before, Mr. Smith placed the dead man's neatly folded clothes on his lap, with his wallet on top. He then put the sandwich bag that contained the flash drive in Jarrett's severed right hand and another in his left, holding the written confession, then set one on each side of his wallet. Once he was sure that all was perfect, he gathered his loppers and blind and quickly made his way to his car.

There was a close call when someone merged onto westbound I-69 off Webber Road. Mr. Smith dropped into the grass and pulled the blind in front of him and could only watch as the diver veered too close to his truck and clipped the front fender. The driver then pulled over and got out to check the damage, like any responsible citizen would; much to the dismay of Mr. Smith.

It was soon obvious to Mr. Smith that the man had been drinking heavily, because he stumbled when he neared Smith's truck.

"Hello? Anybody here?" the man slurred.

Mr. Smith was about to take him out when the man bolted for his car, jumped in, and sped off. *Thank God, you can always count on people to avoid punishment for the wrong they do.* He thought. In this case he was okay with it, and truly relieved, as he did not have any desire to kill again that night. He wasn't at all worried about his vehicle, as it was only a throwaway, just like the men he'd killed.

Chapter 5

At around six thirty, State Trooper Ronnie Fisher pulled onto the off-ramp to Webber Road so he could call his wife, who was just weeks away from giving him his second child. He was delighted to hear that his son was kicking away, and he headed down the on-ramp with a smile on his face, on his way to Lansing to fuel up the *Blue Goose*. Near the end of the ramp, he veered to miss some glass on the road. While he didn't really want to bother, he was a man of the law and a good citizen, so he decided to clean it up.

Fisher had just finished sweeping the bigger pieces into an old box when something caught his eye, something a few hundred feet away, past the end of the ramp, propped up against a tree. The hairs stood up on the back of his neck as he focused on the shirtless man, and he felt even more uneasy when he yelled at the man and heard no response. His hand instinctively moved to the grip of his gun as he walked toward the man. When he was within ten feet, he realized the victim was completely naked but covered with blood. A closer look told him the man's hands were not connected to his arms. *Oh shit*, he thought and ran back to his patrol car and called it in.

"Lock down the scene," First Lt. Edwin Beckman told Fisher. "I'll be there ASAP." He hung up and informed the captain of what he knew and what he suspected, then put in a call to Ingham County Medical Examiner Sandy Randolph, then ran out the door. On his way, Beckman made a courtesy call to the Port Huron Police Department and filled Lt.

Pembrook in on what little he knew. He was well aware of the body that was found outside Port Huron, and the stories of the two corpses now bore a shocking resemblance.

When Beckman arrived, there were three Ingham County deputies directing traffic to make sure no one got near the crime scene. Beckman was more than happy to give the first body to the Port Huron Police, but with the new body found on I-69, he knew he was now neck deep in it. *Not random. We've got ourselves a killer with a plan, damn it,* he thought, *and that's a whole different animal.*

Within twenty minutes, Sandy Randolph made it to the scene and headed straight for the body while the forensics team snapped photos and collected anything that might be important in helping police solve the murder. Sandy handed Beckman the dead man's wallet in a clear evidence bag, then continued her examination.

"Just 26, Randall Alan Jarrett, from Lansing," Beckman said, shaking his head.

"Ed, it looks like our cause of death is blood loss, from his arms, after his hands were severed. I'll know more when I get him on the table."

"Did you find anything, uh...in his hands?" Beckman asked, though he was pretty sure he already knew the answer.

Sandy took a picture, then carefully picked up one hand and opened the stiff fingers to release a baggie containing a folded piece of paper. She laid it back down on the dead man's lap while the tech took a picture of the other hand. Sure enough, the baggie in that hand held a flash drive.

"Damn!" Beckman said, exhaling the curse reactively. He knew all too well what it meant: There was something in that note and on that flash drive that would paint a very different picture of the young man, something no one who knew him would believe.

After Sandy and her team bagged and tagged everything that was deemed important, she headed for her SUV. Beckman decided to follow her to her lab, as he was eager for her to clear the baggies and what they held. Without the items in those bags, he had no way to proceed with his investigation;

except to find out what everyone already knew about their victim.

While Beckman waited in Sandy's office, Port Huron Detective Lt. Pembrook knocked on the door. Beckman knew him, as he was originally from Port Huron, and they attended Northern High School together. Beckman was a year younger, but they'd played football and hockey together during his junior year.

"You didn't have to show up. I still woulda kept you in the loop, buddy. I am glad you're here though. Go Huskies!"

Pembrook smiled, "Go Huskies!" Then he asked, "Anything yet?"

Just as he was about to answer, Medical Examiner Sandy Randolph walked in, carrying a photocopy of the note and copy of the flash drive. "From what I see so far, the only difference from the Conrad case is that this one had a high level of acetylsalicylic acid in his system."

"Acetywhatic acid?" Pembrook asked.

"Aspirin. I believe it was used to prevent deep vein thrombosis."

"What?" Beckman asked.

"Blood clotting. I just did that one for fun," Sandy said, offering a smile that quickly morphed into a rather somber expression. "Be careful when you open the files on the flash drive. You aren't gonna like what you see," she said matter-of-factly and left.

Beckman sighed and then reached for the note. He and Pembrook both just stared at the flash drive and note for a moment before Beckman sighed again, unfolded the note, and read it out loud:

"I, Randall Alan Jarrett, am guilty of unspeakable crimes against children. For this, I must be punished. I will not ask for forgiveness, for I deserve none. To my father, my mother, and my Granny B, I am sorry."

Pembrook noticed right away that the note was basically a form letter, a copy of the one found with Conrad, with the specifics changed to fit Jarrett. "Look at this," he said, pulling the copy of Conrad's note from the file. "Either we've got a real psychotic bastard on our hand, or else we're chasin' a damn good copycat."

"Damn! I'm not sure which is worse," Beckman cursed as he reached for the flash drive and reluctantly plugged it into his laptop. He navigated through the files and found three folders containing a diary, pictures, and videos. Seeking what he thought would be the least disturbing of the three; he opted to open the diary and discovered entries dating back eight years. He clicked on "2016" and found Word files created for each day. He clicked on a random one, without even really looking at the date, and began to read about a boy named Mark. Beckman stopped reading a few sentences in because the words painted graphic pictures in his mind, ones he feared might never leave, and Pembrook's reaction was the same.

"You ready for...worse?" Beckman asked.

"As ready as I'll never be," Pembrook said with a nod.

Beckman forced himself to open one of the picture files but had to immediately close it down, for fear he might vomit. Nothing could have prepared him for the image that would surely haunt him forever, and a tear actually coursed down his face, a tear for the little boy Jarrett harmed. He had seen and heard about molestation and mankind's depravity more than once, but it never seemed to get any easier. Somehow, someway, though, he managed to push all that from his thoughts and became a lawman again. "Face it, Archie. We've got a serial killer here."

"Looks like it." Pembrook nodded in agreement. "What do we do now?"

"I took some courses at Quantico a few years back. I think we should give them a call."

Chapter 6

It's been over a year since we stopped the Fingertip Killer, and I still have nightmares about my time in his chair. Although they're less frequent than before, they are just as real. I find myself rubbing my reattached finger whenever I'm in deep concentration about a case, the digit Seth Avery cut off as his last act before he died. For whatever reason, it helps me focus in my thought processes, especially when investigating criminals.

Surprisingly, Crystal and I are still holding on to our long-distance relationship. I visit her, she comes to see me, or we meet halfway. If it ever ends, I don't know what I'll do. She's talked about moving out here and joining the DC Metropolitan PD or possibly applying at the FBI, and I wish she would. We've never discussed being exclusive, but the only other girls I spend time with are Zee, Noah's wife and daughter, Danielle and Juelle, and of course the love of my life Grandma.

Zee and Vernon are still friends with benefits, but they also date others. They have thrown around the idea of getting serious, but both agree that what they have is fine for now. Marty is dating a new girl, a doctor, I think. He has a picture of her hanging in his Fortress of the Technodude, and she's every bit as attractive as all the girls who I've seen Marty with since I've known him. How he does it, I can't figure out, but more power to him. As far as the picture hanging in the Fortress is concerned, that is a first. I have met a few of the girls he's dated, and, surprisingly enough, all were successful professionals; he is definitely not your average geek.

I really miss spending time with Bradford, Crystal's boss. In the short time we spent together, he became one of my best friends. Besides being a good friend, he is a very insightful lawman. He knows when to be a sounding board and when to offer his thoughts, so I still call him every once in a while, just to get his take on the cases I'm working.

Speaking of work, it's been pretty steady. It seems that whenever we solve one case, another is waiting just around the corner. Sometimes it really gets to me that there are so many broken people out there, and I often wish I could just bury my head in the sand. I wish I could be totally unaware of the sheer number of deviants that roam the United States at any given time. When we catch one, though, it jolts me back to focus on the positive part. It's a dirty job, but somebody's got to do it, right?

I was shooting hoops at the Barber Physical Activity Center (BPAC), the BAU's weekly game against some Marine sergeants, and we were getting our asses handed to us, so I wasn't too pissed when my phone rang. Since it was the ringtone of my boss, Supervisory Agent Noah Bennett, I had to answer right away; the only other ringtone that demanded my attention like that was my grandparents.

I knocked and walked into Noah's office, still wearing my sweats. "You rang?"

"Shut the door," Noah said, looking up only briefly from what he was reading. His office was impeccably neat, as always, and the only thing that was not in its proper place was the file opened on his desk.

"I really don't understand why the good Lord thought *you* deserve such a beautiful family," I said with a shake of my head, looking at new photographs of his wife and daughter.

"It's probably 'because he made me so damn good-looking. Now, sit your ass down," he said, smiling.

"What's up, Noah?" I asked as soon as the door was closed, careful to use his first name only when no one else was within earshot.

"We got a call from the Michigan State Police. There have been two murders along Interstate 69, both involving a certain *m.o.*"

"What *m.o.*?" I asked, though I almost dreaded the answer.

"Severed hands, and both vic's were involved in, um... child pornography. The first body was found near Port Huron, and the second on 69, just outside Lansing. They want us to take a look."

"Child pornography?"

"Yeah. Both were considered model citizens before their bodies were found. One was a highly respected educator, even scored Teacher of the Year last year. The second was a trusted youth minister. When their bodies were found, their severed hands were in their laps, holding written confessions and flash drives that contain proof of their nasty involvement with children. It looks as though both were ambushed in their homes and taken to where they were found. Their hands were cut off, and they bled out."

I studied the disgusting photos as Noah detailed what he knew. The pictures of the hands in their laps were unsettling, but those were not nearly as horrifying as the photos of the victims and the children they molested.

"Are you sure we *want* to stop this person? It seems like he might be doing the world a favor, kinda like that guy who was killing the lawyers down in Florida." I looked into the air, then straight at Noah. "Damn it, Noah, I'm not doing it."

Noah smiled. "We both know better than that. State Police Lt. Beckman was here a couple years ago for some training, seemingly a really good lawman. You won't have any trouble with him. Besides, if you don't go check these murders out, I'll tell Danielle what you said about her meatloaf."

"Shit, no! You can't just—"

"Blackmail you? Oh yes. I can, and I will," Noah said, without a shred of humor in his voice over his pun or his threat.

"Okay, okay. You win," I said, hanging my head in shame. "Just give me all you've got. I'll give Marty a crack at those flash drives, and I know he can figure out who originally posted the pictures and videos on the internet. Zee and I'll head out in the morning."

Noah knew full well that I would have begged to take this case if need be. I had a feeling that there was more to it than just the murder of closeted child molesters. "And, Kroh," he said as I got up to leave, "these murders happened exactly two weeks apart, so we have to assume we may have less than two weeks before he strikes again. Hopefully not, but we can't take that chance."

"Noted, my lord," I teased. "I'll see ya when I see ya, and for God's sake, if one decent bone in your muscle-bound body exists, you'll keep your mouth shut about my opinion of your wife's meatloaf."

* * *

Zee and I flew into Lansing, checked in at the FBI resident agency on Eyde Parkway, and headed straight for the State Police post on Canal Road. When we entered Lt. Beckman's office, we found him there with Archie Pembrook, studying a whiteboard that contained everything they knew about the case so far.

I had to smile as I watched the two catch their breath when Zee walked in behind me. Zee's beauty was no secret to anyone. In fact, she was one of the most stunning women I'd ever met, but that was not what landed her on my team. She could be the proverbial mud fence, and I would still want her at my side. She is also one of the most competent and intuitive people I knew, and she was the one person I always wanted at my side in times of trouble. She is well aware of her beauty but never uses it unless she was sure it would work to her advantage on a case. She could have been on the fast track at the Bureau but was content to stay where she was for the time being, for reasons known only to her and me. I could not imagine being without Zee. She could take it and dish it with the best of them.

"I am Special Agent Benjamin Kroh, but please call me Kroh. This is Special Agent Zindzhi Cole."

The two lawmen made their introductions, and we got down to business. For the next hour, they filled Zee and me in on the most recent discoveries of the forensics team. Other than a few shoe impressions and a best guess on what was used to cut off the victims' hands, there was not much else to go on. The fingerprints on the baggies, flash drives, and confessions belonged only to the victims themselves.

"Can we check out the crime scenes?" I asked. "I'd like to see them for myself, so I can get a feel of what our killer experienced."

"Yeah, let's do it," Beckman said, standing.

"We need to get all the information to our computer expert, Martin Owens. He'll add it all to his database and run some careful analysis," Zee added as she walked to the door. "If you find anything new, send it to him immediately. Right now, he's our best chance to connect the two murders and to find something we can use to catch this killer." She handed each a card with Marty's info.

Marty is our resident computer geek, a Native American who began his life on the Navajo Reservation in Arizona. I'd gladly pit his skills against anyone, and I have no doubt that he'd prevail. Marty did not share my penchant for casual attire; he always donned a suit and tie. In fact, it was the generally accepted opinion Marty was the best dressed agent at Quantico.

After Zee left the room, Beckman, whose wife had died ten years back, touched me on the shoulder. "Your partner seems like a very capable agent, but she's also damn gorgeous. Don't you find that a bit...distracting?"

Feigning anguish, I said, "Yes, yes, I do, but it's a cross I must bear."

We decided to drive separately, since I also needed to visit the first crime scene. We planned to stay in Port Huron so I could get a feel for the first murder.

I looked at Zee as we headed east on I-69. "After we find a place to stay, I'll take you out for a nice dinner. How does that sound?"

"Sounds good to me."

"Ain't life grand? You're one lucky girl, having me for a boss."

"Yeah, well, it's a cross I must bear," Zee said with a roll of her eyes, feigning anguish even more exaggeratedly than I had earlier.

"Huh?" I said, a bit surprised that she'd overheard that.

"Well, you're, uh...still a lucky girl."

"Ass," Zee said calmly, as if stating a well-known fact, then punched my shoulder.

We were both still laughing when we made it to the second crime scene a few miles east of Lansing. Zee and I followed Beckman to where the body was found.

At the crime scene, I knelt in the grass to get a closer look. It had not rained, so the bloodstains from the man's arms were still visible, despite the insects that dutifully carried his fluids back to nature.

"Other than the shoe impressions, there was little else to ID the killer." Pembrook offered.

"Do they know what kind of shoe made the prints?" Zee asked.

"Yes. According to the pattern, they're Merrell Men's Moab 2 Ventilator Mid Hiking Boots, same shoes worn at the scene with the Port Huron victim. That doesn't narrow it down much, I'm afraid. It's a pretty common hiking boot," Beckman responded quickly, as if he was still trying to impress Zee.

"Yeah, well, it's something." I agreed.

Zee stopped and looked closer. "Check this out, Kroh," she said, pointing out six holes around where the body was. "I don't remember anything about that in the crime scene reports."

"Good catch!" Beckman offered, though he likely would have replied with the same enthusiasm if she noted that the grass was green.

While Pembrook helped Zee take measurements, I stood a few feet back and held up a picture of the crime scene with the body in place. We spent another half-hour looking around the scene, then headed to the first dump site.

The first thing we looked for were more holes, and we certainly found them. When measurements were taken, it became obvious that the distance between the holes was the same, though connecting the dots did not lend itself to the same shape.

"Blind," I blurted.

"What?" Pembrook asked. "I saw them as soon as I got here. What are you talking about?"

"No, you're not blind. A blind—you know something to hide him and his victims while he set up his little macabre display."

"Of course! He couldn't take the chance of being seen. Just one flash of a headlight could've ruined everything for him. Damn!" Beckman offered as he made the call to order the forensic teams to go over both crime scenes again. As soon as he ended that call, he hurriedly placed another to put some troopers at both crime scenes to keep everyone away.

"Wait a minute. When Zee found a few holes, you said it was a good catch. I practically solve the whole case, and you just say, 'Of course.' What the hell?" I beamed my signature shit-eating grin, and Beckman's face flushed red.

"Don't worry about him. He's just jealous." Zee smiled as she put her arm around Beckman's shoulder and gave him a one-armed hug.

That evening, at Pembrook's advice, Zee and I went to the Vintage Tavern in Port Huron. I enjoyed the ribeye, and Zee ordered the yellowfin tuna, both entrées grilled to perfection. Halfway through the meal, though, my phone blared in to interrupt.

"Hey, Marty, what's up?" I asked.

"Not me," he said. "Looking at this garbage just has me down. All I can say is yuck!"

"Yeah, I know."

"Well, I won't go into the gory details," Marty continued, "but other than their hobbies, I haven't yet found anything concrete, no common link between them." Then, after a pause, Marty asked, "Hey, do I smell a medium-well ribeye?"

"As a matter of fact, Marty, you do. It's a hard life out here on the road. While you sit in the Fortress of The Technodude, surrounded by your beloved electronics and everything a man could want, I must suffer through a meal in this very fine eating establishment far away from home," I said feigning distress.

"Waaa!" The sound of a baby crying suddenly came from my phone that sat between us on the table, drawing stares from all the other diners in the restaurant.

While Zee laughed, I picked up my phone and pointed at it, smiled, and shrugged. While some patrons looked annoyed, most just smiled and went back to what they were doing.

"Okay, okay. You win. Have you got anything else for us?"

"I sure do. It looks as if loppers or some sort of hedge trimmers were used to remove the hands. I just got that from Lansing. Oh, and one more thing. Based on those dimensions you sent me, I'm thinking he used a portable five-panel blind made by Hunter's Paradise based in upstate New York. I'm looking into purchasers over the last couple years, and I'll let you know when I find something. Enjoy your meal. Bye for now."

"Good work, Marty, as always," I said.

"Bye, Marty. Love you," Zee added.

"Waa-waa-waa!" Then, with a brief burst of crying baby, Marty was gone.

Chapter 7

Tuesday morning, Zee and I met with Pembrook in his office to go over our notes on the Conrad case. Whoever had committed the crime was very careful not to leave any evidence behind; it was as if the murderer knew about forensics and, therefore, avoided any and all mistakes that could lead us to him.

We went over everything Marty found buried in Conrad's home and office computers, and all of it was beyond disturbing. For me, it was hard to believe that no one ever suspected anything, considering the sheer amount of pornography that both computers contained. As I looked at it, one thought came to mind time and time again: *What a sick bastard.*

Pembrook escorted us to Conrad's office at the school, and I noticed a small camera that faced the man's desk. Once that was found, it didn't take long for us to find three more at various locations in the room *Was this Conrad's doing? I had to wonder. Did that slimy monster actually film children here?* I was sure no one would have been stupid enough to hunt where he taught, but that only made the cameras more of a mystery. Fortunately, with a little help from Marty, the crime scene techs were able to find the frequency and activate the cameras. From what they could tell, there was not a place in the room that was hidden from view. I had my suspicions that Conrad knew nothing about the spying lenses, but I had no idea who had placed them and why. One thought came to mind: *Maybe someone at the school suspected what Conrad was doing and was collecting evidence.*

Just as it did with Conrad, the internet exploded with visions of Jarrett's debauchery. In fact, it soon became the top story on the evening news. Pictures of Jarrett, his home, and even his church filled the screen. Reporters knocked on Jarrett's parents' door but were denied an interview. When the journalists spoke to the preacher at Pearly Gates Christian Church, his only comment was, "This is a tragedy. We are praying for his soul and the souls of the children involved."

For the next two days, Zee and I followed every lead we had, only to be led to a series of dead ends. We really had no choice but to move beyond Lansing. From a respected educator to a well-liked and trusted youth minister, the case certainly was not getting any better.

The more I looked into the murders of Conrad and Jarrett, the more my feeling of unease grew. Clearly, the murderer felt his victims deserved it. Nevertheless, my job was to capture a lawbreaker, even if that person felt righteous in ridding the world of the most evil products of humanity. I often caught myself unconsciously rubbing my little finger.

Although there was nothing at all to give credence to my unsettled feelings, I just knew there was more to the story. I truly believed there was. The murders of child molesters, in particular, felt like some sort of diversion, just breadcrumbs that would lead to what our killer was really after. I wasn't sure, though, so I decided to keep that to myself for a while.

For the next few days, I made sure to talk to as many of Jarrett's relatives, friends, and fellow congregants as I could. Sadly, just before I was to interview her, Granny B's heart finally gave out. Whether it was just her time, or the heartache brought on by the revelations of her grandson's indiscretions, no one would ever know. Either way, it was a tragic loss, for her loved ones. It was nothing that would hinder our investigation, but I felt terrible for the double-whammy his family had to endure.

No matter how much digging we did or how much evidence we collected, we were getting no closer to solving the murders. If the killer kept to a timetable, we knew there was a likely threat that another body would be found, handless and disgraced.

Die by Proxy

On a Saturday night, I sat in my room at the Courtyard by Marriott, with pictures and documents spread out all over the bed, again examining everything we had so far. It was beyond frustrating that we had no real leads on the identity of a vicious killer. A smile finally crossed my face, though, when my phone came alive with Led Zeppelin's "Stairway to Heaven."

"Hey, big stuff. How's it going?" Crystal said with as much sex as she could shovel into her voice, a sultry greeting that had me picturing her in her well-worn Zeppelin tee and nothing else.

"Hey, beautiful. It's great to hear your voice." The smile on my face threatened to tear it in half. I hadn't talked to Crystal in three days and hadn't seen her in over a month.

"Are you busy? Can you talk?"

"No and yes. I just got back to the hotel here in beautiful downtown Lansing."

"Lansing?"

"Yeah. Somebody in Michigan has taken to killing child molesters."

"How many so far?"

"Just two, a respected teacher found just outside Port Huron and a youth minister found a few miles from here. Both were left along Interstate 69, with their severed hands sitting in their laps, holding evidence of what the bastards did to children."

"Damn! It's always someone we're supposed to trust with kids. Look, I know you've got a job to do, but the way I see it, anyone who would molest a child deserves to die, in the worst possible way."

"I know," I said with a sigh, as it was a moral dilemma, I'd been struggling with myself. "I really hope the Immoral Crusader is over it, though, because we have no leads. Either the guy's very lucky or is very good in a very bad way. There were two weeks between finding the teacher and the minister, and if he keeps to that schedule, next Saturday could be D-day for someone else."

"Do you think the distance between body dumps is an attempt to hide the connection? Crystal asked.

"I don't think so, since he's splashing his deeds and their crimes all over the internet in the days following their discovery."

We talked for a half-hour longer, and I promised I'd see her as soon as I could. I hung up the phone, stared at the information scattered all over the bed, and lay back on the pillows stacked against the headboard. I put my hands behind my head and fell into deep thought, rehashing the same thoughts I'd been thinking for days. After ten minutes of running the case through my mind, I sat up. "Fuck it!" I said to no one in particular. "I'm tired of spinning my damn wheels here, and nothing is coming together," I complained to the walls. "I need to get away from it for a while, to clear my head."

The next morning, Sunday, after a promise from Beckman and Pembrook to keep me up to date and to watch out for Zee, I drove to Anderson, Indiana to spend some quality time with Crystal.

* * *

Near the end of Mr. Smith's weekend with his kids, he had a bit of a close call when his son Jeremy asked, "Dad, who is Mr. Smith?" It was only then that he realized he had left some mail addressed to Mr. Smith, with his alternate address, on the table next to his computer. "Oh, they sometimes mess up and deliver other people's mail to the wrong address. I'll give it back to the mailman the next time I see him."

Jeremy seemed to accept the lie with a shrug and casually continued his computer game.

Mr. Smith loved his children beyond words, but his wife was one of the many objects of his hatred. His children loved him, too, but they had noticed a change in their father since the divorce. Occasionally, he hugged them close and cried, but most of the time, he seemed to drift off mentally, as if they weren't even there. They loved to spend time with him at first, but as time went on, they began to find him distant and hard to be around.

It was all especially hard on his daughter, Lacy, since she was in her temperamental teens and prone to angst anyway.

Jeremy did not seem to be affected that much, but he sensed his sister's frustration. After a while, they started finding any excuse to forgo his weekends. When they could not get out of it, they moped around the entire time while they were condemned to be with him, and they were openly excited when it was time to go home to their mother, where they received far more attention and emotional stability.

Like many disgruntled, divorced fathers, Mr. Smith took that as a sign that his bitch of an ex-wife was slowly turning his beautiful children against him. Thoughts of adding her to his list of those undeserving of life often danced at the edge of his mind. He had given his life to her, his heart and soul, but as soon as his career took a turn for the worse and they were forced to move, she left him. The more he thought about it, the higher up on that list her name moved.

As soon as his children were safe and sound with their mother again, Mr. Smith got back to business. The third name on his list begged for his attention, but he only had a few days to make the kill, what he hoped would be the best of the bunch so far. It would set up the fourth murder, the kingpin of his plan.

* * *

I made the trip to Anderson, Indiana in about three hours, with Crystal and a warm meal on my mind. The ringing of her doorbell seemed to sing in tune with the growling of my stomach. I forgot all about my hunger pangs, though, when she opened the door just as I imagined her, in that tattered rocker t-shirt and nothing else. It barely covered her, especially when she raised her arms, and even Victoria's Secret couldn't have come up with anything sexier.

"Oh, it's just you," she said, fully aware that she had already turned me on.

"Daaamn, girl!" escaped my mouth before I regained blood flow to my brain. "Hey, what if it wasn't me? Would you still be wearing...*that*?"

"What makes you think I was waiting for you?" Crystal said with a smirk before she turned and started to move away with an exaggerated swing of her hips. As she did, she pulled up the back of her shirt, exposing her world-class ass.

That was all it took; in an instant, I followed her like she was the Pied Piper.

As soon as she reached the bed, she turned, knelt, and started unbuckling my belt. "Oh, Larry," she said, placing her hand on me, "did you miss me?" She loved making my manhood feel special, and saying my college nickname for it, through those beautiful lips of hers did the trick.

After a few moments of Crystal's attention, I pulled her into my arms and kissed her hard. I didn't know what it was, but there was something about that girl. I had never felt that way with anyone else. I picked her up and placed her on the bed. In a blur of long-overdue passion, our bodies were one, and the world was lost to us. Our symbiotic desire took control, and our lust consumed us.

Afterward, we lay exhausted in each other's arms. After a while, we got up and showered, only to find that neither of us was quite satisfied. With water dripping to the floor with my every step, I carried her to the bed again, and our lovemaking took on a slower, more deliberate tone. The air-conditioning chilled on our damp skin, but that only intensified our desire. Upon finishing that second round, we both fell into a deep slumber.

Don't get me wrong: With Crystal, it wasn't just about sex. I enjoyed just being with her, and she was a great friend. Sure, we were in a long-distance relationship and didn't see each other often, so it was difficult not to let the sex take over when we could get away and be together, but I really cherished every moment we shared, even just sitting together for a little TV. Lord help the girl, I thought, since I was sure she felt the same.

Crystal awoke to the smell of bacon, and I'm sure she was surprised that morning had arrived already. She was usually up before the alarm buzzed, but it was an evening of insatiable desire, and it had worn us both out. As she entered the kitchen, I was just sitting the wonderful-smelling breakfast on the table.

"Hungry, milady?" I asked, then bowed and pulled her chair out for her.

"Well, you certainly know how to make a girl work up an

appetite, sir," she said with a wink as she sat down.

* * *

I followed Crystal to work. I needed to see Bradford, and it wasn't just because I missed my friend. I also needed some fresh eyes on the I-69 case. It was one of the reasons I made the trip to Anderson. Things were a little slow for a Monday, so Bradford was glad for the distraction.

"I'm not so sure it's as much about the child abusers as it seems," I told him, to which he simply responded, "Hmm..."

At noon, we headed for the Kroh's Nest. As always, my grandmother hugged me every chance she got.

"Give him some air, Mama. The boy's trying to eat," Pops said.

"It's okay. I'm here for the hugs, not the grub," I said as I stuffed in the last bite of the perfect cheeseburger and patted my grandma's hand.

My grandparents meant the world to me. Not often would elderly folks so wholeheartedly step in to act as mother and father again after a tragic accident. Pops was a hands-on guardian who took an active role in my upbringing. Although I was a good kid for the most part, he wasn't one to spare the rod, and he always took the time to explain why my actions were unacceptable. I owed my life to those two beautiful people, and I cherished those hugs as much as I savored those burgers.

After lunch, Crystal, Bradford, and I headed back to the Anderson Police Department.

"I've got to head back to Lansing tonight. Thanks for your insight," I said as I shook Bradford's hand.

"I'm sorry I couldn't help more," Bradford said. "You got yourself a real mind-bender there."

"Anything is more than I had when I came here," I said shaking my head.

* * *

As Saturday approached, the Michigan State Police stepped up patrols along the interstate. County and local law enforcement also made periodic runs along the areas where it ran through their jurisdictions, as law enforcement was not about to make it easy for any more killing to occur along I-69.

Every vehicle that stopped along the side of the road was tagged and searched, especially after dark. It definitely pissed a lot of drivers off, but if nothing else, it also eliminated a lot of alcohol-enhanced drivers from swerving down the highway.

Chapter 8

Mr. Smith sat watching Andy Reese in a Starbucks on the north side of Ft. Wayne, Indiana, the third name on the list of deviants that Curtis Meyer had found for him. The pictures and videos of Reese and Jarrett ruining the innocence of young the boys who trusted them were sickening. Mr. Smith was very careful to leave any hint of Reese off the flash drive he left in Jarrett's hand. *No need to spoil the surprise too early for those boys in blue,* he mused.

Andy Reese was a nice-looking, brown-haired, blue-eyed kid who came from money, a little overweight but definitely clean-cut. Mr. Smith wondered where he got his hunger for young boys, and he finally chalked it up to bad relations with a perverted uncle or maybe his father. His parents owned a string of daycare centers in Indiana, Michigan, and Ohio, and the three in Ft. Wayne were ones that were under his management, providing him with a stream of victims. Of course, he was careful to wait till the boys were no longer in his care and were living out of state. It was the practice of the George Reese Daycare Centers to photograph and fingerprint every child, just in case of child abduction. Unfortunately, Andy Reese loved to peruse that file of photos and fingerprints the way most people would peruse a menu at a gourmet restaurant.

The videos of Andy Reese alone were even more disturbing than those in which he co-starred with Randy Jarrett. He had some strange fetishes, with taste lingering in the downright bizarre. The things he did with and to the children would never be unseen or forgotten by Mr. Smith; they were simply not possible to disremember. The deviate was not only an abuser but also an abductor. For those reasons, Mr. Smith determined that he did not deserve to be a quickie, a grab and kill. *This one requires...time and more attention,* he thought. He was sure Reese had taken some little ones and disposed of them somehow, because there was no way he could do what he did and then risk sending them home.

"He will tell me where they are, and they will be returned to their parents before I'll allow him to die," Mr. Smith swore to himself. Still, he had to work fast, because once word got out about Randy Jarrett, Reese would likely destroy any remaining evidence, including the little boys he was holding in some dingy chamber of horrors somewhere. If worse came to worst, though, and Reese did make the children disappear, Mr. Smith already had enough evidence in the form of pictures and videos to ensure that Andy Reese would be known for what he was. He also decided to check out missing person reports for young boys in and around the areas surrounding those daycare centers, because he was sure Reese knew a thing or two about some of those little faces on the backs of milk cartons.

That was one thing that never left Mr. Smith's mind, the pained and dead looks on the faces of the young boys the pervert abused. Their disturbed and hopeless expressions spoke volumes. The children could not understand the gravity of the evil that was inflicted upon them; they only knew the humiliation and mental and physical pain. *Hell is too good for the fucking bastards I've killed and will kill,* Smith surmised, and as he traveled deeper into the world of child abuse, his justification for his current undertaking only grew.

His world changed after Eric Conrad, and his resolve strengthened after Randy Jarrett. His ultimate goal was still in place, but he now had a mission, one he felt benefited all mankind. His next righteous kill would be that of a George Reese Daycare executive, and once he saved the sex slaves of that monster, he would be a hero. He was sure no one would want him caught, besides those who had to, because he was doing the whole world a favor.

Die by Proxy

Once everything was set up, Mr. Smith only needed to collect his prey. A week earlier, he placed a GPS tracker on Reese's car, for two reasons: First, he wanted to know where he was at all times, so that when the time came, he could grab him without much effort; Second, he hoped he would get lucky and find out where Reese was keeping the children he kidnapped.

At eleven o'clock in the evening, he drove to a very nice neighborhood just off St. Joe Center Road, on the northeast side of Ft. Wayne. He pulled onto the access road that led to some maintenance buildings next to a golf club and parked his car where it would not be easily seen. A bit of a trek through a small patch of woods was required, followed by a fifty-yard hike across the golf green to get to Reese's house.

Because it worked out so well for Smith with Jarrett's house, he made sure to scope out Reese's a few nights before. Disarming the home security system was easier than he thought, and he quickly went through every inch of the home, searching for any place a child might be hidden. He found nothing, so he just waited for Reese to come home. As he did, he fired up the laptop in the home office and quickly typed up the confession, that form letter that just rolled right off his fingers with ease. He then loosened all the bulbs in the kitchen, and he didn't have to wait long after that. At ten minutes till one, he heard the garage door activate.

As Reese walked into the kitchen from the garage, he reached for the light switch. When nothing happened, he flipped it up and down a couple times. "Shit!" he said, then looked across the room and noticed the clock on the microwave. "What the...? Can't be a power outage then," he reasoned, a little tipsy. "Fuck it. I'll call maintenance in the morning." Then, just as he turned to head for bed, Mr. Smith punched him as hard as he could, square in the face.

For a moment, Smith feared his rage had gone a bit too far, because Andy Reese was instantly down and out. He knelt to feel for a pulse, and once he was satisfied that his victim was not dead, he dropped enough Rohypnol in his gaping mouth to keep him out for a while. He stuffed some dirty underwear from Reese's hamper into his mouth, then zip-tied his hands and ankles, just in case.

As much as he wished he was, Smith was in no physical condition to lug almost 170 pounds of dead weight back to his car, at least not without a few rest stops along the way. By the time he reached his well-hidden vehicle, he was quite tired, breathing heavily, and he made a promise to himself to work out more. Once Reese was tucked safely in the trunk, he drove to a Meijer department store not far from there. In the corner of the parking lot, he sat in his car and caught his breath.

After fifteen minutes, he headed for a house in a wooded area, far enough away from any neighbors so he could work undisturbed. Thirty minutes later, he was strapping Andy Reese to a chair, preparing him for the interrogation. When he was ready, he put the smelling salts under Andy's nose. "Welcome back, Mr. Reese," he said. "I'm afraid you've been a very bad boy. I need you to tell me something."

"Wh-Who are you?" Reese said, the squinted as he darted his eyes around, trying to get a grip on where he was. The room was dark and nearly empty, with little furniture, and the only light was the small glow of a desk lamp shining right in his face. "Wh-What do you want?"

"I only need one thing from you."

"M-My parents have money. They'll pay anything you want."

"The only thing I want from you is the location of the children you have locked away to play out your deviant games."

"Children? What children? What games? Mister, I've got no idea what you are talking about." Reese faltered for a second, but he quickly regained his stride. "You must have me confused with someone else or—"

Mr. Smith slapped him hard across the face, so hard that a little trickle of blood came from the split on his lip that had reopened from the previous punch to the face. "For your sake, I hope you remember soon, or else you will be doing a lot of screaming for nothing," he said with a menacing growl.

"No! I... You can't! Let me go. Let me go right now. If you don't, I'll—"

"You'll do nothing," Smith said, interrupting him with

a backhand that knocked his head the other way, glad that he'd worn his training gloves to protect his hands from the blood and filth. "My patience is running thin, asshole. Where are the children?" he asked again, though he secretly hoped the man would continue to be stubborn. He quite enjoyed smacking the pervert around, and he was thrilled with the prospect of trying something he had used before, with excellent results.

Mr. Smith had studied waterboarding, seen it in movies, and even used it successfully. It would be the proverbial icing on the cake, but more than anything, he wanted to punish the pond scum first. He tried several forms of enticements to get Reese to talk, but nothing seemed to draw out a confession. Reese was stronger than he ever would have imagined, but the fear in his eyes told a different story. Mr. Smith was sure he had those children locked away somewhere, and he knew how to convince him to spill that location. *Time to drown this fucker.*

He remained masked throughout the questioning, only because he wanted Reese to think there was a reason to hide his identity; it was really just a ruse, to make the fool believe he might actually live to tell the tale. If Reese knew for sure that he was going to die, he would only let the children die too.

"One can learn many things on the internet," Mr. Smith said as he tipped the chair over, with Reese still tied to it. He carefully placed his head on a decline, between two boards that kept him from turning away. "This is your last chance, asshole."

"What are you—"

He placed a cloth over Reese's face and grabbed the pitcher of water from a nearby table. He poured it slowly, taking great delight in forcing Reese to inhale much of it into his lungs and gag.

When Reese struggled to breathe, Mr. Smith stopped and removed the cloth. "Where are the children?"

"P-Please stop. Please," Reese begged, coughing and spitting up water.

"Where!?" Smith yelled, mere inches from his face.

"I-I don't know what you're talking about. Please, mister!" Reese pleaded before the cloth was placed over his wide-eyed face again.

This time, Smith extended the duration of the waterboarding, which only heightened Reese's mental distress. When the cloth was finally removed, Reese was coughing and choking up more water than seemed possible.

"Where are the children? If you want to get out of this alive, you will tell me where you are keeping them," Mr. Smith said, more calmly this time. He could see that this pervert was beginning to break, and the thought of teasing the condemned man with the chance of life made him smile.

"I-I... I c-can't," he forced out through his coughing. Then, when Mr. Smith started to put the cloth back in place on his face, Reese finally opted to cooperate. "Okay! Okay, if you'll just stop."

"Mr. Reese, where are the children?"

Reese, now a broken man, told him everything.

Mr. Smith removed his mask but was still careful to hide his face as he sat Reese up and patted him on the shoulder. "You've done the right thing, Mr. Reese. I will check out what you have told me. For your sake, I hope it was the truth. I do not tolerate liars, and I assure you the punishment for that will be far beyond any pain you think you felt before. If the children are not there, I will show you real pain, and I will make it last for as long as I can keep you alive." He could not help hitting Reese once more. He pulled some brass knuckles from his pocket, that he had been saving for an occasion like this, and hit him hard in the face. It thrilled him to hear the sound of his fist shattering the nasty human being's jaw. "Damn, that felt good!"

After securing Reese and giving him enough Rohypnol to keep him out until he returned, Mr. Smith left to find the children. Of course, more than anything, he wanted to save them, but he still wanted to teach Reese a lesson, no matter the outcome.

Chapter 9

As Mr. Smith drove to the address Reese gave him, his excitement was palpable. He would ultimately take care of Reese, but for the time being, he wanted more than anything for the children to be alive. He drove past the property that was a few miles from the Pokagan State Park in northern Indiana. Once he was sure no one was around, he pulled into the drive and slowly drove around the back of the house, where his car would not be seen from the street. He sat still for a moment, just taking in the scene.

He left the car with gun in hand and frowned. The wind coming across the farmland was quite a bit warmer than his air-conditioned car. Then his mind moved to the reason he was there, and he cautiously, walked to the back door. He used the key that once hung around Jarrett's neck, entered gun first, and found himself in the mudroom. He placed his full concentration on the sounds of the house. At the far end of the kitchen, he saw the door that led to the basement.

But first things first. He quickly yet carefully explored the rest of the house. Once he was satisfied that he was the only adult in the farmhouse, and after one last check of the outside, he moved back to the kitchen. The same key that worked on the back door opened the basement. He stood at the top of the stairs and listened, then slowly descended.

From the bottom of the stairs, he shined his flashlight around the room. About ten feet ahead he saw a big metal door. The key to that door was exactly where he was told it would be. The flashlight shook as he pushed the key in the lock, his nerves getting the best of him. The anticipation was like a child's on Christmas morning, and he hoped he'd have the gift he wanted.

Mr. Smith pulled the door open; it was thick but not as heavy as it looked. When he found the light switch, the room came alive. His stomach turned at the sight of a king-sized bed surrounded by three cameras, as well as a fourth mounted to the ceiling, so the degenerate's exploits could be videoed from every angle. He began to picture what had happened in that room, but he quickly pushed those disturbing thoughts out of his mind.

He heard a noise and turned toward another metal door. "Hello?" he said.

There was no answer. *Please be there. Please be alive,* he thought.

Mr. Smith cautiously walked over to the door, unlocked it, and opened it slowly. "Hello?" he repeated.

Sobbing was coming from a corner of the room, and as he walked in, he noticed two jail cells. In the one on the right was a little brown-haired boy, about 9 years old. To the left were two blonds, about 7 or 8, crying heavily; they appeared to be brothers. All the children looked like they'd missed a meal or two, but they were clean. They were also terrified, crammed back as far as they could get in their cells.

As he looked into their cells, he saw something that really disturbed him, something resembling cat boxes, full of litter-covered feces. Then the faint smell of the slightly floral stench wafted to his nose. All at once, he was both saddened by the circumstances the children were in and repulsed and full of rage that anyone could do such a thing to defenseless human beings.

"Please don't be afraid," Mr. Smith said consolingly. "You're safe now, boys. "I know there is no reason you should believe me, a stranger, but I am telling the truth. Excuse me for a minute, and I'll be right back."

When the boys heard the man climbing up the stairs, they hurried to the bars and craned their necks to try to peer through the open door. When Mr. Smith returned a few minutes later, as promised, they quickly retreated to the backs of their cells, but the smell of burgers and fries loomed thick in the air. Smith noticed the older boy hiding a smile when he caught sight of a big, familiar M on a bag in the man's hand.

"I thought you might be hungry, so I stopped on the way," Mr. Smith said as he set the fast food sacks in front of their cells and retreated so they would feel comfortable enough to grab them.

The boys' hunger outweighed their fear. The older one was the first to cautiously move toward the heavenly smelling treasure, as if he feared it might be a trap. Once he successfully claimed his prize without being snatched up, the blonds quickly rushed over, grabbed the food, and hurried to the back corner again. Keeping their eyes on Mr. Smith, they voraciously tore into the bags and devoured the hamburgers, chicken nuggets, and fries as if they hadn't eaten in months.

"What are your names?"

Not one of them was willing to answer that question.

"C'mon, fellas! Haven't I proven that I'm not here to hurt you? At least tell me who you are."

The boy in the cell on the right side spoke first. "M-My name is Eric Dennis," he said, so quietly that Smith almost couldn't hear him.

"And you two?"

The two fare-haired boys looked at each other, then answered, "C-Conner Simpson," and, "Hayden, Hayden Marks."

"It is nice to meet you, boys. I am Mr. Smith. You will all be back with your parents very soon."

The younger boys started to cry, as they'd missed their parents immensely. For the first time since Smith entered the room, hope danced in their faces, but something about that soured him a bit. Somehow, for some reason, he felt closer to those boys than he did his own children, and he had to put that bitter thought out of his mind.

"I cannot take you with me right now, but there will be someone here within the next two days to take you home. I promise."

Almost in unison, the voices cried, "No!"

"I'm sorry. I have my reasons, but God is my witness, you will be with your parents again very soon."

"Please take us with you now," Eric said with a whimper. "We don't wanna be here two more days."

"I'm sorry, but I can't. I will leave the lights on, and this should tide you over for a while," he said as he set two more sacks of food for each boy down by their cells. "Don't eat it all at once. It'll give you a bellyache. Besides, you should save some for tomorrow."

"Nooo!" they chorused, desperate.

"Mister, if you leave us here, he'll come back and hurt us. He'll hurt us like he hurt Jack," Eric begged.

Jack? Mr. Smith remembered that name. "You know what happened to him?"

"No, but about a week ago, before the scary man came and talked to Daddy, he did things to Jack, bad things."

"Daddy?"

"He makes us call him that."

I looked over at the young ones, and they were shaking her heads.

"He did bad things. What do you mean by that?" Mr. Smith wasn't sure he wanted to hear what Reese had done to Jack, but at that point, he had to know.

"He tied him to the bed in there and made us watch as he burned an A and an R on his stomach with cigarettes. When we turned away, he threatened to burn us too. It was awful."

Smith noticed tears forming in Eric's eyes. The thought of Reese burning his initials into the poor boy's stomach, like carving his name into a tree, stoked the fire of hatred that burned in Mr. Smith's being. He wasn't sure if his imagination was playing tricks with him or not, but it was then that Smith noticed the faint order of burning flesh, a stench that threatened to make him sick. "Did this scary man have a name?" Smith asked, as he very much wanted to know who the scary man was, and where he could find him.

"I don't know, but after he talked to Daddy, Jack left with him. Jack didn't wanna go, so the scary man hit him really hard and dragged him out of the room. Jack never came back."

Smith forced himself to break free of the evil thoughts that threatened to consume him. "Like I said, boys, I really need to go now. I promise you that within two days, you'll be back with your parents."

"Please don't leave us! If you take us with you, we'll be good. We promise." The boys were openly crying, and their sobs tore at Smith's heart.

"The man who put you here will never bother you or anyone else again. I promise, boys. In the days to come, you will hear about what I am going to do to this evil man tonight after I leave you. Remember that I am doing it for you and for every child who has ever been hurt by someone they trusted. It is very important that you know none of this is your fault. That man is sick, and he is wrong. He is not your daddy, because a real daddy loves his children and would never hurt them. Don't let that sick, twisted bastard rule your lives. Be strong, and you will get past all this and have great lives. I'll be watching over you, and no one will ever hurt you again."

With that, he backed out of the room and shut the door but left it unlocked, the boys' cries echoing behind him. That broke his heart, but there was a smile on his face as he climbed the stairs. He had saved them, and countless others would be spared, children that might have also fallen prey to the bastard he was about to kill.

He drove back to the house in the woods and was happy to find that Reese was still unconscious. If his calculations were correct, he would be unconscious till they arrived at the site he had picked out for him. He gave Reese an aspirin injection, so the deviant's wrists would bleed, undeterred by clotting when his filthy hands were removed.

As he removed Reese's clothes, the smell of cigarette smoke wafted into his nose. His anger raged. After he wrapped a naked Reese in an army green tarp, he lifted him over his shoulder and carried him out to his car. He was still pissed as he placed Reese not too gently into the trunk. He went back in to make sure he had left nothing behind that might leave a trail to him. He was sure there was little chance of anyone tying that place to Reese's death, but his paranoid and careful nature forced him to be sure.

It was 3:15 when Smith pulled out of the driveway, and the site, some twenty miles north, would be reached within a half-hour. *This death will be a game-changer,* he thought as he drove. Although it was not the goal he'd started with, it was quickly becoming quite the fun little diversion.

As he passed the 340 exit on I-69 near Ashley, Indiana, he readied himself to pull over. He drove about a mile and three-quarters more, then parked about 100 feet before the third dumpsite. There were two reasons for it: First, he did not want to park in front of the place he would leave Reese's body, and second, his car would obscure the line of sight for oncoming traffic. He placed an orange sticker on the car to indicate that it would be towed if not moved soon.

He pulled the blind from the trunk and set it up in a hurry, then camouflaged it by covering the base with some of the surrounding vegetation. It did not take him long to fetch Reese, though he did struggle with his weight a bit. Once he was tied securely to the fencepost, with his arms at his sides, he rolled up Reese's dirty underwear once again and stuffed it in the pervert's mouth. *Damn! He must have worn these to the gym,* he thought as he waved the air in front of his nose.

Reese awoke with a start when the smelling salts passed below his nostrils. His face hurt terribly from the punch, and his mind raced to take stock of his surroundings. It was a bright, moonlit night, and he could see fairly well in the darkness.

"Welcome back, Mr. Reese."

Reese looked into the unfamiliar face and tried in vain to move away from the sound of the voice of his masked torturer.

"Andrew Reese, I frankly have no idea why any fair and just God would allow parasites like you to exist. It is entirely unfathomable to me to think that you or someone like you could possibly harm my children. Why? Why are you still here, still taking up space on this planet, using up oxygen you don't deserve to breathe? Don't get me wrong. I do not wish to act as the hand of God nor to deny His sovereignty and wisdom, but for what you have done, you must die. Justice will be served here and now."

A car approached, and Mr. Smith looked through the peephole in the blind to watch it pass. When Reese screamed into fetid underwear stuffed in his mouth, Mr. Smith backhanded him, and the pervert fell silent.

Once his speech was completed, he moved on to the part he most enjoyed, ready to give the self-serving pervert some clear insight into the aftermath of the evil he had done. "Once you are gone," he said, "I will share your perverted acts with the world." He held up the flash drive. "This contains all the videos you have made of those unfortunate children who were unlucky enough to spark your deviant desires. I can only imagine how this will affect your parents and siblings, Amy and Jordan. Along with the crushing embarrassment, I am sure your parents' businesses will suffer greatly. Why, they might have to close down altogether, thanks to you and the very justifiable lawsuits the families will bring once they find out that many of the children were once in their care. This will surely bankrupt your parents. They will be lucky to stay out of jail. At the very least, their lives will soon be in ruin, all because of you."

Mr. Smith was happy to see the distress in Reese's face, something he had grown to anticipate and appreciate. He dreaded the day when he would come upon a psychopath devoid of guilt or emotion, for that would be a tremendous letdown indeed.

"I commend you for telling me the truth, for I have rescued the children. They will soon be home with their families, and those boys will be the driving force behind the demise of your not-so-good name," he said before a thought suddenly occurred to him. "How many others have there been?

Reese shook his head and growled into the sock, "Fuuk ooh!"

"Wrong answer, asshole," Mr. Smith said, then reached back and casually grabbed the loppers. He opened the cutters wide, fit them around Reese's left wrist, and tightened them until they almost cut into his skin. "Now, how many did you say?"

Reese nodded. "Oak, oak!"

"I am going to take your nasty underwear out of your mouth. If you try to scream, I will cut your hand off. Do you understand?" Mr. Smith asked, then waited till Reese gave him another nod before he pulled the gag from the pervert's mouth. "How many?"

"F-Fourteen or fifteen. I-I can't remember."

"What did you do with the others? There were only three in the house," Mr. Smith demanded. He dreaded the answer, but he had to know. He tightened the grip of the loppers on Reese's wrist, as added incentive.

"I-I sold them. I sold them," Reese admitted and hung his head.

"You *sold* them?" He grimaced, unable to mask his surprise. "To whom?"

"I don't know, man! No names on the internet for that kind of stuff," Reese said. "Those are the rules."

"Who took Jack? Tell me, and you just might get out of this alive." Smith leaned in closer and smiled.

"He is a middleman. He delivers the children and payments," he said hopefully.

"I need a name, goddamn it!" Smith growled. "You want to live or not?"

"Jay Mercer! He was my roommate in college."

"How do I find this Mercer?"

"I think he lives in Kalamazoo. I don't remember his number, but if you let me go, I can get it for you."

"No need. I'll find him. It's time to die, asshole!"

"What?" Reese's eyes went wide as Smith stuffed the underwear back into his mouth and cut off his hand. His scream was deafening inside the blind.

Mr. Smith looked through the peephole to see if any cars were near. When he was sure there were none, he turned back toward the pervert. "You don't deserve to live," he growled as he quickly moved to the other wrist and cut it off. The crunching noise that once threatened to derail his mission was now like music to his ears, the moment he anticipated and savored.

Reese didn't say another word before he fell into shock and bled out moments later, thanks to the aspirin that helped the process along.

After Mr. Smith was sure his victim was dead, he went about his ritual of setting Reese's folded cloths, the wallet, and his hands in place, holding the flash drive and confession in the pervert's lap. He studied the scene before him, decided that it was good, then made his way back to his car and left. He was sure the Michigan authorities were watching I-69 closely, and the thought of leaving a body in Indiana, far from the vigilant eyes of Michigan's finest, made him smile.

His mirth was short-lived, however, as visions of boys being bought and sold like cattle forced their way into his mind. They were not slaughtered for food, but their lives were butchered beyond repair by the very worst of humankind. That disgust overshadowed all the good he felt he had done, sickening him to his core and stirring up great conflict within him during his drive home.

Finally, Mr. Smith's dark thoughts moved to the light again as he remembered the hope in the faces of Conner, Hayden, and Eric. By the time he pulled up to his apartment near I-69 on the northeast side of Indy, he knew that he would sleep well that night.

Chapter 10

Rollie Simmons, a Lansing gun dealer, headed to the Allen County War Memorial Coliseum in Ft. Wayne for a gun and knife show, eager to replenish his supply. He had just passed Ashley, Indiana, The Home of the Smiley Face, as it was known, because just over the tree line was a tower bearing that iconic symbol, in one of the parks. As silly as it was, it was something Rollie always unconsciously looked for every time he drove south on 69.

Another thing he had been doing without much thought lately was gazing at the sides of the interstate. After all the news he'd seen about handless perverts being left along I-69, he couldn't help himself, and he couldn't believe it when, just a mile or so past Ashley, he spotted something that caught his attention. He tapped his brakes to free up the cruise control, then moved carefully from the passing lane to the side of the road. Not the most observant driver in the world, Rollie neglected to check his mirrors and almost hit a Mazda that was hovering in his blind spot.

After quickly pulling back into the passing lane and waving a brief sorry to the middle finger of the pissed driver of the CX-5, he looked to make sure no one was behind him. This time, he made it safely to the side of the road and carefully backed his car along the shoulder until he was directly beside what he could now see was a naked man sitting in the tall grass, next to a couple trees.

"By God, I found one," Rollie muttered as he opened the door of his Chevy van, stood on the floorboard, and looked over the roof for a better view. "I do believe I found one!" As a cool morning breeze moved through the tall grass that blocked his view, he saw the blood that covered the lower part of the naked man's body.

Rollie quickly climbed back in his van, grabbed his phone, and started to dial 911 but stopped. "They ain't gonna believe this. I need proof," he said, as he wanted to take a couple personal snapshots before the cops were swarming all over the place and refusing to let him past the yellow tape.

Ashley Town Marshal Morris Billings was in his office having his first cup of coffee on a beautiful summer morning. He didn't normally go in on Saturdays, but there was a small pile of neglected paperwork forming on the corner of his desk.

Suddenly, Deputy Marshal Kerry Mills burst into his office, followed by the Chief Deputy Larry Corbin. "Marshal, we just got a 911 transfer about a male body out on the interstate, a couple miles south. It's like those ones we heard about in Michigan, naked with his hands cut off."

"Shit! Call the State boys, Sheriff Farmer, and Lawrence Ross, our DeKalb County coroner, and give 'em the location."

"Should I call the Michigan Staties?" Kerry asked as the marshal strapped on his gun.

"No. Let our State boys handle that. For now, let's concentrate on what we can do ourselves," he said before he left his office in a run, nearly missing the trashcan with a quick toss of his almost full cup of coffee.

Within forty-five minutes, every agency was represented at the crime scene. Less than an hour later, Beckman and I were there. The body had already been processed but remained as it was found, and I was glad for that; I needed to see things the way the killer did.

I badged my way through to the victim and was taken aback by the sight of the severed hands sitting in the victim's lap. I had seen pictures of such a macabre scene, but it was ten times worse to see it in person. As I looked at the handless man sitting in the late morning sun, I checked the area around him and found the characteristic holes. "Beckman check this out," I said, pointing to the obvious blind marks.

"It's our unsub all right."

"Yeah. I wonder what this poor, sick bastard was into."

"Well, it looks like it's your case now. I'll continue to work on the Michigan murders, but you're the new man in charge. God, it must suck to be you."

"Sometimes, yeah," I said, shaking my head.

"You need a ride back to Lansing?" Beckman put his hand on my shoulder.

"No, Zee's on her way. I'll let you know if anything comes up. It's been a pleasure working with you, Beckman."

"Well, if ya want, I can stick around for a little while longer. There are a few things I'd like to talk over with the Indiana boys," Beckman offered, trying pitifully to mask his real intentions.

"You're full of shit, you old dog," I said, grinning and shaking my head.

"C'mon, man! Can you blame me?" Beckman retorted, his face a bit flushed.

"Hell no. After all, you *are* a man, and she *is* one of the most beautiful women I've ever known." I paused. "Wait. You *are* a man, right?" I asked, displaying my signature shit-eating grin before I headed over to talk to Marshal Billings. "Marshal Billings, I'm Special Agent Benjamin Kroh from the BAU, but please call me Kroh. Do we have an identity on the victim yet?"

"Yes, I believe we do." He turned and called the county coroner over. "I need to see the note that was in the victim's hand," he said then handed the note to me in a protective bag.

"I, Andrew Robert Reese, am guilty of unspeakable crimes against children. For this, I must be punished. I will not ask for forgiveness, for I deserve none. To my father, my mother, and the families I have destroyed, I am truly sorry," I read out loud. I then turned back to the marshal. "Have them put a rush on the flash drive. I need to see what this guy was into. Do we have a positive ID on Mr. Reese?"

Marshal Billings showed me a DMV printout.

"That's him, all right. What do we know about him so far?"

"Well, he lived in Ft. Wayne and came from money."

"What kind of money?" I asked warily, arching an eyebrow.

"The honest kind, I hope. His family owns the George Reese Daycare centers in Michigan, Indiana, and Ohio."

"Daycare centers? Shit!" I said, grimacing and rubbing my temples. "This is gonna get really bad, real fast." Another question popped into my head. "Who found the body?"

"Some gun dealer from Lansing, Rollie Simmons. He was heading to a gun and knife show in Ft. Wayne. He was running late, so we got his information and his statement, then let him go."

After Zee arrived, we followed the coroner to his office and waited for the flash drive, along with Marshal Billings. Once it was dusted for prints and checked for any trace evidence, it was copied for viewing. Ross plugged the flash drive into his laptop, and, for the next few minutes, his computer treated us to horrible images we knew we would never, ever forget.

"Fuck!" I said, looking away, unable to bear another moment of it.

"Don't you mean fucked, as in totally fucked up?" Ross said, looking as if he might vomit.

Chapter 11

Paul Meecham, FBI Forensic Scientist, arrived around one, driving from Indy, with Agent Vernon. I had worked with both of them on the Fingertip case. Meecham was a very capable, rail-thin agent full of lame jokes, but I liked him just because he made me laugh. For anyone unaware of the circumstances, the humor might have been a bit high schoolish, but it was just another way to cope in the macabre situations we had to deal with.

Armed with all the files on the two previous cases, they sifted through the items collected at the crime scene. While they got familiar with the case, Zee and I headed to Reese's house, a beautiful, half-million-dollar estate on the north side of Ft. Wayne. The first things I noticed were the evidence tents around the blood spots on the kitchen floor. A team of forensic techs were already hard at work, tearing the place apart.

As I looked around, visions of what I saw Reese doing forced their way into my brain, and I noticed Zee looking at me strangely. "What is it?" I asked.

"You're doing it again."

"What?"

"That thing with your finger. What's on your mind?"

After a laugh, because she knew me so well, I answered, "Well, the children Reese molested could not have been returned to their parents. There is no way, because they would have known something was wrong with their kids. What did he do with them once they, uh…served their purpose?"

"I'm not sure. You think he has them stashed somewhere?"

"Or...worse," I thought. "Maybe our killer did him in before he mentioned where they are."

"That would be horrible," Zee said, shaking her head.

I grabbed the lead tech by the elbow. "I want you to tear this place apart, every nook and cranny. This bastard might have had secret passages or rooms, even some sort of dungeon. I'm pretty sure Reese was not stupid. He would have known better than to send those kids home after what he did. We have to check the property for any survivors or...bodies."

"What can I do?" Zee asked.

"Get Marty on the horn. Tell him to do his best to identify the children in those videos. He might be able to use some of that facial recognition and run it against missing children in the area. First, though, I need to know about any properties Reese owned or even those owned by his family. We need to check them all for any children who might be waiting for Reese to return."

I knew it wouldn't be long before our vigilante posted the evils of Robert Reese on the internet. If he stuck to the same timeline, we really only had less than a day to solve the case. Unless our unsub decided to surrender, there was no chance in hell for us to stop him at that point. It was obvious that he carefully planned and executed each murder, and I had the feeling he was really beginning to enjoy his misplaced fame. *This one is gonna get national attention for sure.* I thought, as I wondered where I put my oar, the one I would need to paddle up Shit Creek once it all became public.

I had to get away for a while, because the thought of starving abused children threatened to mess with my head in a very bad way. The only thing I could think to do was to visit the man in Ft. Wayne who had discovered Reese, to get the gun dealer's take on what he saw before the police were called.

It wasn't difficult for us to get into the gun show at the Coliseum once we flashed our badges, though it was obvious that we were not exactly welcome there. After several assurances that we were not there to bust anyone or hassle the dealers or the shoppers, we soon found someone to direct us to Rollie's booth in the packed exposition hall. As we followed our guide, I couldn't help but fear the people I watched buying firearms. I wasn't a normal lawman, as I'd never been a fan of guns. I only had one because I was required to. Furthermore, if it was up to me, I wouldn't sell a gun to 99 percent of these buyers. I really wanted to talk to Mr. Simmons while the crime scene was fresh in his mind, and I had a couple questions I was sure only he could answer.

Simmons, a camo-wearing businessman with a two-day growth, had a lot of nice firearms for sale, but I like I said, not a fan. Being shot in the leg and in the shoulder not long ago, did nothing to change my mind. My collecting passion is straight razors, the kind men used to shave with. My grandfather on my mother's side was a barber, and he gave me my first razor when I was 16, so I'd been collecting them ever since.

The first thing I noticed as we walked up to Rollie's booth was a stack of eight-by-tens of Reese tied to the fence. I could not believe the dumb bastard was selling them for five dollars apiece. When I identified myself, Rollie moved to hide the photos.

"Don't bother, Rollie. Just tell me what happened this morning."

After a moment of embarrassed confusion, he blurted, "I-I was drivin' down I-69, just past Ashley, when I noticed something on the side of the road. I almost had a wreck trying to stop. I couldn't help but notice all that blood," he said. After a hard swallow, he continued, "I ain't never seen anything like that before, so I took a few pictures. When I started showin' 'em around, a few people suggested that I sell them. I-I guess I got carried away."

"Yeah, I guess you did," I said, not trying to hide my disgust. "Anyway, please continue with what you saw this morning."

"Well, when I realized that this might be part of them I-69 killings I been hearin' about, I called the cops, then waited till they got there so I could flag 'em down. That was about it."

"That's a good story, Rollie, but I have another one. You

found the body, took some pictures, then saw the wallet just sitting there. You just couldn't help yourself, could you, Rollie? You had to get a souvenir, so you took his driver's license, didn't you?"

"I-I didn't do anything of the sort!" Rollie said as he unconsciously looked toward his cashbox.

I looked toward Zee with a smile, as both of us were highly familiar with the idea that people inadvertently telegraphed information, as long as we knew what to look for.

"So, Mr. Simmons," she said, taking over, "if we look in your cashbox, what you think we will find?"

"Y-You can't do that. I know my rights," he said, trying to sound stern but quite visibly shaken.

"What if we just arrest you here for hindering an ongoing investigation?"

"You can't do that neither."

"Oh, but we *can*," Zee said, then pulled out her cuffs and stepped toward Rollie.

"Okay, okay! You caught me. I took the damn license," he said, then reached over to open the cashbox, retrieve the stolen license, and handed it to Zee.

"That's not all you took, is it, Rollie?" I pushed.

"No, that's it. That's everything."

"What about the $500 he had?" I said, even though I was reaching on the amount.

"Wait! Th-There was only $250 when..." Rollie trailed off and gave me that oh-shit look when he suddenly realized he fell for my fishing hook, line, and sinker.

"Rollie Simmons, you're under arrest," Zee said, snapping the cuffs shut and giving him his Miranda warning.

"Can't I at least pack up my stuff?"

"Fat chance. How stupid do you think we are? You think we're going to let you handle piles of firearms while you're in custody? Not hardly," I said. "We'll find somebody else to box up all this shit, except those pictures. I'm sure they'll make a great exhibit at your trial."

To that, Rollie had no answer but rolled his eyes and snorted.

After we passed him off to the locals, Zee and I went

on a bit of a shopping spree. She was delighted to find a Glock Nineteen G-Four for a little under $500, and I actually found a couple of nice razors for my collection, one Wade and Butcher 7/8-inch wedge for $275 and a Sheffield's Ankor 6/8-inch wedge for $325. It might not have thrilled most people, but I was practically floating on air by the time we left the show.

* * *

A little after nine p.m., Mr. Smith sat in the parking lot of a run-down strip mall, just a five-minute drive from Ball State University, in Muncie, Indiana. When he was sure no one was nosing around, he headed for Bauhaus Computer Repair, one of the few remaining businesses, happy that he'd made arrangements to meet the owner at the late hour.

He pushed open the door and was hit by the smell of Patchouli incense, along with the smell of the weed the incense was supposed to mask. Ryan Barstow, who preferred to be called Mantis, was somewhat of a computer genius, but his front room décor matched his Goth lifestyle. Mr. Smith found Mantis sitting behind a glass display case full of Goth jewelry.

Once Mantis was sure it was only Mr. Smith, he pulled out the joint he'd hidden behind his display counter and inhaled from it deeply. Then, in a voice that allowed him to hold in his breath as long as he could to maximize the effect of his toke, he said, "Welcome, Mr. Smith."

"Hello, Mr. Barstow."

Mantis bristled at the use of his real name, but it was quickly forgotten in the haze of his high.

Mr. Smith continued, "You said you found what I was looking for. Is that right?"

"Yeah, man. This fucker's real messed up, and his girlfriend's as much of a freak as he is."

"So, you found a couple?"

"Yeah, but I don't think they're married. That'd be real long distance, man, 'cause he lives in Indy, and she's in Muncie."

"Really?" Mr. Smith said with more than a hint of interest.

"I think he's into little dudes, but she seems like...well,

everything. Damn, those two are into some nasty shit!" He slid the flash drive across the counter, then pulled his hand back to wipe it on a napkin, as if the pothead was glad to be rid of the evidence. He also didn't want to take the chance of being touched by Mr. Smith, who seriously gave him the creeps.

"Is this everything?"

"Yeah. There are videos, a few emails, and even that psycho bitch's diary. From what I read in there; it sounds like they've been into this sick shit for a long time."

"Does anyone else know about this?"

"No, man. I did everything you asked, and I kept it on the downlow."

As Mantis took another deep toke, Mr. Smith moved around the counter and reached inside his coat. He pulled out a fat envelope. "Here," he said, but at the last second, he let it fall to the floor.

"Clumsy much?" Mantis laughed. "And *I'm* the one smoking pot."

Mantis bent down to retrieve his payment, but as he started to stand, Smith punched him squarely in the temple. Mantis was down and out with the first hit, but Smith hit him twice more, just to make sure.

Just as Mr. Smith did with Curtis Meyer, his first computer tech, he quickly went through the shop to erase all hint of his presence there. Once he was sure, he moved toward the unconscious Mantis and prepared for the only part of his plan he still felt uneasy about.

Since it seemed to have worked the first time, he found a foam plate, stuck his knife through the middle of it, and pushed it into Ryan Barstow's heart. After the rush of blood lessened, he stabbed him multiple times, hoping to make it appear like a crime of passion rather than a calculated act of necessity.

Mr. Smith then turned off the lights and looked out into the parking lot. Once he was sure he would not be seen, he left the computer shop and made sure to lock the door behind him.

Once again, as he drove toward his Indianapolis apartment, conflict stormed inside him. He was not happy about what he had just done, but it was necessary. He also felt a bit buzzed, which he assumed was a bit of a contact high from Barstow's pot. He had experienced alcohol before but never pot. Somehow, his mission took on a new grandeur in his mind, but after catching himself driving ten miles under the speed limit, paranoia set in. Terrified that he would be pulled over and questioned, even arrested for drug use, he set the cruise control at the appropriate speed and tried to concentrate on making it home. He knew it would be impossible to explain some of the things in his car.

When he finally made it home, which seemed like an eternity later, his mind was weary enough that he wanted to go straight to bed. Mr. Smith was asleep almost before his head hit the pillow, dreaming only of the next step in his plan.

Chapter 12

The next day, at precisely six o'clock, the unsub posted the evils of Andrew Robert Reese on the internet. As graphic as it was, he was careful not to exploit the children, but there was one particularly shocking element in the exposure. In an obviously distorted voice, he narrated, "Before Andrew's fortunate demise, I located the three missing boys he locked away for his perverted pleasure. Authorities are being notified of that location as I speak. The children are understandably frightened but alive. I am only sorry I did not stop this one sooner. I can only hope the parents of this sick individual are ready and willing to pay for the crimes of their son. Justice must be served."

True to his word, the killer notified the Ft. Wayne PD of the boys' whereabouts via an anonymous 911 call. The call also contained a warning: "If you do not give me credit for finding the boys, I will release their names to the public."

As soon as I was informed of the location, Zee and I headed north. It took almost an hour to get to the house, and by the time we arrived, at least eight law enforcement vehicles were already there, along with an ambulance. Zee and I quickly jumped out of the car and headed toward the house.

As the trio of terrorized boys was brought out, their faces were covered, just in case any nosy press or random looky-loos happened to be lurking around. We made our way to the ambulance to speak with them before we headed inside, but they were so shaken up that they couldn't tell us much that we didn't already know.

Inside, we were directed to the basement, and we slowly descended the stairs. It felt like walking into a nightmare. I was sickened at the sight of the messy bed, surrounded by cameras. Knowing such evil went on in that room where I stood forced bitter bile into my throat, so horrible that I had to put a couple breath strips in my mouth just to stave off the taste and sting of the acid. I'd seen some very sick things in my career, but that topped the list, and after only a few minutes of perusing the crime scene, and finally smelling the well used litter boxes, I had to get the hell out of there.

When Zee came out, she found me sitting on the front step, just staring at the sky. "You okay?" she asked as she sat down next to me and put her arm around me for a hug.

"Yeah. That was just... God, that stuff messes with my head, you know? Worse, this stuff is happening all around the world, no matter what we do to try to stop it. It's almost too much to handle. I can't stop thinking about those poor kids. They'll be messed up forever from this," I said. When I dropped my head, the tears started to flow, and I didn't care who saw me.

Zee pulled me in closer and let me cry on her shoulder. After I let it all out, she pulled my face up and forced me to look into her eyes. "Hey, three boys are alive and will be well, soon to be reunited with their families. That's got to count for something, right?"

"You're right. I'll be okay, Zee, but..."

"But what?" she asked, arching an eyebrow of caution at me, as if she already knew what I was thinking.

"It really makes me question whether we should even try to stop this guy. As far as I can tell, he's doing the world a favor, taking out the garbage."

"I know what you mean, but that's not up to us. Our job is to put his ass behind bars, and that's what we'll do." With that, Zee stood and reached out to offer me a hand. When I was on my feet, she pulled me into another friendly embrace. "Let me buy you a drink. Three kids were saved today, and that's worth celebrating. C'mon, Boss."

"I can't argue with that," I said and mustered a crooked smile.

Die by Proxy

* * *

The very next day, I was able to talk to the boys again, after they were reunited with their parents. Their reunion had already worked wonders for their shattered souls. The two younger boys still did not seem to know or remember much; for the duration of the interviews, they just clung to their parents and cried a lot. The information they provided was sketchy at best. Eric, however, the oldest of the three, had a little more to tell.

"The first boy must've left while I was asleep, because when I got up, he was gone. Jack left after a scary man came and talked to Daddy." he said about the two boys who were there before him. "They were older than me, and I kinda think Daddy didn't like that. A few days later, Connor and Hayden showed up."

I knew Reese made the children call him Daddy, so I didn't push him on it, hoping not to open some sore memories. Based on when Eric was abducted, we calculated that he was in Reese's possession for over nine months. Although I tried not to show it, it made me cringe to imagine what that boy had to endure during that time. Since I had to focus on Reese's killer, though, I moved our conversation toward more recent events. "Okay, Eric," I coaxed, "tell me what happened when the other man came to see you."

"He just showed up last night with some food from McDonald's. He fed us, but then he just left us down there."

"What does the man look like?"

"I don't know. He's just…a guy, I guess."

"Do you remember any details about him? Maybe you recall the color of his eyes or hair. Does he even have hair? Did anything about his face seem different or unique? Anything you can remember would help."

"Oh, okay. Well, he has brown hair, but I got no idea 'bout his eyes."

"Anything else?"

"Hmm," Eric said, taking a moment to think. "Oh, yeah! He has a mustache too. That's all I remember."

"Did he say anything?"

"Only that we were safe and that someone would come to

get us soon. Then he gave us more sacks of food and told us to not eat it all at once. I had to yell at the boys. They were being pigs."

"Did he say anything else? Anything that might clue us in to who he is?"

After another moment of thought, Eric beamed a smile. "He mentioned that his name is Mr. Smith. Does that help?"

"You've been a huge help, Eric," I said, and thanked the boy. "Do you think you could talk to our artist about Mr. Smith, to help him come up with a picture?"

"Yeah, I guess."

I left Eric and his parents with the sketch artist and let him work his magic. I found Meecham and said, "Try to determine what he ordered, and maybe we can track down the franchise where he bought it. Nine bags would be a big order, one a drive-thru worker might remember. Maybe we'll get lucky and catch this bastard before he kills again."

Meecham nodded, then went on to confirm Eric's story about the fast food, three bags for each of the boys.

Just as I signed off, I got a call from Marty. "Hey, Boss," he said, "it seems your boy's good karma is on the rise."

"How so?"

"He's an internet sensation, man, and needless to say, the mainstream media is picking up on it. I sent the links to your tablet, but it's probably going to piss you off. See ya."

"Wait, Marty!" I shouted before he hung up. "One of the boys gave us a name. It's not much to go on, sort of generic, but I need you to run a Mr. Smith against anything in the proximity of our dumpsites."

"Smith? Sort of generic? The upper Midwest is a pretty big haystack, Boss."

"Yeah, I know it's an unusual name, so it shouldn't be that hard. Unfortunately, it's all we've got right now. See if you can do that thing you do and turn up a Smith link in more than one location."

"Gee, that's no problem at all. I'm sure there aren't more than a handful of Smiths in that area, right?" he said, his voice thick with sarcasm. "Smith? I'll do what I can, Boss."

"Attaboy!" I said, jokingly, even though I felt his pain.

Marty responded with a word I didn't know, likely Navajo, which I have a suspicion translated into, "Asshole."

"What was that?" I dared to ask.

"Yes, sir. Anything you need, sir." he fibbed.

I could see him smiling in his Fortress of the Technodude. "Yeah right!" I said with a laugh. "Thanks, Marty."

As I had feared, the unsub was becoming something of a hero, with various internet sites singing the praises of his deeds. The Guardian Angle of I-69 became a popular subject on all forms of social media, so he was becoming a superhero on the national scale. At that moment, I vowed to be the kryptonite to that particular superhero.

* * *

Although it had only started as a means to an end, Mr. Smith couldn't help but enjoy his newfound fame. He had no intention of deserting his original plan, but the boost to his sense of self-worth was addicting. *My family will probably never know how freaking famous I am. If only they saw the good I'm doing,* he thought. Even my bitch of a wife would be proud.

* * *

As the sun was pushing away the darkness in the eastern sky, a newspaper boy pedaling his bike tossed the daily edition of the *Muncie Star* onto the porches on his route. Soon, the citizens of the college town would turn to the second page and read a story about the death of the owner of Bauhaus Computer Repair. Authorities suspected that it had to do with a drug deal gone wrong, but the benign report barely registered with anyone except local law enforcement.

Chapter 13

We had nothing but three murders—no suspects, no witnesses, and no real leads. The sketch the artist came up with in talking with Eric Dennis looked more like Andrew Reese than not. I couldn't blame the kid; I knew the face of his perpetrator would be burned into the poor kid's mind for a long, long time, thanks to the repeated abuse he and the others suffered at the hands of the Goddamn pervert. We had quite a bit of information about the murders of three very sick individuals, but we didn't have one shred of evidence that would lead us to the so-called Guardian.

We were spinning our wheels, and the clock was ticking; everyone knew another body would be found inside the two-week window, likely holding the characteristic confession on one of its separated hands. Whoever Mr. Smith was, there was no shortage of child molesters in the world for him to destroy. "The path to hell," I had to mutter to myself over and over again, to remind myself that Mr. Smith's alleged good intentions still didn't justify heinous murder.

Zee and I sat in my new favorite hotdog place, Mr. Coney, on Coldwater Road in Ft. Wayne, enjoying our meal, when Vernon and Crystal walked in.

"What are *you* doing here?" I said, astonished when I saw her.

"Well, Vernon called to ask if I was hungry."

Vernon simply shrugged and nodded.

"I told him I know this little place in Ft. Wayne, so…"

"What?" I asked, not believing a word of it.

Die by Proxy

"It's true," Vernon confirmed.

"You're full of shit, both of you, but I won't say I'm not glad to see you guys." I shook Vernon's hand and hugged Crystal. "It was you, wasn't it? You told them, didn't you?" I asked, looking suspiciously at Zee.

She shrugged, as nonchalantly as Vernon had. "I have no idea what you're talking about."

For the next forty-five minutes, we devoured amazing dogs smothered in cheese and chili sauce and enjoyed each other's company. Just as we were about to leave, my phone rang.

"Hey, Marty. What's up?" I said, lifting a finger to tell the others to hold on a minute.

"I found something strange, Boss."

"Shoot."

"You got your tablet with you?"

"Yeah, why?"

"Turn it on. You got to see this for yourself."

"Okay," I said, firing it up. "Go on, Marty."

"Well, I've been looking at the placements of the bodies on I-69. As an afterthought, I thought I'd check the mileage between each dumpsite. It turns out that the dead guys were left almost exactly 111 miles apart. You're not gonna believe this, but precisely 111 miles south of Ashley is the city of—"

"Anderson!" I blurted.

"Damn it, Kroh, do you always have to do that?"

"Sorry, Marty, but this case is messing with my mind... and not in a good way. As always, great work. You really are the best, when it comes to geeks. You keep this up, and I just might keep you around a while."

"Working for you is a little boring."

"The money is nice, though, right?"

"Well, if you continue to pay me, I just might stay. Bye."

All along, I'd had a gut feeling that there was something more to the killings than just an urge to eliminate perverts. The Guardian was leading us to Anderson, and I couldn't help feeling that the case was connected to me or the Fingertip Killer somehow. I had to consider that Avery might have had a partner. There was an answer, but for the life of me, I could not figure out what it could be.

"Anderson? What about Anderson?" Crystal asked, a little concerned.

I pushed away the remnants of our Coney dogs and fries and placed the tablet where everyone could see the screen. "Marty's been doing what he does best, and he found something interesting. All the bodies along the interstate were almost exactly 111 miles apart. If that pattern continues, the next dumpsite will be—"

"Anderson!" everyone chorused.

"You got it. For the first time since Conrad's body was found, we may be one step ahead of our unsub. We might not be able to stop him from killing the next pervert on his hit list, but we might be able to catch him when he puts the nasty bastard on display."

"So, what now?" Vernon asked, grabbing a couple more fries for the road.

"We need to keep this new intel under wraps. It will work to our advantage if he thinks we're still clueless."

"Don't show our hand, right?" Zee offered.

"Right," I said, smiling over at Zee, "now that we've got an ace up our sleeve."

"You better call Bradford," Crystal advised, and I quickly took her up on that advice.

"Bradford," I said, "I need you to set up a meeting tomorrow, with the sheriff and the Staties. I'll arrange things on my end."

After I hung up, as a courtesy, I called Beckman and Pembrook and asked them to meet us in Anderson. I was glad they both agreed, especially since I couldn't give them any details.

* * *

Great! A two-fer, Mr. Smith thought as he pondered Garret Munson, owner of a youth athletic training center, and Julie Miller, an instructor at that center. It was something new, and the thought of it sent shivers up his spine. *If this works out, as I know it will, I'll be even more popular. Maybe I should run for president!* The thought of himself sitting in the Oval Office made him smile. *Wait your turn Mr. President. I just might come after you next.* That thought made him smile. He didn't much like the president, but his hatred for two others was all consuming; he despised his wife and Agent Kroh. An audible growl escaped him as he wondered which one, he detested more.

Mr. Smith spent the next few days just watching his prey, Garrett Munson one day and Julie Miller the next. He typed and printed all the information he knew about them and everything he could find on Google and all he'd collected from his now-dead source, but he needed to know their daily routines, so he could determine the best time and place to take them. It was a bit of a challenge, since the two did not live together, but as the days passed, he found the perfect opportunities.

In the evening hours, when his surveillance for the day was done, he studied the flash drive. Julie's diary was an unabridged version of their lives together, a detailed account of every experience they'd shared since the day they met. It was hard to understand the joy the woman took in documenting all they had done, but Mr. Smith learned to skip over the nastier details as he fell into the foul pit that was their union.

The malignant duo met at a camp where they served as counselors, and they found a certain commonality among themselves: Both got off on abusing the children in their care and savored the chance to make little ones do unspeakable things. It was easy enough to keep their victims quiet; they only had to threaten to expose the children to their friends and promise harm to their parents if anyone uttered a word. During their two years as camp counselors, they managed to abuse over a dozen children, without raising the slightest suspicion about their activities.

After earning a physical education degree, Garrett began teaching and coaching at various Midwest middle schools, but he did not feel whole without his muse. The remedy for his pain was the death of his mother, which Julie seemed to think was the work of Munson, because once she was out of the way, all she had fell right into Garrett's lap. He quickly sold the farmland for a nice profit but kept the farmhouse and five acres of woodland for himself.

The inheritance from his unfortunate mother allowed Garrett to finance and open Munson's Youth Athletic Center, a place for adolescents to improve and enhance their sports skills before moving on to high school. The facility was located on the northeast side of Indianapolis, which gave him access to boys in central Indiana. While Munson would settle for younger boys, opening a club for 11- to 14-year-olds perfectly hit his sweet spot.

He wasted no time before hiring Julie as his first instructor, and no one questioned the decision, since she specialized in gymnastics and track and field. The two also wasted no time before preying on the children in their care. Certain students were chosen for campouts on his forested property, where they were taught lessons that were not strictly athletic.

The couple lavished those boys with gifts and just the right amount of threat to keep them from tattling, telling the boys, "As long as you keep this to yourselves, your family and friends will never know what you have done. It will only hurt them if you tell anyone. Imagine what would happen if your friends saw these." They showed the young ones pictures of the sex acts they had forced them to perform. For years the silent shame of what happened on that property was unknown to anyone but the victims, and the two who had no shame.

The dumb bitch has times, dates, and names of every person they ever molested and a few who, through no fault of their own, made Munson's property their final resting place. This thought disgusted him, but then his thoughts brightened. *My fame is going to skyrocket when I display this diseased couple! They may as well go ahead and put my name on that ballot,* Smith thought, with a smile on his face.

Chapter 14

I walked into the conference room with Crystal, Zee, and Vernon right on my heels. Already seated around the twelve-foot table were: Daniel Cates, Superintendent of the Indiana State police, as well as five of his boys; Sheriff Bradley Smith; Chief of Police Eric Bennett; and my friend Lt. Bradford. I was happy to see Archie Pembrook from Port Huron PD and Lt. Edward Beckman from Michigan State Police, sitting at the far end of the table. The mayor was purposely left out because we didn't want to involve or inform him until we had a plan. North Zone Commander Major Aaron Scott brought with him Lt. Jasper Fanning from District 22 and Lt. Joanna Bennett from District 16. The South Zone was represented by Commandeer Errol Parker and Lt. Terrence Daltrey, from District 51, and all seemed to be serious lawmen, there to help out in any way they could.

After the introductions, I commenced, "Before I start, there is something everyone must understand. What I am about to tell you cannot leave this room. If you think of anyone who can help us with this operation, let me know before you say a word to them. If I feel they can make a valuable contribution, *I'll* bring them in. Confidentiality is crucial here. Is that clear?"

After nods of agreement, I introduced Marty, who appeared on the Smartboard. His findings caused a lot of dropped jaws and wide eyes, and the room erupted in whispers and questions as soon as he was finished.

"Everyone! Please calm down," I said, struggling to bring

order to the room.

Zee whistled loudly, silencing them all like well-trained dogs. "Ladies and gentlemen, we'll get nowhere with this if we don't let Kroh explain how he wants to proceed."

"Thank you, Zee," I said, grinning at her. "Folks, we have an awesome opportunity here. For the first time in this investigation, we have a chance to get ahead of our unsub. It is unfortunate that we probably won't be able to stop the next murder, but we just might catch this guy when he dumps that body. I'll share my plan now, and I've invited you all here to see if you can think of any ways to improve it. First and foremost, we need to stake out the site that is exactly 111 miles from Ashley."

Superintendent Cates chimed in, "We ought to put some unmarked cars moving north and south on I-69, at least a quarter-mile apart. At the north end, we can use Exit 241 at Indiana 332, and on the south, we can use Exit 119 at Indiana 38."

As Cates pointed at both exits on the map, I smiled. "Excellent idea. This is what I'm talking about. If we put our heads together, we have a really good chance of stopping this so-called Guardian."

Sheriff Smith spoke next: "I know just where that dumpsite is, and we can put a couple people on both sides of the road, well hidden from view."

"It may be helpful to have a helicopter nearby; in case our unsub runs." Lt. Beckman added.

An unfamiliar sensation rolled through me as their suggestions and ideas poured in: hope. For the first time since we started, I felt hope. I cast Bradford a smile, and he greeted it with a thumbs-up of his own, just as pumped as I was.

We spent the rest of the afternoon ironing out details of the operation, and by dinnertime, our plan was set, ready to get underway, as long as the mayor and no higher-ups threw a wrench in it.

* * *

At eight thirty on Thursday evening, Julie Miller left the youth center. True to her dull routine, she stopped at Meijer in Anderson before heading home. As always, she parked her car well away from the door, then headed into the store. Mr. Smith pulled his van next to her parked car, with his sliding door facing the driver side. When she walked out with her groceries twenty minutes later, Smith was ready. As she placed them in her back seat, then turned to get into her vehicle, she felt the stinging sensation of his Taser. Her well-toned body convulsed violently as she crumbled to the pavement, too stunned to scream.

With one more casual look around to make sure no onlookers were watching, Mr. Smith slid open the door of the van, climbed out, and threw the woman inside. He attacked her with the Taser once more, then administered enough Rohypnol to keep her out until they got back to this place. A half-hour later, he decided she was well enough under, and he tied her securely and drove away, leaving her butter pecan ice cream melting all over the upholstery in her abandoned automobile.

Garrett Munson was a different story, because he was simply not a creature of habit. On Friday night, Mr. Smith waited in Munson's home, and by a little after midnight, he began to doubt that the man was even going to return. He was relieved when he finally heard the garage door, but he knew he had to be careful, because Munson was physically fit; if push came to shove, he believed Munson could take him, so he couldn't afford to let it get to that point.

As soon as Munson waltzed casually into his house singing Queen's "We Are the Champions," Mr. Smith wasted no time and Tasered him. For a moment, he seemed unaffected. Munson turned and reached for Smith. Fear suddenly rose up in Smith, but in the next instant, Munson fell to his knees and toppled over on his side, convulsing. Mr. Smith quickly balled up his fist and hit Munson as hard as he could in the temple, Tasered him again, then employed the help of the Taser once again. He didn't have time to wait for the drug to take effect, so he Tasered him once more and punched him again, this time at the base of his thick neck.

While Munson was disoriented and hurting, Smith zip-tied his hands behind his back and did the same with his ankles, then zip-tied those together as an added precaution.

Only then did he force a dose of Rohypnol down Munson's throat. Once he was sure Munson could give him no more trouble, he grabbed the keys from the door, then carried him into the garage. Even though he had been working out, he struggled to handle Munson's muscular frame. He placed the pervert in his own trunk, then quickly drove to the place where he left his van, so he could exchange vehicles and transfer his cargo.

Back at his rented farmhouse, Smith unloaded Munson from his van and moved him into the basement with the help of a hand truck and placed him next to Miller. "I have big plans for you two Saturday night," he said, smiling at them before he wandered off to get some well-deserved sleep.

The next afternoon, the couple was wide awake and more than a little confused.

"Thanks to your very detailed diary, Miss Miller, I am well aware of all you've done since you've been together," Mr. Smith said as he stepped off the last stair.

Munson glared at Julie and growled, "You stupid bitch! I *told* you to delete that."

Mr. Smith smiled. "It doesn't matter now. Your days of hurting children are over. I'm afraid there won't be a sequel to that little life story of yours."

"You bastard! Let us out of here now!" Munson yelled. One of his fears was realized; neither Munson nor Miller felt any remorse over the horrendous things they'd done.

It was obvious to Smith that they were both heartless, without any propensity for coming to a revelation of just how evil they were. Since it would fit better into his plan, he decided to kill them right there in the basement and display them later. He forced some more Rohypnol into them both, waited until they were under, stripped them naked, and went upstairs to wait.

Early Saturday evening, both Munson and Miller were wide awake and naked, filled with liquid aspirin and were seated on plastic-covered cinderblocks, strapped down so movement was nearly impossible, with only their hands free. In Miller's mouth, Mr. Smith placed Munson's dirty workout underwear, and since her panties were too thin and skimpy to do any good, he simply wrapped them around one of her dirty socks and shoved it between her partner's lips. The humiliation he heaped upon them in that unsanitary act brought a smile to his face.

With their focus on their captor, they barely noticed the plastic tarp beneath them, nor did they pay any attention to the pans placed beneath their arms.

"Garret Munson and Julie Miller," Smith said to the perverted pair when he was finished with his preparations, "I frankly have no idea why any fair and just God would allow parasites like you to exist. It is entirely unfathomable to me to think that you or someone like you could possibly harm my children. Why? Why are you still here, still taking up space on this planet, using up oxygen you don't deserve to breathe? Don't get me wrong. I do not wish to act as the hand of God nor to deny His sovereignty and wisdom, but for what you have done, you must die. Justice will be served here and now."

Julie's eyes filled with tears, but Garrett's face simply hardened with anger, wrinkles of hate forming in his sweaty brow as he choked on his curses that were halted by the sweaty sock and lingerie.

Although he was certain the presentation of the evidence would not have the desired effect, Mr. Smith continued anyway, "On this flash drive are videos, times, dates, and her beautiful diary. After you are dead, the world will know of everything you did to those poor children who were trusted to your care."

Miller's eyes glistened with even more tears, as if she feared her loved ones being hurt by the revelation of her deeds, but Munson acted stoic, almost rebellious, as if he didn't care at all.

Mr. Smith turned and walked over to the worktable to fetch his trusty loppers. As he walked back toward Munson, he was happy to see that there was finally something other than contempt in the pervert's eyes. *Is that fear I see?* He thought with a grin. *Let's have a little more of that. I'll take her hands first!*

Julie's screams were muffled by the dirty underwear,

but that did not matter. Munson watched as Miller's hands dropped into their respective pans below, one sickening thud after the other. The blood drained quickly from Julie's thin arms, with the help of the liquid aspirin, and she soon fell into shock. Mr. Smith stared at her neck and watched her carotid artery pulse rapidly, a side effect of her shock, followed by faster breathing, as her panicking lungs tried to compensate for the hyperactivity of the dying heart muscle. He reached out and touched her forehead and found it cool to the touch, as he expected.

Mr. Smith then smiled over at Munson as nature took its course, enjoyed watching him writhe and squirm against the restraints that held him. "Where is that cocky-ass bravado now? Have you learned your lesson? If I let you go, will you leave the children alone from now on?"

Munson nodded vigorously, and a thin ray of hope lit up his eyes, as if he thought there was some chance, he might be set free with his bulky body intact.

"Fat chance, asshole!" Mr. Smith yelled, and with that, he placed the sharp loppers around Munson's wrist and closed them. He paused momentarily for Munson to process that agony before he removed the other hand.

A small whimper emitted from Julie, whose head was hanging, her eyes closed, her breath shallow and slow.

Mr. Smith glanced back at Munson. "It's almost show time," he said, even more pleased with himself when the big man began to cry.

Chapter 15

In preparation for the stakeout, five officers drove their vehicles from the starting point of the Ashley, Indiana dumpsite. Four recorded GPS coordinates within 100 feet of each other, after driving 111 miles, so we were frankly certain we had pinpointed the place. It was a good feeling to think we were one step ahead; as wrong as I knew it was, I couldn't get too worked up about being unable to stop another molester's death. If the Guardian continued his *MO*, it was probable that the one who died was yet another scum bucket, responsible for destroying the lives of innocent children.

On Saturday, we set up the stakeout an hour after sunset, being very careful not to raise any suspicions of why we were there. Two deputies, a state trooper, Pembrook, and I sat in a cornfield across the interstate from our target. Vernon was on the other side, with two of Anderson's finest, Beckman, and two more troopers.

I made it clear to the locals that there was to be no talk about the stakeout on the radio, because I was sure Mr. Smith had access to a scanner and surely liked to listen in for anything out of the ordinary. There was always a chance that someone might say the wrong thing, but I felt our chances were good. Many officers in unmarked cars discreetly covered every road that went over, under, and exited the interstate on both sides, in case our unsub decided to run.

I'd been on many stakeouts in my lifetime, but sitting in the middle of a cornfield on a hot, windless summer night had to be the worst. The tall stalks that surrounded us effectively cut off any breeze that happened by, and our body heat and the stench of sweat were like dinner bells to mosquitoes that were small but plentiful. Even though we drenched ourselves from head to toe with repellent, I spent the next four hours slapping the pesky predators away from my face, killing the ones who bravely tried to feast on me. I could have taken a more command position and sat in a car away from the ravenous insects, but I wouldn't ask anyone to do something that I wasn't prepared to do myself.

A little after two a.m., a car slowed and pulled off the road about fifty feet from our suspected spot. It slowly crept forward until it was adjacent to the 227 mile marker, then stopped. We quietly made our way through the maze of maize and cautiously positioned ourselves right across from the vehicle, and I was sure Vernon and his team did the same on the other side.

A man climbed out of the dark, late-model Ford Bronco, darted his eyes up and down the interstate, then went to the back hatch. He lifted it and pulled out something that resembled the blind we were sure our killer used. He walked to the fence about twenty feet from the roadside, set up the blind, then turned to walk back to his vehicle.

"Go, go, go!" I said into my radio.

Vernon and three deputies emerged from the wooded field behind the blind, as my team and I were already making our way across from the opposite side of the interstate. Three cars in both lanes came in fast, with sirens and lights blaring.

"Down on your knees! Hands behind your head!" I yelled.

"What the...?" the man started.

"I said get down...now!" I shouted again.

The man slowly went to his knees. As I held my gun on the suspect, Vernon pushed him down on his belly, pulled his hands behind his back, and cuffed him. The scene was a veritable light show as cruisers continued to arrive on the scene.

Once the suspect was secured, we headed for the Bronco. I beamed my flashlight into the back and saw something covered by a blanket. I bit my bottom lip when I spotted a foot sticking out at the far edge. After a look at Vernon and a deep breath, I pulled the cover back.

"What the hell?" I said, almost to myself, as I saw a couple pillows, sacks of newspapers, and a volleyball, along with a Halloween body part that exactly mocked a human foot. "Why, hello, Wilson. What are you doing here?" I said to the volleyball that had the same face as the friend of Tom Hanks in *Castaway*. My gut was going crazy. I turned toward the suspect, who was kneeling on crossed legs, handcuffed, and none too happy.

Bradford handed me the man driver's license. "Jerry Pence, from Muncie," he said.

I knelt down in front of the suspect. "Mr. Pence, you're in a lot of trouble."

"For what? Why are you doing this to me? I didn't do anything," Pence snapped, with little confidence.

"Have you been read your rights?"

"Yes, but—"

"You, sir, are about to be arrested," I interrupted. "Do you have anything to say for yourself?"

"Yes, sir! For starters, I didn't *do* anything."

"Then why are you here, and why did you set up the blind?"

"Look, some guy named Smith paid me a grand, all right? All I had to do was stop right here, in this precise spot. He even gave me the damn GPS coordinates. He said it'd be easy to set up that camo thing, and it was."

"What?" I said, trying to catch up, even though I knew the situation.

"He said it's some kinda joke he's playing on one of his hunting buddies. For $1,000, I wasn't gonna ask any questions, especially since he didn't ask me to do anything illegal."

We loaded Mr. Pence into the APD police cruiser and headed into town.

As I rode with Vernon, Beckman, and Pembroke, my mind raced: *Is this guy telling the truth, or is he already working on his defense?*

* * *

At just about the same time when Jerry Pence stopped on the interstate, Mr. Smith arrived at his preferred location, a park in downtown Anderson. *My display will be so much better than that one they found here a year ago,* he thought with a satisfied smile. He felt no fear about being caught, because he knew law enforcement was focusing on I-69. His decoy would do what he was required to do, since he was afraid that his wife would find out about the loss of money and kill him.

He had even driven by the dumpsite on the interstate and watched as law enforcement moved into place. The operation was practically invisible to anyone who didn't know what to look for, but since Smith orchestrated the event, he saw things no one else could see.

He opened the side door of the van and grabbed two lawn chairs exactly like the ones the Fingertip Killer had used; this was one of those details he refused to omit. *Damn, I'm good!* he thought. Once the chairs were in place, he returned to the van to collect his centerpieces. He first carried Julie Miller, and then Garrett Munson to the center of the gazebo. Once they were properly placed, he retrieved the rest of the supplies he needed.

With their handless arms hanging at their sides, he placed their folded clothes on their laps. He placed Munson's wallet on top of his and Julie's purse on top of hers. In Munson's disconnected hand, he placed the baggie that contained the flash drive, and Miller's hand held the confession. Finally, he opened the milk jugs of blood, carefully marked his and hers, and poured them near the ends of each arm. He knew the forensics experts would figure out that the two were killed elsewhere, but the blood was a detail he simply could not leave out.

Perfect, he thought as he stood back to admire his display. He then quickly made his way back to the van and left without a hint of police anywhere. "Now to take Highway 32 to Noblesville," he muttered, deciding it would be prudent to take the back-way home."

* * *

At four a.m., Bradford and I sat across from Mr. Pence

in the Anderson PD interrogation room. I had a bad feeling about him because everything about the guy screamed extreme fear and honesty. We had already confiscated his money, the GPS, and his Bronco, and Meecham and Crystal checked those for prints as we sat across the table from Mr. Pence.

Bradford started, "As we told you at the scene, you're in a lot of trouble here, Mr. Pence. You need to be honest with me, tell me everything you know. Why were you at that particular place at that particular time?"

"I told you already! Some guy said he would pay me 1,000 bucks to put that blind out there at that exact place at that exact time," he said, with fear in his eyes.

"Some guy? If you don't even know him, why'd he ask *you*?" Bradford continued.

"I don't know. Karma, I guess," he said, sporting a stupid smile. "A couple nights ago, I was in Waffle House out on 67. There's this waitress out there, a hot little redhead I have known for a while. I was just telling her I lost 750 bucks at the casino and that my wife's gonna kill me. I think I was a little tipsy, but you understand why."

"Yes, I suppose, with a loss like that. Go on," Bradford pushed.

"Well, that guy must have overheard me, 'cause he walked up to me as I was getting into my car and told me he could help me out. I was a little suspicious, but he gave me $500 right there on the spot, in cash. He promised to give me the other half once it was done." With that, he offered us a foolish smile, as if he knew we all would have done the same thing.

"Did he give you any way to contact him? Tell you his name?" Bradford asked.

"He only told me his name's Smith, just Mr. Smith."

"How were you supposed to get the other $500?" Bradford asked. "Didn't he give you his number or anything?"

"Look, mister, if you met my old lady... Well, let's just say it was better to go home $500 ahead than $750 in the toilet," he said, smiling weakly.

"Why didn't you just take the money and run?" Bradford

asked.

"I thought about it, but he made me show him my driver's license just in case I skipped out on the deal. He threatened to tell my wife."

I had a feeling the man would sooner kill someone than face the wrath of his wife. Playing the typical game, I was the bad cop, so it was finally my turn. "Mr. Pence, you are here because you are suspected of killing three people."

"What!? Wait...what did you say? I didn't kill anybody," he said, genuinely taken aback by our suspicions, overcome with that deer-in-the-headlights look. The fear emanating from him was palpable.

"You set up that blind at that place, at that time," I pressed. "I think you know exactly why we suspect you."

"I told you that guy hired me to do it! I didn't hurt anybody, man. I-I don't even own a gun. I was just trying to keep my wife from killing me for losing the money."

Hmm. Either this guy's innocent or really good at the game, I surmised, since he had made sure to mention a gun when a gun was not even used as the murder weapon in any of the killings. It was one of those things I had learned to listen for during interrogations. "Mr. Pence, I'm gonna ask you where you were on three different occasions. It is in your best interest to answer honestly," I continued.

"I've been honest with you all along," he said, pleading.

"Good," I said, then went on to ask about the three dates of the body dumps.

While Mr. Pence's answer about the first time and location was a bit sketchy, he was able to give us definitive answers on the last two, and he sounded entirely sincere.

"Mr. Pence, you had better hope we can substantiate your whereabouts during the murders, or you're going to have far more than your wife to worry about," Bradford said as we got up to leave.

"Starting with a long time behind bars...or worse," I finished, causing the man to squirm in his chair, so badly that I thought he might have wet his pants. I had the feeling he was just a guy who was in the wrong place at the wrong time, someone Mr. Smith took advantage of to throw us off the trail.

"Wait!" Mr. Pence said just as we reached the door.

"Yes?" Bradford said over his shoulder, arching his brow at our suspect.

"I can keep the $500, right? Otherwise, I might be safer locked up!"

Chapter 16

It had been almost a year and a half since Calvin Mann discovered the body of Erica Roark, a news reporter, but he was still leery of the downtown park. She was the forty-sixth victim of the Fingertip Killer, and it took at least a year for him to break the habit of staring at the gazebo whenever he passed it. *That was then, and this is now,* he told himself sternly, for now he was on a mission. After all, it was Sunday, the wrap-up of a weekend, and he knew there would be plenty of cans to harvest from the trash.

A little past seven a.m., Calvin found his courage and started down the path, pushed on by his need for money to give him nicotine. To calm his nerves, he jammed out to "Let's Get It On" by Marvin Gaye on an old MP3 player he found in the park a couple weeks earlier. He danced from can to can, digging through the smelly garbage to collect his aluminum treasures that either reeked of stale beer or were sticky with soda sugar.

When Calvin braved the can closest to the gazebo, his worst fears came true. There, staring at him, was a naked couple, just sitting there in the gazebo. "Damn, kids! You scared the shit outta me. You'd better get up and put some clothes on. They'll lock y'all up for sure, foolin' 'round the park like that."

Neither the man nor the woman said a word.

"Did you hear me?" Calvin said, his voice shaking as he neared the bodies. "You ain't high, are ya? They're gonna…" He swallowed his words when he saw the puddle of coagulating blood around their feet. "Fuck! Lord Jesus! Help! Fuck! Help! My God! Not again. Not fucking again!"

The sweet sound of Marvin Gaye's 'Sexual Healing" was lost to Calvin. He dropped his bag of cans, and ran as fast as his tattered shoes would carry him, out of the park and toward the police station down the block. He didn't even notice when his cherished MP3 player smacked against his thigh and fell to the curb a half-block from the station, shattering into several pieces.

Crystal and I were in much need of sleep when we walked out of the station, but our yawns were interrupted by screaming coming from somewhere down the street. I squinted to see who it was and saw a local homeless man running toward us in a full-on panic. Once I calmed him to the point where he could speak rationally, I looked over at Crystal. "Grab Bradford," I said, "and meet me in that park."

I had a sinking suspicion of what I might find there, but even I wasn't prepared for the reality. *The fucker played us.* I thought, and I announced to Bradford and Crystal as soon as they set foot on the scene, "He fucking played us in a big way."

"Oh shit! *Two* of them?" Bradford said, shaking his head.

"We need to close this area off quickly and get some tarps to cover the crime scene," I said.

Within fifteen minutes, roadblocks were set up to deter any onlookers from invading the crime scene. Yellow tape and tarps were placed all around the gazebo to hide the macabre sight from press and pedestrians, and Meecham, fresh off the examination of Pence's car, was busy collecting evidence with Crystal.

"He fucking played us, Chuck. He knew all eyes would be on the interstate, giving him the golden ticket to set this up," I said to Bradford and Zee, pissed. "He could've set up searchlights and set off fireworks and still accomplished this without interruption."

Bradford placed his hand on my shoulder, but that did nothing to calm or console me.

"He's orchestrated everything up to this point," I said, seemingly bent on stating the obvious. "Whoever this Smith is, he's a fucking genius. Not only that, his attention to detail is phenomenal. Can't we ever deal with dumbasses for a change? At least they are easy to catch."

"Yeah, I know what you mean," Bradford said. "I'm sick of us being made out to look like the dumbasses by this maniac."

A few thoughts dangled in the darkness of my mind, but I just could not bring them to light. Deep down in my gut, even if I didn't want to admit it to myself or anyone else, I felt somehow, it was all about me. "It's so...coincidental, being here and all."

"What do you mean, Kroh?" Zee asked.

"I don't know why, but I think this guy is trying to get to *me*."

"Hmm," Bradford said. "If that's true, that might be a lead we haven't thought about."

"Yeah...maybe," I said, now even more confused and unnerved.

* * *

Around four o'clock, since we could think of nothing more to do for the case, Crystal and I swung through Arby's, then headed to her place. After gulping down our roast beef sandwiches showering the itchy cornfield stakeout residue away, we headed to bed. All carnal desire was overruled by the need for rest, and we both slept soundly until morning.

I awoke around six, and the first thing I saw was Crystal stretching, dressed in nothing but her well-worn Zeppelin tee. Every time she raised her arms, the shirt lifted to reveal her world-class ass. I couldn't help but prop myself up on one elbow just to watch the show. "I don't care how old that shirt gets. Don't ever get rid of it," I said as I admired her.

She looked over her shoulder and smiled. "Good morning, Agent Kroh. I trust you slept well."

When she began doing toe touches, I threw the sheets back. "I need a cold shower...now!"

"Really? I think *Larry* wants something else."

I looked down at myself and found that she was quite right. Without further ado, she pushed me back on the bed, pulled off my shorts, and climbed on top of me. I tried to put my arms around her, but she held them down to my sides and ever so slowly lowered herself onto me. Her slow, up-and-down rhythm fulfilled every fantasy any man in his right mind could have. The tempo of her lovemaking was perfection, but just when I thought I could take it no longer, she suddenly stopped.

"Okay, that's it," Crystal still said, with me still inside her, before she taunted me with kisses. "Time for breakfast."

"Breakfast? *Now*?"

"Now."

"Girl, you're so rotten." I grabbed her and rolled on top of her, then mimicked her same rhythmic tempo.

Soon, she pushed hard against me as wave after wave of pleasure shook her body. When I was unable to hold it any longer, our bodies became one in an orgasmic dance.

I hoped that moment would never end, but there were other things we had to do. We hit the shower and were somehow able to resist soapy sex, then dressed and joined Vernon and Zee at the Waffle House for that breakfast Crystal mentioned earlier.

"Good morning?" I asked Vernon as I sat down across from him and noticed a cheesy grin on his face.

"Let's just say the day started off on a good note," Vernon answered and smiled.

After we placed our orders with our favorite waitress, Verna, making sure to ask for a huge pot of coffee, we decided it was time to talk about the case. For many people, it wouldn't have been good breakfast table conversation, but we were used to that sort of thing.

"Pence's whereabouts during the last two murders has been verified," Vernon said. "Also, his wife can prove where he was during the first. He's not our guy, Kroh."

"Yeah, I figured that was the case. My money is on his wife kicking his ass up one side and down the other for losing that $750," I said.

"About that. She was actually tickled pink."

"Huh? About what?"

"She was worried about him sleeping around, so she was just glad to hear it wasn't that he was hiding from her."

"Not even with that redheaded waitress he went on and on about?" I asked.

"Not that I can confirm," Vernon said. "His ol' lady might use the gambling against him in the future, but for now, I think she'll let him live. You know how the womenfolk are about never forgetting anything," he teased with a smile, earning a scowl from Crystal and an elbow in the ribs from Zee.

"Do we know anything new about the two in the park?" I asked.

"Well, we know what the freaks were into, a little more than I want to know actually."

"Freaks, huh?"

"Yeah, our killer has a type, and Munson and Miller were partners in perversion."

"Don't tell me. Kids?" I asked, already certain of the answer.

"You got it. Garrett owns a youth training center, and they've been using that to lock down their prey. The sickos even killed some of the children, the ones they couldn't control or keep quiet. We're looking for bodies on some wooded acreage Munson owns."

"How do you know all this? The flash drive?"

"Yep. On it, there's even a diary Miller kept, detailing everything they did. I could only get through some of it. It's really sick shit," Zee said, scrunching up her face as if she'd just eaten something extremely unpleasant.

"I know we've got to abide by the law, but when I think of these monsters, it's hard to really want to stop our unsub," Crystal added.

"No shit," I said, sharing everyone's thoughts, "but now he's made it personal. He's hitting us here, on home turf, and I'm not sure why."

Just as Verna placed our waffles and eggs and bacon on our table, filling the air with a salty, savory aroma that blended perfectly with the warm maple syrup and coffee, my phone rang.

"I feel really bad, Kroh," Marty said.

"Why? What's up?" I asked before I shoveled a huge bite

of jalapeno hash browns in my mouth.

"I played right into his plan, wasted a lot of time and money. If I hadn't misled you guys with that 111-mile tip, maybe—"

"Whoa! Marty, you found something no one else did. Dangling carrot or not, it had to be found."

"Yeah, but it gave him a chance to set up his display without being caught."

"It's all part of the investigation. You just did your job, and you know you do it damn well, kid. There's no blame here. Mark my words, Marty. When we catch this guy—and I do mean *when*—it will be due, in part, to the major part you played in our success. Don't beat yourself up. Be pissed at this guy if you want, but focus. If nothing else, Pence gave us a better idea of what Smith looks like."

"If you say so," Marty said, sounding a little better.

"I do say so, and speaking of that, I've got another chore for you. It's a long shot, but Crystal said Munson and Miller were killed elsewhere and then brought to the crime scene. It had to be someplace private, far enough off the beaten path so no one would suspect anything. I need you to check rural areas around I-69, between Indianapolis and Ft. Wayne, for any property rented or sold to a Smith. Can you do that for me, Marty?"

"A Smith with a rental. Gee. You really love those needles in the haystack, don't you?" Marty said with a laugh.

"If anyone can find that needle, it's you, Marty. You're the best. Remember that."

"If you say so," he said, sounding quite pathetic again.

"I do say so. If you don't believe me, talk to Zee. Oh, but before I hand you over to her, there's one more thing. I need you to check out everyone I helped put away. Someone is mad enough at me to orchestrate this elaborate plan just to lure me here. See if any of those convicts were recently released from prison. You know the drill. Thanks, buddy." I then handed my phone to Zee with a smile, knowing that if anyone could make him feel better it was her.

* * *

The Guardian posted everything on the web and also

found a way to share it with most major media outlets. Marty did what he could to trace those posts, but even he was stymied at every turn. We were able to temporarily shut down many of the sites, but that didn't matter; by the time we pulled the plug, the damage was already read, copied, shared, and viral.

In my temporary office, otherwise known as the conference room, Bradford turned the TV to Channel 3. "Tanner's coming on," he said.

Zach Tanner looked the part of a seasoned field reporter, even though he was just a local beat reporter for a newspaper just a year and a half earlier. He was a good kid, bright and ambitious, and his work with us on the Fingertip Killer case really put him on the map in journalism. "Yesterday morning," he began, "two bodies were found, apparent victims of the Guardian Angel of I-69. The case differs from others, as these victims were discovered not on the interstate but, rather, in the same location where Erica Roark, Channel 15 reporter, was found eighteen months ago, at a park in downtown Anderson. It is presumed that while authorities were busy arresting a suspect on the interstate, the Guardian placed the bodies in the gazebo. The identity of the male victim is Garrett Munson, the owner of Munson's Youth Athletic Training Center. The female is Julie Miller, who was a trainer at that youth center," Tanner said as photos of Munson, Miller, and the youth center were displayed on the screen. "Authorities have declined to comment, but it is believed that there is evidence that the two committed crimes against children, as suggested by posts on the internet, hailing the Guardian as a hero yet ago. As of yet, the Guardian has been very careful not to reveal the identities of the children involved. Internet posts, tweets, and likes, regard the Guardian as a crusader of good, and dozens of websites have recently been created to celebrate his so-called achievements. The vigilante is becoming something of a folk hero among Listen to what some of the people that I've talked to on the street had to say:

A local man appeared on the screen with a microphone in his face, a real looker who was missing an incisor and sporting a mullet. "He's a hero, man. The cops oughtta leave him alone and let him do his job. He's sure as hell doin' a better job of it than they are, takin' these freaks off our streets. Yeah, he's a goddamn hero."

A lady who resembled Frances Bavier, Andy Griffith's famed Aunt Bee, was the next to be interviewed. "The Guardian is the right hand of God, sent to smite the wicked. God bless you, Guardian."

Next, a far more clean-cut man in a proper suit and tie interjected, as articulate as any lawyer's closing argument, "This man must be stopped. No matter the alleged crimes of his victims, that doesn't justify murder in cold blood. What makes him think he's the ultimate judge and jury anyway? Who's to say he won't kill an innocent person just because he suspects them of harming children? Justice and punishment are best left to the authorities."

Behind the interviewees, a teenager walked down the crowded Indianapolis street, photobombing at every opportunity to flash his "Go Guardian!" sign, with an entourage of young people chanting the same behind him. "Go, Guardian! Save the children!" That made it all the clearer that we had to catch the guy and catch him soon, before the entire public turned against us.

The most damning interview of all was Zach Tanner's exclusive with the parents of Eric Dennis, even if careful measures were taken to conceal their identities. "Earlier today," Zach said, "I had the privilege of speaking with the mother and father of one of the three children abducted by the pederast Andrew Reese, an alleged Guardian victim. Presumably, the killer intended to render punishment for Reese's crimes against children." Zach then silenced as a recording of the interview popped up on the screen.

"Our hearts go out to you and your son," Tanner said to Mr. and Mrs. Dennis. "The trauma he must have faced at the hands of Reese is unimaginable. How is your son doing?"

"He is very happy to be home, and he's a strong little man. With the help of therapy and our support, we're hopeful that he can live a normal life and leave this behind him."

It was obvious to me that she was fighting tears as she

spoke, but just as obvious was her husband's silence. While his face was hidden from view, his tense body language spoke volumes. His hands were clenched in tight fists, and he fidgeted and squirmed in his chair throughout the interview.

By the end of the painful interview, Eric's mother was crying. "I thank God every day for bringing my precious little boy home...and I thank God for the Guardian."

At that point, Eric's father could no longer hold his tongue. "Guardian, if you are out there hearing this, know that we owe you our son's life. If there is anything you need from us, anything at all, we are here for you."

On the live report, Zach Tanner just shook his head. "Heartbreaking! We all hope the best for any child who has suffered abuse. One thing we can be sure of is that if the Guardian does nothing else, he has definitely provided a better future for the children he has saved. Channel 3 will continue to bring you all the latest details on this heartbreaking yet disturbing story," he said. "If anyone out there knows anything about these murders or the identity of the man known as The Guardian, please contact the FBI at the number at the bottom of the screen. We will continue to bring you updates on this story. I'm Zach Tanner. Stay safe out there, folks."

* * *

Mr. Smith watched the news on his thirty-six-inch RCA, a far cry from the sixty-inch, high-definition he enjoyed while he was married. His lack of modern technology didn't bother him in the least though; he beamed a smile from ear to ear, basking in the compliments of strangers, his reward for saving Eric Dennis and the others. He wanted nothing more than to celebrate, even if he had to do so alone. "To a truly great man, a goddamn hero!" he said, lifting his scotch to toast himself. He drank it down, then poured another and vowed that he was not ready to give up on his quest as the Guardian. "They still need me," he told himself after another gulp. "They always will."

Not only did the world deserve his continued service, but he found working outside the law to be quite exhilarating, simply because it was so dangerous and risky. "I'll save those kids. I'll save them all," he declared, but just for a moment, he felt a bit morose. *All I ever wanted to do was be a good provider, husband, and father to my own kids. I was good once, a natural-born leader. I was vice president of my junior and senior class, for God's sake, then active in student government all throughout my college years. I excelled in my career, moved through the ranks quickly, and made a name for myself. I guess that was then and this is now...but I'm still making a new name for myself, aren't I? That bitch won't let me do anything for my kids, but I can sure as hell be the Guardian for others.*

After the news, Mr. Smith flipped through the channels, looking for something to watch. He finally settled on a 1949 Warner Brothers film, *White Heat*, starring James Cagney, already halfway over. He enjoyed another glass of scotch as the movie reached his favorite part, when Cody Jarrett climbed to the top of a gas storage tank, trying to elude the law. Before igniting the gas tank with shots of his own, Cagney was shot a couple times. Just before the tank ruptured to consume him in a ball of fire, he looked to the sky and yelled, "Made it, Ma! Top of the world!" As the credits rolled, the scotch finally took its toll on him. With his words slurred and fading, he muttered, "Made it, Pa! Top..."

He passed out in the chair. His half-full glass slipped from his hand, but it was cushioned by the carpet that prevented it from breaking. Even if it had shattered, it would not have broken into his alcohol-fueled slumber and his heroic dreams. His heavy snoring was the only sound that broke the silence in his empty apartment, except for the infomercial about the latest weight-loss health supplement.

* * *

The very next morning, we felt a huge kick in the ego, when several major newspapers felt it was within their freedom of speech to run the transcript of the Guardian's web post after the most recent bodies discovery. As usual, he disclosed the names of the victims and condemned them openly for the crimes they committed. The worst part was the final quote: "I have been very careful not to reveal the names of the children who were victims of these deviants, for they have suffered enough. Just know that I have removed the makers of the mess, and I will leave it to authorities to clean that mess up." The last line was a clever and purposeful two-way slap. On one side, it put the pressure on us, and on the other, it made him look like a hero.

"This guy is fucking genius," I said, none too happy that it was true.

Die by Proxy

PART TWO

Setting the Trap

Chapter 17

Although the death of the child abusers was merely a distraction at first, really only vital to the first phase of his plan, Mr. Smith soon found that it had become part of him. His fame as a defender of the young had grown to an unbelievable level. It was like a drug, an addiction he could not possibly give up.

Time for Phase 2, he told himself, though he had no intention of giving up his good fight as the Guardian. In fact, he was quite sure he could manage both projects easily. *If I am to continue as the Guardian, I will need more deviants.* To that end, Mr. Smith had already found two possible computer repair shops that would fit his needs.

The first tech he contacted was located in the south end of Indy. Slater Tech was a highly rated but small, home-based operation. Max Slater, the owner, had all the makings of a sexual predator himself, but Mr. Smith doubted the man capable of subduing even a 2-year-old. He was barely five feet tall, rail thin, and so pale that it appeared he'd never once set foot in the sun. He was also obnoxious geeky know-it-all who got off on making others feel stupid and unworthy when it came to computer knowledge. That snide arrogance was almost a deal breaker, but it would also make killing the computer whiz much easier. *I might actually like deleting this one,* Smith thought with a smile.

Since the Guardian was a hot topic and one Slater would surely hone in on, Mr. Smith had to resort to a new technique. "I'm with the FBI, and we are currently conducting a sting operation that targets child molesters in your area. Can we count on you, Mr. Slater?" he asked, certain that it would feed the know-it-all prick's ego.

"Does this have something to do with that Guardian guy?" he asked, pretty sure he knew the answer.

"As a matter of fact, it has everything to do with The Guardian." He smiled his first smile since he walked into the computer shop. "You will, of course, be well compensated for your contributions to the investigation." At the mention of payment, Mr. Smith knew he had the scrawny computer nerd's full attention, though he went as far as demanding that he sign a confidentiality agreement printed on fake official FBI letterhead. "Remember one thing, Mr. Slater. Any failure to comply with this nondisclosure will result in serious jail time," he stated with all the matter-of-factness of any seasoned agent. The plan worked well, which brought another smile to Smith's face. *As long as the previous tech boy murders aren't connected, I can use this ploy all the way to the end of I-69 at the border of Mexico in Texas.*

Luckily, Slater already had somebody already in mind, because he noticed something quite unsettling on a computer that was dropped off for repairs the day before. Even though he assured his customers that their privacy was absolute, going as far as to point to a sign that said as much, he quite enjoyed snooping through their private online lives. In doing so, he discovered countless meaningless online affairs and dabbles into porn sites, even a few involving freak shows like animals or sadism, but his findings on Jeremy Wayne Kenney's machine were much darker.

"You've got two days," Mr. Smith said to Slater. "I need as much information as possible on Kenney. Just remember that it must all be conducted under the radar."

His next stop was Mosby's Computer and Games in Henderson, Kentucky. Cassondra Mosby was an interesting-looking, rough-around-the edges blonde, with toned arms sleeved in tattoos. A delicate blue rose seemed to grow right out of her cleavage, its roots nestled somewhere beneath her low-cut top. Mr. Smith was impressed by her natural, self-assured confidence. She wasn't cocky or belittling like Slater, but she made it clear that she had plenty of expertise to offer.

When he told her what he needed, her willingness to participate was immediately evident, with good reason. As they sat in her small but neat back office, she told Mr. Smith, "I have a niece who was abducted and abused, found naked and near death in a park just outside town. She survived, but she's never been the same, ya know?"

"Did they catch him?" Mr. Smith questioned.

"Unfortunately, no. She wasn't able to identify her abuser, so they had no real leads. You've met her. She's my assistant."

"Oh," Mr. Smith said, troubled that an 11-year-old could be so world weary already.

"Leslie's never quite been able to put it behind her and move on. Since Aunt Sara died two years ago, I'm really all she has," Cassondra said, wiping a tear from her face.

Mr. Smith was so taken by her passion that he paused to enjoy a brief fantasy of taking her on as a partner, a female Guardian, but that was short-lived. "Ms. Mosby, we must be very careful that no one finds out about this investigation," he said. "The operation depends on our complete secrecy. We're dealing with people who are somewhat paranoid about being caught." He smiled, then continued, "They thrive on keeping their sexual perversions hidden. Thankfully, nearly everyone owns at least one computer or gadget these days. The world is very connected, and that works to our advantage."

Until then, Cassondra had never even considered vengeance, never even thought of digging into her customers' lives to render payback for the horrible atrocity heaped upon her beloved niece, but as she thought about it, she recalled an odd happening in her shop. "You know, about a week ago, this guy named Stephen Montgomery brought his PC in here for repairs. He's big in politics around here. Leslie waited on him. When he spoke to her, I noticed that her whole demeanor changed. She turned white and looked as if she might throw up, and she subtly begged me to take over. She came back here in the office and didn't go back out there till Mr. Montgomery was gone. I asked her what was wrong, but she wouldn't tell me. She just said that she felt some sort of déjà vu, like the world was closing in around her when he spoke. It was something about his voice, but she didn't know what."

"Hmm. That is very strange," Mr. Smith said, then paused to think for a moment. He quite liked Cassondra and was eager to help her. "Ms. Mosby, if you're up to it, I would be glad to offer my help in checking out this Mr. Montgomery. What would you say to that?"

"I say hell yeah!" she exclaimed, without a second of hesitation. Then, a look of concern came over her, "We may have a problem though."

"What's that?"

"Montgomery asked me how to wipe a hard drive."

"Cassondra, I'm sorry. Can I call you Cassondra?"

She nodded.

He continued, as you know, a drive is never truly wiped. We will address that problem when and if it comes up," Mr. Smith said, sounding very official and knowledgeable. He then outlined a preliminary plan. "Find out everything you can about Montgomery, and I'll do the same. We have a lot of resources at the Bureau for this sort of thing," he fibbed. "I'll return in four days, and we'll get started. Remember, you mustn't talk to anyone, and use the utmost discretion."

"Mum's the word," she said, mimicking a lock and key on her lips before he smiled, and he walked out of her shop.

* * *

As promised, Mr. Smith returned to pick up the data on Kenney, just before closing time in the evening. There were no other customers in Slater's shop; he had made sure of that.

"Oh! It's you. I've got what you asked for. Follow me," Slater said, then locked the door behind Mr. Smith and turned the "Closed" sign around in the window.

Mr. Smith followed Slater to his office next to the kitchen. Then, as soon as he was in possession of the Jeremy Wayne Kenney flash drive, he made short work of eliminating the computer tech. Slater died no better beneath the Styrofoam plate than the others, but unlike those killings, Mr. Smith quite enjoyed watching that arrogant prick die. He enjoyed it so much, in fact, that he inadvertently pushed too hard, ramming the knife all the way through the skinny bastard's heart and into the carpet pad in the floor beneath him.

The moment Slater's scrawny little heart took its last beat, Mr. Smith moved to his computer. He navigated easily to Microsoft Word and created a large-font sign: "I will be out of town for the next three weeks due to a family emergency. If you need assistance, please call the number below. I am sorry for the inconvenience."

Mr. Smith had done a little digging of his own, so he knew Slater had no relatives living any closer than in California, and his friends were few and far between. *Likely because of the pasty prick's personality...or lack thereof,* he reasoned. He turned up the air conditioning, hoping to preserve the corpse and stave off the stench a little longer. He also made sure the body was not visible from the outside. "With any luck, you won't be missed for a month or more," he said to the dead man in the puddle of blood on the floor.

The following day, Mr. Smith started his research on Kenney and found out everything he could on Montgomery. Since he had to reunite with Cassondra in a few days, he concentrated on the politician. Montgomery was a busy boy, to say the least. Interestingly enough, he had taken several junkets to Cambodia, a country that relied heavily on tourism. Unfortunately, much of that tourism had to do with the buying and selling of children for sex; that had been the case for at least two decades, since the powers-that-were could easily be bribed to look the other way. That sickened Smith, but the next thing he learned brought a smile to his face.

Montgomery and his family were currently enjoying the Orlando experience, and that would make his job much easier. He marveled at the ease with which he was able to enter both Montgomery's residence and office, and he had ample time to check every nook and cranny of both, examining all hidden spaces and digging through drawers and closets and shelves. In the house, he concentrated on the home office, the bedroom, and the basement. In Montgomery's government office, which didn't even require special clearance for entry since it was unguarded most of the time, he checked the bookcase, walls, and desk. He found nothing damning in either location, but he did clone the hard drives and swap them out. He almost didn't want those hard drives to come up clean, but he knew that if anything was left lingering on them, Cassondra would easily find it. Mr. Smith also checked for any property Montgomery owned or rented, and he looked into home renovations, any alterations made on the home since it was built, just in case a secret room or dungeon had been added somewhere for the deviant's nasty pleasure.

The next evening, when he sat in Cassondra's office and shared what he had learned, she marveled at his findings and apologized for her meager offering.

"Don't worry," he said with a consoling smile. "It's what I do. Now it's time for you to do what *you* do."

Without another word, she got to work, and within just a few minutes, she'd unearthed some password-protected files. She looked up at Mr. Smith and grinned. "Most people don't realize how vulnerable their data is. It's really rather simple to get around passwords." She perused what she was able to open on the screen, and her next glance at Smith was a wide-eyed, sickened one. "This Montgomery is one sick puppy," she said, pointing at files that made her stomach turn.

In a main folder were several others, organized by date. The first, labeled "In the Beginning," contained yet another folder labeled with her niece's name.

"Oh my God," she said as she clicked on it and sat back in her chair, sniffling as tears began to flow. "Leslie?"

"Are you sure it's her?" Mr. Smith asked.

Cassondra was horrified and speechless and could only lift a weak finger to point at the picture of her blindfolded niece, a once happy, carefree girl. The sick bastard was in the photo with the terrified child, offering a smiling thumbs-up.

Mr. Smith was instantly angrier than he had ever been before, filled with even more fury than he'd ever felt for his wife. He placed his hand on her shoulder reassuringly, and she put her hand on his in an attempt to steady her grief-stricken nerves, looking as if she might faint.

The sad but tender moment was not wasted on Mr. Smith. For the first time in a long time, he felt a deep connection to someone; it had been so long, something he'd missed, especially with his own children. She needed him, but if Mr. Smith could be honest with himself, he had to admit that he needed her, too, at least in that moment. In his former life, he would not have given the tattooed girl a second thought, but his worldview had changed. Even though he barely knew her, Cassondra was the closest thing to a friend he had, and it felt good.

"We have to get him, Mr. Smith," she said.

"I agree, Cassondra," he said, fully aware of her resolve, "but you must promise that you will not do anything until I say so."

"We need to get him now!"

"We must first make sure everything is in place," he cautioned. "We cannot afford to rush. He must answer for *all* his crimes, not just what he did to your niece. Justice must be served."

"Screw justice! He's a monster, and he needs to suffer," she said, wiping a tear from her face.

"Oh, he will. I promise you, that man will suffer," he said, giving her inked shoulder a tender squeeze.

Chapter 18

It was Sunday, and another Kroh Family picnic was in full swing. Life could not be any better than all that fun, food, and family. Bradford and Lillie brought their grandson Charlie, and it was a nice surprise to see Noah and his family as well. *This is going to be a great day,* I thought. Noah was one of my oldest friends, as well as my boss. We met at Parris Island boot camp in South Carolina and had remained close, but I maintained a line of respect at work, because Pops taught me never to take advantage of personal relationships in the workplace.

Pops worked his magic on the grill as Grandma, Lillie, Zee, Danielle, and Crystal created to-die-for side dishes and accompaniments: salads, potatoes, and beans, just to name a few. Plenty of cakes and pies had been made the day before. "If anyone goes home hungry today, it's their own fault!" I declared, looking around at the delicious feast.

Bradford, Vernon, Noah, and I kept the young ones busy in a game of flag football, but the kids didn't seem to have any trouble tackling me, laughing all the while, regardless of whose team they were on.

"Hey, can you guys swim?" I asked when I finally had enough.

"Yeah. Why?" they said, looking at me suspiciously.

"Good!" I shouted before I grabbed two of the kids and playfully threw them in the pool, one at a time. I didn't have time to think as the rest ran at me in a mob, eager to gang up on me and push me in the pool, only to soak themselves when their forward momentum sent them splashing in behind me.

Bradford, who had a body as fit as a man half his age, perfectly executed a cannonball. The resulting splash was strong enough to reach the nearby picnic table, where Zee was setting out food, and she squealed as the cool, unexpected shower rained down on her. Everyone laughed as she balled up her fist, feigning anger, but when she could no longer keep from laughing herself, she shrugged and made a beeline to the pool. She retaliated against Bradford with the best cannonball a petite body could make, just enough to leave him soaked and sputtering, much to the children's delight. For the next half-hour, we were all engaged in splashing, dunking, and cannonball lessons.

When Grandma, wearing her "I always thought growing old would take longer" t-shirt, rang the dinner bell, everyone was ready. Personally, I was famished after expending all my energy trying to keep up with the kids.

Just as we sat down to eat, Marty graced us with his presence, and he brought a date. She was attractive but not as pretty as a lot of the women Marty had been with before, though she did have a killer smile. Regardless, I knew that if he was dating her, she had to be someone pretty special.

I got up and walked straight past Marty and introduced myself. "Hi. I'm Benjamin Kroh, but *you* can call me Kroh."

"Down, boy," Marty said, laughing. He then went on to introduce Andrea to everyone else but purposely left me out. When his introductions reached Pops, he warned, "Oh, and be careful with this one. He's trouble."

"Don't listen to him," Pops retorted as he took her hand to lead her to the seat next to his. "He's just worried about the competition, *and you* now have something wonderful to compare him to."

When we were all finished laughing at Pops' remark, we learned quite a bit about Andrea, a pediatric physician at George Washington University Hospital in DC. Marty met her while volunteering there, installing a new software program.

"I decided to take a CPR class while I was there," he said, winking at Andrea. "How could I resist, with a teacher like this?"

The feast was everything the aroma promised. I know it isn't in my best interest, but I bypassed the big bowl of salad and grabbed a beautifully grill-marked ribeye and a pile of mashed potatoes covered in butter. I convinced myself that two ears of corn would be healthy, even if they were glazed with far too much butter melting over each juicy kernel. *Heaven!* I thought, as I closed my eyes and let every nuance of the ribeye thrill my taste buds.

After we ate, Bradford, Vernon, Noah, Marty, and I were on KP duty. As we busied ourselves putting away leftovers and cleaning up, we briefly talked about the Guardian. It was interesting and cool to see Noah and Bradford bonding, two of the most important friends and co-workers in my life. Everyone was as frustrated as I was, but when a couple of the kids ran through the kitchen, the shop talk was over just like that.

As we were finishing up, Bradford hit the restroom, and Noah took the opportunity to let me know what he thought of Bradford. "He's quite an intriguing fellow. I can see why you like him," he said, then paused briefly. "Of course, we all know you have exceptional taste in friends."

"That's nice of you to say, considering that Bradford thinks you're a tremendously boring asshole," I said, laughing.

"Right," he said, then popped me on the arm, rocking me pretty good.

"Hey, what's going on?" Bradford asked when he walked back in the kitchen and saw me rubbing the sore spot.

"Oh, Noah just said he thinks you're a racist shithead."

Noah hit me again.

"Ow! Shit, stop that! Damn! What he really said is that he wants to have your children," I said to Bradford. I then turned to Noah. "There. Is that better?"

This time, when Noah reared back to hit me again, he saw the fear in my face but just laughed and clapped me on the shoulder. That had us all laughing for the next five minutes.

As the sun kissed the horizon in the west, I sat by the fire pit, enjoying a cold glass of iced tea. We talked, laughed, and just enjoyed the fellowship, and I knew there was nothing better than getting together with friends and family. For the second time that day, I just shut my eyes and let the moment wash over me.

As I took another drink of my tea, my thoughts moved to my deserted island list. Iced sweet tea was a must on my frivolous list, along with ribeye steaks and popcorn. As I took another drink, I looked over my glass at Crystal and instantly added her to my list of essentials. *God, she's beautiful,* I thought with a smile.

"What?" she said coyly when she caught me looking at her.

"Have you ever thought about your deserted island list?"

"Huh?" she asked, a little confused.

"Never mind. I'll explain later."

For the rest of the evening, we just sat around the dwindling fire, enjoying one another's company. At eight, Marty and Andrea had to head to Indy to catch their flight back to DC.

Just before they left, Pops pulled Andrea aside and, in a voice loud enough for everyone to hear, announced, "Andrea, it was very nice to meet you. You're welcome anytime…and if that Marty ever disrespects you, just let me know. I'll tan his puny Injun hide."

Everybody laughed, including Marty, and Andrea gave Pops a farewell with a hug and a peck on the cheek. After handshakes and hugs all around, they took off. I was really sad that he had to leave. Although Marty was part of my team, I had come to think of him as family, the brother I never had.

A while later, as the children were preparing for bed and the girls were inside watching a popular reality show, the guys gathered around the fire. Talk soon turned to the military. Pops told us about his time at the US Combat base in Khe Sanh, Vietnam, during the Tet offensive in '68. Bradford was part of the invasion of Panama ousting Noriega in '89. Noah and I talked about our time in Kosovo, and Vernon spent time in the Middle East, helping train the Iraqi military.

While we all served in different areas and eras, our reasons were the same: We wanted to fight for our country. We each answered the call of duty and ended up in some foreign land, fighting an enemy we really didn't know; serving in good faith that our government had good reason to be involved in each conflict. We had all killed people who were deemed our enemies, and we'd all seen friends die in the line of duty. That was part of our military service that remain locked within each of us, but that part, we shared in silence.

Things wrapped up soon thereafter, since everyone but Noah had to work in the morning. Since his flight didn't leave till five Monday and the Kroh compound was a big place and knowing that Grandma would not have it any other way, he and his family opted to stay there for the night. After promising to meet at the Kroh's Nest for lunch, Crystal and I headed back to her place.

Immediately, I made my way to the shower. While I loved bonfires, before I climbed into bed, I really needed clean off the smoke smell that lingered in my clothes and hair.

As I was busying myself in the bathroom, Crystal walked in. "Strange," she said.

"What?"

"I just got a call from Gordon Jacks," Crystal said with a puzzled look on her beautiful face.

"Turd?" I said with a laugh, mocking the Goth medical assistant who almost derailed the Fingertip Killer case for us by leaking information to the press, which caused unnecessary panic throughout central Indiana.

"Yeah, Turd."

"What the hell did he want?" I asked, still irritated by the thought of him.

"He claims he knows something about the I-69 murders."

"What?"

"Yep, he's absolutely convinced he knows something. I really don't like the guy, but I think we ought to at least listen what he has to say."

"Fine. We'll see him tomorrow, if you think he might have something we can use," I said as I flushed the toilet and pretended to wave goodbye to a swirling piece of shit that was quick to disappear. "That's the last I want to hear about him tonight though." A thought suddenly entered my mind, and I couldn't help literally laughing out loud.

"What's so funny?" Crystal asked.

"I was just picturing Jacks rotating clockwise and struggling in vain, being pulled down into the sewer.

At that, Crystal tried to hold back a smile of her own.

I shed the rest of my clothes and beckoned her to follow me into the shower. "Let the games begin!"

"No games tonight," she said as she slid into the shower.

"No games?" I asked.

"Nope. Tonight, feeb, I am *seriously* going to screw your brains out."

It was glorious blur from that point on.

Chapter 19

After breakfast, we headed to Muncie, where we met Turd in the same cafeteria where I first wanted to rip his head off. As we approached his table, he excused himself from the girl he was talking to and led us to a more secluded place near the back. I'd never really been one to hold a grudge, but just the sight of Turd made me anxious in a very bad way. In my mind, he was indirectly responsible for the death of Channel 15 News Anchor Erica Roark, even if it was ultimately at the hands of the Fingertip Killer a little over a year ago.

"Okay, Jacks, what is this so-called *information* you have for us? And it had better be good," I said with more anger in my voice than I meant to express.

Turd did not look at me at all; he obviously preferred to talk to Crystal, but that was fine with me. I wanted him to fear me, to be intimidated by me, and I hoped that would keep him honest, if he was even capable of honesty.

When he began to speak, it became clear that he was a little scared of Crystal as well. "Officer Markum," he said, heeding her earlier warning not to call her by her first name, "I-I have... Well, this friend of mine was murdered a few days ago. His name was Randy Barstow, but everybody called him Mantis. He was a badass on computers, and they found him stabbed to death in his shop. They're saying it was a drug deal or something, but I am sure they are wrong."

"I'm sorry about your friend," Crystal said in a tone far more sympathetic than I was ready to use, "but what does this have to do with the I-69 murders?"

"Well, we were hanging out one night, Mantis and me, and he told me about this dude who hired him to find some child molesters in the area."

"Go on," I said, as my gut told me it was important for some reason.

"Mantis found a couple names to give to this guy." He looked up at me and paused for a minute, as if he wasn't sure he should say the words that were about to tumble out of his mouth. Finally, he continued, "We were, uh...smoking a little weed, so the details aren't clear, but I seem to remember him saying something about a man and a woman. Please don't tell Dr. Simpson."

My interest piqued; I took a seat across from Turd at the table. "You remember anything else?" I asked.

"Um, no, I don't think... Wait! Yeah, now that I think about it, I'm pretty sure Mantis said the guy's name was a real common one, like Johnson or White or... No, Smith was the name. I'm sure of it."

"Smith?"

"Yeah! That's it. I'm positive." Turd said, his eyes lighting up with recognition.

The coincidence hit me like a lightning bolt when Turd said the same name given to us by Eric Dennis and Jerry Pence, the same man who delivered the McDonald's food to the three abducted boys and paid a man off to serve as a distraction to the police while he did his dirty work elsewhere.

We questioned Turd for about twenty more minutes, dragging as much information as we could out of the Goth pothead.

"Listen, Turd, I need you to keep your mouth shut about this. You got that?"

"Yes, sir."

"Good, because if I hear about you speaking one damn syllable of any of this to anyone else, I'll personally find you and kick your ass so hard you'll have to do your toking out of your—"

"Kroh!" Crystal warned, though I could see she was working hard to stifle her laugh.

"Shit, I ain't gonna say nothing. I have been scared as

hell since I heard about Mantis. Matter fact, you think I could get some police protection?" he asked, completely sincere.

"I'll see what we can do," I said, then nodded at Crystal.

Bradford made arrangements with the Muncie PD to have someone meet us at Barstow's computer shop. A half-hour later, as a favor to Bradford, Chief of Detectives Jerry Brennan gave us a personal tour of the crime scene, and he also shared everything they'd found so far. Bradford had already made it clear that he was to keep what we shared with them on the down low. We all knew it was best to keep our investigation on a need-to-know basis, to keep a lid on it until we could use all our discoveries to our advantage.

"I need you to do what you do at the crime scene, then look at the report and photos obtained by Muncie police," I told Meecham when I called him.

At the same time, Crystal arranged for Ryan Barstow's body to be exhumed and reexamined by Dr. Simpson at Ball Memorial.

* * *

By two o'clock the next afternoon, Crystal and Dr. Simpson had finished the autopsy. We gathered in the conference room of the Anderson PD so they could fill us in. It wasn't a case buster like we hoped, but it did reveal some interesting things.

"Along with the presence of THC in his system," Crystal said, "we found seven stab wounds in Barstow's chest. We believe those were just a cover-up to mask the fatal one to the heart. It was delivered first, killing the victim almost instantly."

After Crystal finished, Meecham interjected, "First off, Barstow's computers were wiped, and there were no security cameras anywhere." He went on to elaborate on the physical evidence found around the shop, which wasn't much, then moved on to the body, pointing at several grotesque pictures on the Smartboard, taken from several angles. "Notice anything peculiar here, folks?" he asked. Then, when no one answered, he continued, "Since we know the first wound was inflicted on the heart, we should expect blood spatter higher on the wall and the sides of the counter, but that is not the case. Another interesting thing is that the blood spatter we did find on the wall is sort of...curved." He paused and used his pointer to indicate the highest blood spatter. "Wouldn't you agree that this is odd, Detective Markum?"

Crystal nodded when we all looked at her.

"Exactly," Meecham said. "With that in mind, I had to search a little deeper. In the trashcan, I found a foam plate with a hole in the middle. That hole matches the size and shape of the knife used to kill Barstow. Our killer tried to wash it but got sloppy, because we found trace evidence of blood. That also explains why the spatter is so low on the wall, because the plate acted like a shield, deflecting the mess downward. It's only a guess, but I believe our unsub might've used it to try to keep the blood off his hands, so to speak."

Those highlights were quite interesting, but we really only had Turd's word to connect the dots to link it to our I-69 serial killer. To complicate matters even further, if it was the work of our unsub, he could no longer be considered a vigilante, because as far as we knew, the dead computer geek was innocent, not a child molester or kidnapper or abuser. We were so close, but the truth was that what we had was mere speculation at best.

"Is there anything that connects Mantis to Munson or Miller, maybe a receipt or a business card?" I asked, desperate for answers.

"Not at this time, but we're conducting a more in-depth search that we hope will reveal something. As you probably realize, more often than not, child predators disguise their true identities when dealing with the outside world."

"I think we can all agree, based on the information the Guardian spilled to the press, if Barstow worked on one of their computers, it was hers," I offered. "The diary was on that flash drive, a diary authored by our female vic'."

"We conducted a thorough search of Miller's residence and office, but we found nothing. Our forensic accountants are still looking into Barstow's books and bank accounts. If they discover a name that cannot be linked to a real person, we may at least have a date and time when the computer was serviced."

After the meeting, I walked up to Meecham. "If that's all you've got, what the hell good are you?"

He looked me straight in the eyes, without a hint of humor on his face. "If you'd get that thumb out of your ass, you might be able to catch this sick bastard."

We shared a laugh at that; as crude as he was, Meecham was real, and that was something I appreciated in my co-workers.

As the room hummed with continued conversations about Barstow's death and the lackluster evidence presented, I rubbed my finger and just sat there, deep in thought. *We must make the connection*, I realized, *and then this Guardian's growing fame will be at an end.*

Chapter 20

It had been more than two weeks since the Guardian left Munson and Miller in the downtown park. If the internet was any indication, his fans seemed extremely anxious for another macabre display, almost demanding another pervert sacrifice. I was certain his ever-growing band of supporters were the same kind of people who would have flocked to a public hanging in days gone by.

Although I, too, felt the only justice for a child predator was the death sentence, I knew in my heart that cold-blooded murder wasn't the right way to go about it. On one hand, though, I had to admit to myself that I understood the general public's need for a blood fix. The Guardian had provided a show every two weeks for a month and a half, and his audience was growing impatient as he denied their desired stimulation. *Withdrawals are a bitch, no matter your addiction,* I thought to myself.

While his fan club wanted to see more, the media was trying to strike it rich by exploiting the situation. All the crime channels scurried to slap together documentaries about the Guardian's reign of what one even called "justifiable terror." Experts speculated about his motives, trying to decide why he felt such a strong urge to kill child predators, and it was a race to Amazon to see who could publish the first book on the topic. Questions about what prompted him to kill these perverts were trending on all the social media sites: "Was he abused as a child? Was his child abused? Were any of his victims responsible for some horrific event in his life? Why hasn't he killed again, when it's been over two weeks? Has he been arrested for some other crime?" No matter what the answers to those questions were, he was more popular than ever.

"We have to find this guy soon. Either that, or we've got to nail down something to tarnish his image. If we don't, even if we do catch the salty bastard, no jury is going to want to convict him," I spat at Bradford in frustration as we sat in his office, combing over the details of the case once again.

"You know he's seeing the same thing we are, and the pressure to please his fans must be overwhelming. He must be feeling the heat from the public to kill another," Bradford said, and I knew that was a wise assumption.

"Maybe he thinks that in giving us two bodies, he can now wait for four weeks before he offers his next display for his adoring fans," I said with a grimace.

"We can only hope," Bradford replied, with a shake of his head.

* * *

Mr. Smith was indeed basking in the limelight, but he also felt a great deal of pressure to entertain his supporters. He had to be careful, but if he failed to deliver the corpse of another pervert, his eager audience would simply move on to the next big thing. He did like the sensation of his life being full and busy again, and his mind quickly moved to Jeremy Wayne Kenney, the sixth predator on his list.

Fortunately, Kenney kept a journal, and that helped immensely with the planning. Originally from Park City, Kansas, Kenney was a registered molester in that state, but he did not register as a sex offender when he moved to Indianapolis. His Indiana neighbors had no idea he was caught with an 8-year-old girl in a Wichita hotel room, nor were they aware that he spent a measly two years in the Hutchinson Correctional Facility, some forty miles northwest of Wichita.

In Indiana, Kenney was determined to start with a clean slate. He was lucky enough to find an old farmhouse to rent, near Shelbyville, far from the closest neighbor, so he had all the privacy he wanted. The cornfield bordered the property on three sides, and the stand of trees in the front only allowed a glimpse of the house to any cars that passed by.

It was easy enough for Kenney to falsify his records and find work as a substitute teacher. For over two years, he had access to plenty of students, and with the right amount of enticement, he lured several into a world their young minds simply could not grasp.

Soon, he resumed his molesting ways, with one major difference: His years in Hutchinson hardened him, so he approached his new victims with a new violent streak. While he was aware that he was trying to make others suffer the pain and humiliation he endured in prison, it still felt right, added a bit of an edge to his sexual thrill. His time in jail also broadened his perspective, so his gender preference was wide open. Behind bars and in secret corners of the prison shower, he was forced to do vile, painful, mind-warping things, and he now found an outlet to shove that suffering onto the young people he was supposed to educate.

Kenney was not a fool though. He was very careful not to grab the students he taught. He was also careful to never show any interest in them during school hours. Any child who suited his interests and desires was in danger only when they were vulnerable, away from the safety of parents, school staff and faculty, and witnesses. When he could not snatch them up like a lion grabbing an unsuspecting gazelle, he simply found ways to lure them into his arms.

He had abducted four children since his move to Indiana. The first two were released, bruised, violated, and traumatized but alive, just a few days after they were taken. When he observed Cora Winfield and Lindsey Brooks at the local mall, he had to have them, and he donned a mask to hide his true identity. The next child he took was a student at a school where he substituted many weeks prior. He kept little Amy Jordan for six months and only let her go after he went too far one evening; the girl died crying for her mommy.

Timmy Andrews was really a victim of opportunity. As he was biking home from a friend's house, he was grabbed on a lonely street just a block away from his home. The boy was then forced to bear witness to Amy's horrible death, but that only cemented his fear and kept him from trying to run away.

Mr. Smith skimmed over the part of the journal in which Kenney described Amy's death. It was written there in gory detail, and Mr. Smith knew if he read it too closely, those words would forever haunt him. As he read, though, he noticed hints that Kenney was toying with the idea of killing Timmy to satisfy a growing desire to watch the boy die. His journal also indicated that he had already found his next victim. "The boy will soon no longer be necessary anyway," he wrote, without a shred of remorse or emotion in his cold confessions.

The thought of Kenney abducting another child chilled Mr. Smith to the bone. "I can't let this happen. I won't!" he vowed aloud.

Two days later, with his car well hidden, Mr. Smith waited inside the farmhouse for Kenney to return. As he waited, he released Timmy from the locked basement. "Hello, Timmy," he greeted softly. "I am Mr. Smith."

It took a while for the boy to trust him enough to talk, but Timmy's need to feel safe won out, and that gave them a chance to bond.

"Soon, you will be home with your parents, and Mr. Kenney will bother no one else again. I promise," Mr. Smith said with a smile. "Are you hungry?" When Timmy nodded, he gave the child a sandwich and a Pepsi, and they talked at length about him, his friends, and his family. Mr. Smith was glad to discover that Timmy seemed like a strong boy, one who would likely be able to put the trauma behind him and make a real life for himself, albeit after a little therapy.

"I want to show you something, Timmy." Smith reached in his jacket pocket and pulled out a gun. Smith could see that it seemed to surprise the little guy, but Timmy smiled and asked if he could touch it. Smith showed the boy how to handle the gun. "Just hold it straight out and keep your arms stiff. "Good, Timmy. Good."

A few minutes past ten, Kenney pulled into the gravel drive; his headlights poured through the front picture window, momentarily bringing the sparsely decorated room alive. As Kenney parked beside the fading blue farmhouse, Mr. Smith had to make sure little Timmy was safe, in the event that things went south.

"Timmy, I want you to take this gun, go to the bedroom, and shut the door. If Kenney walks through that door, point the gun at him and pull the trigger. Do not come out until I call for you, okay?" Mr. Smith whispered to Timmy, and the boy quickly complied.

When Kenney came through the door, he attempted to turn on the light, but that was futile for reasons he did not understand. "Damn!" he cursed. He shook his head and headed straight for the kitchen to access the basement. Mr. Smith, standing in the dark and ready to pounce, hit the man hard with the sap, and Kenney crumbled to the floor.

Thump! Smith thrilled at the sound the leather bag of lead shot made as it hit the deviant's temple. *Thump! Thump!*

Mr. Smith continued to pummel Kenney until he was sure he was unconscious. When the molester was lying still on the linoleum, bleeding here and there from the blows that broke the skin, Mr. Smith darted his eyes around the kitchen and spotted just what he needed. He walked over to the heavy oak table, turned it on its side, then pushed it up against the wall. He secured Kenney's back to the underside, forcing him into a seated position. He also put a rope around his neck that would tighten it if the man tried to pull himself loose. He smiled as he tied Kenney's arms and legs to opposite legs of the table, spreading his limbs wide. Finally, he stuffed some dirty underwear from Kenney's bathroom floor into his mouth.

When Kenney inhaled the smelling salts under his nose, his eyes fluttered open. "What the...?"

"Timmy! Come in here," Mr. Smith called. "It's okay."

The boy slowly opened the bedroom door and stepped out, unsure of what was to come. He shied away from Kenney, even though he could see that he was tied up.

"Don't worry, Timmy. He won't hurt you again, not now and not ever," Mr. Smith said, gesturing him closer. "Timmy, listen to me. I want you to kick him in the balls, as hard as you can."

Timmy looked at Mr. Smith and shook his head. It was clear that even bound tightly, Kenney still held sway over the child.

"Don't worry, Timmy. He cannot harm you. I will not let him."

Timmy moved tentatively forward, as if anticipating a monster's attack. Finally, Timmy kicked him in the crotch. The blow from the small boy's shoe didn't pack much power, of course, but his abuser still registered the pain. Smith involuntarily moved his knees together. Mr. Smith saw a change in the boy's face when Kenney winced. In the next second, without further prompting, Timmy reared back and kicked with all his might. Kenney's scream only encouraged the boy, and he continued kicking his assaulter, harder and harder, until Mr. Smith was sure that Kenney's balls were probably mush.

"Feel better?" Mr. Smith asked, smiling as he pulled Timmy back and struggled to calm him down.

Timmy just looked up at him and returned his smile, his face flushed from the exertion. As far as Mr. Smith was concerned, Timmy had regained some control over his life once again, and he was a boy well on his way to recovery.

Mr. Smith looked down at the pervert writhing in pain, his face covered with sweat and tears. Mr. Smith looked at Kenney, then at Timmy, smiled again, then gave Kenney a kick of his own, smacking the man's most sensitive parts so hard that Kenney's eyes rolled back in his head and he passed out cold once again.

After forcing Kenney to drink a glass of liquid aspirin, Mr. Smith placed duct tape over his mouth and ensured that the zip ties were secure, so escape was impossible. He doubted that his captive was in any condition to even try, but he knew it was wise to be sure. Once he was sure Kenney was going nowhere, it was time to take Timmy home.

He parked a block away from Timmy's house, and before he let the boy out of the car, he shook his hand. "It was nice to meet you, Timmy, but I need you to promise me one thing."

"Okay."

"You must promise that you will never think any of this was your fault, I am proud of you, just as your parents are.

Always do your best to mind them and give them as much love as you can."

"I will," the boy said with a sheepish smile. I won't go out riding my bike by myself either. Mom was always worried about that, and now I know why."

"Very good," Mr. Smith said with a nod. "It is obvious that your mother loves you. Now, will you please give this to your parents?" he asked, placing a note in the boy's hand.

"Okay," Timmy said. He seemed conflicted for a moment, as if he wasn't sure what to do, but then turned to hug his hero. "Thank you, Mr. Smith. If you didn't come, I woulda—"

"But I *did* come," Mr. Smith said, "and now you're going to be just fine. Go on now."

Just as the clock struck midnight, Mr. Smith watched as a light came on in an upstairs window. A moment later, the door opened, and he heard Mr. Andrews call up to his wife, "Honey, get down here! It's Timmy! Our boy is home!"

As Mr. Smith drove away with tears forcing him to blink, he heard the joyous squeals of the boy's mom. "Tell 'em The Guardian sent ya, kid," he said with a grin into his rearview mirror.

* * *

Whether it was because they felt they owed their son's rescuer or simply because they were distracted by the joy they felt in having their son back, Mr. and Mrs. Andrews did not call the authorities until morning. For Mr. Smith, that afforded him plenty of time to leave his present for the world, in a preselected location.

On his drive back to the farmhouse by the silvery light of the moon, he was on top of the world. When he walked in, he was happy to find Kenney awake and still moaning from the pain between his legs. "You're one sick motherfucker...but not for long."

Smith secured Kenney's arms to his sides and placed plastic containers under each arm. He decided to forego his ritual, because he knew Kenney would not be moved by the display of the confession and flash drive. He was a man beyond shame, so there was no use wasting precious time to try to conjure up any. Instead, Mr. Smith thought it best to simply cut off his hands and watch the bastard die.

He poured the blood from the plastic containers into gallon jugs. He packed them away, then untied Kenney and let him collapse to the floor. He dragged the lifeless pervert into the bathroom to wash him down, as he didn't want the mess in his vehicle. He was glad to see that Kenney's crotch was smashed, bruised, and bleeding. *Timmy boy, you done good,* he thought.

He cleaned the hands and stashed them in baggies. He also tied baggies around each arm, to catch any leftover blood leakage. He rolled the dead deviant up in a plastic tarp and his own living room throw rug, then carried him out and stuffed him into his primer-black van.

Since Anderson was 333 miles from Port Huron, Michigan, he knew the authorities had staked out at the 444-mile location since before the two-week timeline, in an area where I-69 was under construction. When he did not stick to his schedule, the popular opinion was that the Anderson bodies might have been his swan song. In fact, many wondered if The Guardian was ready to retire.

One day, he had a chance to watch the watchers. He knew the stakeouts alternated between locals, State Police, and federal personnel. No one believed he would leave a body in such an easily anticipated location, but that was exactly what he was going to do. *The best place to hide is out in the open, where no one thinks to look!* he mused. Thus, almost three weeks after he left two bodies in the downtown Anderson park, Mr. Smith placed his sixth victim, Jeremy Wayne Kenney, just 150 feet away from the overpass, basically right under the nose of the coffee-slurping, donut-munching, sleeping stakeout.

Mr. Smith drove by and saw the men sitting in their car. He traveled little farther, until he was out of sight, then turned around and drove by again. He continued a few miles north of the site, then took the long way around to end up within a couple miles of his destination. Before he turned onto East Joe Smith Road, he cut the lights and relied on his night-vision goggles. He pulled onto a dirt construction road and traveled to within a football field away from the overpass, then parked next to a wooded area, where his van would not be noticed.

He pulled Kenney out, set him on a dolly, and strapped him down. He hooked a bag around Kenney's neck, one that contained the gallons of blood. Once his package was ready, he headed toward Kenney's final destination. He tied the dead man against a post and placed his hands, along with a confession and flash drive, in his lap. He poured the blood on the ends of Kenney's arms. Then, without the least bit of ceremony, Mr. Smith sighed and walked back to his van to head home. He dreaded the day when his efforts to rid the world of vermin would become routine. He was enjoying his quest, especially the accolades of the parents and children of the world.

Chapter 21

At 6:45, Adam Drake, the supervisor, pulled into the I-69 construction site just a couple miles south of Cincinnati, Indiana. Perked up with extra-strong coffee and a little morning loving from his wife, he felt pretty good. His crew had been busting their asses all week, and he brought donuts to celebrate their success. As he climbed out of his F-150 Limited, though, something caught his eye, about 150 feet beyond the overpass. Regardless of what his eyes told him, his mind didn't want to go there. *It's just too damned early for this shit*, he thought as he set the donuts back on the seat and reached into the glove box to retrieve his handgun.

Adam walked closer, navigating his way around the uneven landscape of ruts and dirt piles. His suspicions were confirmed when he saw that it *was* a naked man, sitting by a post. "Hey, you can't be here, buddy. Did you party too much last night or something? You look like hell."

Of course, the person didn't move.

"You need to get the hell outta here!" he yelled, fingering the gun in his jacket pocket. "You're trespassing, mister, in a damn construction zone."

Adam moved to within about twenty feet away, and he could see the man clearly. The man's arms were bound at his sides, and there were bloody stumps where his hands used to be. He looked around fearfully, as if the killer might still be there, but he saw no one. While he had brought his gun, he was horrified to discover that he'd left his phone in his truck. "Damn," he uttered, backing away slowly at first but then hightailing back under the overpass.

Other workers were pulling in by the time Adam reached his truck. "You okay there, Boss?" one of them asked.

"No! Yeah, I mean... Hell no! There's a dead man over there," he said, pointing beyond the overpass.

"What?" the worker said, then grabbed a few of his buddies and headed in that direction. "It ain't one of ours, is it?" he yelled over his shoulder.

"No, but whatever the fuck you do, don't get too close," the supervisor warned, "and, for God's sake, don't touch anything!" Drake yelled after them. "If you have a weak stomach, don't look, or you'll end up puking your guts out. I'm calling 911."

* * *

The stakeout team was the closest, so they were the first to arrive, pulling in just ahead of a Greene County deputy. After the sheriff took heat for letting it all happen right under his nose, the two locals who were supposed to be keeping an eye out were going to have some explaining to do. Nevertheless, considering how much area they had to cover, they would probably receive little more than a reprimand and a bit of harassing from their co-workers.

We called ahead and let the local authorities along our route to the crime scene know that we were coming. At ten o'clock, Vernon, Zee, Crystal, and I pulled in, to a swarm of law enforcement securing the area, and Meecham and his team were right on our heels. As I found the person in charge, Meecham found the coroner. Sheriff Donnie Gert was a tall, balding man. At first, he seemed wary of me, but he softened when he realized I wasn't there to take over and throw my federal badge in his face. He was happy to fill me in on what little they knew, and it wasn't long before Mary Jenkins, their coroner, walked over to hand him a bag of evidence.

"It seems to be the victim's wallet, Sheriff," she said, pointing to the license that was already pulled out of it.

When I approached the body, Meecham's team was already busy working the scene. Crystal was taking pictures and helping bag more evidence. "Do we know anything about this Kenney?" I asked, looking at his license, which didn't reveal anything but a normal-looking man.

"Nope, not yet," Sheriff Gert said. "We'll dig into that flash drive though. For now, we're heading over to Greene County General Hospital in Linton with the body. See you there?"

"Yep, but I need to talk to the forensics team to see what they found." I started to walk away but asked, "Would you mind if my forensics guys and gals handle the flash drive and the confession?"

The sheriff thought for a moment. "I guess that'd be all right. After all, getting down to brass tacks, it really is your case. Here. Take my card, just in case you need something... or find anything."

I was shaking his hand when Zee walked up. "Kroh, we found something."

Meecham broke out in a smile as we arrived at the crime scene. "It is pretty much the same as the others, except this man's genitals suffered some severe trauma."

I winced, as did every male at the scene. The thought of what the man went through resonated in all of us who happened to be within earshot of Meecham's statement.

"It's not exactly a case breaker, but the shoe impressions we spotted are unique, not from anyone here. They appear to match the Moab 2 Ventilators we found at the previous body dumps. Since there's a lot of loose dirt around here, we may be able to get a weight range for our unsub. We also got wheel impressions."

"Wheels? Like...a vehicle?"

"No," he said. "Probably a dolly, used to haul the body to the display. There are shoe *and* wheel impressions coming but only shoe impressions going back," he said, pointing east, to a wooded area.

"So, he carried the dolly back?" I asked.

"Looks like it. We haven't found anything here that matches the wheel pattern," Meecham answered.

Crystal yelled over from a place beside the woods. "Hey, I think I found his parking space!"

We walked over and saw where the dolly impressions started. The tire marks stopped, then backed up, then headed back the way they came. It wasn't much to go on, but it was more than we had before.

"What's the nearest access road to the east?" I asked, directing my inquiry toward the sheriff.

He thought for moment. "Hmm. I figure that'd be East Joe Smith Road, a little over a half-mile away."

"Could you have someone check with the residents out that way, just in case anyone witnessed anything...out of the ordinary?"

"You got it," the sheriff said with a grin, happy to have a lead to follow.

Before we left, Meecham asked Sheriff Gert and I to step in the loose dirt near our unsub's prints, to help determine our mystery man's approximate weight. Meecham may have been full of cheesy humor, but he was always a skillful, thorough investigator.

* * *

A couple hours later, we were waiting outside the medical examiner's office. We had already collected everything we could about Kenney, and what we knew of his life was piled on the desk before me.

Meecham walked in the office, threw a copy of the flash drive to me, and handed a copy of the confession to Sheriff Gert. "I nailed down Kenney's residence. I'm heading there now. See ya later." Then, with a wave, Meecham was gone.

While Zee plugged the drive into her computer, Sheriff Gert read the confession aloud, "I, Jeremy Wayne Kenney, am guilty of unspeakable crimes against children. For this, I must be punished. I will not ask for forgiveness, for I deserve none. I have not only most certainly caused irreparable harm to the minds of my victims, but I am also guilty of the murder of Amy Jordan. Although you might want to hear that I am truly sorry for what I have done, the truth is that I am not. The only thing I am sorry for is that I was caught."

We all sat in silence as the meaning of the words sank in. When we opened the flash drive, we already knew that Kenney had served time for crimes in Wichita; Marty had given us all the dirt on that.

Crystal opened a folder called 'The Evil of Kenney," then

navigated to another, simply labeled, "Wichita."

"Damn!" I cursed when we laid eyes on a video of the little girl in Wichita. Just then, the police entered the room on the video. "Wait. If he was arrested at the hotel, how did he get this video?"

"Vernon, was there a video on the evidence log of that case?" Crystal asked, just as confused as I was.

Vernon dug through the pile and found the log. A moment later, he shook his head, "No, no mention at all."

The others thought for a moment before Zee blurted, "Whoa. That can only mean that someone either found it after the forensics team left or that someone *knew* it was there."

"Are you suggesting that he had a partner?" Crystal asked.

"That would explain why Kenney had a copy," I said, then turned to Vernon. "Send our Wichita agents to the hotel to check the room out. I know it's been a while, but maybe the camera is still there. Send them a picture to give them an idea of where to look."

We watched a little more of the disgusting life of Jeremy Wayne Kenney, and even with my strong stomach, I was the first to turn away. I sat in the corner with my head back, doing everything in my power to unsee what I'd seen and to push away the thoughts of the torment those innocent children went through.

About an hour later, the coroner walked in, shaking her head. "I've been on the job for twenty years," she said, "and I've never seen anything like this." As hard as she tried to hide her feelings and maintain her professionalism, it was easy to see that she was more than a little shaken.

"Go on," I said, though I wasn't really ready to hear it after what I'd already seen.

"Well, although the crime scene was made to look like Kenney was killed at the dumpsite, I don't believe that was the case. I found carpet fibers in his arm stumps. It is my opinion that the killer captured the blood as it drained from the victim's body, then brought it to the crime scene. I discussed this with Special Agent Meecham, and we believe the blood was poured under each arm at the scene, not that it drained from the body there."

"Anything else?" Crystal asked.

"Yes. The hands hand wounds are consistent with tools used for cutting tree limbs, pinched on one side and cut through the other. The only other interesting finding is that Kenney suffered severe trauma to his genitals before he died. I found small, round, evenly spaced impressions consistent with shoe eyelets in that area."

"Shoe eyelets?" Vernon asked, arching an eyebrow.

"Yes, the kind found in tennis shoes. I believe the trauma was caused by our victim being kicked repeatedly in the genitals."

She went on for a little while longer but didn't add much to what she already said, but every time she mentioned the kicks to the crotch, every man in the room began to squirm in his chair, including me. In fact, when she finished that part, I looked down and was surprised to discover that my hand was instinctively covering Larry and the twins.

"Got a little problem there, Kroh boy?" Crystal asked with a smirk, placing her hand on my shoulder.

* * *

As we pulled up to the farmhouse Kenney rented just northwest of Shelbyville, Indiana, I saw Meecham's vehicle, parked alongside three Shelby County cruisers. I badged my way past the deputy guarding the driveway and drove up to the small but well-kept home.

When we carefully entered the house, I saw Meecham on his knees, placing an A-frame evidence-marking tent and taking pictures. "Meecham, are we clear?" I asked.

"Yeah, just stay away from this area over here. You might want to check downstairs, but be careful. They're still wrapping up."

Zee, Vernon, and Crystal followed me to the basement door and down the steps. What we found there was something like the dungeon we discovered at Reese's place, though not nearly as elaborate. This one was furnished with a futon, a bookshelf, and even an electronic game sitting on the nightstand by the bed.

"Did you find the camera?" I asked one of the technicians

working the room.

"Sure did." She pointed to the upper corner near the ceiling, opposite the bed.

"God, I'm glad this fucker's dead," I announced to no one in particular. "I know I shouldn't be, but I am."

Back upstairs, Meecham was wrapping up, and what he found seemed to back up all that the coroner had shared with his. "I believe Kenney was tied to these oak table legs," he said. "This is probably where he was kicked repeatedly in the balls, due to this blood smear here," he continued, pointing to a spot on the linoleum. "There is also a shoe print, consistent with a child's size sneaker. I think our unsub let one of the children take a little...revenge."

"Can't say I'm not happy about that," I said quietly, earning a silent nod of agreement from Meecham. "If there was a child here, though, where is he or she now?" I spoke, mostly to myself as I reasoned it all out in my head. "Vernon, check out any missing-persons reports involving children between 8 and 13 in central Indiana. Zee, check Kenney's journal and see if he mentioned a child he was still holding."

Zee quickly found the name, Timothy Andrews, and Vernon confirmed the boy's name on the list of missing children.

* * *

We pulled into the driveway of a gray aluminum-sided, split-level house in an upper-class neighborhood on the west side of Indy, a home situated on a half-acre lot and surrounded by perfectly trimmed hedges. Crystal and Vernon stayed in the car, while Zee and I headed for the front door.

"Thank you for coming," Mr. Andrews said when he answered the door, obviously expecting our visit.

"Mr. Andrews, I'm sure you know why we're here."

"I do," he said.

"Well, I am Special Agent Ben Kroh, and this is Special Agent Zindzhi Cole. We need to talk. Is Timothy here?" I asked hopefully.

"Yes, he is," he said with a nod. He then stood back and motioned us inside.

As soon as we were comfortably seated in the well-appointed living room, I asked, "When did your son get home,

Mr. Andrews?"

"Right around midnight. Timmy just... Well, we heard a knock on the door, and there he was," he said as a tear rolled down his cheek.

"Is he okay?" Zee asked.

"He was a little shaken, but he's happy to be home. We would have called last night, but we wanted to give Tim a little time to settle in before...you know."

"I understand," I said with all honesty.

"He sent Timmy home with this," Mr. Andrews said, holding out a plastic bag.

I examined the note, pulled it out, and read it aloud: "Mr. and Mrs. Andrews, your son has suffered at the hands of a very bad man. That man is now dead. Timmy is a strong boy and will be okay in time. Let him know this was not his fault. Timmy will need therapy and as much love as you can give him. Your humble servant, The Guardian." I then turned my attention back to Mr. Andrews as I handed the note to Zee, and she placed it in an evidence bag. "Is your wife home, sir?" I asked.

"Of course. She has not left Timmy's side since he returned."

"Do you mind if we talk to Timmy? It's important."

"Just a moment," Mr. Andrews said, then left the room. A few minutes later, he returned, trailed by his wife, with Tim hugging her tightly.

After we talked together for a while, so Timmy would see that I was not a threat, I asked, "Tim, I need to talk to you alone, away from your mom and dad. Is that okay?"

The book looked nervously at his dad.

Mr. Andrews nodded approvingly. "Go ahead, son. These people are safe, and your mom and I will be right here waiting."

Timmy then looked back at me, bit his lower lip, then stuttered, "I-I guess it's okay."

"Great! Show me your room."

I made sure to leave his door slightly ajar, so he would feel more comfortable. I also showed my badge to him as a distraction, so he wouldn't feel threatened by me. "Hey, it's cool that you like *Dr. Who*," I said, nodding to a Tardis poster on his wall. I saw a slight smile, so I continued, "Who's your favorite doctor?"

"The eleventh."

"Amy and Rory are really good companions, don't you think?"

"Yeah, Rory's cool," he said, relaxing a little. "I kinda like the Daleks sometimes, even though they're the bad guys."

I had to laugh at that. "How did you like the twelfth doctor...and Clara?"

"I think Clara is cool." When he said Clara and gave me that smile, I was sure he was smitten with Dr. Who's companion. "The new Doctor was a little grumpy at first, but after a few episodes, he mellowed out. I hear the next one's gonna be a girl."

"Yeah, I heard that too. I'm sure it will still be worth watching."

At that point, once his defenses were down a bit, I said, "First of all, Tim, I want you to know that none of this was your fault. Mr. Kenney was a very bad man. Okay?"

He nodded, drawing back in a little.

"I do need to ask you about what happened at the farmhouse though."

"Um...okay," he said.

Little by little, he revealed more and more to me, glancing at his poster of Dr. Who's TARDIS every so often, as if he wished that time machine could whisk him away. We talked for about twenty minutes.

"I-I saw him kill Amy," he finally said, out of the blue.

"Oh," I said, somewhat startled and definitely saddened by that news. "I am sorry you had to see that."

"I wanted to stop him, but he was so much bigger than me. I just... I couldn't do anything. I couldn't help her."

"Tim, as I said, none of it was your fault. Mr. Kenney was a very sick man."

"Wait. Was?" he asked, obviously a bright kid. "Is he really gone now, like that man promised?"

"Yes, Mr. Kenney is dead," I said, feeling better when his face broke into a small smile.

"Tim, do you remember the man who saved you, the one who made that promise to you?"

He nodded.

"Tell me about him."

"Well, he said his name is Mr. Smith. He's a really nice man. He got me out of there and brought me home."

"You are a brave little man, Tim," I said after we talked a while longer. "If you need me, I'll be here," I finished, giving him one of my cards and a pat on the shoulder. Then, just before we left the room, I asked, "Just between you and me, how did it feel to kick that asshole in the balls?"

"It was awesome," he said, beaming and offering me a high-five I simply had to accept. "Asshole!" he said and giggled.

"Tim," I explained once we rejoined his parents in the living room, "you're going to have to talk to the authorities and tell them what happened. I need you to do something else for me though."

"What?"

"I need you to stay strong, okay?"

"W-Will you be there?"

"Do you *want* me there?"

"Yes, please."

"In that case, I wouldn't miss it for the world."

Tim smiled.

Before we left, I informed the boy's parents, "I have arranged for you to meet with authorities at our FBI headquarters in Indy to file the report. I think that would be far better than police parading in and out of your home, making a spectacle of his bad experience."

"We appreciate that," Mr. Andrews said.

"Tim, you will have an opportunity to talk to a sketch artist, so we can create a picture of the man who saved you. We really want to find him," I said.

"So, we can thank him for bringing you home," I lied. I hated doing that, but I didn't have the nerve to tell the kid that the man who saved him was, in many ways, as bad as the man who abused him.

After we left, Zee told me about her conversation with Mr.

and Mrs. Andrews. "I gave them the general rundown of the road ahead for their son," she said. "I made sure they understood that he's gonna need a whole lot of understanding, therapy, support, and a whole lot of love."

"You worked wonders in there, Zee," I said, and I meant it. I could tell by the way they acted before we left that she had helped them feel less like victims and more like empowered parents who could face the truth. She had a special way about her, and she gave them the confidence to see the whole mess through, yet another thing I admired about her.

As we headed for the car, she held up a brown grocery bag.

"What's that?" I asked.

"Oh, just the clothes he was wearing when he got home, along with his bloody shoes that I'm sure have crotch residue on them."

"You are the best," I said with a smile.

"I know. I know."

Chapter 22

At eight o'clock that evening, The Guardian posted the edited diary and pictures of Kenney, just as he had done in the aftermath of his other killings. Also, as before, he was very careful not to reveal the identities of the children involved. In fact, everything about his *modus operandi* was identical to the previous cases, except for one thing: At the end of his post, in all caps and a one-inch font, he wrote a stern command: "Check your email, Kroh."

I grabbed my tablet, accessed my email, and immediately saw one from Jeremy Wayne Kenney, sent at about the same time when we were at the construction site crime scene. I read it in a muttered voice: "I know the news reporter Zach Tanner is a friend of yours. If he does not credit me for saving little Timmy's life, I will reveal his name publicly, along with all the names of all the children my victims have molested."

For a moment, we all stared at one another, dumbfounded by the threat, but in the end, there was only one thing I could do.

"Hey, Zach," I said as soon as he picked up the phone. "We've got a bit of a problem here…"

* * *

At eleven, we all gathered in the conference room to watch the top story.

After a few commercials and lead-ins, Zach's handsome face filled the screen, and he began, "This morning, a man was found dead near Cincinnati, Indiana, another apparent victim of The Guardian Angel of Interstate 69. The victim has been identified as Jeremy Wayne Kenney, a generally well-liked substitute teacher who worked in the Indianapolis area," he continued, as photographs of Kenney and his rented farmhouse appeared on the screen behind him. "Authorities have declined to comment, but as has been the case with other Guardian victims, the obvious evidence of Kenney's crimes has been posted on the internet. Thankfully, The Guardian has been very careful not to reveal the identities of the children involved." Tanner paused, glanced at his notes, then turned his face toward the camera again. "Kenney was originally from Plains, Kansas and spent two years in the Hutchinson Correctional Facility, after he was caught with an 8-year-old child in a Wichita hotel room. Following his release, Kenney moved to the Indianapolis area. He failed to register as a sex offender and falsified documents, allowing him to teach in area schools. While Mr. Kenney is an example of someone slipping through the cracks of the criminal justice system, we are happy to report that his last victim was rescued and reunited with his parents last evening, the fourth child to be saved and returned by The Guardian. Whether this vigilante is sinner or saint, I can't say, but we want to warn our viewers that, due to the violent nature of these vigilante murders, it would be wise for anyone who has insight into the identity of The Guardian to contact the authorities right away. We will continue to follow this story and keep you up to date as we learn more. For Channel 3, I'm Zach Tanner."

I switched off the television and sighed. "Great. With every news report, this killer looks more and more like a goddamn hero."

Marty, who had been watching the news with us from D.C., broke in. "We got to catch this guy, Boss."

"No shit. No fucking shit!" I said, exasperated and disgusted.

"I do have some news about the email," Marty said. "It was sent from Kenney's computer, presumably by The Guardian, while you were out checking on his handiwork. We're dealing with one bold, arrogant son-of-a-bitch, and..." He paused when he realized he was speaking in mixed company. "Oh! Hi, Crystal. By the way, if you ever get tired of that white man, let me know."

"You're first on my list, Marty," she answered with a sly smile.

"Okay, okay, you two," I scolded. "Marty, get your ass back to work and find something I can use. Otherwise, I'm gonna hire your grandpa. He's a man who can get things done."

"Well, hell, that might be the smartest thing you've said all day, Kroh," Marty teased. "I'll take that threat as a compliment. Gramps is the best, and we're all proud of him."

"As you should be," I said.

During World War II, Marty's grandfather worked with the Navajo Code Talkers. He, along with other Navajo men, created a secret code to confound the Japanese. I was honored to talk to him a couple times, as he was an impressive individual, a real, live hero, and I saw a lot of him in his grandson. Gramps was very proud of Marty, and I had to agree with him on that too.

"Anything else, Boss?"

"Not right now, Marty. Thanks for the email info, but just keep digging, cowboy," I said, then signed off quickly with a smile.

It was late, and everyone was tired and ready to go, but as I gathered my things, Meecham hurried up to me. "Hey, Kroh, I got one for you," he announced.

I said nothing but definitely cast him an oh-no-here-we-go look.

"A psychology student from a local university was sent out on a class assignment at a psychiatric hospital. He asked if he could talk to a few of the patients there, and the director was happy to oblige. When he opened the door to the first room, he saw a man swinging an invisible baseball bat. With the director's permission, he asked the guy what he was doing, and the man kept swinging and looking into the distance, with his hand shading his eyes. The patient answered, 'If I hit a homerun, they're gonna let me outta here.' The student simply replied, 'Oh, that's nice,' then shut the door and went to the next room. In that room, he saw another man swinging an imaginary golf club. He asked what he was doing, and the man had a similar answer, just, 'If I hit a hole-in-one, they're gonna let me outta here.' Again, the student replied, 'Oh, that's nice,' then smiled at him, shut the door.

I had to smile, because Meecham was enjoying himself just telling the joke.

"Finally, in the third room, there was a naked man lying on his back in the middle of the room, with a cashew on the end of his erect penis. The confused student asked, 'Excuse me, sir, may I ask what you are doing?' The patient looked at him with a maniacal grin, and said, 'I'm fucking nuts. They're never letting me outta here.'"

I couldn't help but laugh, as did everyone within earshot. I had heard a version of that joke a long time ago, but his take on it with the cashew was inspired. "No, *you're* fucking nuts, Meecham," I said, shaking my head as I walked out the door. Sure, it was a stupid, adolescent joke, but we had to find some way to counterbalance the awful things we saw, and we all loved Meecham's punchlines, the cheesier, the better.

We were due back at FBI Headquarters at nine a.m., so Crystal and I decided to stay at the Hampton Inn in Castleton. Besides, I needed to relieve some tension. Apparently, Crystal was in need of a little unwinding herself, because she started in on me before we entered the room.

"Whoa, girl!" I said, turning to face her.

"Shut up now," she said, pushing me roughly onto the bed and jumping on top of me. "Just let Larry do the talking."

The rest of the evening was a blur of lust and desire. I tried to roll her over a couple times, but she insisted on being on control, riding me like she was busting a bronco. It was all I could to keep up, but I had no complaints about that. When we finished, all I could say was, "Wow!"

"You like that?" she asked, panting from the exertion.

"Yeah. I think I'm gonna have to let you in the driver seat more often. Damn, girl!"

We showered and climbed back in bed, and this time, we just snuggled close and fell asleep in one another's arms, completely spent but thankful for the sweet release and the togetherness we shared.

Chapter 23

As I sat in the meeting, I could not keep my mind on the proceedings. Meecham thoroughly explained everything he found at the construction site and Kenney's house, but I couldn't help focusing on what we didn't know. Mr. Smith was highly intelligent, a planner, and at that point, it seemed the only way we would catch him was if he made an unlikely mistake.

Something at the edge of my mind jerked me back to reality. I finally realized I was unconsciously rubbing my little finger, and my phone was vibrating against my leg. When I saw that it was Marty, I felt justified in stepping out of the meeting to answer it; I had a gut feeling it was far more important than what I was learning in the conference room. I was also sure we would not learn much from the crime scenes; Mr. Smith was way too smart for that.

"Call me in the conference room. I might have something you need," Marty said, with audible excitement in his voice.

As I walked back into the conference room, I missed catching the door, and it slammed against the wall, startling the shit out of everyone. "Sorry!" I apologized, hoping I didn't cause anyone to pee a little. "Zee, pull Marty up, would ya? He says he has something for us."

"Okay," she said, and she made the connection in seconds.

"What you got for us, Marty?" I asked straightaway.

"Well, Kroh, cliché as it sounds, I've got good news and bad news. Which do want first?"

I could tell by the sound of his voice that he had found something big. "Okay, I'll play. What's the bad news?"

"I could not find any connection between the name Smith and the areas around the dumpsites. Sorry about that."

"Well, that was a long shot anyway. What's the good news?" I asked, finding it difficult to keep the desperation out of my voice.

"I did a search for murders in Michigan and Indiana, and one in Flint caught my eye. It might not be anything, but a computer tech named Curtis Meyer was stabbed to death in his shop soon after Eric Conrad's body was found. The police report indicates wounds are consistent with those found on Ryan Barstow."

"Holy shit! That *is* good news," I blurted.

"You *like* geeks getting stabbed to death, do you?" Marty asked, smiling.

"No, smartass. It's just that you may have just given me the key to shutting down The Guardian's killing spree and his love fest with the public."

"I already called the Flint chief of police, and he promised to email me everything they've got, ASAP. He said he's happy to cooperate and that he won't share this information with anyone till he talks to you. His name is Alex Masters, and he's expecting your call."

After Marty gave me the phone number, I thanked him for the information and signed off. I was floating on a cloud as I dialed Masters's number, and I knew, beyond a shadow of a doubt, that the Flint case was somehow connected to Barstow's death.

I talked to Chief Masters for about twenty minutes, and he sounded just as excited as I was that we might be able to put a lid on our respective cases.

"Nobody has been in the computer shop since the murder," Chief Masters said.

"Good. Please keep it that way till I arrive with my team."

"You got it," he said. "We're all the good guys here. We may as well work together to tie this nasty business up."

I thanked him again, unable to hide my excitement, then disconnected the call.

After signing off with Masters, I called the FBI field office in Detroit and asked them to dig up whatever they could on Curtis Meyer. Because of the nature of our suspicions, but I warned them to keep quiet about their search.

As Crystal, Meecham, and I made our way to Flint, Meecham studied the crime scene photos. "If these are accurate, I'd bet a year's pay that we'll find a foam plate in the trash," Meecham said. "Look at that blood spatter on the wall beside the body," he said, handing the pictures to Crystal.

"It barely goes higher than the baseboard." Crystal said.

"Yeah, I know. See the curve at the top?"

"Yeah, that could have easily been formed by the round edge of a foam plate," Crystal deduced.

"Not only that, but it's hauntingly similar to the pattern we found after Barstow's murder," Meecham offered with a deliberate smile.

As soon as we arrived in Flint, we stopped by the Police Department as a courtesy. Chief Masters was a no-nonsense lawman, and he immediately ordered Detective Hansen, the one who had worked the crime scene, to escort us to Tech Masters Computer Repair.

As we walked the crime scene, I held up photos taken when the body was still in place.

While I did that, Meecham did a little trash digging; of course, he found the Styrofoam plate he expected, and he burst out of the back room with a proud smile on his face and the plate in a plastic evidence bag. "Told ya," he said.

"Good call, Meecham. We need to tear this place apart, and then check out this guy's home. If we find anything that connects Meyer to any of the predator murders, we can expose The Guardian for what he is, just another cold-blooded homicidal maniac with a twisted sense of vengeance," I said.

"You won't find anything on either computer. Our guys checked them thoroughly, and they've been wiped clean," Detective Hansen offered.

"Do you still have the drives from both?" I asked hopefully.

"Yeah, why? They're just paperweights by now," he said, a bit confused.

"At the risk of sounding insulting, there may be something still lurking around on them. I've got a miracle worker who can find all sorts of things, even on paperweights," I said proudly.

We examined the business and the home thoroughly, every square inch, but after a couple hours of that, we still didn't find anything to link Meyer to any of the victims.

"Goddamn fucking hell!" I ranted; my frustration palpable.

Crystal gave me a hug, but I was too pissed to respond.

As we walked out to the car to leave, Detective Hansen said, "You know, maybe there's something in the box."

"What box?" I asked, confused.

"The box of stuff found with the body. It's in evidence lockup at the station."

"What!?" I said, having trouble wrapping my head around what he said. "Why didn't you mention that before?"

"Sorry. I guess I just got caught up in the hunt and totally forgot about the stuff we already collected."

We headed for the station with our sirens blaring. Now, I was too excited to be pissed.

At the station, Detective Hansen brought the box in the conference room, and the chief was right on his heels.

"What the hell are we doing here, folks?" Chief Masters asked.

As he dumped the contents of the box on the table, Hansen explained everything to the chief, and everyone grabbed a pile and dug in. Chief Masters happily joined in. For ten minutes, we discovered nothing important, but then Crystal looked up at me with a delighted expression on her face.

"Hey, this might be something," she said, withdrawing a journal from her pile and laying it on the table. "Look at this page," she said, pointing. She then read aloud, "EC 2 MS." She flipped a couple pages over and read, "RJ AR 2 MS," then asked, "What do you think it means?"

"I don't... Wait! Maybe MS stands for Mr. Smith. If that's the case, EC could be Eric Conrad," I noted.

"And RJ could be Randy Jarrett," Crystal added.

"And AR is...Andrew Reese!" we said together.

"This is it, people!" I declared; with the biggest smile I'd been able to wear for several weeks. "This is just what we need to tie these two murders to Mr. Smith." I high-fived everyone and gave Crystal a hug.

Even Chief Masters managed to break out with a big-ass grin as he clapped his detective on the back. "Good thing you remembered this damn box, Hansen," he said. "Next time, don't forget to check out *all* the evidence, or I might just murder you myself!"

Before we left, I made sure everyone here knew it was to remain on a need-to-know basis, and there were very few who actually needed to know. "We have to use this to our advantage," I said. "This is our best chance to discredit this asshole."

* * *

Mr. Smith felt great. Now that he had regained his status, with the death of Kenney and the saving of another child, he was on top of the world again. The news outlets were singing his praises, and the internet was abuzz, with his name showing up all over Facebook and saturating the world of tweets. He was excited and inspired to continue with other projects, one minor and the other bigger than big.

The minor project was Stephen Montgomery. Mr. Smith had promised Cassondra that they would expose Montgomery for what he was, a depraved deviant. He drove to Henderson to see Cassondra and waited outside her shop until everyone was gone. When he was confident no one was around, he left his car and put on the jacket that made him look like a real FBI agent. After he entered the shop, he locked the door and flipped the sign around to indicate that it was closing time.

When Cassondra heard the door, she came out of the back to see who it was. "Oh! Hi, Mr. Smith," she said. She liked the man, but she sensed there was something off about him, something broken. *I wonder if all FBI agents are a little broken*, she thought as she glanced across the room at her troubled visitor.

Cassondra had been keeping tabs on Montgomery since she found out he was the man who molested her niece. She was careful; Mr. Smith had told her it was absolutely vital that Montgomery remained unaware of their suspicions. Otherwise, he would bolt and sink into the woodwork, and they would never be able to find them again to exact her revenge. She couldn't help but wonder if Montgomery had another child hidden somewhere, a little one being forced to do God-knew-what. *The bastard has children of his own,* she thought, and her mind was powerless to stop the image of him and her niece from wafting through again. Above all, she wanted him punished for what he had done, so she was very careful to keep her investigation under wraps.

"How have you been, Cassondra?"

"Fine, but I really want to nail Montgomery's ass, ASAP."

"Soon, my dear. Soon."

"Why do we have to wait?"

"As I told you, if we rush things, he might flee and escape justice. We cannot let that happen, can we?"

She nodded but looked more than a little dejected and frustrated. "Yeah, I guess. I just wish The Guardian would get him. That would solve everything," she blurted.

That remark startled Mr. Smith, but he recovered with a smile and a calm voice. "I suppose it would, wouldn't it?"

"You're an FBI guy. You got any inside information, stuff they aren't saying on the news? Are they getting any closer to catching The Guardian?"

"Not yet. He always seems to be one step ahead of the... er, us, if not two."

Rather than appearing angry about that, Mr. Smith almost seemed pleased, but she dismissed it as a bad read. Cassondra thought of herself as a good judge of people, but she'd been wrong before. Case in point: Her last boyfriend had turned out to be a real tool bag.

Mr. Smith was not sure how to handle Montgomery. He wanted to involve Cassondra, because she deserved her revenge, but that went entirely against his normal protocol. He was torn between letting The Guardian do his thing or teaming up with Cassondra and letting the molester have his day in court. He stared into her eyes for a moment and came to a decision. "This is going to be great, Cassondra. You and I are going to take this bastard down," he said, with a gentle touch on her shoulder. He could not let her be part of what he would ultimately do to Montgomery, but he thought it might be fun to have a partner to help with the planning, and she deserved that much. He liked her and had decided already that he would never hurt her. He was pretty sure she would hold her tongue, because she would not want the authorities to know she had conspired with The Guardian.

"So, we're gonna get him, right?"

"Yes, my dear, we are, but we have some planning to do first."

Chapter 24

At six o'clock the next evening, I stood outside the front gate of the FBI field office in Indianapolis. Zach Tanner was giving his cameraman last-minute instructions next to the Channel 3 news van that was parked in the lot. *This is going to be a great day,* I thought as he began his intro for this live special report.

"First, I must warn you that the following may not be suitable for children. For weeks, the self-proclaimed Guardian of I-69 has been leaving the bodies of those guilty of crimes against children along the interstate. He has become something of a cult hero, having removed several criminals from society and returned four children to their families. It is presumed he also saved countless others from the deviants and sex offenders he killed. Sadly, however, there is another side to this story." He then turned to me. "We are here at the Indianapolis FBI headquarters, with Special Agent Benjamin Kroh from the *Behavioral Analysis Unit. Agent Kroh and his team* are best known for their efforts in stopping the infamous Fingertip Killer, nearly two years ago. Thank you for speaking with us today, Agent Kroh."

"I'm happy to be here, Zach," I said.

"Can you tell us a little more about The Guardian investigation?" Zach asked, getting right to the point.

"Sure," I said, turning to the camera. "Many of you have heard of The Guardian of I-69, who has been killing child predators. Several have offered public praise of him, making online claims that he is fulfilling a purpose, ridding the world of sick individuals. To be honest, on some level and considering my line of work, I have to agree. However, we operate under the law, under a justice system of crime and punishment, and while these sick individuals must be stopped, a vigilante bent on killing is not the answer. Like it or not, in the United States, everyone has a right to a fair trial. It is one of the many reasons our country stands above the rest. This is not a case of a parent losing perspective and seeking revenge. Rather, this killer meticulously plans and carries out his brutal, premeditated murders, and that, too, is a crime and a violent one by a disturbed human being. Whether these people deserved to die or not, it was not his decision to make."

"Do you have any new leads, Agent Kroh?" Zach chimed in.

"Well, we have just discovered something about the individual known as The Guardian. He is not an all-knowing protector of children, and he did not find his predators-turned-prey on his own. He had help."

"Help?" Zach asked, arching a brow. "So, we're talking about a team of killers here? Maybe a Bonnie and Clyde situation?"

"Not exactly, Zach. From what we know, The Guardian hired computer repair technicians in the areas around where the bodies were discovered, to run illegal scans of their customers' computers to find evidence of child exploitation. The unfortunate techs were led to believe they were helping to save the lives of the children involved. This is the one thing The Guardian did not lie about, per se, but it is also where the true evil is realized."

"How so? Playing the devil's advocate here," Zach said, "doesn't this just mean he's resourceful, using others to help him with his self-assigned mission?"

"You could say that, I guess, but once the computer techs gave The Guardian the information about the predators, he killed them in their shops, in cold blood. Without mercy, he stabbed them in the chest multiple times, then methodically went about destroying all evidence of his presence there."

"Wow," Zach said. "This is a shocking new development."

"Indeed. He has killed two computer techs that we know

of, Curtis Meyer, owner of Tech Master Computer Repair Shop in Flint, Michigan, and Ryan Barstow, owner of Bauhaus Computer Repair in Muncie, Indiana. We are positive that there are others. These were innocent victims, folks. Their only crime was being naïve, easily tricked into breaking client confidentiality and too quickly believing that the person they sold that info to, was a good man. He took their lives for vanity, because he has a sick need to feed his own ego, to be acknowledged as a hero, a righteous defender of children. We know now that The Guardian is as sick as the deviants he murders. He administers cruel and unusual punishment."

"Cruel and unusual?" Zach pressed.

"Yes. He cuts his victims' hands off at the wrists while they are still alive, then watches them die." I paused for a moment, prepared to release my lie to the public, the bait that I hoped The Guardian would take. "There is one other thing as well," I said, then hesitated for dramatic effect.

"And what's that?"

"There is evidence of postmortem sexual acts against the bodies of his victims. He is truly a monster, and now *he* must be brought to justice for his crimes against society. He has used a vague name, Mr. Smith, in his dealings with computer techs. If anyone has any details about him, we implore you to contact your local authorities or the FBI at once. Your life and the lives of others may depend on it. Thank you," I said, then gave a quick nod and walked away.

Zach quickly wrapped up the segment and walked over to me. "Is that necrophilia bit true?" he asked.

I smirked. "The good guys wear white hats, right?"

"I guess, but what's that got to do with—"

"Well, occasionally, we have to tell little white lies too," I said with a wink. "That's off the record though, or you won't think me such a good guy anymore."

"You got it, Kroh. You're one sly bastard. I hope it works."

"Me too," I said to him, then softly repeated to myself, "Me too."

* * *

By the end of the day, many of the websites created as a tribute to The Guardian were closed down, and only the hardcore ones remained. Their cold rationale seemed to be that the lives of a few geeks were a fine price to pay to save children from molesters, and there was a lot of debate about whether or not that equation was true.

Mr. Smith was beside himself, beyond furious. It wasn't that Agent Kroh had revealed that The Guardian had killed innocent people. That part was inevitable. What he couldn't stomach was being accused of having sexual relations with corpses, as if he was warped in the head. He knew exactly what Kroh was up to, trying to throw him off his game by humiliating him and destroying his fan base, but knowing that didn't make him feel any better. He felt it was all over, that he could no longer continue his quest to rid the world of child predators. He could've weathered the death of the techs by somehow tarnishing their reputations, but that blatant lie took it all away.

Because of Kroh, he had to call Cassondra right away. When it went to voicemail, he decided not to leave a message; he wanted to break the news to her face to face. He wasn't even sure if he could explain, and he didn't know if he should. Everything in his being cried out for her death, so she wouldn't expose him now that the heat was on, but he liked her. Something about the young woman just struck a chord in him, made him feel things he hadn't felt in a long, long time. *If I just talk to her, I think I can make her see the light,* he told himself.

He climbed in a vehicle she had never seen before and drove quickly to her shop. He passed by once, peering in to see if she was there. He couldn't tell, so he pulled into the parking lot of a little shopping center across the street. Through his binoculars, he read a sign on the front door: "CLOSED! I will be out of town until further notice, due to a family emergency. If you need emergency help, call the number below. I am sorry for the inconvenience."

The sign was almost a replica of the one he's posted at Slater's shop, which he found ironic. He also felt a twinge of satisfaction in knowing his fake sign mimicked an actual one, but that elation was short-lived. Cassondra wasn't there when he needed her to be, and he had to leave and come back later.

* * *

Cassondra checked on the tilapia in the oven while her niece Leslie chopped up vegetables for a salad. She was only half-listening to the news, but the story about murdered computer techs caught her attention. She stood upright, with her oven mitt in one hand and a bottle of paprika in the other and stared at the TV. "That sick, fucking bastard!" she exclaimed with a grimace as she listened to the part about the necrophilia.

"Aunt Cassie! Language!" Leslie scolded. "And close the oven. It stinks like fish in here."

"Well, there are no other words for it," she said, shaking her head as she sprinkled seasoning on the baking fish and slammed the oven door closed.

"He has used a vague name, Mr. Smith, in his dealings with computer techs…"

Cassondra gasped and dropped the paprika as fear shook every part of her. "Holy fucking shit!"

Leslie looked up at her again, wondering why her usually in-control aunt was standing there with her mouth agape, trembling as she stared at the TV. "What's the matter, Cassie?" she said.

Cassondra managed to move beyond her shock and answered, "I'll explain it later. Just pack up what you need for the next two weeks. Hurry!"

"I-I don't understand," Leslie said, more terrified than she'd been in a long, long time. "What about the tilapia and—"

"It can burn! Now please just do what I say, quickly."

A half-hour later, the two of them were in the car, ready to leave, with two quickly packed bags of wadded clothes on the seat behind them.

For a brief moment, Cassondra wondered if she remembered to turn off the oven, but she didn't really care. "Give me your phone," she said, urgently holding her hand out.

"What? Why?"

"Please, Leslie!"

The girl looked at her pink smartphone with the Hello

Kitty sticker on it, then reluctantly handed it to her aunt.

Cassondra quickly pressed a few buttons, disabling the GPS tracker she'd installed.

"Oh my God! Have you been spying on me?" Leslie asked.

"No. I've been looking out for you," Cassondra said, then sped across the Twin Bridges, quickly passing the sign that indicated Evansville, Indiana, she made a quick call to a friend. She knew if anyone checked her phone records, it would reveal her last location somewhere near the Indiana border. As she approached the end of bridge, she opened the window and casually flung her phone and Leslie's into the deep Ohio River below.

"What the hell are you doing? That phone had all my pictures in it, all my friends' numbers and texts and… Tell me what's going on," Leslie demanded.

"We just need to be off the grid for a while. I'll explain later."

"But I loved that phone!"

"I'll buy you a new damn phone! Now, just be quiet. I need to think."

As soon as Cassondra crossed the bridge, she seemed to change her mind; she made a U-turn and crossed back over, heading toward Henderson. She drove to Owensboro and crossed into Indiana on the Glover Cary Bridge. For the next forty minutes, they drove in silence. Leslie was brooding over her phone but knew her aunt wouldn't act in such a strange way if not for good reason.

Finally, she pulled into the drive of a property owned by a friend, near Santa Claus, Indiana. "We should be safe here for a while. The owner's in South America, doing one of those Doctors Without Borders programs," she said.

"Define a while," Leslie said.

"Maybe a week, maybe a few months, as long as it takes," Cassondra said, to a smattering of half-hearted complaints from her niece. Inside, once they were settled down, she finally told Leslie the whole story.

Leslie hugged Cassondra. "Are we still gonna go after that guy who hurt me?"

"Damn right, we are! You can count on it." She gave her a

squeeze.

After a few moments, Leslie moved her head from Aunt Cassie's chest. "Just remember you owe me a phone, Aunt Cassie…and what's for dinner?"

* * *

At one in the morning, Mr. Smith returned to Mosby's Computer and Games. He easily disarmed her security and made quick work of searching the house and shop for any indication of Cassondra's whereabouts, but came up empty. One thing that was very telling was the fish still in the oven, as well as the paprika bottle, its red contents spilled all over the floor. "Must have left in a hurry," he said to himself, popping a grape tomato in his mouth from the unfinished but relatively fresh salad on the counter. "Fucking Kroh!" he yelled when he realized that the laptop in her office was also gone.

One thing that bothered him almost as much as not knowing where to find Cassondra was the knowledge that Montgomery was probably a no-go. If, by some off chance, Cassondra remained quiet, he could follow through with his plan to give that heathen what he deserved, but the chances were slim to none.

As he was getting ready to leave, he noticed a folded piece of paper by the laptop with "MS" written on it, an origami fortune teller or chatterbox, a children's game. His mind reflexively traveled to the past as he remembered his daughter, Lacy, playing with one just like it. He pushed the bittersweet memory from his thoughts and picked it up, then worked it to discover the messages she had left for him.

"Thank you for trying to help me with my problem," she wrote.

He worked it once more and read, "Please do not try to find me." It was simply signed, "C".

Fucking Kroh! he thought. *He's ruined everything…again.*

After cleaning the food away that was beginning to stink, he grabbed the trash bag, and left. Otherwise he left it as he found it.

It was now time to complete the final act of the first part of his plan, and that upset him beyond belief. He was just starting to enjoy the hero worship. Nevertheless, he had bigger fish to fry, and his only real regret was that it might become necessary to kill Cassondra sometime in the future.

Chapter 25

At seven p.m., Mr. Smith sat in the bushes near a dog park, just a couple miles beyond Exit 210 on southbound I-69. He was sweating profusely in the humid heat of early evening, swatting away an endless multitude of mosquitoes that saw him as a great feast; none of the hungry insects seemed the least bit deterred by the insect repellant, and they were as hungry for his blood as Kroh was. It didn't really bother him much, though, because he was there for a very important purpose, a pivotal event that would change everything.

His excitement was as thick as the damp, heavy air. Everything he had done in the past few weeks had led up to that moment, to the end of Special Agent Benjamin Kroh. Although he preferred to get up close and personal, he knew that was not an option. His plan would be effective, but the one disadvantage was that it would keep him well out of Kroh's reach when he breathed his last. His body hummed with anticipation as he thought about it. The months of planning and the perfect execution of each step bordered on genius. *Only I could have accomplished a great feat such as this. Only the Guardian!* He thought, stroking his own ego.

He checked the tracker on his phone and silently thanked the GPS satellites above for letting him know that his quarry was approaching from the FBI office in Indy, heading back to Anderson. It was a simple thing to place the tracking unit on Kroh's car, but sometimes, Mr. Smith surprised himself. *I really am a genius,* he thought with a smile.

It's not bragging when it's a fact.

When the time was right, he got into position and readied his silenced rifle for a little payback. In a moment, Kroh would be dead. The agent drove at his typical seventy-four miles per hour, and it was a sure bet that anyone who was with him would soon join Kroh in the afterlife when his car lost control. The thought of Kroh, forced backward by the impact of the bullet, slamming against the seat, then slumping dead over the wheel, brought a major smile to his face.

Among the other skills on his dossier, Mr. Smith was a skilled marksman, courtesy of the many hunting trips he and his father took on his Uncle Jake's property. In high school, he even lettered as an all-county champion in target shooting. Still, he was nervous now, and he knew he had only one chance. He could not miss, for that would mean chaos he was not sure he would be able to handle.

His weapon of choice for the long-awaited adventure was an XM-21 7.62mm NATO Sniper Rifle with silencer, like the kind used in Vietnam. It was one of his most prized possessions, and he'd spent many afternoons with it at his uncle's cabin, which he now also owned. He used a solid black camera tripod he purchased from Walmart for just a few dollars as a rest, a cheap but effective means of steadying his shot. He smiled as he thought of putting a bullet hole in the middle of Kroh's forehead, the would-be fitting end to that phase of his plan. Mr. Smith took aim at approaching cars, as practice and to settle his nerves, but he had no desire to shoot any innocent persons. *Only if it's necessary,* he reminded himself. *They were all meant to be.*

When Kroh's car neared, Mr. Smith activated the light he secretly attached to the underside of the target vehicle. He looked as far down the northbound interstate as he could see, and suddenly, there it was. He looked through the high-powered site and focused, then mentally counted down as he readied to shoot. *Five...four... Almost there. C'mon, Kroh.*

He pressed his finger against the trigger, but just as the hammer was about to send a projectile toward Kroh's head, a mosquito buzzed in his eye. Reflexively, he shook his head to shake the pesky insect away, and that caused him to hesitate for just a second, forced him to take a quick shot, with a less-than-optimal angle.

The shot was away, and he watched as Kroh's vehicle swerved across the lanes, but he didn't wait for the aftermath because he was busy tearing down and couldn't afford to stick around. He had just taken down one of the Bureau's darlings, and he knew they would soon swarm every square inch near the shooting.

As he ran for his car, he listened for the inevitable sound of a car veering out of control, rolling, and finally coming to rest in the middle of the interstate, possibly upside down. All he heard, though, was screeching tires, followed by a flurry of honks and even some curse words yelled out windows. *Doesn't matter. He's dead*, he told himself but felt cheated that he couldn't look into Kroh's dying eyes.

* * *

Thwack!

There was a loud, sharp sound like a rock hitting the windshield just before a small hole suddenly appeared in the glass in front of me. An imperceptible moment later, the passenger-side window shattered, and shards of glass struck me in the face. In the seconds that followed, I tried to make sense of it. I was barely able to control the car as I focused on the hole in the glass, but when I finally pulled safely to the roadside, looking back at a long line of middle fingers and angry drivers who had to slow down or swerve away from me, I could finally breathe again.

"What the fuck! For a moment there, I thought I was gonna lose it. That was a close one, huh, Zee?" I reached up and felt the spot on my face that stung a little.

Only silence answered me.

"Zee? Zee!" I wailed when I turned and saw a crimson river running down her forehead. "Oh my God! Stay with me, girl. Stay with me!"

I grabbed my phone and quickly dialed Vernon with one hand and threw the car in drive again with the other, then stomped on the gas. St. Vincent's Fishers Hospital was a couple miles up the road, and I didn't dare wait for them to send an ambulance to us. As I raced through traffic, ignoring the protesting honks and squeals of tires, I held Zee's head so it would not flop around, hoping to minimize the damage.

Worst-case scenarios mocked me, rolling through my head one after the other. The thought of not having Zee with me, my right hand, was terrifying, and I refused to believe that was going to be the case.

I screeched to a halt in front of the emergency room entrance, nearly colliding with an overweight woman in a blue bathroom, stuffed into a wheelchair in front of me and drawing a furious scowl from the orderly tasked with pushing her. Apparently, Vernon managed to call ahead, because ER staff was already racing out the door when I pulled up, and they didn't hesitate to lift Zee out of the car, place her carefully on a gurney, and race back inside.

"Damn it, Zee, don't you die on me!" I pleaded as I ran behind the nurses who were wheeling her toward the operating room. I couldn't tell if she was breathing or not, and they stopped me as I tried to follow them into the operating room.

"Sorry, sir. We'll have to take it from here. You can wait there," a brunette nurse said, placing a hand on my chest and pointing at the closest waiting room.

I felt as helpless as I did the day my parents died, and all I could do was wait and wonder. *What the fuck just happened?* I asked myself, struggling to make sense of it in my head, playing the trip over again and again in my head. As I thought of the moments just before the hole appeared in the windshield, just after I adjusted the radio to one of our favorite oldies, I remembered a thought that occurred to me then: *Wait. Was that a muzzle flash?* I remembered exactly where I saw it, and I wanted to run over there and check the spot out, but I couldn't bear to leave Zee alone.

While I waited, I called Crystal and told her what happened. "Call Bradford," I said before I made the two hardest calls at all.

Marty and Zee were more than close, and I knew he was not going to take it well, which he didn't. Next was the obligatory call to my grandparents, because she was like a daughter to them. I hoped to have some details about her condition before I called her family, but it didn't seem I was going to be informed anytime soon. After I'd passed the message along to all the appropriate parties, I shoved the phone back in my pocket and found myself waiting once again, feeling very alone in that ugly orange chair, surrounded by other miserable people who were also hoping for good news about their loved ones.

Twenty minutes later, Vernon sprinted in the emergency room door, and the look of fear on his face was devastating. "Is she okay? Where is she?" he asked, darting his eyes around and pacing the floor like a caged animal. "She's got to be okay, Kroh. She's just got to be!" he said, with tears running down his cheeks as he slumped into the waiting room chair.

"Vernon, we don't know anything yet. The doctors are with her now," I said, grabbing him by the shoulders to calm him down. "She's strong. I'm sure she'll be fine."

When Crystal and Bradford finally arrived, we had no choice but to leave Vernon to watch over Zee and head to the spot I was sure was the origin of the shot. We pulled onto a road near the dog park entrance, a tree-lined, shaded space that was perfect for anyone who wanted to remain concealed. Just on the other side of the fence was a clearing, with a perfect view of the interstate.

I peered closer at the spot where the shooter stood not more than an hour earlier, the matted grass a telltale sign of his presence. I wanted to move in closer still, but Crystal stopped me.

"We need to wait. It's a crime scene, Kroh."

Meecham showed up half an hour later, and he and Crystal got to work. I felt useless just standing there, fantasizing that the shooter foolishly left some evidence behind, maybe a fingerprint or a cigarette slathered with his DNA, maybe even a dropped wallet. Sadly, I already knew they'd find nothing. *This is the Guardian,* I was sure, *and he's always too damn careful.* I had finally given in to calling our unsub by his press-generated nickname, but he was really a killer, a murderer, and I liked to think of him as a dead man walking. It was so much more than personal now. *Hurting me is one thing, but hurting someone I love is...unforgivable.*

I called Vernon for the tenth time, only to discover nothing new. "Damn it to hell! It's been hours. What's with those doctors anyway?"

"No news is sort of good news," Crystal told me, consolingly rubbing my arm. "If they're still working on her, at least it means she isn't...you know."

"Yeah, I guess," I said with a shrug.

"We all know Zee's a fighter," she said.

"Right," I said flatly, hoping the medical team who was working to save her was truly up to the task. I was scared, and I didn't care who knew it, so I didn't even try to disguise the tremble in my voice. A tear pushed its way out of the corner of my eye and burned a cooked path down my face.

"Kroh! Over here," Meecham said, breaking me away from my horrible thoughts of an upcoming funeral I didn't want to attend.

"What you got?" I asked.

"I'm not sure, but I think it's one of those camera stands. Let me check it out," he said, then walked over to where the shooter had stood. "Yep," he said, turning back to me. "I'm pretty sure the guy used this to steady his shot. It fits the hole I found."

Once we thoroughly combed the crime scene, we hurried back to the hospital, but there was still no word on Zee. Grandma and Pops were there, and while he did his best to hide his worry, she was openly beside herself.

Chapter 26

The scene yielded nothing other than the partial shoeprint and the camera stand, an inexpensive piece of junk that could have been bought at any discount store. The straight line from the shooter's standing spot to where the stand was found led to the parking lot of the dog park. One slight bit of hope was that it was a members-only park, and a keycard had to be swiped for entry to the caged area, though that didn't really affect the parking area at all.

FBI agents were dispatched to speak with anyone who was there walking their dogs, as it was considered an all-hands-on-deck operation since one of our own was injured. Although they were professional and tried to do things by the book, following the letter of the law, they were all out for blood, and I couldn't blame them.

Within an hour, the officers determined, with help from the owners, that six card-carrying members had been there.

Agent Ray Sparks was sent to speak with a potential witness, Randolph Singleton. When he knocked on the door, he was greeted by a forty-something, latter-day yuppie, holding his Pomeranian in his arms. "Mr. Singleton, I am Agent Ray Sparks, with the FBI. May I ask you a few questions?"

"Sure. Come on in."

Once Agent Sparks was seated on the couch in Singleton's well-appointed living room, he began, "I understand that you were at the dog park around seven today. Is that right?"

Singleton nodded and patted the head of his little dog.

"Did you happen to see anything out of the ordinary?"

"Well, Hercules and I weren't there long. My boy's been a bit tired lately."

Sparks grimaced at the dog's name.

"It's such a cute name for my big boy, isn't it, Hercules?" Singleton defended, kissing the animal on its head and speaking to it in baby-talk.

Trying to mask his repulsion, Sparks continued, "Please continue, Mr. Singleton."

Singleton frowned. "You must be a cat person. Anyway, I did see a car parked back in the far corner of the lot. It struck me as odd, because the place is never that busy, and no one ever parks that far away. It was a dark car, fairly new, but I can't tell you what kind. All I know about cars is that you have to change the gasoline every so many miles," he said with a wink and a smile.

"Anything else?" Sparks impatiently asked, scribbling notes on a small pad in his hand.

"Well, as I was getting into my Corolla to leave, I saw a man come out of the trees at the far corner, obviously the owner of that dark car. I've never seen him before, and I thought I should inform him that only members were aloud, but he was quick to jump in his car. He drove out of the parking lot like a madman. I hope he got a ticket on the way home."

"Did you get a license plate number, by any chance?"

"Uh...no. Why would I do that?"

"I just thought that if he was driving erratically or seemed strange... Never mind," the agent said with a sigh when he caught Singleton staring at him in disbelief. "Did you happen to see what the man looked like?"

"That, I can tell you. He's about my height, with brown hair and a mustache, carrying some long thing wrapped in a blanket. Other than that, I can't remember much more, but I know he wasn't supposed to be there. I know all the members. They all love Hercules, except that Spot. I swear, that Chihuahua's bark is bigger than his bite, and one of these days, a collie's gonna make a chew toy out of him. That mangy thing jumped on me once, knocked the latte right out of my hand and scared my little Hercules to death."

Sparks wanted to punch the dickhead in the face and might have if he mentioned members only or his pet's name again. "Can you remember anything else, anything a little off about the man?" he asked.

"Well, truth be told, I noticed that his hair wasn't sitting right on his head."

"Excuse me?"

"He was wearing a wig, some sort of toupee; I think...a cheap one without enough adhesive. He looked like roadkill died on his head."

"Do you think you could work with a sketch artist and offer a description while the memory's still fresh in your mind?" Sparks asked.

"That depends. Will it take long?" Singleton asked with undisguised irritation. "I am the president of our Neighborhood Association, and we have a meeting at ten o'clock tonight."

Great! Another self-important asshole, Sparks thought, fantasizing about rubbing his nose in a fresh pile of Hercules's poo, but he resisted the urge to assault the witness. "He can be here in fifteen minutes, and it shouldn't take long at all. I'll just wait in my car until he arrives."

"Whatever floats your boat," Singleton said with a sigh and a shrug.

I'd like to see you floating, mister...facedown, in a river, Sparks said but faked a smile and reached his hand out for a shake. "Thanks. I'll just be right outside," he mustered.

Once the sketch was made, Sparks emailed it to the FBI field office and sent it to Vernon as well, who absently handed his phone to Kroh.

"Damn. This is no better than any of the sketches we got from the kids," Kroh barked.

Vernon just shrugged, said nothing, and quickly resumed his silent worrying about Zee.

Around ten thirty, Marty rushed through the door, trailed by Zee's parents, Bob and Jana. The look on his face brought another tear to my eye, and I pulled him into a hug. We were a team, and when one of us was hurt, it pained us all.

"Mr. and Mrs. Cole, please have a seat," I said, gesturing to those awful orange chairs, then went on to tell them what we knew so far, which was embarrassingly little.

Until someone in a white coat found time to speak to us, all we could do was huddle there in that waiting room, mostly in silence, working our way through tissues and drinking the watered-down coffee that didn't seem to have any taste at all.

Chapter 27

Mr. Smith lost his balance and fell as he climbed over the fence to return to the parking lot. He had to stop to make sure his flesh wasn't torn, because he didn't want to leave any DNA for the FBI sniffers to find. When he was sure he was not leaking any evidence, he gathered up the rifle he'd wrapped in a blanket, and made a beeline for the car.

On the way to his vehicle, he spotted another man just leaving the park, a nosy person who looked like he wanted to say something, with one of those yappy little puffball dogs tucked snugly under his arm, dressed in an obnoxious argyle doggie sweater. Mr. Smith jumped in his car, threw it in gear, and sped past the man, not even daring to look him in the eye.

He turned left when he reached 131st Street and continued on as it turned onto Marilyn Road. He looked in the mirror and noticed that his brown wig had shifted slightly, and he frowned and pulled it back in place. He stayed on Marilyn Road until he finally turned left on 146th, then drove into Indianapolis.

He was sure no one had noticed him, other than the man in the parking lot, and he knew that uppity idiot couldn't possibly identify him, because crooked wig or not, his disguise was good enough to obscure his true identification. His vehicle, however, was another thing, and he feared that the man would remember the make and model, if not his license plate number. No worries, he told himself, as he had a contingency plan for that. In fact, he had six vehicles to choose from, and the loss of one was really of no consequence.

He drove to Indianapolis International Airport, parked in the garage, and walked to another automobile that was stashed in the long-term economy lot. It would be a while before they found the other one, and the chance that they would connect it with Kroh's death were negligible. Even if they did, there was nothing to lead them back to him.

Just over two hours after he took his shot, he sat in his apartment, eating Vietnamese takeout and eagerly awaiting the eleven-o'clock news. He wanted to pat himself on the back, but he couldn't officially do that till Zach Tanner announced to the world that Kroh was dead. An hour before the news came on; he decided to take a shower.

At eleven, Mr. Smith parked himself in front of the TV, with his celebratory scotch in hand, ready for an announcement that never came. He couldn't believe the news came and went with no mention of Kroh or his certain death. *Are they intentionally holding back the information?* He wondered. *That must be it, the sneaky bastards.* He wanted to make some calls but knew better. *That's probably just what they want, for me to blow my own cover by doing something stupid.* He knew the FBI would be all over the death of one of their own, and he just had to wait patiently for the good news to be revealed. "Damn it!" he barked to no one in particular, but even as he complained, he recalled that he had sources. In time, he would have all the secret information the Bureau insisted on withholding, but he still desired the instant gratification he deserved for his efforts.

He went to bed but failed to sleep, because his mind continued to race with thoughts about the future. He first thought about his family. More than anything, he wanted to go back in time, to the days before his life went to shit, to the time when his wife and children loved him and were proud of who he was and where he was headed. Those wishes only turned to grim thoughts of his wife abandoning him, and he recollected when things went south. *That was when I needed her the most, but she divorced me and moved on,* he thought. Then, like the proverbial salt in the wound, less than a month after it was legally over, she was already seeing someone new; a man named Brad, ten years her junior. *Fuck that muscle head,* he thought, but he was sickened when he recalled that that was precisely what she was doing.

His children, who once thought their dad could do no wrong, now wanted nothing to do with him. *My bitch of an ex has turned my own flesh and blood against me.* The last time they were supposed to be with him, her new boyfriend had the gall to take them to an Indianapolis Indians game. *It was my weekend, damn it!*

A fantasy of killing her brought a wide smile to his face in his dark bedroom. *If she's gone, out of the picture, Jeremy and Lacy will have to come back to Daddy. Then I can tell them what a lying bitch their mother has been, what a bastard that Brad is.*

Next, his thoughts drifted to Cassondra, a tattooed, self-assured, intelligent woman. He usually despised those qualities, but either she was different, or his views had simply changed. He really, truly liked her, and he wasn't sure he could find it in himself to end her life. *If I kill Montgomery for her, will she keep my secret? If she will, I can let her live.*

Finally, he thought about the death of Kroh, and Phase Two of his plan. "It's really been a glorious day, hasn't it, Mr. Guardian?" he asked himself. "Let's sleep on it, and tomorrow, we'll begin a new chapter, one that will shake the world," he decided before he drifted to sleep, to dark dreams that echoed all the success he was sure he would have.

* * *

At eleven thirty, Dr. Leyla Shankar walked into the waiting room, and we all jumped up to greet her with a chorus of, "Is Zee okay?"

The doctor smiled. "I'm sorry for the delay, folks, but it was touch and go there for a while. Fortunately, the projectile did not pierce the skull."

Everyone sighed, and Zee's mother collapsed to a chair in relief, sobbing uncontrollably.

The doctor continued, "The shot did hit with enough force to fracture the frontal bone. This resulted in coup and countercoup injuries." When she realized her medical jargon made no sense to most of us, she explained, "The brain was suddenly forced against the front and the back of the skull, causing bruising and bleeding that leaked into the brain tissue. Frankly, this is of great concern, but we're doing everything we can to reduce the swelling. Thankfully, no bone fragments resulted from the injury, for that would have greatly amplified the danger. We will continue to monitor her condition, and we're as prepared as we can be for any scenario. It may sound cliché, but she's not out of the woods yet. The next ten hours are critical, but we'll know more by tomorrow morning."

"What should we do, Doctor?" Zee's father bravely asked.

"Go home and get some rest. We'll let you know if anything changes."

I wasn't sure about anyone else, but I wasn't about to leave, so I plopped down in a chair beside her mother and put my arm around her. I wasn't sure who benefited most, her or me.

Around midnight, Bradford took Crystal home, and my grandparents left after embracing everyone. The Coles, Vernon, Marty, and I stuck around, and the medical staff eventually allowed us in to see her.

As I sat there watching Zee breathe, I once again recalled losing my parents, and I had to stave off my tears in the darkness.

* * *

In the morning, Zee had still not opened her eyes, and the doctors seemed as worried as we were which was disconcerting. The pressure in her skull had gone down, but for whatever reason, she just couldn't come out of her state of unconsciousness.

At nine, Vernon had to reluctantly leave her side to take care of some paperwork at the FBI field office. Marty tagged along; he needed to see some files he could not access remotely. Bob and Jana tore themselves away to go to the cafeteria for some breakfast, knowing they needed their strength to deal with their heartbreak over their daughter.

At ten, a soft knock came at the door.

"Come in," I said quietly.

"How's she doing?" Meecham asked as he stepped in.

"Not sure yet. She's still out."

"Damn. I'm sorry, Kroh."

"It isn't your fault, and the docs are doing the best they can. Anyway, what's going on? Any news on the case"

"Yeah," Meecham said, keeping his voice low. "We checked out your car, and it's clear from the ballistics that you were the intended target. If you had been speeding even a bit more or the guy fired just a second earlier, it'd be you with a hole in your head," he said, pointing at me. "As it happened, the bullet hit the windshield at just the right angle to deflect it. Either our shooter's a bad shot, or he made a mistake and fired too late. You were lucky, Kroh."

"Well, she sure wasn't."

"Actually, she was," Meecham said, "except for the fact that she has to work with the likes of you."

"Funny," I said, but I couldn't even smile.

"Actually, it appears her head was turned at the time, looking out the window. Otherwise, instead of glancing off her forehead, the bullet would have gone straight through. Like I said, she's a lucky woman."

"It should've been me."

"Way to dodge a bullet, asshole," a weak but sweet voice said beside us. "Pun intended."

I turned so fast that the tablet that was resting on my lap crashed to the floor. "Zee? You're awake! Thank God."

As I stood next to her bed, holding her hand and grinning, she slowly opened her eyes and smiled. "You look like shit," Zee said softly.

I blinked through my tears and leaned down to hug her. "Yeah, well, I've had a rough few hours."

"A few hours? How long have I been out?"

"Since about seven last evening, so you've been out about sixteen hours."

"God, really?"

"Just about."

"The Guardian," she said, more of a statement than a question.

"I'm sure of it."

Marty and Vernon almost knocked Meecham down as

they crowded back into the room. I pulled myself away from Zee and let the other men in her life welcome her back.

I walked with Meecham to the nurses' station, and we informed them that Zee was awake. I thanked Meecham before he left, then headed to the cafeteria to tell her parents their baby girl was awake and talking.

The nurse shooed everyone out as I made all the necessary calls to Crystal, Bradford, and my grandparents. "Can you bring me some fresh clothes?" I asked Crystal. "Zee says I smell like, uh..."

"Yeah, well, I don't blame her," Crystal said with a smile in her voice. "I'll be there soon."

Within an hour, Zee's entire fan club was there to see her. Unfortunately, the professionals had to run many tests, and Zee was so tired that she fell asleep before we could visit again. We were all bummed about that, but we wanted what was best for her, so we hung around the waiting room again till we had our chance.

Around six, Zee's dad walked in. "She's awake again," he said, "and she wants to see you all."

We all crowded into her room; the love meter maxed out. All seemed right in the crazy world again, and we found happiness, if only for a moment. For at least a little while, The Guardian didn't enter our thoughts, even though he was the one who put her there.

Chapter 28

Later that evening, I received a call, and at my request, Crystal answered.

"It's from the Sioux City field office in Iowa. Supervisory Special Agent Jordan Drake would like to speak to you."

"Hey, Jordy. What's up?"

"I'm afraid our Firstborn Killer is back. We just found a body with the same *M.O.*, the second one in less than two months.

"Are you sure?"

"Absolutely. Can you come out and put some fresh eyes on the case?"

"Damn, Jordy, I would if I could, but I'm underwater on my own case, and Zee is in the hospital."

"Yeah, I heard about that. How's she doing?"

"It was pretty hairy for a while, but now the doctor says she'll be fine."

"That's great. Glad to hear it, Kroh. I know you've got a lot going on, and I wouldn't ask if I didn't really need you on this. I'm only asking' for a couple days."

"I'll have to talk to Noah to see if—"

"Way ahead of you there. Noah's fine with it, if you agree."

"Okay. Send me everything you've got and copy Marty."

"Thanks, Kroh. I'll owe ya one."

"Just one, Jordy?"

"Well, maybe a few more than that," he said before he hung up.

The Firstborn Killer had terrorized the Sioux City area for five years, but it suddenly stopped. In all, he'd killed ten people, seven men and three women, all with bullets to their hearts. The victims ranged in age from 18 to 63, and the only correlation was that they were all the oldest siblings in their families. Other than that, I didn't know much about the case.

"Have you ever been to Sioux City?" I asked when Crystal walked into the room.

"What? Why?"

"I have been asked to help out on a case. I figured you might want to tag along."

"Oh, well, I'd love to, but I have to talk to Bradford first."

"Do that, and I'll go ahead and tell Marty to book our tickets."

"What if Bradford says no?"

"Please," I said with a smile. "Do you really think any man can turn *you* down?"

"Hmm. Well, I guess you have a point," she said, then shook her fine hips as she walked out of the room.

We spent the rest of the evening enjoying Zee. She was still weak, but she was alive, and that couldn't have made me happier.

When we had a little time alone, I had to offer my apologies. "I'm sorry, Zee. Really."

"What for?"

"For getting you shot."

"Hey, the doctor said it was your quick thinking that made all the difference. You saved my life by getting me here in a hurry, Kroh."

"Actually, Zee, you were shot because of me."

"Bullshit!" she said, glaring at me. "This is Mr. Smith's fault. Anyway, it's probably better that he got me."

"Why?"

"Because we all know what a big pussy you are when it comes to pain."

"Yeah, well, you've always been stronger than me."

"Duh!" she said, wincing as she laughed. "Why do you think the good Lord makes us girls have the babies? Y'all couldn't handle pushing an apple out of your assholes, let alone a cantaloupe. Oh, and don't tell my mom I just said that."

When I finished chuckling at that, I grew serious in a hurry. "I'll get the fucker, Zee. I promise."

"Wrong. We'll get the bastard together, and we'll make him pay."

"Whatever you say. I've got to head out town for a couple days. Will you be okay without me?" I blurted.

"Wait. What? You can't just leave me now, Kroh. I-I can't live without you," she said, with hurt in her eyes. How can you just—"

"Okay, okay. I guess I didn't think that through, did I? But I can stay if you really need—"

She laughed again and interrupted, "Calm down, Kroh. I'm just busting your chops. You know I love you, so get out there and do your job. Just promise you'll come back soon, in one piece."

"I will, girl, and I love you too. I got to go. Jordy awaits," I said, then leaned over to give her a kiss on her forehead.

I didn't want to leave her, but too many other people needed me. Vernon had taken a few days off to watch over Zee, and Grandma and Pops would be there if they were needed. In fact, Pops insisted that the Coles stay at the Kroh Compound, so I knew Zee would be in good hands until I returned.

I said my goodbyes, and Crystal and I headed for her place to grab a few things, just in time to catch our eleven-o'clock flight.

As the plane jetted through the sky, I revisited the Firstborn case, and Crystal studied it for the first time. "It never ends, does it?" she said.

"Nope," I said, handing her yet another file of evidence.

* * *

At nine the next morning, after catching a few Z's at the Holiday Inn, we walked into the Sioux City field office. Jordy met us in the lobby. "Thanks for coming, Kroh," he said.

"Good to see again, Jordy. Zee won't be up and around for a while, so I brought Crystal. I hope you don't mind."

"Not at all. The more eyes we have on this, the better. It's really nice to meet you, Crystal. If you're half the agent Zee is, you'll go far in the FBI."

"Oh, I'm not FBI."

"She's a detective with the Anderson PD in Indiana but one of the best forensic tech specialists I know. She gave us our first leads on The Fingertip Killer."

"Nice! Sounds like you could have just sent her, Kroh."

"I don't have one doubt about it. Now, let's see what you got."

Jordy took us to his office and shared the latest files on his case. It wasn't much more than what we already knew, but we needed every last detail if we were to have any chance at helping him.

"The family of our latest vic's coming in today. Would you like to sit in?"

"Glad to, Jordy."

At one o'clock, Robert Humphrey's family sat in the conference room, looking more than a little nervous. Robert's younger brother, Jesse, brought his girlfriend Jillian with him.

"Would anyone like water? Maybe tea or coffee or soda?" Jordy asked, trying to put the family at ease.

"No, thanks. What do you want from us?" Robert's dad asked.

"We just want to ask you a few questions about the days prior to your son's murder," Jordy began.

"I don't understand how we can help," Anne Humphrey interjected.

"Did you notice anything different with Robert in the days before he went missing?" Jordy asked.

They all looked at one another, their expressions blank, but something seemed to be bothering Robert's younger brother.

"Jesse, do you recall something? Anything could be helpful," I coaxed.

"I'm not sure that it matters, but... Well, the day before my brother went missing, we were in a coffee shop downtown, with Josh and Tina, and I was saying a lot of mean stuff about Robert," Jesse said and started to cry.

Something about what he said seemed important and struck a chord in my gut, but I wasn't sure why.

"Jesse, why?" his mother asked, aghast.

"Robert just kicked my ass in fantasy baseball, and I guess that pissed me off. I was just ranting, Mom, over something stupid. I-I really didn't mean it." He sniffed a little and wiped a tear from his face.

"What coffee shop was it?" I asked.

"Why does it matter? My brother's freaking dead. It isn't like I can make it up to him with a damn cappuccino!" he barked, then sniffled again.

"Please just answer my question," I pressed.

"The Last Drop, downtown," he said, staring at the table, seemingly more irritated with himself than he was with me.

"Did you notice anybody there, maybe someone who seemed to take a special interest in what you had to say?"

"No. I was talking to Jillian and my friends," he said, reaching over to give his girlfriend's hand a squeeze.

"How about you, Jillian? Did you see anyone taking an unnatural interest?" Jordy asked.

"No. I was too busy talking to Tina."

What? Talky Tina? I thought, fighting back a smile as I was struck by the thought of an old *Twilight Zone* episode starring Telly Savalas.

"Damn," Jordy complained when the family left. "I hope we learn more from the relatives of the other victims."

"It'll all come together in time," I assured him. "You want me to talk to anyone else?"

"Sure," he said, "if you're offering."

"I am."

"All right. Well, the second-to-last victim was a Raymond Turley, the owner of Turley Construction. The place has been in business for over eighty years. Anyway, according to the interviews we've done, Turley was a tough but fair boss. His brother Eric took over after his death. I found his number in the paperwork, and we're supposed to meet him at his office."

"Sounds like a plan," Crystal said. "Let's go."

When we pulled up to Turley Construction, Eric met us in the parking lot and walked us inside. "I hope we can make this quick, Officers. We got a building inspector coming to one of our downtown sites tomorrow, and we're really busy making sure everything's up to code. Can't afford to lose that contract."

"It'll be as quick and painless as possible," I assured him.

He walked us back to his office, where his father was waiting behind the desk. "This is my dad, Ray. He's helping me out during the transition."

"I am Special Agent Ben Kroh, and this is my partner, Crystal Markham. We'd like to ask you a few questions."

"Go on." Eric's father was a get-straight-to-the-point kind of guy.

"Well, for starters, did you notice anything different about Raymond in the days leading up to his death?"

They looked at each other, and the elder of the two spoke first. "No, not that I could tell. Eric?"

"Nope. If anything, he was more Raymond than usual."

"What you mean?" Crystal asked.

"He just completed a major construction job and was finally able to relax a little. He was smiling more, even joking around."

We talked for a while longer but discovered nothing helpful, not until I asked the question my gut kept telling me to ask: "Have either of you been to The Last Drop?"

"Yeah, I go there all the time. Why?" Eric asked.

"We're just covering all our bases, gathering as much background as we can. This might seem strange, but did you ever happen to mention your brother while you were there?"

"No, but Ray and I had a little disagreement there recently, over a job. I guess it got a bit more heated than it should have. We were…a little loud."

"And how soon before his death was that?"

Eric thought for a second. "Gee, I guess just one or two days. Why?"

"I'm not sure," I said, my gut and head somersaults as I realized the coffee shop had something to do with the case.

We finished the interview, and as we left Turley Construction, I called Jordy and told him what we learned.

"So, you think we should ask the other relatives about

the coffee shop, huh?"

"It might be a good idea," I said.

Next, I called Marty and told him to check out the financials of Eric Turley and Jesse Humphrey, and I hoped he would find credit card transactions confirming trips to The Last Drop. My instincts told me we'd stumbled into something very important to the case, and it was time for us to go to that place and check it out.

The Last Drop was a nice, family-owned little place smack dab in the middle of downtown Sioux City, a fairly popular gathering for hipsters and caffeine addicts. Even at five p.m., there were only two or three tables open, and there was a line at the counter.

When we made it to the front of the line, I asked the barista if I could speak with the manager. When he emerged from the back office, I identified myself and asked if we could speak privately, and he led us into the office.

"Mr. Sutton, we're here to investigate a lead on two recent murders in Sioux City."

"The Firstborn Murders?" he said.

"Yes, sir. How far back do your surveillance tapes go?" I said, pointing up at the camera in the corner.

"Why do you need to know?"

"Just humor me please. I'll explain later."

He walked to the door and yelled out, "Kyle, could you come in here for a moment. He then turned back to us. "He's my son and a tech man," he said. "If anybody knows about those cameras, he does."

A kid in an apron and with a man-bun at the back of his head walked in.

"Son, how far back do our security tapes go?"

"Uh...we have a five-terabyte hard drive, so at least five or six months. Why?"

"These people are with the FBI, and they need to look at our video."

"The FBI? Cool!"

I called Marty again and asked him what was next on the agenda. After a few moments, I could tell he was getting a little frustrated, and he asked me to give the phone to Kyle, and it didn't take long for me to be entirely lost as they spoke geek to one another.

"Fan-fucking-tastic!" Kyle said five minutes later. He handed the phone to me and walked over to their computer. He came back to me, smiling, and handed me the external hard drive. "Here. I'll switch it out with the new one tomorrow."

"Won't you need that?" I asked, then thought about it for a minute. "Wait. What did Marty promise you?"

"He told me to tell you it's none of your business. This is fucking great!"

I knew when to let it go when it came to Marty, so I turned back to Mr. Sutton. "I need you to let our forensic accountants check your business records."

"What? Like an audit?"

"Don't worry, Mr. Sutton. We've got nothing to do with the IRS. I can't stand those pricks myself," I said. "We just need to check your sales transactions, nothing else."

"Of course. I've got nothing to hide."

I smiled and thanked him and left The Last Drop, full of hope. I took the hard drive back to the Sioux City field office and gave it to their techs. The army of accountants was already at the coffee shop, slurping down triple-espressos as they dug into the mountain of paperwork, thankful that the coffee shop was at least using a computerized financial system.

We quickly found when Turley and Humphrey were there, based on their debit card receipts, and that gave us the timelines to search for people who were there the same time. That gave us enough information to cross-check any siblings of the deceased that might have been there before they died, and while I knew it wasn't prudent to start counting our chickens, Ii was a little excited that some seemed to be hatching.

After a long day of crime fighting, Crystal and I were hungry. I asked Jordy for his recommendation, and we ended up at the Diamond Thai. We both settled on pho, a rice noodle soup served with beef or chicken. I topped that off with spring rolls and cold glass of sweet tea.

"Hey, this'll be the first time I ever boinked a girl in Sioux

Die by Proxy

City," I said as we made our way back to our hotel.

"Really? Are you planning on calling a hooker or what?"

"Of course. Hey, maybe they have a buy-one-get-one sale. I could get one for you too."

"Careful, boy. You keep that up, and you might actually need to make that phone call."

Needless to say, much to my delight, I didn't have to hire anyone, and I could check Sioux City off the list.

Chapter 29

The next morning, in the conference room, Marty gave us a rundown of what had found. "I ran the data on Turley and Humphrey, and I came up with six possibles," he announced as six DMV photos appeared on the screen. "It's not a sure thing. I mean, our unsub could be smart enough to avoid the paper trail by paying in cash. Props to the guys in the Sioux City field office though. They found the victims in the videos. First, that's Eric Turley and his entourage. After they ordered, they found a table in the middle of the room. The Humphreys sat close to that same spot. The six people I showed you were present on both occasions," he said, then drew circles around the six seated around Eric Turley.

I studied each person, hoping for a sign that someone was paying a little more attention than normal.

"This is where we believe he started his little rant about fantasy baseball. I didn't see anything unusual, but maybe you guys can spot something."

Next, Marty showed us the video of Jesse Humphrey and went through the same process as before. As he circled each of the six, the first thing we noticed was the change of clothes, but as before, none appeared the least bit interested in Humphrey at all.

"I'm still running financials on the six. So far, I've found no red flags."

By six o'clock, we were all tuckered out from a hard day's work. All day long, agents who interviewed the other families checked in, giving us news that many had frequented the coffee shop.

"Let's shut down for now and pick it up again tomorrow," Jordy said, standing to stretch.

"Hey, Marty, can you send those videos to my tablet?" Crystal asked.

"Your request is my command. They're on their way."

"Thank you, Marty."

"Marty, what would it take for you to come and work for me?" Jordy asked.

"You know my boss, sir. Clearly, it wouldn't take much. Maybe a gift card for that coffee shop, if it wouldn't get me killed."

"Your mouth's going to get you killed if you're not careful," I said with a grin.

We all laughed as we headed out for the night. Crystal and I got something to eat and returned to the hotel, with too much on our minds to entertain each other as we did the night before. Even though the six we identified did not appear to be guilty, I still felt like The Last Drop was the key.

While I watched a little TV, Crystal studied the tapes, but after about an hour we called it quits and hit the sack.

I awoke around eight and found Crystal was already studying the videos. "How long have you been up?" I asked, stretching and yawning.

"About an hour. Hey, I think I found something."

"I've got something over here you can find," I said, wearing my best shit-eating grin.

"Not now, Kroh boy. We need to go see your friend." She smacked me on the stomach and headed for the shower. "And, no, I don't mean *that* little friend!"

"Little? Sorry, Larry. She didn't mean it," I said as I hoped off the bed to get ready.

At nine, Crystal practically dragged me through the front door of the FBI field office. She made a beeline toward Jordy's office, and ten minutes later, we were sitting in the conference room, waiting for Marty. He checked in five minutes later, and Crystal started the meeting.

"I've been looking over the two videos of our last two victims, and I think I found something. Marty, could you play the video of Robert Humphrey?"

"Sure thing, Crystal."

As the video played, we all strained to see what Crystal had found, but nothing dawned on us.

About three minutes in, Crystal said, "Stop right there, Marty. See the guy in the green shirt, on the right?"

We all nodded.

"Okay, now move forward. Stop! See the guy in the brown shirt, just on the other side of Humphrey?"

We nodded again.

"Now, pull up the video of Turley."

Marty obliged and played the second video.

"There!" Jordy almost jumped out of the seat, pointing.

"Yes, and if we move a little forward, there's the other guy," Crystal added.

"Damn, Crystal, great catch. Marty, get me the best picture of each of those guys. We need to identify them right away," I said.

"You got it, Boss. I bet they paid cash, at least on one of the visits. Nice job, Crystal," Marty said, and then he was gone.

Armed with two new suspect photos, Crystal and I headed to The Last Drop. We showed both pictures to the elder Sutton, and he easily identified one of them.

"That's Steve Carson, a regular, but I'm not sure about the other guy. Kyle, do you recognize him?"

"Yeah, that's Jimmy Rector. He's in some band called The Flaccid Dogs. They're actually pretty good. I was thinking of inviting them for our next open mic night."

"Thanks a lot," I said, and I pulled out my phone as I headed for the door. "Marty, I got two names, Jimmy Rector and Steve Carson. Run them quick, would ya? My gut tells me one of them is our killer, and my money's on Carson."

By the time we got to the field office, Marty was ready. "Rector's a no-go," he said. "He left town after starring in the Humphrey video, had some weekend gig for his band at some Denver festival. Carson is another story. He works for his older brother, at Carson Industries, a plastics manufacturer in Sioux City. He was out of the country for two years, at their factory near Cartagena, Colombia. He just got back three months ago. On a hunch, I looked for unsolved murders around Cartagena. Three were single gunshot wounds to the heart. I made a call to the Colombian National Police, and the officer I talked to was Ernesto Hernandez. Although they had not yet made the connection, it was confirmed that all the victims were firstborns. Before I hung up the phone, Hernandez gave the killer a name, Primero Nacido Asesino."

"Firstborn Killer? He's our guy!" Jordy almost yelled. "Let's go."

We pulled up in front of Carson Industries, just in time to see the staff flooding out of the building, horrified and screaming.

"He's crazy! He's shooting the place up!" squealed a woman with only one high-heeled shoe on.

"I saw him in his brother's office," a custodian said, brandishing his mop like a weapon.

We rushed inside and found the office door closed and locked, but we could hear the conversation going on behind it.

"Haven't I always taken care of you?" Bob Carson asked.

"Taken care of me? Taken care of me? I can take care of myself. I'm just as smart as you. Dad should've given us the company, but he gave it to you," Steve Carson whined.

As I listened to Steve through the door, I couldn't help thinking of my favorite movie, *The Godfather*, specifically the conversation between Michael Corleone and his brother Fredo, which mirrored the words coming from the locked office. Bob Carson's stressed response brought me back.

"I know the business, and you don't. I took the time to learn it from Dad, while you chose to play instead. You were too busy running with your buddies, drinking, and chasing the ladies. I don't know how many times Dad said to me that he wished you'd start taking life seriously. Now you burst in here like some maniac, and…"

Crystal and I stood with our guns drawn, near the back of the pack. It was Jordy's show, not mine, and he was on the front lines.

"Steve Carson, this is the FBI. We need you to step out,

with your hands in the air," Jordy yelled at the door.

"Go away!"

A shot broke the silence.

"Dad... He never liked me," Steve said as the bullet tore through the door, sending splinters in our direction.

"Bullshit! He was just worried about you. His one wish was that you'd grow up and settle down, so we can run his company together," Bob replied, the stress evident in his voice.

"Liar!"

Suddenly, there was another shot but no hole in the door.

Jordy was unwilling to wait any longer after the second shot fired, he gave the signal, and the agents breached the door. By the time Crystal and I reached the door, we could only watch as they pulled a crying Steve Carson away from his brother, who was bleeding heavily from his chest.

"I'm sorry, Bobby. I didn't mean to. Bobby!" Steve cried as he struggled against the grip of the agents who held him. "Goddamn it! Let me go!" he screamed, straining to reach his brother. "Let go of me and help my brother!"

As I reached Robert Carson, I saw that it was too late. Just like the other victims, he was taken down by a shot to the heart. The Firstborn Killer was cuffed and crying uncontrollably. He had killed the inspiration behind the twelve other murders he committed and the one person he loved more than anyone else in the world.

* * *

Later that day, Jordy dropped us at the airport. "Thanks, Kroh. Without you two and that Marty—or should I say Crystal and Marty?—we'd probably still be looking for that sick bastard."

"It's too bad about his brother though," I offered.

"Yeah. I guess Carson caught wind of our investigation and lost it. Anyway, thanks again. Are your grandparents still slinging the best burgers in the Midwest?"

"They sure are. I'll tell 'em you said hi. Bye, Jordy."

Then, after Crystal and I bid farewell with a hug and a handshake, we headed for the plane.

Chapter 30

Mr. Smith thought about it and knew it was time to move on. Although he missed Kroh, he still felt good about recent events. *I came close to killing that black bitch who works for him. That has to be worth something, right?* He thought. He was still pissed about Kroh, but he told himself there was plenty of time to take care of that little detail. *At least I put a little fear in his ass.*

He quite enjoyed his role as The Guardian and enjoyed ridding the world of diseased vermin, but he had to set that aside for a bit and concentrate on the future. To do that, he had to think back on something that happened in his past, not long after he killed Conrad.

He thought back to that lucky break that made everything possible. Mr. Smith knew things and had access to information that was not readily available to most people. In the early stages of his planning, he found out that Danil Vetrov, a top-level accountant for the Russian mafia, was visiting his brother in the Lebanon Correctional Institution in Ohio. The convict, Arsenii Vetrov, was incarcerated there for killing a man while visiting friends in Cleveland. Danil loved his brother, so he visited him once a month. It was also suspected that he met with the Aryan Brotherhood leaders to deliver protection payments for his Arsenii.

Danil Vetrov did not look like a typical mobster. He was a clean-cut young man who gave off the impression of a Wall Street investment broker. He had been recruited by his uncle straight out of college and had never known the more violent side of the business. He had never spent a minute behind bars, and his body was free of tattoos. Although his future looked bright in the legitimate world, he had gone to the dark side, chosen to work with the mafia. He proved to be a valuable asset and moved up the ranks quickly.

Mr. Smith's knew Vetrov usually stayed at a Comfort Inn just a short drive west of Lebanon. He was glad to find that the Russian was a creature of habit. He was also thrilled that Vetrov reeked of innocence, that he was one of those undercover troublemakers who never had to look over his shoulder. It was simple to Taser the American-born Russian as he attempted to climb into his car, suspecting nothing.

He quickly pulled Vetrov into the van and slid the door shut, then looked around to make sure no one noticed. As per his usual way, he zip-tied the man's hands behind his back, followed by his ankles, then bound them all together, virtually hog-tying him. He stuck a gag in his mouth and Tasered him twice more before pulling out and heading for Cincinnati. During the drive, every time his prey dared to stir, Mr. Smith zapped him again.

Mr. Smith pulled up to a warehouse that he had rented under the alias Joseph Wayne. He activated the automatic door, pulled the van in, and parked it. After the door was closed and locked, he pulled Vetrov from the van and set him on a rolling cart. He wheeled him to a room at the far end of the open warehouse. In the middle was a two-by-eight board, with one end resting on a cinderblock. He pulled Vetrov from the cart, snipped the zip-tie that connected his hands and feet, and laid him on the board, with his head on the lower end of the incline. After he secured Vetrov to the board, he strapped his head down and placed boards on either side of his head, to keep it still.

"Okay, comrade," he said, loving the fear in the Russian's eyes, "this is what's going to happen today. I will ask you some questions, and every time you refuse to answer, I will attempt to drown you. Do you understand?" he asked, giving Vetrov a knowing smile.

"Why are you doing this to me? Don't you know who I am, who I work for?"

Amused by his uncertain defiance, Mr. Smith continued, "Yes, of course I know who you are and whose payroll you're on. That's precisely why you're here. See, you have something I want, and I'm pretty sure you won't give it to me if I simply ask."

"What is it?" he demanded, truly confused.

"Let's just start the fun, to show you how serious I am," Mr. Smith said, then put a cloth over Vetrov's face. He grabbed a jug of water, then began to pour it on his face.

Vetrov struggled against his restraints, but the boards that flanked his head kept him from turning away, and he was forced to breathe in the water, gagging all the while.

Mr. Smith stopped and patted Vetrov on the shoulder, then pulled the cloth down so that he could see his eyes. "Now that I have your attention, I will tell you what I want from you. I need the access codes to the offshore accounts for the Russian mafia."

"I-I don't kn-know what you're talking about," he sputtered between coughs.

"That is very unfortunate for you," he said as he put the cloth back over Vetrov's face and resumed pouring the water. He had read up on torture methods, and he was delighted to know that Vetrov was just beginning to feel as if he might actually drown.

As the water stopped pouring over his face, Vetrov coughed up what he'd breathed in, and the terror in his eyes was absolute.

"Are you ready to give me those account numbers?"

"I-I can't," Vetrov said, coughing.

"In that case..." Once again, he started pouring, this time longer than before, but still, the accountant said nothing. *This shitty little bean counter is stronger than I thought,* Mr. Smith thought, his patience growing thin. "Give me the account numbers, or I will not stop again."

"Th-They'll kill me."

"*I* will kill you if you don't. On the other hand, if you give me what I want, I will let you go. At least you will have a chance to hide in, say, South America."

"I can't. I—"

At that, Mr. Smith pulled the cloth over his face and shook the bottle so Vetrov could hear the sound of his impending death.

"Okay, okay! Just don't!" Vetrov cried, and even though his face was covered with water, Mr. Smith saw tears escaping the corners of his eyes, the tears of a man who would do anything to make it stop. A second later, he fed Mr. Smith the numbers.

Mr. Smith walked over to a laptop on the counter. For half an hour, he performed several transactions, transferring a total of twenty-five million into Vetrov's personal account. From there, he moved it five more times, until finally leaving it securely in an offshore account under the name Joseph Anthony Wayne. "Thank you, Danil Vetrov," he said, smiling. "Now, regrettably, you must die."

Vetrov's eyes widened as his captor pulled out a knife. "But you said..."

"I lied." Mr. Smith shrugged, then pushed the knife into Danil's heart, staring into the dying man's eyes as the life left his body. "Thanks again," he said while the Russian took his last shuddering breath.

After it was clear that Vetrov had passed on, he went about cleaning up his mess. Mr. Smith knew he would have to dispose of Vetrov so no one would ever find him. It would appear that the Russian embezzled from the mafia and ran, but Mr. Smith was left to do whatever he wanted with the pilfered millions. *I am not only The Guardian. Now I'm God!* He thought, smiling.

* * *

Once Mr. Smith had the money, all he needed was the muscle, people to carry out certain parts of his plan as he moved forward. Randy Mills and Paul Reichart were bad men, willing to do anything if the money was right.

Randy, the smaller of the two, was smart and as mean as they came, an Army Special Forces veteran who'd served in Iraq. After his time in the military, he kept his black hair cropped close to his head on the sides but a little longer on top. He wanted to be a career soldier, because he secretly loved the brute power of it, the free pass to kill at will, but his anger issues made that impossible. He was discharged dishonorably, on bad conduct.

Paul was an ex-semi-pro lineman, an attractive, blue-eyed, blond-haired hunk of a man, like a Greek god. His quick-to-anger nature rendered his football career nothing more than a boyhood fantasy, and that only made him embittered. He outweighed his partner by a muscled thirty pounds, but Randy still scared the shit out of him.

Coincidentally, the two met in the Lebanon Correctional Institution in Ohio. Randy had two years to serve on a four-year sentence for beating a prostitute half to death for trying to steal his wallet. When the police arrived, he violently resisted arrest, breaking the ribs of one officer and the jaw of another. He was a man with a bad reputation, someone no one fucked with. When he arrived in prison, from day one, he made it clear that he refused to affiliate with any gang. The Aryan Brotherhood made several attempts to coerce him to conform, but those attempts ended badly for the white supremacists, and they eventually just gave up. When the Heartless Felons, a particularly violent gang, saw that he posed no threat to them as long as they didn't push him, they also left him alone. He just wanted to do his time and leave.

Paul caught his wife with another man and bludgeoned that man with his fists and a bedside lamp, nearly smashing his skull in. For that crime, he received a divorce and a two-year sentence, and he continued the trend in prison, fighting all the time. The inmates saw him as attractive, fresh meat, but Randy recognized him as a kindred spirit, someone who also just wanted to be left alone. For that reason, Randy stepped in and made it clear to everyone that Paul was off limits, and from that point on, they were fast friends. Randy focused the young man's talents and put them to use.

The leaders of the major gangs at Lebanon recognized Randy's talents and used him as an independent contractor when it came to collecting gambling debts and loans. Randy and Paul spent the next two years free to walk unmolested, to mingle freely, unfettered by gangs. The pair came to Mr. Smith's attention when they were suspected of carrying out numerous gang hits. Before Randy was released, it was rumored that he was given contracts by three major players, hired to remove certain individuals who had, in one way or another, run afoul of the gangs on the outside.

Near the time when they were to be released, it was rumored that they had murdered Arsenii Vetrov, when his brother fell behind in his protection payments. It was also rumored that the Russian mafia paid the Aryans to try to find out where his brother Danil might be hiding, and once that failed, they were instructed to kill him as painfully as possible. Since nothing about the murder could be verified, Mills and Reichart were never charged.

They were released a month apart, Paul first, then Randy. Once they were out, they made good on their promises to the Aryans, the Heartless Felons, and the Gangster Disciples. Those seven homicides went unsolved in the Cleveland area, and their new career that had started in prison was well underway outside those bars.

Mr. Smith kept tabs on the duo and had great plans for them. While he knew all about them, they knew nothing of him. In fact, they never laid eyes on him. At first, their only communication was by phone, and when the job required it, he sent diagrams or detailed instructions by email.

He tested their commitment to their tasks with minor assignments, and then moved on to tougher tasks. The only thing required to hold their loyalty was money, and Mr. Smith now had access to millions. Soon, they were ready for the ultimate assignment, one that would help Mr. Smith rock the world.

"Mr. Mills, I have a little chore for you," Mr. Smith said.

"I got one question first."

"Okay..." Mr. Smith said nervously, not sure where things were headed.

"Are you the same Mr. Smith who's been killin' those creepers, those kid-molesting freaks?"

After a pause, Mr. Smith answered, "Yes, but contrary to what you might've heard, there was no sex with the dead."

"That's good to know."

"Does my past make any difference to you?"

"No, not really. They deserved what they got. We put the

smack down on lots of those animals in lockup. Anyway, what's the job?"

"It will be the most difficult, riskiest assignment you will ever do," Mr. Smith warned. "If you are caught, you will never again see the light of day. You may be shot in the process."

"That bad, huh?" Randy said with a snicker.

"Yeah, it's that bad," Mr. Smith said, then went on to outline his plan.

"Whoa, man," Mills said after he heard all the details, taken aback not by what they had to do but rather, by the target. "I'm not sure if—"

"Is there some sort of problem?" Mr. Smith said, cutting him off.

"I just don't think you have enough money to warrant the risk, pal. This is gonna cost you, big time."

"Money is of no consequence. Name your price."

Mills thought for a moment, then threw out a figure he was sure would shock Mr. Smith. "A million," he said, then thought for a moment and finished, "each. This ain't a two-for-one sale."

"Fair enough. I'll send you all you need to know, and I'll let you know when it's go time," Mr. Smith said, and then hung up.

Randy Mills was dumbfounded. Mr. Smith had always paid, but he never imagined the man would fork out two million bucks, just for this one job. *Am I really up to this?* he deliberated, knowing that if he went through with it, he'd have to leave the country. *A million dollars and a tropical island? Hmm. I guess that doesn't sound too bad.* He smiled an uncertain smile.

Chapter 31

It had been a little over a week since Zee was shot, and she was still not 100 percent. As she recovered at the Kroh Compound, she suffered from frequent headaches, but she refused to let them stop her. She hated all the attention she was getting from all of us, as she was an independent woman. While she made that clear to Crystal, Vernon, and me, though, when Grandma and Pops fretted over her, she acted like their little baby. Go figure!

Marty spent the day at George Washington University Hospital, upgrading the software he installed on the computers in the pediatric wing. He enjoyed the work and likely would've done it freely, even without dating Andrea. While we appreciate his ability to help us catch the evil of the world, there was something refreshing about him putting that knowledge to work to save the lives of the innocent, all those babies whose health was monitored by the machines he tended to.

As he worked, Marty thought back to when he first started there. He recalled walking past the bulletin board and seeing a flyer for the CPR class Andrea was teaching. He wanted to believe he took the classes for the educational benefit, but even he highly suspected that he really took it to impress her.

He desperately wanted to kiss her while they were working in such close proximity, but she insisted on maintaining her professionalism at work. He truly admired that, but he still tried to make her smile when she was trying to be serious, even if it meant making a face, crossing his eyes, or walking in some ridiculous, clowny gait. There was something about the girl that made him feel complete; she'd taught him how to breathe life into others, and she'd somehow breathed life into him too.

It was a special day in the pediatric unit, as the president's grandson, Christopher, was there for his routine checkup.

"He's just a few doors down," Andrea said. "I'll be back." She checked to see if anyone was looking, then gave Marty a quick kiss and headed out to check out the little VIP.

It was early evening, and the sun was already setting in the west. Eager to finish his upgrades, Marty ran the last diagnostic program and was relieved to find that the software worked perfectly. He looked forward to taking Andrea to dinner, even if they'd already spent a lot of time together over the last few weeks.

Marty walked down to the room where Andrea was examining Christopher. Since Marty was an FBI agent, as soon as he entered the room, the mother and the agent sent to watch over them took their opportunity for a restroom break.

Marty watched as Andrea went about her important work, and he found another thing he admired about her: her bedside manner and efficiency, even when dealing with a squirming, scared child. Just as he was about to ask how much longer she'd be, he heard commotion outside. He hurried to the door, looked out, and saw someone lying on the floor, a fellow FBI agent, the one sent to protect the infant. There was a man standing over the agent, and when he caught sight of Marty, he quickly moved toward the room.

"Sit on the floor and don't move," Marty ordered Andrea as he locked the door. His mind began to race, and he couldn't believe what was happening. He was locked in a hospital room with his girlfriend and the president's grandbaby, and he was not armed to defend himself or them.

Within seconds, the intruder began beating on the door.

"Marty, what's—"

"Just stay down," he said, then ran to push a chair under the door handle to secure it, though he knew that wouldn't last long. He figured he had less than a minute to come up with a plan.

When Marty looked up at the door again, he saw it bend and fracture, kicked in with great force, the lock set ripped right out of the frame. Two men entered, cleverly disguised in a way that hid their features but didn't render them too noticeable, which allowed them to whisk right by security and the nurses' station.

Marty was not a field agent, so he was something of a fish out of water, with no keyboard or computer screen to work his magic. As the two kidnappers moved toward the baby, he kicked a rolling cart of medical equipment toward them.

The cart hit the bigger of the two, but he angrily pushed it away, spilling syringes and gadgets all over the sterile linoleum. Furious, he backhanded Marty and knocked him to the floor.

Marty lay stunned on the floor for a minute, watching helplessly as both men moved toward the baby. When he snapped to his senses, he scrambled to find anything he could use as a weapon, and the wrecked medical cart came to his aid. He picked up something shiny and looked it over, struggling to focus. When he realized what he had, he instantly rolled toward the bigger man. The scalpel was sharp and cut right through the man's Achilles tendon.

"Ah!" the brute screamed as he toppled over, right on top of Marty.

Trapped under the weight of the mountain of a man, Marty could only lie there as he saw the smaller attacker move toward the carrier that contained the crying baby. He snatched up the carrier and turned toward the door. He stopped, set the crying baby down, and turned toward Marty.

"I'm hurt! This little bastard cut me," the man on top of Marty cried. "You have to help me. I-I can't walk, and I'm bleedin' all over!"

"Mr. Smith ain't gonna be happy about this," the other man said, raising the gun.

"Nooo!" Andrea screamed. "Please stop!"

Marty closed his eyes and waited for the shot that would end his life. *Ironic that I'll die here, surrounded by life support machines and personnel,* he thought with a grimace.

The high-pitched crack of the silenced shot echoed in his ear.

Marty felt no pain but felt the warm blood running down his face. At that point, all he could do was wait for the world to slip away. One regret rang out above all others: He hated that Andrea had to see it.

A second later, much to his own surprise, Marty opened his eyes. He couldn't believe he was still alive, but he saw the man with the baby running out the door. He looked at the colossus on top of him and saw a single hole in the middle of his forehead. A trickle of crimson poured from the wound and dripped down into the matching red puddle that was forming around his lacerated ankle. "What the...?" Marty wondered aloud. "Not that I'm fucking complaining about the dude's bad aim, but still."

"M-Marty," Andrea said, her voice trembling, "Thank God you're okay, but h-he took the baby!"

* * *

Randy Mills was on automatic. The moment he put a bullet through Paul's forehead, he switched into survival mode. If it wasn't for the million dollars he was promised by Mr. Smith, he would have left the cumbersome brat behind. The money was the only thing that would keep him out of jail, keep him hidden. The world would be after him now, and it was his only chance of escape: to take that kid, get the hell out of there, and then let that million buy him a whole new life and identity somewhere very far away.

He thought about killing the man under Paul, but he was contained, and he needed to conserve bullets. He did shoot one agent, on his way to the pediatric wing, and he didn't want to complicate matters by becoming a double-cop killer. On his way out, as he headed for the service entrance where his car was parked, he encountered another agent, but he used the crying baby as a human shield. The boy was the most precious hostage in the world, and Randy knew it. "I'll put a bullet in him if you don't back the fuck off," he said, and as soon as that agent lowered his weapon, he shrugged and shot him in the chest.

Frustrated that things had not gone smoothly, Randy

kicked open the service door and rushed through, barely noticing as he banged the baby carrier on the doorframe on the way out. He bounded down four steps, practically threw the carrier in the passenger side front seat, and didn't even bother to buckle the child in before he climbed in the driver seat, jammed the key in the ignition, jerked the car into gear, and stepped on the gas. He barely missed a delivery truck that threatened to block his escape.

He tore out of the hospital parking lot as fast as he could, picking up the plan where he left off. He drove a short distance, pulled into a parking garage, and quickly switched vehicles; Mr. Smith had wisely determined that if anyone caught a glimpse of the dark blue Ford Taurus that left the hospital, they would not be looking for the white Chevy van that pulled out five minutes later. Randy knew he needed to get out of DC as soon as possible, so he quickly made his way to Rhode Island Avenue West and continued north on Highway One, but he was careful not to drive too fast or erratically. *The last thing I need is some pig pulling me over to give me a traffic ticket,* he thought. His destination was a warehouse district just outside south Baltimore.

Once he was sure that no one was following, he tried to handle the baby in a gentler manner. To soothe the terrified child, he even sang "Rock-a-bye Baby" as he drove, though his off-key rendition didn't seem to quiet the boy. He was in survival mode, and the baby's crying only served as a distraction. Unable to pacify the shrieking infant, and with his nerves already on edge, Mills turned up the radio in an attempt to drown out the wailing.

As he drove north, enjoying Alice Cooper's "School's Out," he worried that there might be a roadblock ahead. He knew that would leave him with only two choices: make a quick U-turn and hope the authorities did not catch it or do whatever it took to shut the baby up, even if he had to shove a sock in his little bastard's mouth and cram him in the tool chest in the back of the van, at least till he got out of earshot of the cops. He looked over at the car seat that contained the sobbing baby, and he wondered, *maybe it would just be better to turn myself in and spend the rest of my life in prison.* Then

Die by Proxy

he thought of fresh air, women, and the million he would soon have, of lying on a deserted beach somewhere with a little umbrella drink melting in his hand, without a care in the world. "I deserve this, you brat, so shut the hell up," he said.

He drove around for a while before he found the address Mr. Smith had given him. After the automatic door rose to grant him access, he pulled in and quickly closed it behind him. He got out of the van and closed the door, glad that he could no longer hear the bawling that had been driving him crazy for the last hour and a half. His head ached from the constant crying and the even louder music, and he hoped he could soon find some aspirin or some hard liquor to take the edge off.

In the weak light of the overhead garage door opener, Randy quickly found the light switch. As the lights came up, he saw the car Mr. Smith had promised; he was delighted to see that it was a black Cadillac Escalade. About thirty feet to the left was a small office, and Randy walked over and tried the door. It opened easily, and the light switch was right inside the door. There was a desk there, accompanied by a ratty office chair that had seen better days. On top of the desk was an intriguing shoebox, topped with a note that simply instructed, "Open."

Randy smiled, then walked over, plopped down in the creaky chair, and opened the box. Inside it, he found a note, a cellphone, some keys, and small black leather shaving bag. He opened the bag carefully, as if it might contain a rattle snake. Instead, he found two envelopes, one bearing his name and one reserved for Paul Reichart, who had decided not to show.

He pulled out the note first, unfolded it, and read it aloud: "If you have gotten this far, I applaud you. Use this phone to call the only number in the contact list. When the call is picked up, simply say, 'Done,' and hang up. You are to leave the baby in this office, then take the car I have left you and drive to the location written below. You will stay in that safe house till it is feasible to leave the country. You will find the balance of your payment there. It was a pleasure doing business with you. P.S.: In case you are worried, after you make this call, someone will be there within the hour to retrieve the child."

Next, he opened the envelope addressed to him. Inside, he found $250,000. He stashed the cash in the bag, along with Paul's envelope, zipped it up, and started for the van. "Damn," he thought when he realized he'd forgotten to kill the engine. "If this place was any smaller, me and that kid woulda been killed by the exhaust."

"Walk this way..." Aerosmith screamed as Randy neared the running van, the baby still crying in awkward harmony with the rock music. He reached in, cut the engine, then walked around and opened the side door. He looked down at the carrier and, now that he was not in such a panic and a frantic state of mind, he felt something was off. "Oh well. What the hell do I know about kids? This ain't no daddy daycare," he said dismissively, then picked up the carrier and took it to the office, where he sat it on the desk beside the shoebox. "There ya go, kid. Have a nice life, you little bawlin' bastard...and if you ever get the chance, tell your damn grandpa I didn't vote for his sorry ass."

He pressed call on the phone provided by Mr. Smith, waited for it to be answered, and spoke one word. "Done." He started to leave, but something compelled him to pull the blanket off the infant's face. It was a little warm in the office, after all.

After he pulled the blanket down, something caught his eye, and he had to take a closer look. "What the...?" he said as anger intensified the pounding in his head. He suddenly realized that, although the thing in the carrier was really close, it was not a real baby. "Son-of-a-bitch! Jesus fucking Christ!" he said as he pulled the little one roughly out of the car seat. "Fuck, fuck, fuck!" he screamed, then let out a growl of frustration.

Are you tellin' me I just became the most wanted man in the fucking world over a fucking Cabbage Patch Kid, some fucking little robot doll? I'm royally fucked! Then, another grim thought pushed its way into his mind. *Wait. There it is again, the crying. It's not coming from this thing.*

He tore through the blankets and padding in the carrier and found a phone. He stared at it for a long moment as it cried again, louder and louder. "You sneaky assholes!" he yelled, then stomped on it till the crying died. "Mr. Smith ain't gonna be happy about this."

It was then that another cruel reality smacked him in the face, bringing with it a chill that flooded through his body from head to toe. *GPS?* The crying phone was a high-end Samsung, and he knew there was a good chance it contained a locator chip.

Instantly, he was back in survival mode. He grabbed the bag and keys and ran out of the office as fast as his legs would carry him. He went to the van and grabbed the garage door controller, then ran to the Escalade. *I guess a brand-new SUV and $500,000 will have to do, 'cause I'm gettin' the hell outta Dodge. Screw you, Smith! And screw the whole damn FBI and the president too!*

Chapter 32

Andrea crawled over to Marty and helped push the dead weight off him.

Marty slowly got to his feet, still shocked that two men had so easily entered a relatively well-secured medical facility to kidnap the president's grandson. He stood there for a moment, just trying to make sense of the last few minutes. Once he was sure the man was gone, and knowing it was probably redundant, he quickly found a phone and called 911. Within minutes, every hospital corridor was crawling with agents.

Once Marty was sure everything was secure, he rushed over to a bank of drawers on the left side of the room. When he opened the largest drawer, a little, wide-eyed baby looked up at him and cooed, then smiled. He gently picked up the child, handed him to Andrea, and cautiously moved to the door.

An agent with a bullet wound in his shoulder ran up and was very relieved when he saw the infant in Andrea's arms. "Little Slugger's safe," he said into his radio, with a smile on his face. "I repeat, Little Slugger is safe." He then turned to Marty. "What the hell happened here anyway? How... I mean, I *saw* the man running from the building with the crying baby."

Marty let out a sigh for the ages, then told the story he would find himself repeating twenty times in the hours to come. After that, he just sat there, with his head in his hands, trying to recover from the shock of it all but secretly wondered to himself how in the hell his security measures worked.

Soon, a hand touched Marty's shoulder. "I must thank you for your quick thinking. You saved my little boy," said Melissa, the president's daughter, smiling down at him. She then pulled Marty to his feet and hugged him tightly as they cried together.

When they separated from their sniffling embrace, Marty said humbly, "I was just doing my job, ma'am."

"Well, thank you for doing it so well," the woman said, then kissed her son on the head.

Marty smiled and nodded, but the lump in his throat prevented him from speaking again.

Agent Harris was the next to give Marty an actual pat on the back. "She's right. Great job, Marty. That was a neat trick with your phone. Thanks, buddy. Not only did you save the baby, but you also probably saved my job."

My phone? he thought. "My phone!" he almost screamed.

"What?" Agent Harris asked.

"My phone's got GPS," Marty said, almost running to his laptop.

It had been almost an hour since the man left with what he believed was the president's grandbaby, and Marty cursed himself for not thinking of the GPS sooner. All along, he was just glad the fake baby was taken instead of the real one, but it didn't occur to him that the kidnapper could be tracked.

Agent Harris looked over Marty's shoulder as his fingers worked their magic on the keyboard. Within a moment or two, they saw a blinking light moving north on Highway 1, toward Baltimore, and Agent Harris was calling it in.

* * *

As Randy Mills climbed into his new ride, he had no idea that agents from the Baltimore FBI office were converging on the warehouse. He forced a little smile. "Fuck you, Mr. Smith. This is all your fault, so the car and the money are mine. It's the least you can do, you sick bastard. You probably did fuck those dead guys."

He put the key in the ignition and started the Escalade. In an instant, the would-be kidnapper and the shiny black Cadillac were suddenly no more, as an explosion ripped through the warehouse.

The automatic door blew outward, as if the fire that followed pushed it away, knocking back the three agents that were moving to set their own explosives. Once it was safe to move, the other agents who were standing on opposite sides of the door picked themselves up and hurried to check on their fallen comrades. Thankfully, two of the agents would require only minor medical attention, but the third man was hit solidly with the door, knocked unconscious, and it was obvious that his body was broken.

The warehouse was engulfed with fire, and the agents surrounding the building were quick to call in and inform the agent in charge that no one left the structure before the blast. "I'm pretty sure he's gone if he was in there, sir," the agent said. "I don't think anybody coulda survived that blast."

Within twenty minutes, fire trucks arrived to fight the inferno, and since the place was almost vacant, with little flammable material, the fire was contained quickly.

* * *

Later that evening, Marty and Andrea sat in his living room on a videoconference with us about the day's events. "Kroh, how's the agent who got hurt at the warehouse?" he asked

"He's pretty banged up, but the doc says he'll be fine."

"I feel bad. If I would have thought about my GPS sooner, no one would have gotten hurt."

"Marty, listen to me. If you would've done anything differently, those agents might've been inside the building when everything was blown to hell. You did everything right, everything you could, and we're all proud of you."

"Thanks, Boss."

"Marty, tell us what happened at the hospital," Crystal said, smiling.

"Nothin' much. I didn't do anything you wouldn't have done," Marty said, feigning humility for the umpteenth time that day.

"Just shut the hell up and tell us," I said, grinning.

"Which is it, Boss? I mean, if I shut the hell up, how can I—"

"Marty!"

"Okay, okay. While the would-be kidnappers kicked at the door, I was scrambling for any way to save the baby. My eye happened upon a drawer marked 'CPR Mannequin.' I quickly crossed the room and yanked it open, and I saw that the thing was very realistic. Andrea said it was a Simulaids CPR Billy Manikin, the brand closest to a real baby."

"So, you like to play with dolls? We get it. Let's move on," I teased.

"Very funny. Anyway, I pulled it from the drawer and whispered for Andrea to put the baby in the drawer, replacing the mannequin. She put some towels next to the baby's ears to keep the loud noises from scaring him, then carefully closed the drawer, leaving plenty of space for air. We prayed he'd keep quiet, and he did. I wrapped the mannequin in the real baby's blanket and put it in the car seat."

"Weren't you afraid he'd notice your trick?" Crystal asked.

"Yeah, and that made me realize that he'd never buy it unless the baby cried, so I pulled out my smartphone and set a crying app on continuous, then stuffed it way down in the blankets. Then came the hard part. I knew I had to put up enough resistance, so they'd believe they were actually taking the real kid, and I thought the big guy was going to tear me apart. I know you can't tell by looking at me, but I'm not exactly a black belt or a pro boxer," he said.

"Say it's not so. I was sure you took out Bruce Lee and Sugar Ray a time or two," I said with a smirk.

"Real funny, Boss. Anyway, so I pushed a medical cart at him, but he just pushed it out of the way, dumping everything on the floor He backhanded me, and I fell to the floor, along with the cart. It rocked me pretty good, I tell ya, but I was lucky enough to grab a scalpel. I lashed out and cut deep into the big guy's ankle. He fell on me, and I could hardly move. When he hit me, it knocked the wind out of me, and his weight made it hard to breathe. Since I couldn't move with that Jabba the Asshole smothering me, I thought it was all over when I saw the little guy pointing a gun at my head. Of course, he wasn't really a little guy either."

"Hey, was that the same crying baby app you used on

me when Zee and I were eating in that crowded restaurant in Port Huron?" I asked.

"That's the one...and by the way, you owe me a new phone," Marty said with a laugh that we all parroted.

"That's quite a shiner you got there," I said with a smile.

Marty reached up to touch his face and winced. "Yeah, and it hurts like hell."

"Welcome to working in the field, my friend," I said, then smiled again.

Suddenly, Marty stopped laughing and sat up. "Kroh, I just remembered something. When the man was pointing the gun, about to shoot the other guy, he said, 'Mr. Smith's not going to be happy.' I should have caught that before, but things just happened so fast. I guess I'm still trying to catch up."

"What? Are you sure he said Mr. Smith, Marty?" I asked, literally on the edge of my seat as I moved closer to the screen.

Marty looked at Andrea, and after she nodded, he looked back at the camera. "Yes, we're positive. That was the name he said."

My mind swirled with questions, coming at me from every direction, the most prominent one being whether or not it could be real. "It could be an incredible coincidence, Marty, but my gut tells me they're connected in some way. God, you're a genius! Not only did you save the president's grandbaby, but you might have just given us what we need to solve our case against The Guardian. I've got a lot of thinking to do, so you get some rest, and we'll talk tomorrow."

Andrea leaned into the camera. "Marty is a real hero. I couldn't be prouder of him for saving us," she said, then hugged him and gave him a kiss on the cheek, "even if he is just a computer geek and not a boxing champion." He winced, but he was smiling.

"I guess someone's getting some he-saved-the-president's-grandbaby-and-me sex tonight', huh?" I joked.

"Damn right, he's getting some he-saved-the-president's-grandbaby-and-me sex tonight," she said with a smile, and the last thing I saw before she closed the laptop was Marty leaning back on the couch, with his hands behind his head and big shit-eating grin on his face.

* * *

Marty sent me his full report, along with everything we knew about the men who attempted to kidnap the president's grandson. The big guy who backhanded Marty and died on top of him was Paul Reichart, a football lineman who ruined his chances at a pro career because of his violent anger issues. That bad attitude also didn't carry him far in life, except to prison.

We are pretty sure his partner was a man he met at the Lebanon Correctional Institution in Ohio, while he was in there for a two-year stint for beating a man half to death. Randy Mills was a real bad ass. He had spent time in Iraq and was known for his fearlessness. The two were known to be freelance enforcers for various Lebanon gangs, and while they didn't claim loyalty to any of them, they were also suspected of seven gang-related deaths on the outside after their respective releases.

In spite of the fact that the Cadillac was blown to bits, a nationwide manhunt was still underway for Randy Mills, just in case. There was nowhere to hide for a man who tried to kidnap an infant, particularly when that infant was a relative of the U.S. president. I hoped against hope that we were able to capture him alive, because I really needed to talk to him about Mr. Smith.

I made a mental note to have Marty check the backgrounds of the inmates who were at Lebanon while Mills and Reichert were, as well as anyone who ever paid them visits. I knew it was a long shot, but I also knew it was wise to leave no stone unturned.

"Who are you, Mr. Smith?" I asked aloud but mostly to myself.

PART THREE

Full Disclosure

Chapter 33

Mr. Smith thought long and hard about ending his sick leave and reentering his increasingly mundane life as Special Agent Donald Calder. Most FBI personnel held that same title, so it didn't exactly make him feel special. It was a far cry from what he was just a year and a half ago, when he was the special agent in charge of the Indianapolis field office. Not only that, based on his record and his many connections, he was on the fast track to lead the Bureau. Now, for reasons beyond his control, the FBI had downgraded him to little more than a desk jockey in the Cincinnati field office.

He felt the gazes of the others around him there. All his colleagues knew what had happened to him. *What you fuckers don't know is that Kroh fucked me royally.* He was sure Kroh manipulated him into moving too fast on The Fingertip Killer case, and he blamed the man for his downward spiral. *That jackass let me take the fall for the mistakes he made. It was Kroh who arrested The Cowboy, locked him up in a cell that would become his tomb. He and he alone is responsible for the death of the wrong suspect, and I don't see why in the hell everyone still loves the man.*

Then there was the one person in the world he thought would never leave his side, his former best friend, John Burns, President of the United States. He was sure Kroh somehow got to him, possibly through Noah Bennett, and put an end to that friendship that he valued by once again damaging his reputation.

The events of that day in Washington were still clear in

his mind. He was summoned to the FBI director's office for a verbal dressing-down over his faux pas in The Fingertip Killer case. The last words of the director still echoed in his mind: *"Donald, we have lost confidence that you can effectively lead the Indianapolis office. You will be reassigned to the Cincinnati field office as a special agent, until further notice. That will be all."*

Calder tried to talk to the president, confident that his oldest, best friend could make the mess go away, but that was not the case. That conversation also played over in his head time and time again:

"Make this quick, Don. I have a meeting in ten minutes."

"John, I need your help."

"If this is about Fingertip, my hands are tied."

"But, John, I—"

"There is really nothing I can do. Sorry, Don. The director was very clear about how we must proceed."

"But you are the president...and my friend."

"I'm afraid that won't cut it this time. You really screwed the pooch. Really Don, there is nothing I can do. Now, if there is nothing else, I have to go."

"But, John..."

"I'm sorry, Don. I'm late for a meeting. Jeanine will show you out."

With that, the president was off to his meeting, surrounded by Secret Service and seemingly uncaring that he'd effectively shoved his good friend under the bus. *Fuck you, John!* Calder thought then and Mr. Smith still thought now. *I don't need you.*

From there, it just got worse, and the year and a half that followed was full of pain and loss for Calder. The move to southwest Ohio was hard enough, but the demotion was an embarrassment he simply could not handle. He was exiled to menial tasks, grunt work like data collection, and his star was no longer in ascendance. Unwilling to accept fault embittered him, and his resentment manifested itself in his life at home.

Although his wife Sandra had long since given up on the love she had once felt for the man she married, she, like many women, continued to carry on with their family duties, trying to hold on to the life she and her children had grown accustomed to. It was not only hard for her; the children also suffered because of their father. They resented having to move away from their home and their friends. Once that life was threatened by the loss of social status and the arguments that seemed commonplace, Sandra decided it was time to move on.

After his wife filed for divorce and moved back to Indianapolis, Calder fell into a deep depression. Even now, he remembered sitting in his Chevy cargo van outside the Fashion Mall at Keystone in Indy, sweating in the summer heat and waiting for his wife to finish shopping. At 5:40, he watched as she exited the mall, carrying two handfuls of stuff she didn't need, and then happily strolled to her brand-new Lexus with a smile on her face. He didn't want to care that she was probably buying something to impress her pissant boyfriend Brad, but he did care. After all, she started seeing the man only a month after they separated, and he was sure she bought that luxury car with the money he scraped up for child support. *Bitch, that money's for the fucking kids,* he thought, his mood darkening.

There was no introspection in his depression; all blame was focused outward. He just could not see that the fault was his own. He targeted his rage on Special Agent Benjamin Kroh and a man who was once his best friend. For months, he just wanted his life back, but one night, while drowning his sorrows in his favorite scotch and toying with the idea of ending it all, an epiphany exploded into his alcohol-shrouded thoughts. He suddenly realized the one thing that would make him happy: *Kroh must die, and I must kill him myself!*

Gone was the depression, and in its place grew the happiness that could only come from exiting a dark tunnel, into the light. From that moment on, his life took on new meaning, and he felt alive again. Although it was easy enough to research Kroh and spy on him, every plan required funding, money he did not have because he was too busy financing his wife's new love affair.

He took what little he did have from various accounts

and stashes he had kept secret from his wife and began to meticulously lure Kroh to his death. Even in that determined state, though, he could not bring himself to murder innocent people, unless it was an absolute must. Kroh, however, was not innocent, not in the least, so Calder spent his lonely days coming up with ideas. Then one night, a news segment spoke about a local child molester, and Calder had another epiphany. The diagram of his plan came to him in one explosive thought. *Ah, a few dead child molesters. Yes, that's the perfect bait to catch a Kroh!* he thought. *Not only will I lure him to his well-deserved death,* he thought, *I will also do a great service to humanity in the process!*

There was always a chance that Kroh would not be assigned to the case, but he had a Plan B for that: *I'll simply invite Kroh to join the fun, dangle a carrot he can't resist, and like the horse's ass he is, he'll come running.* Then, at the proper time, Kroh would die.

Once he started down the path, it seemed the gods of vengeance were on his side. Just two days after he set Eric Conrad on I-69, just outside Port Huron, Michigan, some paperwork crossed his desk; documents concerning an accountant involved with the Russian mob, a man who made monthly visits to his brother at Lebanon Correctional Institution, which was only a half-hour from the Cincinnati field office. Thanks to the very thorough and constantly updated FBI database, Calder learned much about that man and his routine movements.

That part of his stroll down Memory Lane made him smile. *Talk about rags to riches! Now I've more money than I can ever use, and I'm free to do anything I want.* In time, he would still kill Kroh for turning him into a laughingstock, and the president would answer for his betrayal, but Smith had nothing if not time. No one knew who he was, and he had over twenty million dollars to use as he pleased. He had moved the fortune eleven times since he first opened the account in the name Joseph Anthony Wayne, and in the months that followed, the money traveled through Monaco, Singapore and Switzerland. The bulk of it now rested in an offshore account in Luxembourg, under the name Jason Alan

Wainscott.

He had over ten aliases, as solid as could be and able to withstand even the closest scrutiny. If the FBI did take an interest in any of them, it wouldn't take long for them to realize something didn't add up, but as long as he covered his tracks and made sure not to screw up and leave evidence or a paper trail, there was no reason for them to investigate. Even if they did, he would just move to the next one, as simple as changing his clothes.

Calder also became proficient in changing his looks. With unlimited funds, he was able to buy the best, most realistic silicone masks. He also modified his stance, his gait, his voice, and his mannerisms, and the internet taught him how to do much of that, even without the aid of full disguises. With carefully applied makeup, wigs, and with the precise application of facial hair from blond to black, he could fool even an up-close observer.

He bought or rented homes and apartments in various locations around the U.S. under those aliases. When possible, he made it known that he traveled a lot, informing the landlords that he might not be around very often. As Fred Posner, he purchased a farmhouse, the safest of all his properties and the one he took the most care in obtaining.

The property was owned by the real Posner family for over 150 years. It was three miles outside of Atlanta, Indiana, less than an hour from both Anderson and Indianapolis. Jacob Posner had no one to pass it down to, and since he was getting on in years, he needed the kind of care that only a senior citizens home could provide. Jacob was glad when another Posner expressed interest in purchasing it, even though Calder assured him they were probably not related. "At least she'll stay in the Posner name for a little longer," Jacob said as he happily signed the deed over.

That real estate deal worked well for Calder in two ways: First, mail delivery would continue under the Posner name, and second, any friends or neighbors who wandered by would take comfort in the fact that the property was still in the family, and no one would ask too many questions as long as a Posner still owned it. Calder didn't expect that latter problem, since the old man Posner told him that no one ever visited and that most of his neighbors were "city folk with them nice, big houses, people who don't want nothin' to do with a dusty ol' place like mine."

If the worst-case scenario occurred and he could no longer remain in the United States, Calder already had an escape route in place. He set up identities in Veracruz and *Mazatlán, Mexico. If those didn't prove safe enough, he could easily travel to* Montenegro or even Taiwan, where there were no extradition treaties. He was fairly confident that he would never have to rely on any of that, but his FBI work had taught him that it was crucial to expect the unexpected and plan accordingly.

Thinking back on all that, on all he had done, he smirked as he recalled something Kroh once said to him, a passive-aggressive attack he would never forget: *"There's a very good reason you're behind that desk and not in the field, Calder. There are really only three kinds of agents, those who are good at administration, those who are good in the field, and the rare few who can manage both. I must admit that you excel at administration, but you could never be a field agent. You just don't have what it takes."*

Look at me now, Kroh! I have more identities than most spies, more faces, and unlimited funds. Best of all, I answer to no one. I'm more than a field agent, you smug, uppity son-of-a-bitch. I'm the rogue agent you only dream of being, so suck it!

"One more week," he finally decided, opting to use a few more days of sick leave before he returned to work, as he was sure it was prudent to lie low for a while. He also thought it might be wise to call a false truce with his ex and reconnect with his children. He really didn't care about her, and he wanted to kill her so he could have his kids to himself, but he wasn't quite ready to take that step. *When I do finally get rid of her, then they'll see. Without their mother's evil input, my kids will finally see what a great dad I really am.*

Chapter 34

There was still the matter of Cassondra as well. He promised that he would take care of Montgomery, the man who harmed her niece and others, but Indiana was now a hot zone. He wanted so much to assure her that she was safe, that he would not hurt her and that he didn't blame her for hiding from him. On the news, Kroh openly painted him as a monster, a sexual freak, but he would not harm her in any way, and he wanted very much for her to know that. He could not figure out why, but she was the closest thing to a friend that he had, and he truly missed her deeply.

Calder used his last week of sick leave to plan. In the very near future, Kroh would be dead, the president would suffer greatly, but he had two things to do first. One of them was to prove to Cassondra that he truly cared, and to do that, he had to fulfill his promise to the pretty, tattooed lady, even if she wasn't around to help him.

Calder's research informed him that Montgomery stayed late at the office on Thursday nights. As the day surrendered to darkness, he left his van that was parked at the public library and walked the few blocks to the government building. Once he was sure no one was watching, he quickly unlocked and climbed into the back seat of Montgomery's car.

A half-hour later, Montgomery left the office and climbed in his car to go home. Before he could even start the engine, he felt the cold steel of a weapon at the base of his neck.

"I only want your money," Calder said, pressing the muzzle of his .22 against him. "As long as you don't try anything stupid, you'll soon be home, safe with your family and only a few dollars poorer. On the other hand, if you choose to try anything, I'm afraid your family will be planning your funeral."

"Okay, okay. Anything you want, mister! Just please don't kill me!"

"Good. Then start the car and drive to the library."

"The library?"

Calder jammed the muzzle harder against the thin skin of his neck. "Do you want to die?"

"No, no. I-I'm sorry," Montgomery said, then started the car and slowly left the parking lot.

"Park over there, next to that white van," Calder said, directing him to the back. After Montgomery complied, Calder continued, "Now, here's where it gets interesting, where we really find out if you want to live or die."

"Live!" Montgomery shouted. "Of course, I want to live."

"Then you'll slowly reach in your back pocket and give me your wallet."

As Montgomery obeyed, Calder quickly surveyed the parking lot and noted that no one was around. He pulled out his stun gun and pushed it against Montgomery's shoulder. The rapid electric popping seemed amplified in the closed vehicle, but he held it there until he was sure the miniature lightning storm had incapacitated his prey. Then he grabbed Montgomery by the hair, jerked his head back, and dosed him with Rohypnol. Just to make sure, he reached over the seat and pushed the stun gun against Montgomery's ribcage, then held it there for a long moment.

Certain that Montgomery would give him no trouble, he climbed out, slid the side door of the van open, and pulled the man from his vehicle, then piled him in his own. Calder then zip-tied his wrist and ankles, as he did with all the others. He also gave him an injection of concentrated liquid aspirin. Then, just to show the pervert how much he hated him, Calder took his sap out and smacked him, administering two hard blows to his temple. "That's for Leslie, pervert."

As he drove, he heard his prey struggling to free himself, but it wasn't long before the Rohypnol took effect. After that, the sound of his wheels rolling across the pavement was all the music he needed.

A little after three in the morning, Calder parked on I-69, also known as Pennywise Parkway, just under the Adams Lane overpass in Henderson. He did a little prep work in the van, then left to set up his display. He placed the blind just north of the overpass, in an overgrown area, then hurried back to the van and grabbed the unconscious, naked molester and carried him to where the world would soon find him. His arms were already secured at his sides, and all that was left to be done was to tie him to the waiting post.

When Calder put the smelling salts under his nose, Montgomery awoke with a start and found that he was unable to speak, because something was stuffed in his mouth. The taste was anything but pleasant, and he struggled to dislodge the object. It also occurred to him that he was naked and unable to move. A faint light illuminated a face before him, but try as he did, he could not remember ever seeing that face before. It was the voice he recognized, the voice of the man who was hiding in the back seat of his car, some mugger demanding money.

"Stephen Montgomery, I have no idea why God allows people like you to exist. That is unfathomable to me. To think that you or a person like you might have harmed my children makes me ask, 'Why, God? Why?' Now don't get me wrong. I am not acting as the hand of God here, but for what you have done, you are going to die right here, right now."

"Mo...ee..." Montgomery blubbered around the blockade between his lips. "Ah, goh mo...ee!"

"Mr. Montgomery, I'm afraid I have no need of money, and it is time for me to go." With that, Calder pulled out the loppers, held them in front of Montgomery's eyes, and then set them down again. Calder leaned in close, held up a flash drive, and whispered into the pervert's ear, "Once you're dead, I'm going to take this and share your diary, pictures, and videos with your family and friends. Can you imagine what they'll think?"

Montgomery's eyes went wide, and he screamed into the sweaty sock stuffed in his mouth, pleading with the stranger for his life.

"Your wife Cynthia will have a hard time looking anyone in the eye ever again. She will always wonder if people think she knew about your perversion. After all, how can a woman live with someone for fourteen years and be unaware of these terrible deeds? Your four children will forever live with the stigma of what you've done. Why, little Kira and Justin are no older than the kids you molested, and your wife will wonder whether you preyed on them with your sick desires. It will be a quick social death for Janice and Steve Jr. in middle school. No longer will they be the darlings of a respected politician. They'll become social pariahs, to be ridiculed and haunted forever by your evil. After all, kids are cruel." With that, Calder reached back and grabbed the heavy-duty loppers.

Montgomery could only watch as his captor positioned the high-quality pruners around his wrist, just an inch above his right hand, and cut it off.

"It makes me nauseous to think about what these hands have touched. You're a sick motherfucker, Montgomery. You destroyed those children's innocence, forced them to know the darkest of humanity. What those poor little children must have experienced at your hand, I can only imagine." He shook his head in disgust.

As Montgomery screamed into the putrid sock, Calder moved the loppers to the other arm. Montgomery struggled violently, but Calder only smiled and followed suit with the left. As Calder watched Montgomery slowly drift away, he again held up the flash drive and waved it in front of the dying man's eyes, taunting him.

Then, Montgomery weakly shook his head and was gone.

Calder worked quickly to complete the display. He placed the hands in Montgomery's lap, along with the two baggies containing confession and flash drive. He gave the site a onceover and was pleased, so he gathered up his blind, his trusty loppers, and other belongings and climbed up to the van, proud of a job well done. His only regret was that it might be the last time he would use them for the good of mankind.

Die by Proxy

As he drove north to the farmhouse, Calder was overcome by two emotions, excitement and exhaustion. It had been a long couple of months, and he had accomplished much, but it had taken a lot out of him. Nevertheless, he couldn't wait to see what tomorrow would bring. *I have just one more thing to do, just one,* he thought with a smile as he drove on.

On his way, he dropped a letter off at Mosby's Computer and Games. He wasn't sure she would get it, but he really liked her, and he had to communicate to her somehow, to let her know she had nothing to fear from him, no matter what lies the media and Agent Kroh had to tell.

* * *

Early the next morning, as I was readying myself for the drive to the Cincinnati field office, I received a call from Vernon with a grim announcement: "We got another body."

"Where?"

"Just outside Henderson, Kentucky. I'm heading there now."

"See you there," I said, then signed off and called Marty, so he could spread the word. Then, within fifteen minutes, Crystal and I were heading to Henderson.

We arrived at the crime scene around noon, and as we got out of the car, Vernon and Meecham walked up to meet us.

"We've already processed the scene. The coroner's ready to take the body, but I figured you'd want to see it in place first."

"Everything the same?" I asked, already sure of his answer.

"Yep, down to the last detail," Meecham said, shaking his head.

As I walked up to the body, I saw that he was right. The flags were even there to mark where the blind was placed.

"Looks like he parked up on the Adams Lane overpass," Meecham explained, pointing as he spoke.

"Who's our vic'?" I asked as I surveyed the scene.

"His name is Stephen Montgomery, a respected local politician," Vernon answered

"Respected politician? Isn't that an oxymoron?" I asked.

"Sometimes, Kroh, *you're* the moron, with those corny jokes of yours." He tried really hard not to smile the guiltier-than-Kroh smile but failed miserably.

"*My* jokes? You're a real shit. You know that?" I said, laughing.

"That really hurts, Kroh." He tried to feign offense, but he made the mistake of looking at me, and we both broke out laughing. "Anyway, they're packing the body up now. Let's head over to the coroner's office and check out that flash drive."

It didn't take Meecham long to open the contents of the flash drive. As we suspected, we didn't have any material evidence against the killer, but the grotesque and unsettling files we saw confirmed that the dead man just off the highway had been a very, very bad boy for a very, very long time.

"Nothing respected about that," I said, and Meecham readily agreed.

Chapter 35

President John Burns was eager to thank Marty personally for saving little Christopher. Marty asked me to attend the White House with him, and that was a grand opportunity I couldn't turn down, because I had some questions for the president myself.

"I'd be honored to be your date. I've got the perfect sequined gown for the occasion," I teased, batting my eyes at him.

I could see that Marty was a little apprehensive about meeting the commander-in-chief, considering that he only offered a very uncharacteristic, unenthusiastic retort, simply, "Thanks."

At four that evening, we pulled up to 1600 Pennsylvania Avenue Northwest. After a thorough head-to-toe body search of us and a complete check of every nook and cranny of our vehicle, we were finally allowed inside. Considering the kidnapping and the crazies always trying to shoot at the White House, jump the fence, or assassinate someone, it was entirely understandable that they were cautious about the people they let through, and the Secret Service were out in droves, standing around in their dark suits and sunglasses. A half-hour later, we were ushered into the Oval Office. The room was pristine, and even a white glove test wouldn't have rendered a trace off lint or dirt.

The president was standing in front of his desk and walked over to greet us. "Agents Owens and Kroh, thanks for coming," Burns said as he shook my hand, then Marty's, then pulled him in for a hug. After a few pats on the back, he let him go and asked us to be seated. "Agent Owens, I owe you a great debt, one I can never repay. Your quick thinking most assuredly saved my little grandson. Christopher is the light of my life. Do you have children?"

"No, sir."

"Well, if you do someday, you will understand. They will be the best things that ever happen to you...till your grandkids come along!"

"I appreciate your gratitude, Mr. President," Marty humbly said, "but truth be told, I was merely doing my job. Anyone in that situation would have done the same."

"Nonsense! Switching Christopher with the CPR mannequin was one thing, but having the sense to add the crying app was just inspired. I wish I had quick thinkers like you on my cabinet, or in the House or Congress. Maybe then they'd get off their collective asses and do something."

Marty smiled. "Thank you, sir."

"I want to give you a little something to show my appreciation."

Marty started to object, but he was rendered speechless when his grandfather walked in. I was not surprised to see that the man had the same fashion sense as his grandson; standing next to them, even the president looked as if he shopped at Kmart.

"It was a true pleasure to meet and talk with your grandfather, Marty, a very interesting man. His stories about what was done during the war by the Navajo talkers are the stuff of legends. I also know he's as proud of you as you are of him."

Tears flowed as Marty stood to embrace his grandfather, and I shed a few myself as I watched two generations of Navajo warriors hug it out.

When they finally separated, the old man put his hand on his grandson's shoulder. "The president wants you to have this," he said, handing a box to Marty.

At everyone's insistence, Marty opened the box and saw that it was a limited-edition Gresso Regal titanium smartphone, accentuated with eighteen-karat gold.

"Please, whatever you do, don't tell my wife, or she'll want one too!" the president said, causing us to laugh through the tears.

As Marty sat and talked with his grandfather, I took the opportunity to interview the president, hoping it would shed some light on our investigation. "Mr. President, as you know, my team's been working on The Guardian of I-69 case. We're certain it is somehow connected with what almost happened to your grandson."

"Really? How so?"

"Well, we know that in the case of The Guardian, there have been references to a Mr. Smith. When one intruder killed the other during the attempted kidnapping at the hospital, he mentioned his boss, also a Mr. Smith. Mr. President, can you think of anyone specifically who wishes to do you harm?"

"You mean other than the usual horde of party haters or extremists?" President Burns asked rhetorically with a smirk. "I don't know any individuals who would go to such lengths to hurt me personally, no."

"We must also consider the possibility that this Mr. Smith or his affiliates were out to harm or seek revenge on your son or his wife, sir. With your permission I would like to have agents talk to them also."

"You got it, Agent Kroh, whatever you need. We need to wrap this up as soon as possible."

"Thank you, Mr. President. If you think of anyone or anything that might be helpful, please let me know. In the meantime, I'll keep you apprised of what we find."

The president was understandably a busy man, with other duties to perform, so in short time, Marty, his grandfather, and I were ushered out of the office and pulling onto Pennsylvania Avenue again. We had a few hours to kill before Marty's grandfather had to catch his plane for home, so we decided to get a bite to eat. His grandfather was a simple man with simple taste, so we ended up at Arby's.

All too soon, we were at the airport saying our goodbyes.

"You be good to my grandson, white man, or you'll be needing a wig!" Marty's grandfather said as he shook my hand, exercising his great sense of humor.

"No wampum, no promises," I replied, and we all laughed.

After my big hug with the man, he had another for Marty, and then we both watched him enter the plane. I was moved to tears by the ones running down my friend's face.

As we headed for the terminal for my flight, I said, "Hey, I guess I got you a new cellphone after all, huh?"

"*You?* Bullshit!"

We probably looked pretty silly walking through Dulles, looking like a couple Little Leaguers who just won the big game and laughing hysterically.

Chapter 36

The next morning, I was a little jetlagged as I headed for Cincinnati, but my mind didn't pay much attention to that; I was too busy hoping Ohio law enforcement had more information on Paul Reichart and Randy Mills than we already had. I could have asked them to fax or email it, but I had a specific reason for wanting to be there in person.

As I walked into the Cincinnati FBI field office, I spotted Colleen O'Neal, an old friend and the newest special agent in charge. I smiled, fondly recalling our training days at Quantico. "Hey, Colleen. Nice to see you," I said nonchalantly, as if we'd only been apart for a couple weeks instead of years.

"Kroh! Why didn't you let me know you were coming?" she asked, truly stunned and clearly as happy to see me as I was to see her.

"I wanted to surprise you." I pulled her in for an unprofessionally long hug, then finally let her go.

"I'm just about to head to Arby's. Hungry?"

Arby's again? Does everyone love that now, I thought. "I can always eat," I answered.

At the restaurant, she tore into her Caesar salad, I drank a Pepsi, and we caught up on our lives since Quantico.

"I hear you're making quite a name for yourself at the BAU," she said.

"Yeah, I guess. I've got a great team. They make me look good."

"Kind of like how Noah and I made you look good during training, huh?" she teased, and then popped a tomato in her mouth.

"You're probably right about that," I answered, then shared a laugh with her. "Hey, are you still with, uh…Brady?"

"Hell no! I caught his ass cheating with a girl who worked for him."

"Hmm. I guess he wasn't too intelligent if he thought he could get away with that while he was dating an FBI agent. I'm sorry to hear it though."

"Don't be. It was the best thing that ever happened to me, truly a good riddance. Two days after I threw him out, I met Kyle, and we've been happily married for three years now."

"Really? Wow. Congratulations. If you're happy, I'm happy for you."

"How about you? I don't see a ring on that finger yet."

"Nope, not married, but I have been seeing someone for over a year now."

"A whole year? Wow, Kroh. That's like a lifetime for you," she said with a laugh that she punctuated with another tomato.

"Yeah, I guess. If you met Crystal, you'd understand why. She's great."

"Good for you. Hey, how's Noah doing?"

"As buff as ever."

"How are Danielle and the kids?"

"Doin' good. Noah's a great husband and father."

"What brings you to Cincinnati anyway?"

"Oh, just trying to get some info on The Guardian case."

"What kind of info?"

"You heard about the attempt on the president's grandbaby, right?"

"Who hasn't heard about it? But what's that got to do with anything."

I went on to tell her about the Mr. Smith connection and the two men who spent time in the nearby prison.

"Hmm. You might be on to something, Kroh," she said, whipping out her cellphone. She quickly called the local field office, gave them the names Randy Mills and Paul Reichart, and ordered them to gather everything they could find on the two. After she hung up, she turned a smile on me. "They're working on it, but what do you expect them to find?" she asked.

"I really don't know, but I need something. This case is fucking with me. He even tried to kill me, like a sniper, but Zee got hurt instead."

"Kroh? Are you all right?" Colleen said some indeterminable amount of time later, after I zoned out for some reason.

"Huh? Oh, yeah. Sorry. Like I said, this case is fucking with me."

"I can see that. Let's go. Hopefully, my team will have something for you by the time we get there."

On the way back to the field office, she mentioned a name I had not thought of in a long time.

"Oh, that reminds me. It's too bad your boy's out on sick leave."

"What?"

"Calder."

"Calder!?"

"Yeah. The bastard landed right in my lap after he screwed up The Fingertip case. Without the backing of the president, he didn't have any choice. The director sent him here, hoping everything would blow over. He hasn't taken the demotion very well. Calls in sick a lot."

"Really? I haven't thought about him since we caught Avery. Well, Calder did no favors for the FBI. That's for sure."

"You're right about that, but we really got an earful when he got here. It was all 'Fucking Kroh' this and 'Fucking Kroh' that."

"What a dumbass!"

"He also doesn't have very nice things to say about his former bestie, John Burns. I had to call him into my office once and reprimand him about his very outspoken opinions about our president."

"What? You mean he didn't get called to the principal's office for badmouthing me? Don't I count?" I asked, feigning hurt.

"Oh, well, I mostly agree with his opinion of you," she said with a laugh, and I couldn't help but join in.

"Like I said, he's a dumbass."

"About two months ago, things changed."

"What you mean?"

"I don't know if it was our little talk, but it was as if all was forgiven. He hasn't said a bad word about you or the president since. In fact, he's actually starting to be a decent guy."

"That's good," I said, not really believing my own words.

"Maybe, but I still feel like he'd just as soon stab me in the back."

"That's Calder for ya. Why is he on sick leave?"

"According to the paperwork, he had a nervous breakdown or something like that. To tell you the truth, I hope he doesn't come back."

"That's completely understandable."

Back at the field office, once I was settled in and introduced, Colleen said, "I got to get back to work. I have a meeting with the director Monday, and I've got some stuff to review. Evans will help you with everything you need. It was really great to see you, Kroh. You know where I am, so keep in touch."

"Thanks, Colleen," I said and shook her hand before she walked toward her office.

"This is all we got," Evans said, handing me a thick file of their findings on Mills and Reichart.

"Okay. Can you relay this info to Marty, my guy?" I asked, then made my way back Anderson.

Chapter 37

During his last week of sick leave, Calder called his ex and begged to see her and the kids. He was somewhat surprised that she reluctantly agreed.

He arrived around six, and once they were all seated in the living room of a house he bought, he began, "Over the last year and a half, I've been under a lot of strain. As you know, I took a lot of my frustration out on you guys. For that, I am very sorry. You certainly didn't deserve that." Although he really didn't give a shit about what they thought or how they felt about him, he did his best to sound and look sincere. He even managed a tear that escaped the corner of his eye and ran down his cheek; he was proud of himself to being able to cry on command. At that particular moment, he called up the one memory that hurt him the most, the death of his father, and it had the desired effect.

"It's okay, Daddy," Jeremy said, warming up to him.

"No, it wasn't okay, son. I hope I can in some way make it up to you. I really want to be a part of your lives, to be a father you two can love and be proud of. Lacy and Jeremy, you are the greatest things that ever happened to your mom and me."

His ex-wife couldn't help but smile at that.

"Sandra," he said, turning to his ex-wife, "I don't know if we can ever get back to where we were, but I want us to be friends. You are a great mother, and whatever happens, I hope we can work together to raise our children." More tears coursed down his face as he appeared to open his heart to his family.

His wife and daughter shed tears of their own, and his son, who never really resented his dad, was smiling brightly.

"Well, guys, that's all. I'll let you go for now, but please think about what I said. I really hope you can find it in your hearts to forgive me."

Just as he stood to leave, Jeremy rushed over to hug him. "I already forgive you, Dad," he said. "I wish we could come over this weekend, but we're staying with Grandma and Grandpa Welch. Maybe next weekend, okay?"

"Well, if it's okay with your mom, that sounds great to me."

Sandra and Lacy were next to stop him at the door, and his daughter gave him a tentative hug. "I love you, Dad."

After his kids went off to do whatever they did in the evenings, Sandra walked him to the door. "If you really mean what you said, I believe we can work something out. I know Lacy will be watching closely to see if you've really changed, and I guess I will as well. We enjoyed a lot of good years together and made two beautiful children. I do hope we can work this out, at least for their sakes. As far as next weekend, it's okay with me. Take care of yourself, Don."

He leaned in and kissed Sandra on the cheek. "Thank you for letting me be here tonight. I did mean every word. You'll see." He smiled his sweetest, then turned and walked to his car. He noticed that she was still standing in the doorway as he backed out of the drive, so he honked the horn and waved. *Yeah, you'll see all right*, he thought, *you bitch.*

Once he was out of sight, a shiver of repulsion coursed through him. *Oh, how I'd love to twist her head till it pops off, like a dandelion's.* Calder could tell she'd been hitting the gym again, as she looked as fit as she did before she had their children. The fact that she was dressed to go out for the evening did not escape him either. *Fucking Brad and leaving our kids with the grandparents for the weekend? Nice.* Nevertheless, he had done what he wanted to do, and though he wouldn't win any award, he knew that it was an Oscar-worthy performance. *I fucking had them as soon as the tears came,* he thought. *Paging Mr. Spielberg!*

Die by Proxy

As he drove toward his apartment in Cincinnati, still tortured by the fact that his ex was going out for the evening, he received a call. "Hey, Jerry. What's up?" he asked. Jerry Weinberg was one of the few people he associated with at the field office, but it wasn't because he liked the man; it was only because Jerry's cubicle neighbored his, and he had to keep up appearances.

"You're not gonna believe who was here today, Donny boy."

"I'm not in the mood for guessing games, Jerry."

"It was your old buddy, Benjamin Kroh."

"Kroh!?" Surprise ripped through him, and his car swerved till his tires bumped the rumble strips on the side of the road, startling him even more. He overcompensated and almost hit someone. "Do you know why?" he asked when he finally recovered from his near collision with an oncoming gray Nissan.

"He came over to pick up some intel on that guy who tried to kidnap the president's grandbaby. You read that story, right? It's been all over the news."

"He picked it up personally, in Cincinnati. Why didn't he just have you send it over? The dimwit jackass is aware email's been invented, right?"

"Yeah, you'd think, but it seems he and our new boss are old friends. They were at Quantico together."

Just like that, Calder's sense of accomplishment was banished beneath a deep wave of new depression. His knuckles went white as he gripped the steering wheel, his mind raced, and his blood ran cold. *Could that be all it was? Is there any chance he suspects me?* When he finally recalled where he was in the present moment, he continued his conversation with Jerry, trying to remain as civil as possible. "Well, I'm sorry I missed him. I shouldn't be angry at him, and I really do want to apologize. We all know he's one of the good guys."

"That's not what you were saying a couple months ago... or five seconds ago. Didn't you just call him a dimwit jackass?"

"Well, yeah, but a couple months ago, I wasn't myself.

That occasionally comes back on me, I guess."

"Yeah, that's understandable. Anyway, when are you coming back?"

"I feel I'm ready to come back now, but the good doctor thinks I should wait at least a couple weeks. As you can tell, I'm still having some...problems occasionally. Anyway, I really got to get going, Jerry. I'll see you soon."

With that, Calder hung up, pissed beyond belief. *Must that Kroh fuck up every good mood I have?* He felt a pain deep in his gut. While he knew it could've been some indigestion, brought on by the tacos he ate earlier, he knew the acid flowing into his stomach was because of Kroh. He was sure there was nothing to tie him to The Guardian or the attempted kidnapping, but Kroh had pulled off the impossible more than once in his silver-platter life. Calder knew Kroh and his team were well known for piecing together seemingly unrelated facts. He also knew his time as Mr. Smith was coming to an end.

For the next hour and a half, Calder drove around aimlessly, wasting gas and contemplating all possible scenarios. He knew he had to be prepared for the worst case. He wasn't really worried; he was just furious that he now had to hasten things along, because moving too quickly might cause him to deviate from plans and could cause mistakes. *If they're on to me, I can just use one of my aliases and remain in the States indefinitely,* he thought, realizing it wouldn't be wise for him to try to leave the country for a while anyway, since the botched job with the president's grandson had law enforcement carefully watching the borders and keeping tabs on any outgoing international flights.

I wonder if I passed that stupid fuck as he made his way back to Indy, he asked himself, feeling great desperation to put an end to Kroh as soon as possible. The thought brought an uncertain peace to his mind. "This time, I won't miss, Kroh. This time, you'll die!" he said aloud, then finally headed home.

Chapter 38

Something was bothering me as I drove back to Anderson, something lurking right at the edge of my subconscious, something I couldn't quite grasp. My gut told me it was something I had to discover, had to know, but for the life of me, I could not pull it into my conscious thoughts. I hoped against hope that the information I received from the Cincinnati field office would trigger something, that it would give me the one elusive lead that would break the case.

As I drove west on I-74, enjoying a beautiful day and Tony Bennett belting "Rags to Riches," Marty interrupted my reverie with a buzzing cellphone call. "What's happening, Marty?"

"We just got the results on the DNA from the warehouse. They didn't have very much, but it was definitely Randy Mills."

"Is it possible that he left something behind to make us *think* he died in the blast?"

"Not in this case. There were several, uh…pieces of him. No one could fake that. Mills is dead, Kroh, and it's definitely gonna be a closed casket, if not several grocery bags."

"Damn! I was really hoping to talk to him. He would have been our best lead to Mr. Smith."

"Sorry, Boss."

"You've got nothing to apologize for, Marty. At least he didn't take the real baby with him."

"Yeah, I know. There is some good news though."

"What's that?"

"The CPR mannequin is still usable, albeit a little singed."

"That's great, Marty," I said with an eye-roll I was sure he could hear in my voice. "I still can't believe this Mr. Smith had no intention of letting the baby live. That's almost colder than anything he's done so far, especially if he is claiming to be some Guardian who wants to save children. Last night, I had an awful nightmare about the president's grandbaby sitting in that room all alone. Thankfully, I woke up before it reached its end."

"You're bringing me down, dude. I got to go."

"Bye, Marty. Thanks."

When I was about thirty minutes outside Indy, another call came.

"We got another computer tech," Vernon said. "If this guy keeps this up, there won't be any one around to fix computers."

"Another computer tech?"

"Yep. Deleted...permanently, just like the others. His name was Max Slater, owner of Slater Tech. He was found in his shop, but we figure he's been dead for over a month."

As I drove to the south side of Indy, I shook my head in frustration. I parked in front of Slater Tech and noticed that Meecham was already there. As I entered, the stink of death hit me hard, a clear indication that his body had been decaying for weeks.

"Here," Meecham said, throwing some peppermint oil at me.

I shoved a bit under each nostril. While it didn't mask the stomach-turning stench entirely, it helped. I walked over to Meecham and gave him back his bottle. "Find anything new?"

"So far, it's just like the other crime scenes, just a body with multiple chest wounds and a paper plate in the trash, same sort of blood spatter pattern on the walls. The computers are wiped, and can you believe a tech nerd like this guy had no surveillance cameras?"

"Damn! I'm tired of these dead ends, no pun intended. I was hoping there'd be...something."

"Sorry. Hey, I heard you went to Cincinnati today. Did you see my old boss?"

"No. I guess he's on sick leave."

"Well, I'd be sick, too, if I pulled as many numb-nuts stunts as he did. The way I see it, he deserved what he got. Hell, I think they should have kicked him entirely out of the Bureau. He'd make a great Walmart greeter or fry-flipper, wouldn't he?"

"I doubt that," I said, imagining Calder in one of those silly little vests with the smiley face on it. "Anyway, I'm gonna head back to Anderson. Let me know if you find anything new."

"Will do."

As I parked in the lot next to the Anderson PD, I tried to let my bitter and frustrated thoughts slip away. I tucked the files under my arm and headed inside. "I'm back," I said, slipping my head in Bradford's door after a short knock.

"Hey, Kroh, come in and sit for a minute," Bradford said. "It seems our Guardian has posted the information about Montgomery."

For the next thirty minutes, we watched as The Guardian painted the picture in the slime of Montgomery's crimes against children. Not only did the man prey on the children of the people who voted for him, but he also traveled to Cambodia, on the taxpayers' dimes, to have unrestricted sex with the unfortunate children who were torn from their families and forced into the sex trade.

After it was over, we both sat there, feeling the need for a long shower and a great deal of disinfectant.

Bradford finally broke the silence: "Anything interesting about the newest computer tech?" he asked hopefully.

"Nope. It looked the same as the others. As you know, the crime scene on the south side of Indy doesn't exactly lend itself to neighborhood crime watch, so the guy was locked up in there with the summer heat for over a month, baking with no A/C. There probably gonna have to burn the place. I got the stuff from Cincinnati, too, and I'll probably spend the rest of the day going over what they gave me," I said with a yawn.

"Need any help?" Bradford asked.

"If it's not too much to ask, sure."

"I've got a few things to finish up here. I'll meet you in the conference room in about twenty minutes."

I downed a few cups of coffee before Bradford showed up, and we studied the files for the next two hours.

Bradford gave me a look of uncomfortable awe. "If these guys committed even half the murders they were accused of, they were monsters, very dangerous men."

"Yeah, that's the impression I get too. It's probably a good thing for the world that they're dead. They wouldn't have gone down easy."

"I hear ya." Bradford stretched. "Hey, I got to get going. Lillie is expecting me home for dinner."

"Thanks for the help. See you tomorrow," I said as he walked out.

Forty-five minutes later, I was pulling into Crystal's driveway. I intended to continue combing the files there, but all I really wanted was to sit back, have a beer, maybe watch some TV, and rest a little.

When I opened the door, Crystal was there to greet me, again in her tattered Led Zeppelin t-shirt. There was one difference though: She was also wearing one of those little French maid aprons, with high heels. I don't know about you, but that combination had my blood leaving my brain so quickly that I almost fainted.

"Dinner will be ready in a few moments, sir," she said. "Would you like a drink while you wait?"

I only had a Pepsi at Arby's with Colleen, so I was really hungry, but food was the last thing on my mind. I dropped the files, my phone, and my keys on the table by the door, then grabbed her and pulled her in close, as I absently used my foot to close the door. I kissed her feverishly, and it felt like the first time. She pushed her body into mine and kissed me as if she felt the same way.

As we kissed, I carefully maneuvered her to the couch. Once there, and without ending our kiss, I gently laid her down. I was a slave to my lust; with my mind no longer in control, my body was on autopilot. Her body reacted to my every touch. As my hands were about to explore the treasures hidden by the lacy white apron, Crystal's smoke alarm brought to a close what promised to be one of the greatest experiences of my life.

"Goddamn it to hell!" I growled breathlessly. I looked into her eyes and saw that she was feeling the same. Then the corners of her mouth turned up in a smile, and we both broke into laughter. We were still chuckling as she shut off the alarm and I opened the windows to let the smoke of our burning feast clear the house.

I assured her that I would still eat the grossly overcooked food, but she wouldn't have it.

"Order a pizza, and I'll clean up this mess. Don't you, for one minute, think we're not going to continue what we started, Kroh boy."

I went to the table by the door, grabbed my phone, and dialed in the number from the magnet on her refrigerator. "I don't know. I'm pretty tired."

She smiled, straightened her apron, then turned to walk away, revealing that world-class ass. She made sure to bend down slowly to pick up the towel I was sure she intentionally dropped. She stood up with her hand on her hip and stared at me. "You don't look that tired to me."

I glanced down and realized that my manhood had revealed me to be a liar. "Damn you, Larry," I said, then growled and shrugged. "Okay. I guess you can have your way with me."

"Oh, believe me, I *will* have my way with you, mister, and unlike the pizza, I can't guarantee thirty minutes or less," she said with a wink.

After we ate our fill of pizza and cleaned up the box and the greasy napkins, I sat on the couch watching a little TV and drinking a beer. I enjoyed Crystal's company, but I really needed to look over the information from Cincinnati, as I was sure it held the key to Mr. Smith. The guy was smart and very meticulous. He had killed nine people in a little less than two months, then tried to have the president's grandbaby kidnapped, yet we had next to nothing.

While the Guardian captured my thoughts, I couldn't help noticing Crystal on the far side of the room, a vision of a goddess in her t-shirt, apron, and heels, using a feather duster to tend to a lampshade. She seductively moved around the room, tickling random things with those colorful feathers, always making sure she was well within my line of sight.

As hard as I tried, I could not remember a time in my life when I'd seen anything sexier. The high heels worked wonders for her legs and ass, and she was truly something to behold.

She dusted the picture that hung on the wall near the hallway that led to her bedroom. Then, when she was done, she looked over her shoulder, blew me a kiss, and sensuously headed that way.

I jumped up with an intention to follow her, but I tripped on the leg of the coffee table and tumbled to the floor.

She ran back into the living room. "Are you okay?"

"I think I might be dead."

"Dead?"

"Well, based on the view from down here, I must be looking up at Heaven."

"Cheesy, but I like it. Now get your ass up, and let's go."

True to her word, Crystal ravaged me, or maybe I ravaged her, if not a little of both. For the next hour, we discovered our bodies once again. She pushed me back and sat on top of me. As my hands caressed the nuances of her sweet curves, she brought me close to the edge at least three times before she tensed and pushed herself hard against me, moaning. I pushed back and found I could hold it no longer. Our bodies rocked as the more intense orgasmic waves rewarded the glorious moments of primal bonding.

After a while, she leaned down and kissed me deeply as the aftershocks of our lovemaking shook us in glorious, random waves. Crystal rolled to the side and snuggled close to me. A while later, I awoke with her still cradled in my arms, wondering if life could get any better.

Chapter 39

Calder decided it was time to leave. He knew he could no longer be Mr. Smith, but there was one more thing he had to do. He drove past a neighborhood he knew very well. He knew just where to park, in the wooded area just behind where he needed to be. After making sure his car would not be easily noticed, he made his way through the woods and soon found himself looking into the back yard that had been his for fifteen years. Thoughts of the cookouts and of his children running and playing were bittersweet, mostly severely painful, thanks to the ex-wife that stole all that from him.

As he approached the garage, he saw an unfamiliar car in the driveway. Although the color was masked by the neon green hue of the night-vision goggles, he knew in an instant who owned it. *Brad.* An involuntary surge of anger coursed through him.

He entered through the garage, where the darkness seemed absolute, but his high-tech goggles picked up the smallest amount of light and made the unseen seen. He knew the kids were away, with their grandparents, and that was important to him. He loved Lacy and Jeremy with all his heart, and he knew that, deep down, they loved him too. *They'd love me even more if that bitch of an ex-wife didn't turn them against me,* he thought. Oh well. *Garbage in, garbage out. Someday they will see the light.*

Calder had visited the house the day before, while his ex-wife was at work. He was familiar with every creak and noise it made, since he lived there so long, but he had to be very careful. He was methodical about his movements around the house. By the time he finished, he knew every place where a warning sound might be produced.

He moved into the kitchen without a sound. He stopped and listened and heard laughter coming from upstairs. He grimaced as he padded silently across the living room, careful to avoid that danger spot next to the couch. He stood at the bottom of the stairs and took a deep breath. He made his first cautious step and was rewarded with silence, so he skipped the one creaky step and carried on, moving precariously up the minefield of stairs.

Once he reached the landing, he stopped for a moment and let out a breath. Something was different. There was a light in the bedroom, and he knew from the sounds that they were having sex. *In the last ten years of our marriage, she wouldn't let me touch her with the lights on. Now, she's bumping uglies with this stupid fucker in the damn spotlight,* he thought and almost audibly growled. *In the light, goddamn it!*

With the light from the open door, he no longer needed the goggles. There was only one more place on his way to his bedroom that he had to avoid. It still bothered him that the door was open. *Why wouldn't it be? No one else is supposed to be here, right?* he mused. He pushed the door open and stood, transfixed, as he saw his former wife riding her new boyfriend, panting heavily as she pounded herself down again and again on top of his muscled thighs. Brad's eyes were closed as he matched her movements.

"You fucking whore!" Calder said when he could take it no more. He stood at the end of the king-sized bed, seething in anger.

Sandra screamed and peed a little on Brad as she clambered off him. She moved back against the headboard and pulled the covers over herself, as if to hide her shame.

Brad sat up and pushed himself back. "What the fuck's your problem, man?" he asked in a cocky tone. "What gives you the right to—"

Instantly, Calder shot him in the forehead. The sound of the silenced shot, in the quiet that had come over the room, startled him, but the sight of the interloper falling dead into his ex-wife's lap made him smile. He was pleased to see that the bullet did not exit Brad's head; the thought of the bullet ricocheting around in the pissant's skull, shredding his tiny brain, filled him with delight. "I *have* no problem, Braddy boy."

Sandra screamed at the shot, then screamed again when Brad lifelessly crashed into her lap. Mascara-smudged rivers of tears ran down her face as she batted her eyes and sniffled. "Don, what are you—"

"Shut up, you cheating bitch!"

"Donald, why?"

"I gave you my life, and you threw it away, but you couldn't stop there, could you? You had to turn my children against me with your lies too!"

"Please, Don! I-I didn't... Don't..."

"I told you to shut up, you fucking whore!"

"You changed, Don. I gave you every chance, but—"

"Bull-fucking-shit!" he said and put a bullet right between her eyes, not wanting to hear another syllable his ex had to say.

She fell against Brad, a crimson stream of blood leaking from the hole in her head, dripping down onto her dead boyfriend's back, her eyes wide open and staring blankly at the wall.

Calder stood there for a moment, studying what he had

done. He tilted his head to the side like a confused dog unaware of what its maser wanted. When he finally found his voice again, he declared to the deaf ears in the room, "Finally the kids are mine and mine alone. In time, they will appreciate what I did for them here tonight. They'll learn to hate you for tearing our family apart, you fucking whore!"

As he left, he made no attempt to be quiet; in fact, he thrilled with each squeak of the stairs. He left the same way he came in, through the garage. He crossed his back yard and walked through the back gate. It was a short trek to his car in the woods, and he had no reason to rush. He actually danced a little, while he walked, like a man without a care in the world.

Now I can leave. The world is my bitch, he mused.

At seven o'clock the next morning, Calder was on a plane to Rio de Janeiro.

Chapter 40

The next morning, I sat in my makeshift office at the Anderson PD, going over everything from Cincinnati, as well as what Marty had discovered at the latest computer shop crime scene. My gut told me there had to be something there, something that would provide a break in the case. *God knows we need it.*

Near the bottom of the pile, I spotted an odd name, Danil Vetrov. As I continued reading, I found that he was a top-level accountant for the Russian mafia, who disappeared after visiting his brother in the Lebanon correctional institution. It could not be confirmed, but word was that over twenty million bucks disappeared with him. Not long after he vanished, his brother, Arsenii Vetrov, was murdered in his cell at the prison, and Reichert and Mills were suspected of carrying out the hit, but nothing could be proven. They were soon released from Lebanon, only to be accused of killing seven gang members of different affiliations in the months following their release.

What took them from contract killings to attempted kidnapping of the president's grandchild? That's quite a freaking leap, even for homicidal maniacs. I wondered. *What is their connection to Mr. Smith? How did he find out about them, and where did he get the money to hire him? Is our unsub a millionaire or something? If so, wouldn't there be a paper trail leading straight to him?*

As I sat there thinking, a couple of visitors walked in. "Mind if we join you?" Bradford asked.

"Please do. I'm getting nowhere here," I told them.

"Well, six eyes are better than two," Crystal said, then kissed me on the top of my head and sat down.

I divided the files into three equal stacks, then gave them a synopsis of what they contained and what we were looking for.

For the next three hours, not counting occasional interruptions that required Bradford's and Crystal's attention, we studied the files. As each person completed his or her pile, we handed them off to the right, until we all had a chance to peruse all of it. I made sure to take notes of anything of interest that we found, and Crystal pulled those notes up on the smartboard so we could study them together.

"Nothing here gives any clue as to why Reichert and Mills went from contract killers to kidnappers and why they started with such a high-profile victim. There's no doubt that the assholes were very good at killing and leaving no traces," I said, and they nodded in agreement. "I mean, they were suspected in numerous deaths, but not one shred of evidence connected them to those crimes. Nevertheless, not one shred of anything indicates that they'd want to become kidnappers either."

There was a knock on the door, and Zee and Vernon came in.

"Mind if we join you?" Vernon asked.

"That depends. Are you guys into spinning your wheels? That's all we seem to be doing here," I said with a sheepish smile.

"Better to spin wheels in an attempt to move forward than to bring to a standstill the quest for possible futures," Zee said.

"Wow. You should write fortune cookies," Vernon teased as they sat down.

Zee pinched his arm, then dived right into the information on the table.

Vernon rubbed his arm and did the same.

After about an hour, Crystal's stomach growled. "Hey, speaking of fortune cookies…" she said.

"All right, it's settled," I said, stretching. "Crystal has

made it clear that it is time to get something to eat."

Twenty minutes later, we were sitting in the corner booth at the Lemon Drop, and I was thrilled when the waitress placed my toasted cheeseburger, breaded tenderloin, fries, and root beer in front of me. We enjoyed each other's company as we ate.

Although she chowed down on the signature onion burger, Zee seemed fairly quiet, and she insisted on thumbing through one of the files as we ate. "Hey," she finally said as we were about to finish, "did you guys notice who signed off on most of these documents?"

After taking a second to think about it, I answered, "No. Who was it?"

"Your old buddy, Donald Calder."

"What!?" I was surprised and a bit embarrassed that I failed to notice that name that had come up more than once in the last couple days.

"Think that means anything?" Vernon asked.

I knew he was talking to me, but I was already gone. My mind was racing, trying to put together any scenario in which it was impossible for Calder to be involved, but in every case, he was a definite maybe.

Crystal touched my shoulder. "Kroh? What's going on in that head of yours? You're rubbing your finger again."

"This is the second time I've heard his name in the last two days. It's like finding that piece of a puzzle that's been eluding you but not being quite sure where it fits. No matter how I approach it, I-I just can't rule Calder out. I don't want to believe he's gone that far off the deep end, but he does have a motive, no matter how psychotic it is."

"What motive?"

"Well, he has a major grudge against me. That's for sure. Not only that, but his childhood friend, the current POTUS, let him down when he needed him most, basically threw him under the bus and right back to desk duty."

"Wow. That is motive," Crystal said, and everyone nodded in agreement.

As we got up to leave, I called my favorite geek. "Hey, Marty, I got a little side project for you. I need you to get me everything you can find on Donald Calder."

"Calder? Really? What for?"

"I'm not sure, but my gut tells me there's something there. Also, this needs to be one of those, uh…under-the-radar searches. We can't afford to raise any red flags, okay?"

"Okay, I'm on it. Anything else?"

"That's it for now, but please hurry. Thanks, Marty."

By the time we got back to the PD, Marty had sent all that he had discovered already. We were already aware of most of it, but Marty included everything that was known about Calder's demotion, move, family troubles, rough start at the Cincinnati office, and the death of his father.

As far-fetched as it seemed that a fellow agent could be our suspect, everyone was excited that we finally had one. It didn't take us long to connect the dots that should have been obvious, if we had only looked in the right direction.

"To do all the things he needed to do to carry out the predator murders, he would have needed a lot of time," Crystal offered.

"He had plenty of that. He's been out on sick leave since just after the first murder," I let them know.

"Wouldn't *that* have drawn up some red flags?" Zee asked.

"No one cared. His colleagues were just glad he'd been gone, and he pretty much alienated himself from his family long ago. I can't say I blame anyone for not missing him," I said, giving them a look and a shrug.

"How does a man who dedicated his life upholding the law go so far off the edge?" Bradford asked.

"Well, everything hit him in a short amount of time. He screwed up royally at work and was highly humiliated by the demotion. The president, a friend of his, refused to help, and then his wife filed for divorce and moved back to Indy. To top all that off, he lost his father. I really think that death was the turning point."

"Well, it was one thing to carry out those predator murderers, but renting out the warehouse and giving Reichart and Mills enough incentive would have taken a major amount of cash," Bradford said. "I mean, I'm not complaining' about my paycheck here, but I'm not sure the Bureau gives anybody a nest egg that big."

"Marty checked into Calder's finances, and it turns out he received a healthy inheritance when his father passed away. He also squirreled away money for many years, unbeknownst to the missus, but those two put together wouldn't account for what he needed to pay the kidnappers. From what I read in the files on Mills and Reichert, they were high rent criminals, and money was their only motivator. Going after the president's grandbaby wouldn't have come cheap," I said, perplexed.

"No doubt!" Crystal said.

"So... Where did he get that kind of money? If we could figure that out, we might be on to something," I said, proclaiming what everyone was thinking.

While I sat rubbing my finger, Zee continued looking over the files from Cincinnati. "Wait a minute," she finally said, scrunching up her forehead in thought. "I don't know if it means anything, but Calder's name is on this paperwork too."

"Huh? Let me see that," I said, and she slid the file over to me. It was the information about the accountant Danil Vetrov and the over twenty million dollars that the Russian mob lost, and my gut told me that Zee just turned the whole investigation in our favor. "Great catch, Zee! This definitely explains a lot. If what we suspect is true, Calder is a thoroughly dangerous man. He has motive, along with detailed knowledge of the inner workings of the FBI, and he has money. From what I know about him, he's surely planned everything down to the last detail, along with contingencies. I'm sure he's got false identities, multiple places to hide, and various escape routes. He isn't one to be caught off guard, which is why all that shit raining down on him was so devastating for him in the first place."

"And to think, I already didn't like the bastard *before* he shot me in the head," Zee said, rubbing her scar.

At least he didn't hit anything important," I said and was immediately rewarded with a slap.

"Play nice, mister. I technically took a bullet for you."

"But seriously, we need to get eyes on him, like, yesterday."

Chapter 41

I was positive that Calder was Mr. Smith, but I knew my intuition would never hold up in court. So, I did what I could to make our case against Calder solid.

Crystal and I spent the day driving around, showing Calder's picture to people who might have seen him and lived to tell about it. First, we stopped by Rudolph Singleton's place, and he was every bit the yuppie prick Agent Sparks said he was. When I knocked on his door, he answered it with an attitude that clearly told us he didn't feel he had time for us.

"Mr. Singleton, I am Agent Kroh from the FBI. I believe you spoke to Agent Sparks a few days ago. Is that right?"

"Yes, I believe Sparks was his name. Why?"

"We have photograph we'd like you to look at."

He took the photo from me and stared at it for a long moment. "Yes, that very well could have been the person I saw, except... Well, his hair's all wrong, and they man had a mustache. When I saw him climb over the fence, I could tell right away that he was not a member. I was just about to tell him so, but he jumped in his car and took off."

"How could you tell he wasn't a member?"

"He just had that look, you know? Plus, it's a dog park, and he didn't even have a dog with him."

I wanted to smack the shit out of him for his flippant tone, but instead I urged, "Please look at the picture again."

"Like I said, it could be him, if he had brown hair and a mustache. Why is this so important anyway?"

"I'm sorry, but you have to be a member of the FBI for that information. Are you a member of the FBI? No? Sometimes you can just tell."

My insulting remark hit home, because he said with a heightened edge in his voice, "I'm sorry, but I'm going to have cut this short. Hercules has an appointment at the grooming salon."

Once we were in the car, Crystal couldn't hold it any longer and burst out laughing. "Hercules? Really?"

Then, it was my turn to lose it too.

We were still riding the waves of the laughter when we pulled up to Timmy Andrews's house.

Timmy seemed to be doing well, considering what he went through. He was playing catch with his dad when we drove up, and he ran up and gave me a hug that made me feel wonderful.

"How you doing, buddy?"

"Great, Mr. Kroh."

"Hey, we're friends. You can just call me Kroh."

"Okay...Kroh."

"I need you to do something for me, Tim."

"What's that?"

"I need you to look at a picture and let me know if you have seen this man before, okay?"

"Okay," the boy said with a shrug.

I handed him the picture of Calder. "Take a good look now," I said.

"He kinda looks like Mr. Smith, but not really. I-I don't know."

"Mr. Smith talked to you boys quite a bit, didn't he?" I asked as a new idea dawned on me.

"Yes."

Okay, hold on a second," I said, then quickly called Marty. "Hey, can you pull up some video of Calder and send it to my phone?"

"Will do, Boss."

Once Marty sent the video, I hurried back to Timmy and, without showing him the video, let him listen to Calder's voice.

Die by Proxy

"Yep, that's him all right," he said, perking up when he heard Calder's voice. "That's Mr. Smith."

"You did great, Tim."

"Is Mr. Smith in trouble?"

"I'm not sure. He might be. We're trying to find him. With your help, we might be able to before anything happens to him."

"Oh," Tim said. "Well, I hope he doesn't get hurt or anything. If it wasn't for him, we'd...well, you know."

"I know, Tim," I said, torn in two with moral dilemma. "I've got to go for now, but I will come see you when I can. Maybe I'll bring my mitt next time."

Timmy solidified our case, but his word alone would not account for much. The one thing it did do was make me absolutely, irrevocably certain that Calder was our man.

We left the Andrews home and headed for the next place on our agenda, the home of Eric Dennis. Like Timmy Andrews, Eric's contribution would be limited. At just 9 years old, his memories gave us little, but he was just as positive as Timmy was that it was indeed Mr. Smith's voice.

The parents of the two little ones who were confined with Eric refused to let us talk to them, and I completely understood that. I didn't yet have children of my own, but if I did, I would have fought tooth and nail to protect that child from reliving those horrible experiences.

That left only one other person to talk to, and it wasn't long before I knocked on Pence's door.

"Wh-What do you guys want?" Jerry asked when he saw us, all the color draining from his face.

"I need to ask you some questions," I said as his wife walked up behind him.

"What's going on, Jerry?" she said, with a bite in her voice.

"I don't know, baby. It's the FBI," he said, with just a hint of fear.

"I need to talk to your husband, Mrs. Pence. He may have information that will help us with a case we're investigating. May we come in?"

"Yes, of course," she said. She seemed confused and

caught a little off guard, but her curiosity won out in the end.

"Um, it might be better if we talk alone," I said to her.

"I'm not going anywhere," Mrs. Pence barked. "Whatever you have to say to my husband, you can say in front of me."

I looked back at Jerry, and he nodded.

"You talked to Mr. Smith at the Waffle House in Daleville, right?" I asked Jerry Pence.

"Yes. You know that, or you wouldn't be here, right?"

"True. Do you recall what he looks like?"

"It was dark, but I'm pretty sure I remember. Why?"

I want to show you some pictures. I need to see if any of them look like Mr. Smith."

"Whatever," Jerry said and took the stack from me, then started moving through them one by one. Then he backed up a couple and stopped to stare at the one of Calder. "This kinda looks like him, only Mr. Smith has brown hair and a mustache. Who is this guy?"

"I am not at liberty to say at this point in our investigation, but I need you to listen to something." I then played the video clip on my phone, listening carefully so I could stop it before it revealed that the supposed Mr. Smith was actually one of us, an FBI agent.

"Hey, that's him! I don't think I'll ever forget his damn voice, after all the trouble he got me in."

"You mean the trouble *you* got yourself into, Jerry?" his wife said testily.

I smiled at the heat that came from her words, then continued, "Anyway, it's too early to tell if this is actually him, but we thank you for your help, Jerry. You and your wife should know that you're very lucky to be alive. Everyone else who helped Mr. Smith was murdered, so if he contacts you again, it would be in your best interest to call me at once. Here's my card."

Crystal took the wheel as we headed back to her house, and that gave me a chance to make a few phone calls. First, I informed Noah of what we found; I kept him up to date on the goings-on, and he continued talking to the director. For the time being, he seemed to think it was enough to at least watch him.

After I hung up, I called Colleen and told her about our suspicions. I also reminded her, "We need to proceed with extreme caution and secrecy," a warning she didn't really need because she already knew it. She would have laughed at that any other time, but the situation was serious, and she felt a bit foolish and guilty, even though I knew she was neither. Someone under her command may have gone rogue, and she was just now finding out. "You couldn't have known," I assured her, but I knew from our time at Quantico that she would still take Calder's indiscretions personally. Most importantly, I also knew that she would follow my lead. "We need to get eyes on him as soon as possible, but it can't be one of your people. He might recognize them and get spooked," I said. "Just be ready on your end. We may have to move quickly."

Next, I called Vernon and asked him to send some capable agents to Cincinnati as soon as possible. "Just make sure Calder has never seen them before."

"You got it. Hey, at least we know who we're looking for now. It's good to know that mystery is solved."

"Yeah, but it still doesn't really account for much. He's the worst kind of criminal, an FBI agent with a working knowledge of how we hunt. In Calder's case, he's more of a challenge. He has crazy skills in planning and a shitload of money at his disposal. He's never been a great FBI agent, but he's turned into a world-class criminal. Just get those agents on him right away, Vernon."

"Consider it done."

"Thanks, Vernon."

Chapter 42

Calder left the airport in Rio de Janeiro and immediately hailed a cab. "Get me to Rio," he said to the cabbie, with no time for the regular pleasantries.

At a busy intersection with cars and people buzzing about in all directions, he heaved a sigh of frustration, paid the driver for the accumulated fare, and got out.

After Calder left the taxi on the busy street in Rio, he waited ten minutes and hailed another taxi. This one took him to the Novo Rio bus station, where he looked at the schedules to see what buses would depart within the hour. He settled on one that was leaving forty-five minutes later, going to São Paulo, Brazil, and he quickly bought a ticket and climbed aboard. He found a seat near the back, then took out his wallet and discreetly dropped it to the floor. He used his foot to push it back under the seat, where it would not be noticed easily. He then got up, walked to the front of the bus, and indicated to the driver that he had to go to the bathroom. On his way, he avoided the cameras; that was easy enough since he knew where they were from previous trips. In the bathroom, he quickly scanned for prying eyes, then made his transition to someone else. A few minutes later, he left the bus station and caught a taxi back to the airport.

He knew leaving the wallet on the bus would work in his favor in one of two ways. First, if it was found by an honest person, it would be turned in, creating a record of it being found on the bus going to São Paulo. The second scenario, which Calder preferred, was that it would be found by somebody who had larceny in their heart. In that case, his credit cards would be used, and the authorities would waste much valuable time chasing their tails. The more time everyone spent looking in the wrong direction, the more time Calder would have to move freely in the other.

Within an hour, he was back at the airport as Nathan Voss, a sales representative from Chicago. His hair was now dark brown, and wire-rimmed glasses and a close-cropped beard completed his character. He had made the same trip several times in the past few months to work out the kinks, and he didn't feel the least bit nervous about his travels. The only thing he couldn't control or plan for was Mother Nature, and for the moment, she seemed to be cooperating without delaying any flights.

He boarded a charter plane he'd booked for a trip to Lima, Peru. From there, he hopped on an Aeroméxico flight to Monterrey, Mexico. He grabbed the car he'd left there two weeks earlier and drove up Highway 85, then crossed the Rio Bravo into Laredo, Texas. The whole ordeal took just a little over thirty-four hours. He was stoked that it all worked out but was also very tired, so he stopped at a Super Eight just off of I-35 in Laredo and slept hard for the next eight hours.

When he woke, he felt great. *Back in the good ol' USA, and they don't even know I was gone,* he mused. "Deep in the heart of Texas…" he sang, and he considered staying in Laredo until the shit hit the fan, but he wanted a front-row seat. *I deserve at least that,* he told himself. With Kroh's demise on his mind, he took a quick shower, picked up something to eat, and headed east.

* * *

It was another Monday morning, and Crystal and I headed for the Anderson PD. I was still shocked that Calder was our guy, as I didn't think he was capable of stooping that low, but I couldn't seem to think about anything else.

"You gonna get that or what?" Crystal said, distracting me from my thoughts.

"Huh? Oh!" I said as I picked up my buzzing phone and looked at it. "What's happening, Marty?" I answered when I saw who it was. "I really hope you've got something for me."

"Kroh, we may have a problem. Calder is...in the wind," Marty said

"What!?"

"Yeah, his normal daily credit card use stopped two days ago. The last thing he bought was gas at the BP on Montgomery Road in Cincinnati, not far from the field office there. After that, nothing."

"Maybe he's just being thrifty, trying to cut back on spending."

"Very unlikely. From what I've discovered, Calder is a creature of habit, and he never deviates from his routine. He was a no-show at the FBI field office in Cincinnati, AWOL, with no word. It was supposed to be his first day back after his extended sick leave."

I thanked Marty almost inaudibly, and then hung up. "My God. He's on to us. He knows," I muttered.

"What? Who knows what?" Crystal asked.

"Calder. He knows we're on to him."

"How, I don't know, but this is bad."

"So, what now?"

I thought for a moment, then held up my index finger to Crystal and quickly called Coleen back. "Change of plans," I said with great urgency. "If you can find Calder, bring him in. Surely, I don't have to remind you to be careful."

"If we can find him?"

"Yeah, it looks like he's in the wind."

"Don't you mean like a fart in the wind?" Collene said, quoting the ass-hat warden in the *Shawshank Redemption*.

"Well, yeah, that too," I said, but I couldn't muster up a smile at the bitter truth.

"All right, will do," Colleen said, and I could almost hear a smile in her voice. "I'll let you know when we have him."

I called Vernon next and explained that we needed to send some agents over to watch Calder's ex-wife's house. I was sure it was a long shot, but we couldn't take the chance.

Finally, I turned back to Crystal. "I think we'd better bypass Anderson and head straight for Cincinnati. You up for that?"

"Sure," she said. "I want this guy caught as badly as you

do, Kroh."

We all knew we had to locate Calder in a hurry. Personally, I had a very strong feeling that if we didn't grab him quickly, we might never get another chance.

Colleen called me back an hour later. "Sorry, Kroh, but he's nowhere to be found, totally ghosted. We checked his house, and it's clear that he hasn't been there for a few days."

"Shit! Lock it down and have your forensics team tear the place apart. I should be there in less than an hour."

* * *

As promised, we arrived at Calder's house around noon. Although the FBI did not converge on it with sirens blaring, neighbors did gather to see what was going on. When we pulled into the driveway, it only added to the spectacle.

I saw Colleen standing in front of the house, so I quickly walked up to her and introduced Crystal. "You found anything yet?" I asked as she led us into the house. I couldn't help smirking as I saw how torn apart the place was; as anal and OCD as Calder was, I knew he would shit a brick to see his home like that.

Sandy Taylor, one of the techs, came up to Colleen. "We found this among some other papers and documents that fell behind the desk in the den."

Colleen thanked her, and then examined the list. "Looks like somebody was planning a little vacation to Rio," she said.

As soon as I heard that, I called Marty to have him check on all flights leaving Cincinnati under the names Smith and Calder. I stayed on the line, and within a few minutes, Marty confirmed that Calder bought a ticket just two days prior. "Damn it to hell! He fled the country, just...gone."

Within an hour, Marty sent pictures of Calder at the Cincinnati airport, taken just before he boarded his flight. Somehow, he also got his hands on photos of Calder at the airport in Rio de Janeiro, confirming the flight information we found.

Chapter 43

There was not much we could do in Cincinnati, so we headed back to Indy. As we drove, I fell into a deep funk. All along, I knew something was off about The Guardian case, but Calder's involvement was completely unexpected. Though, all along, the clues were right in front of me. The Guardian seemed to have a fixation on me, and he tried to put a bullet in my head but hit poor Zee instead. The attempt on the president's grandbaby should have been our second clue. The third was the careful planning, with meticulous attention to detail and all tracks covered. That had been bothering me during the whole investigation, but all in all, that trifecta was so Calder-like that I should have put two and two together far sooner. I felt like shit and feared I was losing my edge.

Over the last year and a half, Calder had become a thoroughly dangerous man. He had supplemented his skills as a master administrator with a desire to kill. Although I knew deep down that none of it was my fault, that no one died because of me, I couldn't help beating myself up about the way I handled Calder during The Fingertip case. *Maybe I came on a little too strong,* I thought. *Just because I dislike the man and his ways, I didn't have to push him so hard that it turned him into a monster.*

I was so caught up in my self-loathing that I barely registered that Crystal received a call. What I did notice was the firm slap to the back of my head. "Hey! What was that for?"

"Zee just called. She told me to get your attention, so I

did."

"You could have just said something."

"I did, and you didn't even hear me. Besides, that was more fun." Crystal smiled as she handed the phone to me.

I talked to Zee for a while and felt better by the time we hung up; she always had that effect on me, and she wasn't one to mince words.

Before we reached Indy, I decided to drop in on Calder's ex, because I felt she needed to know what was going on. As we pulled up to the home, I could see that it was a beautiful, well-kept place in a really nice neighborhood, a couple steps and one or two leaps above Calder's home in Cincinnati. I was sure that was another thing that must have burned him, losing that place in the bitter divorce.

We had called ahead so the surveillance team could expect our arrival, and I waved as we passed by their car. As we pulled into her drive, I noticed a late-model black Chevy Malibu parked near the garage.

As we were getting out, another car pulled in behind us, and an older gentleman and two children got out. Once we identified ourselves, he informed us that he was Arthur Welch, and Lacy and Jeremy were his grandchildren, Calder's kids.

"What seems to be the problem?" Arthur asked, his expression changing from one of curiosity to one of anxiousness.

"I need to speak with your daughter Sandra," I said. "Is she home?"

"Mom should be, but we just got here," Lacy said. "That's Brad's car over there. He's, like, her best friend lately."

"You mean her boyfriend," Jeremy corrected.

"Whatever," Lacy said, scrunching up her little face, obviously not too thrilled with her mother's new love interest.

"Could you please tell her we're here? I would appreciate it very much."

"Sure," Lacy said, and then opened the door. "Mom, we're home, and there are some people here!" she called. When she got no answer, she called out for her mother again, then shook her head. "Maybe they went somewhere and took mom's car." She went inside, and her brother scurried off to the garage.

Once they were out of hearing range, I pulled Arthur aside and told him the bad news about his ex son-in-law. "Please have your daughter call me as soon as she can. It's very important that I talk to her," I said, handing my card to him.

"You know, this doesn't surprise me. I never really liked Don. I always had the feeling he was just waiting to stab me in the back," Arthur confessed. "If it was like the old days and he actually asked for her hand in marriage, I wouldn't have given it. I just never found him very...honorable. Hell, he's not even tolerable most of the time."

"You're not the first person to tell me that," I said. "Unfortunately, as badly as we need to speak with him, it looks as if he left the country. We think—"

"Hey, Mom's car's still in the garage," Jeremy interrupted, running back to where we stood.

I felt a twinge in my gut, and it only grew worse when I heard a muffled scream coming from the open front door. Crystal and I both ran toward the house and inside. We found Lacy sitting at the top of the stairs, shaking her head and sobbing.

I took the stairs two at a time. When I reached her, I instinctually checked to see if she was hurt. "What's the matter, honey?" I asked, even though I was already sure what the answer was going to be.

She did not say a word and only pointed a trembling hand toward an open door at the end of the hall.

Jeremy started up the stairs, but Crystal, sensing that something bad had happened, grabbed him before could go any farther. "You stay here with Grandpa," she said, then walked Jeremy over to Arthur and looked into the old man's eyes.

"No! Let me go!" Jeremy shouted, but Arthur put his arms around his grandson's shoulders and held him tight, even as his own wrinkled eyes filled with knowing tears.

Crystal climbed the stairs and sat down with Lacy. She put her arm around the hysterical child.

Lacy buried her face in Crystal's shoulder and continued to cry. "Mom's dead. She's really d-dead," she panted out between sobs and sniffles.

"What!?" Jeremy yelled and began to cry as his grandfather tried to console him.

I walked into the bedroom, unsure of what I would find. As I looked through the door, I saw what had devastated the young girl who, just moments before, didn't have a care in the world. There were two people sitting in a king-sized bed, collapsed over one another, with bullet holes in their foreheads, the woman staring lifelessly at the wall.

Since it was obvious that both were dead, I backed out of the room, making sure I touched nothing, and called it in. I met Crystal still trying to console Lacy, and frowned. We helped the girl to her feet and walked her down the stairs. As we met Arthur at the bottom, I shook my head, and a tear escaped the corner of his eye. "I'm sorry," I whispered with a frown on my face.

After Crystal and I walked them from the house, I called Vernon to inform him of the situation. "Get Meecham here ASAP," I said.

The Indianapolis police were first to arrive. I identified myself, and with the surveillance agent's help, we directed them stay out of the house but to form a perimeter. "Watch where you step and keep an eye out for anything suspicious, but do not touch anything. I repeat, do not touch anything. This may have links to a case we've been investigating, and we need to wait for our forensics."

A half-hour later, Meecham arrived. I told him what I found in the bedroom, and he and Crystal disappeared into the house. As they went through the door, Meecham handed her his camera. The list of attendees seemed to grow by the moment, and soon, the coroner, more detectives, and our FBI forensics team were there.

Even though Mrs. Calder's neighborhood was a lot farther up the social ladder than Calder's in Cincinnati, the looky-loos were the same. They gathered in groups, whispering and speculating and trying to find out what it was their neighbors had done. They were probably wondering why their peaceful neighborhood, with its perfectly manicured lawns, was now tainted with FBI and police. It wasn't long before the news vans arrived and joined the ever-growing throng pushing against the crime scene tape.

Chapter 44

We were back at the Indianapolis field office at nine a.m. sharp on Tuesday for a highly anticipated meeting. I invited Bradford, Beckman, and Pembrook to sit in. I figured I owed it to them, and I also wanted and respected their opinions.

After a short intro by Special Agent in Charge Chuck Harris, Meecham started off the meeting. "The cause of death for both was a single shot to the head, with a .22 caliber. We believe they were surprised during sex, and she was on top. We found her urine mixed with the seminal and vaginal fluids on Reynolds. Based on the position of the bodies, we believe the killer surprised her, and she hurried to move against the headboard, as did Reynolds. It is clear that Reynolds was shot first, and his head fell into her lap. Mrs. Calder was shot soon after and collapsed on top of him. We've established that the time of death was sometime Friday night. As close as we can determine, it was likely between eight p.m. and one a.m." He paused, then continued, "'Our forensics team carefully combed the house and found no evidence of any intruder, no forced entry, and nothing left behind by the shooter. The police who interviewed the neighbors discovered no witnesses either."

"What about Calder's home in Cincinnati?" Bradford asked.

"We tore the place apart and found nothing to indicate his specific location. We also came up empty on anything connecting him to the predator killings or the attempt on the president's grandbaby."

When Meecham finished, it was time for Vernon to follow up. "It looks as if he killed them the evening before he left the country. He boarded the plane in Cincinnati to Rio de Janeiro at seven a.m. Saturday morning and arrived in Rio at noon, Eastern Time. Our people in Rio claim he just disappeared. They found a taxi driver who seemed to recognize his photo, but he was not 100 percent positive. The cabbie said he drove that man into the city, but the passenger told him to let him out on a busy street. This cannot be substantiated, and there is no other trace of him after he left the airport. We also reached out to the Brazilian Federal Police. They have agreed to help us in our investigation."

As Vernon continued, videos of Calder entering the terminal in Rio and exiting the airport played behind him on the smartboard. He went on for a while longer, then gave the floor to Marty, who had been hooked in from the Fortress of the Technodude. Marty did not look like the normal geek, as he almost always wore a suit and tie, and not the hipster, skinny-pants type either. His fashion sense was well known at Quantico, and I suspected that was one reason he was so successful with the ladies.

"There has been no activity on any known account owned by Calder," Marty said. "The last transaction was at seven p.m. at the BP on Montgomery Road in Cincinnati, about one hour and a half after he went to his ex-wife's house to ask for forgiveness. It is unclear whether that desire to be forgiven was a ploy or that something happened between his meeting them and killing them later on that evening. At 11:20 p.m., reservations were made on Sandra Calder's computer for a one-way flight from Cincinnati to Rio de Janeiro, using Sandra's credit card. As Meecham mentioned, we did find Calder's fingerprints on his ex-wife's credit card. One other thing I found was that Calder made a trip to Rio once before, about a month ago. He paid cash, which is why it took me so long to find it. I have contacted the agents on location in Rio, as well as the federals, and asked them to be on the lookout for any wealthy American who's set up residence there or in the surrounding area in the last month. Hopefully, our man will stick out like a sore thumb. That is pretty much all

I have right now. We will continue to monitor his financials. If he uses his credit card or anything connected to him, we'll know immediately."

Once Marty finished, the floor was open for questions, and I was the first to oblige. "We can assume Calder is using an alternate identity, with identification, possibly more than one. We can also assume he's staying at some alternate residence that may contain evidence of his crimes. Finding these might be impossible, and we may require luck, especially if he's out of the country. Although I can't say why, I believe he'll eventually find a way to reenter the United States and try to finish what he started."

"What do you mean by that, Kroh?" Bradford chimed in, arching an eyebrow.

"Well, he may not make an attempt on the president, due to the security that surrounds him, but I'm a different story. For some reason, he focuses a great deal of hatred on me. I believe at first, the only reason he killed the child predators was to lure me into an investigation, to involve me with his sick little game. He led us straight to Anderson, then completely blindsided us when he left the bodies of Munson and Miller downtown. He wants me dead, but most of all, he wants to prove he's smarter than me, if only to prove it to himself. Now, I don't know about the rest of you, but I find it very hard to believe that anyone could hate little ol' me so much as to want to kill me. I'm a thoroughly likable guy, right?"

Someone in the room offered one of those pretend coughs to thinly veil his "Bullshit," and everyone laughed, including me.

"Okay, okay, but at least we can all agree that Calder is one sick-ass son-of-a-bitch."

"Now I'd bet on that," said Bradford.

"But what... God, how could a man use children like that? I mean, they think he's their hero, and he's just a psychotic manipulator with grudges to settle," Crystal asked. "And what about his own kids? He killed their mother, for God's sake, left her there for his own little girl to find."

"I told you, he's sick. In his mind, he really does see himself as The Guardian, the savior of the known universe."

"What?" Pembrook asked.

"I'm sure he believes his children are better off without the influence of his ex-wife. He probably expects them to thank him one day," I offered.

"It's hard to believe that a mind could go that far off track," Chuck Harris said, shaking his head.

"I'm with ya there," I agreed.

We spent the next two hours brainstorming. Many excellent points were discussed, but we knew none of that would ultimately matter if we didn't get some kind of a break in the case. What we really needed was for Calder to make a mistake. The chances of that were slim, but it was the only way we would be able to move forward.

* * *

The meeting broke up around noon, and I suggested that we head back toward Anderson and stop at the Kroh's Nest for lunch. Beckman and Pembrook joined us, and I was thrilled to introduce them to Pops. After a delicious lunch, we headed for the Anderson PD. Beckman and Pembrook decided to stick with us for a while, because they were not quite ready to let the case go, so they found lodging to stay in Anderson overnight and head back in the morning.

While the rest of the gang went into the conference room, I decided to have a word with Bradford. I knocked on the door, sat across from him, and pouted.

"At least we know who we're looking for," Bradford offered, trying to cheer me up. "Never in a million years would I have suspected Calder."

I knew it was next to impossible, but I was still kicking myself in the ass for not seeing the connection earlier. "It was right there in front of me all along. Our unsub has an amazing ability to plan, he knew details about The Fingertip Killer case that were not made public, and he definitely has major bones to pick with the president and me. If I had only put two and two together, we could have grabbed Calder before he killed his wife and left the country."

"Be honest with yourself, Kroh. There's no way in the world you could have figured this out any sooner, not with what little we had to go on."

"Yeah, I guess. I think what really bothers me is that he had me running around like a trained seal, baiting me every step of the way. The murders, the 111-mile carrot, and then the display of Miller and Munson... Those were nothing less than genius, all for my benefit. He wants...no, *needs* to show that he's better than me. I think it stems from the time I jumped his ass in front of everyone at the Indy field office. You heard about that, right?"

"Yeah, Crystal told me," Bradford said, smiling at the thought. "I wish I would have been there. The look on his face must have been priceless."

"It was. Anyway, I got to tell you, he's the worst kind of criminal. He's got an FBI background and a working knowledge of how we operate. He excels at planning, and he's apparently bank-rolled."

"Good."

"Good? What's that supposed to mean?" I asked, wrinkling my brow in confusion.

"It means it'll feel damn good to catch the bad guy this time," Bradford said as he stood and walked to the door. "Now let's get to it, shall we?"

We joined the others in the conference room and got busy trying to figure out our next move. After two hours, we decided to call it quits for the evening and made plans to meet at the local casino for a little down time and a few drinks.

With Calder out of the country, everyone relaxed a little. I bought the first round, and we all settled in for what turned out to be a thoroughly enjoyable evening.

Chapter 45

I was in a rush to get back to Quantico, as I knew there was paperwork to tend to on my current case, as well as others that required my attention. I decided to take the rest of the week off and head back to DC on Sunday, but a nagging feeling of dissatisfaction continued to bother me. *Calder committed all those crimes and just left the country? Where's the justice in that?*

By Wednesday, I needed to let off a little steam, so I started up a pick-up game at General Pulaski Park on 38th Street in Anderson. Crystal and Vernon were drafted for my team, and our opponents were Bradford, Zee, and Pops. I made the mistake of mentioning how old Bradford and Pops were, and they proceeded to kick our asses from one end of the court to the other. Pops made a few three-pointers that left me dazed and confused. I had forgotten how good he was, and I was genuinely surprised by Bradford's athletic prowess as well.

When Zee came in for a layup, I wasn't able to plant my feet in time to block, and the petite woman knocked me right on my ass as she moved in to shoot.

"Foul! Foul! Mr. Bradford, Zee is being mean to me."

Bradford looked at me, then at Zee. He raised his arms toward me, palms out. "Leave me out of this. You're on your own."

Pops reached out and helped me up. "Buck up, Benjy. Quit being a pussy and play ball."

He only called me Benjy when he was trying to get my goat, and as I caught a glimpse of his shit-eating grin in the

Die by Proxy

afternoon sunlight, a grin I obviously inherited from him, I couldn't help but smile. After that, we made up some ground, but we ultimately lost when Pops swished it in for another three.

I invited everyone to Gene's Root Beer for some postgame refreshments on me, but Bradford and Pops turned me down, stating they had better things to do than hang out with a bunch of losers.

"Good, because I didn't want you sweaty old cow bastards in my car anyway," I teased.

Pops pulled me into a big bear hug, sweat and all.

"Jeez, Pops, now I'm gonna have to take a shower," I complained, trying to shake my way free. After he let me go, I gave him another hug, and we walked him to his car. "Love you, old man."

Zee, Crystal, Vernon, and I piled into my car. We parked at Gene's, and when the carhop came, we ordered a feast. By myself, I devoured two kraut dogs, one Coney with no onions, and a large root beer. After dinner, I took Zee and Vernon back to their car, and Crystal and I headed to her place.

* * *

Calder watched as Kroh and friends played their silly game, like a bunch of children, their sneakers screeching annoyingly on the asphalt. He walked along the path not more than twenty feet away. He was now Jonathon Fuller, a 67-year-old retired autoworker. He walked with a bit of a limp, helped along by the rock he had placed in his shoe. As he gimped along, he marveled at his ability to be anyone, to go anywhere he pleased, without the fear of being recognized. *If only I would have brought my gun, I could kill them all right here and now,* he thought.

He continued down the path, until he reached his car. He thought about making another pass but decided it was best to return to his farmhouse. While he was at the park, he did glean one useful bit of information, and he made a mental note of it: *Kroh will head back to DC Sunday night.*

* * *

That evening, I sat with Crystal, watching *Criminal Minds,* a show loosely based on our reality. As we watched, I wished that our real cases could so easily be solved in the span of a couple days, with everything wrapping up so neat and tidy. Although some did come together pretty quickly, most took far longer. It was job security in the worst of ways.

Just as the credits started to roll, Marty called, spawning my ringtone for him, Johnny Preston's "Running Bear." It seemed perfect, as the song was about two star-crossed lovers from opposing tribes who were also separated by a raging river. When they attempted to brave the current to be together, they met, kissed, and were pulled into their deaths by the undertow. It was as beautiful as it was tragic, quite like the news Marty often gave me.

"Hey, Marty, what's up?"

"We may have some good news on the Calder front. Seems one of his cards was used to buy a pie from someplace called Braz Pizzaria in São Paulo, Brazil. The same card was used to buy a laptop an hour later, also in São Paulo. Unfortunately, security cameras aren't common in those parts, but the feds down there are checking both locations and talking to potential witnesses. We should know something within the hour. I'll keep you posted."

"Hmm. It looks like our boy is a real jet-setter, on the move. Thanks, Marty."

"You got it, Boss, but damn. Now I want pizza!"

Chapter 46

I called one more meeting at the field office in Indianapolis, as I wanted to deliver a bit of a profile I worked up on Calder. It wasn't complete, but it would serve to help everyone understand what motivated the man to do his dirty deeds. As I did with all the cases that crept across my desk, I did my best to put myself in Calder's shoes, tried to think the way his decrepit mind would. Although the former agent had gone completely off the rails, I understood what drove him to do things that he had done. "It's hard for me to believe Calder will stay away for long. I know he's got unfinished business stateside, and I'm a major part of it. He's not gonna bump into me in Brazil anytime soon. Calder's a detail-oriented person, a planner. He must be in control. In fact, that is what ultimately ended his FBI career.

"When I was placed in the lead on The Fingertip case, he saw that as a threat to his advancement to directorship. Instead of relying on the expertise of the very capable agents at his disposal, he chose to micromanage every aspect of the case. In his mind, he could not afford any mistakes. When I was put in charge, it didn't sit well with his control freak tendencies. That loss of control over the investigation pushed Calder out of his comfort zone. In his desperation, he proceeded without a plan, and there was a high price to pay. Any chance of him becoming director of the FBI was gone in a flash of reckless impulse.

"I know he's already planned his revenge, down to the last gory detail. Something has broken in his mind, but he's still very clever. He aims to punish the people who have wronged him, and that desire has overpowered his common sense. He has all the money he will ever need and an entire world in which he can disappear, with an unknown number of identities to help him do it. Nevertheless, he won't leave things undone. It is likely unfathomable to him to let me and the president get away with it, as he would see it.

"There are three things Calder must do before any other life is possible. First, he must deal with the man in the White House. As for a little history, if not for President Burns, Calder would have probably taken over his father's Chevy dealerships and found a good life selling cars, but that was not to be. He met John Burns in middle school, and they somehow clicked. By the time they reached high school, they were best friends.

"I can only imagine how it must've bothered him to watch his best friend become the most powerful man in the world. Although he will never admit it, and maybe he doesn't even realize it, at some point in their lives, Calder began to see the president as little more than a means to an end. He decided to ride that horse for all he was worth, but when he screwed up The Fingertip case, that ride was abruptly cut short. All Calder sees is that his best friend failed and betrayed him, and he needs to punish him. He believes his former buddy chose to abandon him when he needed him most. In Calder's mind, this is unforgiveable.

"Then there are his kids, Lacy and Jeremy. He does not have the same paternal instincts as others. What coaxes him to hold his kids close is his desire for control. When his wife divorced him and took the kids away from him, he was no longer in a position to influence their destinies. He could not let that continue, so he remedied the problem by killing their mother. Although I am sure he loves them, that distorted love will always come second to his need to be in control.

"Finally, there's me. As I mentioned before, Calder has seen me as a threat from the beginning, someone beyond his control. He saw me as an adversary rather than a colleague. From the start, he attempted to belittle any of my contributions to the case. To Calder, I was a wildcard, someone capable of destroying his reputation and ruining his image. Once I was made lead on The Fingertip case, I attempted to mend fences by telling everyone Calder was still in charge, but it was apparently too little, too late. From that moment on, he was in damage-control mode, desperate to shine the spotlight on himself again. That drove him to hold that ill-timed news conference, in which he told the world that The Fingertip Killer was no longer a threat, something else he holds me responsible for. He thinks I set him up, and now he wants me dead. What is it about me? People either love me or want to put a bullet in me. Surely no one in this room has any reason to not adore me...do you?"

Almost every arm shot up, and the laughter began.

Feigning hurt, I said, "Fine. I'm taking names." I looked over at Crystal, Bradford, Zee, and Vernon, whose arms seemed to be raised the highest. "*Et tu, Brute?*"

After the laughter finally died down, I had to drive home one more important point. "As I said when I started this, Calder will not stay away long. I have nothing to support it, but I sense he's already here."

"Hmm. Do you sense that the Force is strong in that one too?" Vernon teased, chuckling again.

"Very funny," I said. "All I'm saying is that we need to err on the side of caution. I am asking each and every one of you to be mindful, always aware of your surroundings and the people you come across. If anyone seems too interested in the case, if a vehicle feels out of place, or if anything raises the hair on the back your neck, discreetly check it out. We can't afford to spook him, but we need to capture his sick ass before he hurts anyone else. Does everybody understand?"

Everyone nodded.

"I know this has been a long road, folks, but I feel good about our chances now. While Calder is meticulous in his planning, he is still functioning under delusion. Hopefully, this will be his undoing, and we'll be there to catch his first mistake."

Again, the room was filled with nodding heads, everyone as resolute to find our killer as I was.

"I am heading back to DC on Sunday. Since Calder is

apparently out of the country, there were a few other cases on my desk that need my attention, but I won't be backing down on this investigation by any means. Just remain focused and review the evidence we've collected, in case we missed anything. Calder should now be considered a threat to his own children, as well as the president of the United States. Although I joked earlier about being a target, I am not as worried about myself as I am for my friends and family. We cannot afford to rule out any possible clue to where this madman might be, so I thank you for your time and input."

What I didn't dare tell my friends and colleagues was that I felt like I was being watched. My life really was at stake, and that had me on edge, but I needed my team to be calm enough to do their jobs, and I knew they'd give it their best effort, as they always did.

* * *

Before leaving Indy, I decided to drop in on Lacy and Jeremy. I wasn't sure it was a good idea, since they'd so recently gone through a family tragedy, but there was something I wanted the little ones to know, especially Calder's darling daughter. I called ahead so they'd be expecting Crystal and me.

The kids moved in with their grandparents after our grisly discovery. Mr. and Mrs. Welch had a home even nicer than their daughter's, in the Geist area, just off 106th Street. I passed through the six-foot, white stone wall that stretched the length of the front of their property and traveled down the long driveway, at least 400 feet, till I was standing at their front door.

Arthur and his wife Beth met us at the door, looking very suspicious, and they had every right to be. After I told him what I wanted, he let us in. As Crystal went off with Beth, Arthur took me to his den. *Damn!* I thought, looking around. *If I ever shell out this kind of money for a house, I'm going to have a room just like this one.*

As soon as we sat down, a young woman, presumably their maid, walked in. "Can I do anything for you or your guests, sir?"

"Angie, honey, can you send Lacy in here?" he asked,

sounding more like her relative than her boss.

"Certainly, Arthur."

A few moments later, Lacy came through the door and looked at me like I was something right out of her nightmares. Considering that I was connected to such a bad memory, that I was the man she saw on the day she found her mother's dead, naked body, it was understandable.

"Lacy, sweetheart, Agent Kroh is here to talk to you. Is that okay?"

"I-I guess," she said softly, scowling at me.

"Would you like to be alone?" Arthur asked.

"No. I'd very much like you to stay."

"Good, because I wasn't going to leave anyway," Arthur said, with a slight smile.

"Lacy, I am not going to treat like a child. You are a young woman now, and you deserve to know the truth. Your dad is a very sick man. He has lost the ability to determine right from wrong. As hard as this is to believe, in his mind, he did this for you and your brother. I am not trying to excuse what he did, but I want you to know that no matter what he tells you, he is a very, very dangerous man."

"What happened to Da...to him? Why did he go crazy?"

My heart broke when she caught herself calling him by the name he once held in her heart. "I really don't know. I think a lot of things hit him all at once, and he couldn't handle the stress. Most people come to a crossroads in life, but not everyone chooses the path he has taken. He just...lost his way. You need to know that it was not your fault or Jeremy's, not even your mother's. There was nothing you could have done to prevent what took place."

"Am I gonna turn out like him?"

"No, not a chance. You are strong. Look what's happened to you, but you're making it through. You also have your grandparents. When I was young, my parents died in a car accident. If not for my grandpa and grandma, I wouldn't have done so well. Also, you've got one thing I didn't have."

"What?"

"A younger brother. Jeremy is going to need you now more than ever."

We talked for a while longer, and I hoped I gave Lacy a little something to help her make sense of her life in the aftermath of what her horrible father did.

As I was leaving, Arthur shook my hand. "Thank you, Agent Kroh."

"She's a strong girl. Just be there for her."

Back at the front door again, Lacy decided to walk us out.

"Remember what I said," I said, looking seriously into her eyes. We talked for a few minutes during the walk to the car, and I purposely took my time. Before I climbed into my car, I gave her as much advice as I could. "I'm here for you if you ever need to talk. I gave your grandpa my card. Call me anytime."

She nodded and gave me a hug, then turned to walk back to the door, sniffling a little.

"You're a good man, Kroh boy," Crystal said brushing the back of her middle finger across my cheek.

* * *

Pops decided to throw another get-together at the Kroh compound on Saturday, adults only. Although I loved having the kids around, it was really nice to relax with grownups for a while. That is not to say we had no fun; there was a swimming pool, after all, and the sight of Crystal in a swimsuit was almost as much fun as I could handle.

As I was sitting there talking to Vernon, Pops dribbled a basketball over to us. "Care for a quick butt-kicking before dinner, boys?"

"Are you sure you're up for it, old man?" I asked.

Instead of answering, Pops turned and made what would have been a half-court shot, nothing but net.

"Shit," I whispered in Vernon's ear.

After Pops, Bradford, and Zee spanked us again, Pops asked, "One more?"

"Can't you see were just letting you win?" I asked, panting.

He answered that with a basket from the free-throw line, not even looking.

I raised my hands in surrender. "Okay, okay. You win, Pops. We give up."

Die by Proxy

With that, I fell into the pool and enjoyed the rush of the cool water that washed away the heat of the game. In short order, everyone was splashing around beside me. For the next half-hour, we just fooled around, making the most of the pool on a hot summer day.

At five, it was steaks, burgers, dogs, and brew. I couldn't have imagined a better day, and it was clear that my grandma was going to miss me. It seemed like everywhere I turned, she was right there to tend to my every need. The one thing she couldn't do for me was catch Calder, but just for the day, I managed to shove him to the back of my mind.

Against my weak objections, Crystal and Bradford drove me to the airport. Once we arrived, Crystal headed to Starbucks, and I sat down to talk to Bradford.

"It's so hard to leave her," I said. "She makes me feel whole."

"Corny much?" Bradford asked.

"I can't help it."

When Crystal returned, Bradford winked at me and gave us our space until it was time for me to head to the plane. "Have a good flight, my friend," he said, shaking my hand.

Crystal kissed me hard, nearly spilling her latte in the process. "Call me when you get home, Kroh boy."

"Damn, I'm gonna miss you, girl," I said, then gave her one last kiss and headed for the plane.

Chapter 47

I sat in my den and marveled at the beauty of the layout. Of course, it was dominated by books and pictures of my parents and grandparents, as well as Noah's service and family pictures, Zee, Marty, and the newest, Crystal. It was also equipped with state-of-the-art electronics. Marty was responsible for creating a nerdvana of computer, television, and stereo equipment, and he somehow managed to keep the swarm of wires from dominating the warm and homey atmosphere.

My apartment was stylish, yet homey, and I spared no expense to make it my home. Truth be told, I tried to emulate the Marty style. Like his place, mine was the ultimate man cave, albeit without any outward signs of being one. My television was large but not huge. It could accommodate a football party of twenty and was still just right for a night alone. My kitchen was something a professional chef might envy. I was definitely not a great cook, but I wanted the best, just case I caught the bug.

I was lucky enough to have plenty of money, a lot more than the average FBI agent. Pops, wise as he was, invested the payout from my parents' life insurance, and while it wasn't much at the time, it had grown to over a million and a half. Once, a fellow agent that was a real asshole, said to me that I was a lucky man. I wanted to punch him in the face for that, because no amount of money was worth losing my parents, but I managed to somehow laugh it off.

The reason I returned on Saturday instead of Sunday was because Sunday was the day that my parents died so long ago. I could never help feeling down on that day, and I tried to use that day to reflect on my life and talk to them. The few memories I had of Mom and Dad were overshadowed by the loss of what might have been. Since my arrival in Washington, I had attempted to spend this day alone in my apartment, imagining them looking down from wherever they were and hoping they were proud of what their little boy became, of what I managed to accomplish in life.

I still felt the sadness and grief, but it used to be much worse. In those first few years following their deaths, I spent my time in my darkened room at my grandparents' place, frozen with grief. Then, one day, Pops came in to talk to me.

"How are you doing, boy?" he asked as he sat down on the bed next to me and put his hand on my shoulder.

"I miss them, Grandpa. I miss them so very much." I said as tears ran down my face.

"It's okay to miss 'em, son. I miss them too," he said, crying a few tears of his own.

"I'd give anything if they could be here now," I pleaded.

"Yeah, I know. I'd trade all my tomorrows for one single yesterday."

"What?"

"It's a line from a song by Janis Joplin, 'Me and Bobby McGee'."

I was surprised he even knew who Janis Joplin was, let alone that he remembered any lyrics from one of her songs. All that aside, it was exactly how I felt.

"It's okay for you to grieve, Benjamin, but you cannot let it rule your life. Your parents would not want that for you."

"I just want them back, Pops."

"I know, but you must remember one thing. The future is not set, no matter when it starts. Do you remember the stories your grandmother read to you about the genie and the three wishes?"

I shook my head.

"All the wishes backfired in some way."

"Yeah, so what's your point?" I asked wondering where he was going with the weird conversation.

"Okay, well, if you got your wish and your parents didn't

die that day, what would be to stop them from dying the next day or the one after that? Knowing how much it hurts; would you want to go through that again? I know I couldn't. I know you loved your parents beyond compare, son, but you need to start thinking about yourself. How would your parents feel if they saw you now?"

"I just miss them too much, Grandpa."

"Like I said, it's okay to miss your mama and daddy, but you mustn't let that define you. Don't dwell on lost time, on things you can't change. Just keep in your heart the moments you spent with them. Remember that the future starts after every passing moment. Make those starts count for something. Live every day to honor your parents, and you'll make them proud, okay?"

"Okay, Pops. I'll do my best," I said as I hugged him tight.

"That's all me or anyone else can ask," he said, and when he embraced me, I felt the world move forward.

It may sound simplistic, but the world changed for me that day. Although I still missed my parents greatly and always would, I still honored them on one special day every year, and I tried to live every day of my life to make them proud. Sure, I'd walked down a few wrong paths and made a few bad decisions, but for the most part, I'd led a good life.

As the sun went down in DC, I decided to do a little work. I studied the smartboard that was cleverly hidden by a giant picture of my favorite Warner Brothers character, Daffy Duck. All the info we had on Calder and the case was there before me. Still, no matter what scenario I plugged into the case, I didn't seem to be getting anywhere with it, so I called Crystal just to clear my head. "Hey, beautiful. I miss you."

"I miss you, too, James."

"What? Stop," I said, caught off guard for a moment.

"Oh. Kroh? I, uh... I knew it was you," she said, laughing nervously. "I, uh...miss you two."

I laughed. "If you don't stop that, I'll have to spank you when I see you again."

"Ooh. That sounds like fun, James. Why don't you come over right now? My boyfriend is out of town, so we'll have the place to ourselves."

"If you keep it up, I'll tell Larry."

"You wouldn't!"

"I would."

"Fine. You win," she finally agreed with a sweet giggle.

Even though I just left her, we had plenty to talk about. I looked at her picture and wished I was lying next to her right at that moment. We talked for about an hour, but we both had to work in the morning, so we said our goodbyes, and I reluctantly let her go. *God, I really love that girl,* I thought when I hung up, *corny or not.*

At eleven o'clock, I climbed in bed, but sleep completely eluded me. My mind just spun with thoughts of the trail of death that was Calder. Of course, there were the seven deviants, but I couldn't get too worked up about them. The three computer techs were a different story, and in a way, they made me think of Marty. That took him from being a vigilante to being a cold-blooded murderer. He had no intention of the president's grandbaby surviving, and he had no thought about what it would do to his children to find their mother with a bullet hole in her skull. What burned me the most among all the mayhem he had caused was that the crazy fucker almost killed Zee while aiming for me.

I knew Calder was out there somewhere, but I didn't have a clue where. I tossed and turned for hours, till I finally succumbed to physical exhaustion in the wee hours of the morning. I awoke feeling tired, as if I hadn't slept at all, and I walked into Noah's office like a stupefied zombie.

"What are you doing here? And why do you look like hell?"

"I just... I was thinking I should take care of some of the paperwork piling up on my desk."

"No, you stay on Calder. I'll deal with all that red tape bullshit for the filing cabinet. He needs to be your only case, your only focus. The director wants him captured ASAP."

"I'm doing my best, Noah."

"I know you are, but the director is *motivated*, if you know what I mean. The president calls him almost every day."

"I'm motivated, too, you know. That freak shot Zee, for

God's sake!"

"I know. That hurt us all."

"Noah, I really think Calder is here, in the States."

He looked at me for a moment. "Gut feeling, huh?"

"Yeah, but I also think I know a way to draw him out, like a damn fly to manure."

"How? Are you telling me you are volunteering to be our pile of cow shit?"

I wanted to laugh but was too exhausted to even muster half a smile. "Sort of. If I really degrade Calder, publicly and brutally, he might come after me again. Not only that, but I'd very much enjoy such an assignment at this point."

"Hmm. That sounds risky."

"If you can think of any other way, I'm more than glad to listen to it."

Noah thought for a moment. "In the words of a great starship captain, make it so."

"He's smart as hell, but he's also delusional. In his twisted head, he actually believes he is justified in what he's doing, that he really is a Guardian. That misguided arrogance makes him dangerous, and his brilliance in spy games makes him hard to find."

We talked for a half-hour more, some about the case, some about Crystal, and a lot about his family. I looked forward to putting a close on the case, so I could spend some time with them; the thought of chasing Juelle, around Noah's back yard made me smile, and smiling felt good because it was becoming harder and harder to do so.

Noah had one more thing to say as I got up to leave: "Just to reiterate, Calder is job priority one. That crazy fucker is one of our own. We need to shut him down now."

"Yeah, I didn't think he could hurt the Bureau any more than he did with the Fingertip faux pas, but he's doing it in spades."

"I'd like to take a spade to his face."

"So would I, Noah. So would I."

"Get back on the case and just forget the paperwork. Oh, did you get through yesterday okay?"

"Yeah, it was a good day. Thanks for asking. Tell Danielle

and Juelle I said hi," I said, then gave him a fist bump and left the office.

* * *

At two that afternoon, I was on a plane back to Indiana. As the world passed by beneath me, I composed my hate speech, full of truths but sprinkled with a little creative liberty and definitely some poetic justice.

I rested my head against the back of the seat and tried to relax to the hum of the plane engine. My mind was on overdrive, and all I could see when I closed my eyes was Calder's smug face. He had successfully led me along the path he had laid out for me. So far, everything had gone according to his plan. "That stops now!" I mumbled under my breath, hoping we could force Calder to make a mistake and give us the upper hand.

At six o'clock that evening, as the others sat in a conference room awaiting the broadcast of the evening news, I stood in another room not far away, one built for press conferences. There were at least fifteen reporters there, both local and national, eager to hear what I had to say. Those with cameras had signaled go, and those without had their digital recorders ready to catch everything I said. The journalists were practically salivating by the time I stepped up to the mic.

"I'm here tonight to an issue a warning about a man most of you know as The Guardian of I-69. The real name of this man is Donald J. Calder, and he is a former agent of the FBI," I said, and right on cue, a photograph of him appeared on the screen beside me, not a very flattering one at that. "Mr. Calder was, at one time, the special agent in charge of the Indianapolis field office. He has forsaken his duties to the people of the United States to pursue a sick, twisted reign of terror. Under the guise of The Guardian, he murdered and mutilated seven people and placed them along the interstate. As you all know, those victims were all child predators. As such, many believe we should leave him alone and just let him rid the world of harmful degenerates, but it is my job, and the job of the FBI, to stop him. Although some may disagree, justice is justice, and under the law, everyone deserves a fair trial. Mr. Calder is not entitled to dispense his own brand of vigilante justice on anyone, especially since he is guilty of multiple homicides himself.

"Something many of you may not know is that the so-called Guardian also savagely murdered three innocent computer technicians. He killed these unfortunate people merely to cover his tracks and nothing more. In addition to that, we have recently discovered other disturbing notches on his dossier of evil. Calder is responsible for the recent kidnapping attempt on the grandchild of our president of the United States, and we know he had no concern for the child's safety. Christopher is an innocent child who did this man no harm, except for the fact that he is related to President John Burns, yet Calder was willing to let him die."

With that, I paused for dramatic effect and to catch my breath, and I knew my revelations were hitting the audience like a fist to the face, especially when the photo of Calder was replaced with a picture of adorable little Christopher, looking as vulnerable and tiny as could be.

"It is known now that Donald Calder hired two men to take the baby. Luckily, due to the quick thinking of one of our agents, one of the would-be kidnappers was tricked into absconding with a mannequin instead. When the perpetrator arrived at the location chosen by Calder, a warehouse just outside Baltimore, an explosion killed the kidnapper, and it would have blown that child to bits. It is clear that killing the defenseless infant was Calder's plan from the beginning."

The picture of Calder appeared on the screen once more.

"Finally, Calder broke into his ex-wife's house and murdered her and a male friend. These two murders bring Calder's total body count to thirteen. Donald Calder is 39 years old, five-eight, around 157 pounds, with blue eyes and blond hair, but he is often disguised with a bad brown toupee and a mustache. He is cleverly deceptive and should be considered armed and extremely dangerous. If you see this man or anyone who might be him, do not approach him. Please call the authorities right away, as we have initiated a nationwide manhunt to bring him to the right kind of justice. We thank you for your cooperation, and please stay safe out there, folks."

I purposely left out the fact that Calder fled the country, for good reason. Most of all, I was certain he was still looming around the United States somewhere, but it was also because I needed the general public to believe he was in their midst. I knew that would make it harder for him to move about freely, something like a version of the wanted posters they used to post in Old West post offices that had the local sheriffs and saloon girls on high alert.

When I opened the floor for questions, the first came from a pretty reporter from Channel 7. "Agent Kroh, "You referred to Calder as sick and twisted. What do you think turned him from a respected FBI agent to a crazed serial killer?"

"I really can't speak to the reasons, but I do know he has endured a stressful couple of years, with a demotion in the FBI, a bitter divorce and the death of his father."

I fielded a few more questions from the other reporters, and then I pointed to Zach Tanner.

"Mine is a two-part question. First, we've been on a bit of a rollercoaster ride when it comes to The Guardian murders targeting child predators. Do you know his motives in choosing to murder, mutilate, and display those individuals? Second, we know Mr. Calder has children. Are they in danger?"

"As to why he chose those particular victims and why he placed them in such a grotesque way along I-69, I can only speculate that he found them with the help of three unsuspecting computer techs. I suppose if he chose different computer shops, our list of victims might have been different."

Up to that point, I'd offered factual information peppered with opinion, but it was finally time for that creative liberty, so much so that I had to fight the urge to put my hand behind my back and cross my fingers as I said, "To answer your second question, Zach, Calder's children were gone for the weekend. There is evidence that he searched both of their rooms, in an attempt to find them. We believe that if his son and daughter were home at the time, they would have met the same fate as their mother and her guest."

Then, it was time to drop the straw that would have the camel screaming about his back, and I felt I needed to put *both* my hands behind my back to cross my fingers or at least declare Scout's honor, since my lie was for honorable intentions. "As we have investigated Donald Calder," I said, "we have discovered that some or maybe all the child predators he killed were actually co-conspirators in child exploitation in which he was a participant. We believe Mr. Calder killed the computer technicians because they threatened to expose him. We believe his being a child molester stems from abuse suffered at the hands of his father. When his father died, his hatred had to be directed elsewhere, and it is our best guess that he aimed to punish his father through the sick, twisted deaths of the seven Guardian victims.

"I urge each and every one of you to visit the FBI website and check out our ten most wanted. There, you will find a summary of Calder's crimes, a description of him, any known aliases, and photos depicting possible disguises. We are currently offering a reward of up to $200,000 for information leading to the arrest of Donald J Calder. I want to caution you once more that Calder is a very dangerous sexual predator. If you know anything about his whereabouts, please call the FBI or your local police. Do not attempt to apprehend him on your own, because it is highly likely that he is armed and absolutely true that he is very dangerous. Thank you."

The reporters continued firing questions at me as I walked away from the microphone, but I finished what I was there to do. I really hoped Calder was watching this live, because I really wanted to hit him where it hurt now, rather than sometime later, while watching it on replay.

Chapter 48

Safely hidden at the Posner Farm in Indiana, Calder watched Channel 3 as he ate dinner. He had grown quite fond of Zach Tanner's reporting style, but he almost knocked over a TV tray and his dinner when he heard the teaser that promised, "Join us for a news conference with Special Agent Benjamin Kroh, of the FBI." He pushed the tray aside and leaned forward waiting to see his archenemy. *He really is my archenemy,* Calder mused.

Calder actually smiled throughout the first portion of Kroh's speech, as if the man was giving a speech about his many accomplishments. *Everyone I killed deserved to die, no matter what anyone believes.* He thought back to each and every murder, and among them, the sweetest of all was the death of his ex-wife. "And that brainless boyfriend of hers," Calder said, laughing out loud.

His mirth was short-lived though. When the Q&A began, Agent Kroh's answers to Tanner's probing questions had Calder's smile doing a 180. "How dare you say that about my children, you motherfucker! I did it all because I love them, more than anything," he shouted at the television.

He was so upset about the accusation that he planned to murder his offspring that he barely registered Kroh's inference to him being a child predator himself. He had already used that ploy before, in an attempt to piss Calder off, but now he was over it. Then came the words that set him off.

When Kroh blatantly lied to the world about him being molested by his father, Calder went ballistic. In fact, he didn't hear a word after that. His bourbon hit the wall and showered shards of glass and liquid all over the television. He kicked the TV tray, and his dinner hit the floor.

"My dad was a saint!" Calder screamed. "I'm gonna kill you, Kroh! How dare you, you lying motherfucker? Goddamn you! Goddamn you to hell! You don't know a damn thing about my father. That man was a saint, more of a man than you'll ever be!"

After the initial flood of anger subsided, Calder settled into a time of thoughtful hate. "I don't care what you say about me, but you will not get away with slandering my dad's good name. It's time for you to die, Kroh," he said, every word coming out in a growl.

Calder's sense of revenge went into overdrive, and he no longer cared if he was caught, just as long as he killed Kroh before they locked him in the slammer. His hope was that he could somehow take Kroh without being caught, and then kill his friends one by one. Most of all, he wanted Kroh to suffer.

Another thought came to him in that instant, as sinister plans began to roll through his demented mind: *I'll cut of his hands, just like I did to those molesters. Of course, I won't let him bleed to death though. He'll feel the pain as long as possible. Maybe, just for kicks and to remember old times, I'll cut his fingertips off first.*

For the rest the evening and all through the night, Calder *drank his scotch and thought* of nothing but the unavoidable death of Kroh. He was too bent out of shape go to bed, and he decided to save sleep for some other time.

He fought the urge to drive past Crystal's house, since he knew Kroh was there. He also knew there was a strong chance that the agent was just waiting for him to do something stupid. Kroh wanted to drive him mad, to force him into making a mistake, but he refused to give the man that satisfaction.

"I've got time," he convinced himself. "I just have to come up with a plan, a plan they'll never forget." Soon, the result of too much alcohol deteriorated his thoughts from revenge to happier days. What he longed for more than anything in the world was to be a child again, to be held by his father and told everything would be okay, but now Kroh had tarnished those memories. With anger and sadness flooding his soul, former Agent Donald J. Calder, The Guardian of I-69 and the infamous Mr. Smith, bawled like a baby, shedding the tears of someone who was utterly alone and hated all over the world.

* * *

I was not sure I hit the mark, but I was reasonably confident. I knew the part about Calder's children would strike a nerve, because in his own twisted way, he loved them. After all, in his mind, the killing of their mother was to set them free.

Whether Calder's saw the broadcast live or watched a rerun, I also knew the bit about his father would set him on fire. Once we started investigating Calder, it was clear that he placed his dad on a pedestal. As I thought back, I remembered that he had several pictures of the man, his hero, hanging in his office, and I knew they were very close.

In spite of Calder's offenses, I had no doubt that his father was a genuinely decent man. I felt a twinge of regret for saying the evil things I said about him, but Calder had to be stopped. I truly believed we would only catch him by stretching the truth to drive him nuts, so he would do something foolish. I hoped the lies I told to the world would unnerve him enough to render him vulnerable, just long enough for us to slap the cuffs on him.

I walked into the conference room and was surprised to hear a round of insincere applause, followed by laughter. "All right, all right. Settle down," I said, a bit embarrassed by the accolades.

"I laughed. I cried. Then I threw up a little," Meecham said, taking a bow. "God, I hope I never have to witness such bad acting again."

That remark was followed by more laughter, and I had to thank my lucky stars that the room was soundproof, so the media wouldn't overhear the punch line and report at eleven that the whole thing was a ruse.

"Thanks, Paul. It's good to know I can always count on your support. Let me know if you'd like an autograph."

After all the excitement died down, we settled in to discuss what we needed to do going forward. Well aware that we'd stirred up a proverbial hornet's nest, I asked for security details for Crystal, Bradford, Zee, Vernon, and my grandparents, even though the security system we installed at their house was enough to protect the president. I wasn't willing to take any chances with my friends' and loved ones' lives. "Don't be surprised if the teams gain a little weight," I warned. "I'm sure my grandmother will treat them to a lot of delicious home cooking." Of course, there was already a team assigned to me, since the biggest bull's-eye was on my back.

The vehicle I drove toward Anderson was equipped with everything needed to protect all occupants from an all-out attack. The glass could withstand armor-piercing bullets, the body was armor plated, and the tires were Kevlar reinforced. Although it drove well, it did feel a little heavy, like a tank when we took the curves.

We'd had a busy, stressful day, so Crystal and I decided to stay in for the evening. I ordered pizza and a roast beef sandwich from Arts Varsity Pizza and made arrangements for one of the agents to pick it up for us. Fifty minutes later, an agent, dressed like a pizza delivery boy and driving some old beater, delivered our feast. The 'Round the World pizza was truly something to behold, and the Italian roast beef was the best sandwich I'd ever had, so juicy that I had to eat my half with a knife and fork.

After dinner, we settled down on the couch to cuddle and watch a little television. Even though I was in greater danger than I had been since my military days, it felt great to just relax. It had been a while since I could watch *Castle*, one of my favorite shows, a crime thriller about a mystery writer who shadowed a female police detective for research for a heroine in his crime writing. While shadowing the detective, he also became an integral part of solving crimes. The star of the show, Nathan Fillion, also acted in a sci-fi Western called *Firefly*. Both of those roles were adults deeply in touch with their inner child, and I just loved to let the plots carry me away from my everyday crime drama. Crystal, who had never heard of either show before she met me, caught up quickly, and was excited as I was to watch.

Afterward, we decided to head to bed. After brushing and mouth washing the last remnants of pizza and roast beef out of my breath, I kissed her deeply, and it was nice to feel that she was as into it as I was, because she pushed her body against mine and held me tight. "Wait a second, missy," I said when I pulled away. "Aren't you afraid the agents outside will hear the screams of joy?"

"If you weren't such a little girl, they wouldn't hear any screaming, would they?" she retorted, then kissed me again, springing Larry to life.

Around two o'clock, we took a quick shower, and decided to get some sleep. Snuggled in Crystal's arms, I slept like a baby for the next six hours.

I awoke feeling more rested than I had in a long time, and we showered and prepared for another day. We showered together a lot, probably two or three times a day, and I wondered what kind of an effect that had on her water bill.

"What's with that stupid grin, Kroh?" she asked as I climbed into the car. "You look like the Cheshire Cat."

"I was just thinking."

"Does it hurt that much?" she teased.

"No. I was thinking about…sex and water."

"What?"

"How much does your water bill go up when I'm in town?"

"Oh, I don't care. It'd be worth it at twice the price," she said, then winked at me, slid her hand up my thigh, and greeted Larry.

I had to force myself to keep driving to the Anderson PD. Everything in me wanted to turn around, go back, and take another shower.

Chapter 49

Although I wanted Calder to try to kill me, I knew he was too clever to do it without a plan. He was bat-shit crazy, but he was also functionally intelligent, almost frighteningly so, like all infamous serial killers. I hated that he was right up there with the Bundys and Dahmers and BTKs and Gacys and Fingertips of the world, because it made him all the more difficult to catch. For that reason, it wasn't wise to stand around buck naked, blindfolded, and holding a "Kill me" sign up, because I still had a life to live. *And what a life it is, some crazy bastard always out to do me harm*, I thought, as that had been the case pretty much since my days in the military.

That thought reminded me of my first brush with death. I was just 18 when a guy, who thought I had done him wrong, shit-faced drunk or high, pulled up next to me in a van, pointed a pistol at my head, and threatened to shoot me. Since I didn't really know what his problem with me was, I simply said, "If you're going to do it, just do it." Then, after waiting a moment that seemed like forever, I turned and walked away, still expecting a shot that never came. I never saw that guy again, but the experience made me realize that some things were out of my control and could only be faced head on. Such was the case with former Agent Calder.

As I was about to walk into my office at the PD, I saw Zach Tanner coming out of Bradford's. "Nice performance at that news conference, Kroh," he said as he slapped me on the back.

"Thanks...I think."

"You laid it on pretty thick. From what I remember about Calder, that'll push him to the brink."

"Well, that's the plan."

"And here you are, just reporting to another day at the office. Aren't you a little scared?"

"Zach, to tell you the truth, I'm more terrified now than I was in Kosovo. There, I was with a group of guys whose two priorities were to protect each other and to complete the mission. Here, my family and friends are possible targets, and that scares the shit out of me."

"I hear ya there, my friend."

We shook hands, and he headed out of the building, but I quickly called after him, "Zach, it might be wise to lie low for a while. Whatever you do, just be careful."

"Yeah, I will," Zach said, then hurried to his van, darting his eyes around the parking lot in both directions.

Back in my makeshift office, I put my feet up at my desk and fired up my tablet, only to be summoned by Marty's ringtone. "Hey, Marty. What's up?"

"Are you sitting, Kroh? We got some news from South America, and it's not particularly good."

"Lay it on me."

"Well, the authorities in São Paulo grabbed the guy who tried to use Calder's credit card to withdraw some cash from an ATM. From what I gathered; the man found Calder's wallet on a bus headed from Rio de Janeiro to São Paulo. He figured he struck gold, all the cash and cards of some rich gringo."

"Great. Obviously, Calder left the wallet on the bus intentionally, hoping a thief would find it and throw us off his trail."

"Mission accomplished."

"Well, in a way, it is good news."

"It is? How so?"

"At least we know his life and identity as Donald Calder are over now. He has to have a different appearance and name."

"But he could be anyone, anywhere in the world."

"I know but what he wants is here, especially after that news conference that made him and his Daddy Dearest look so shady. My gut tells me he's close by, biding his time until he figures a way to kill me."

"Hey, Boss, if he does kill you, can I have your Monte Carlo? It'd go great with that fancy-ass phone the pres gave me."

"Gee, thanks a lot, asshole!" I said, smiling as I thought about one of my most prized possessions, my black, 1972 Monte Carlo with the Landau roof and 60-series tires all the way around. It was the first nice car I ever owned, a relic of my youth, and I worked plenty of nights and weekends at the Kroh's Nest, saving up my tips to buy it. It was still in pristine condition, my pride and joy, but it seemed everyone around me was always trying to get their hands on it. "I'm afraid you'll have to fight Noah for that one," I finally said before I hung up.

* * *

Although all the evidence we had, which wasn't much, pointed to Calder being out of the country, I knew he wasn't. He had become a very accomplished rogue agent, and his persistence and attention to minutiae made that transition possible. His micromanagement of his subordinates as a supervisory special agent and his meticulous planning for career advancement melted well into his life as a bat-shit crazy, vengeance-seeking killer.

I sat back on Crystal's couch, shut my eyes, raised my arms, willed my mind to reach out into the psychic void, and looked for any evil aura that resided in the central Indiana area.

A moment later, Crystal sat down beside me and slapped my stomach.

I jerked up, smiling sheepishly.

"What the hell are you doing?" she asked, looking at me as if I was the nut job.

"I-I was just connecting with my spirit guide, asking for some clue to where Calder is hiding."

"Should I be worried about you? Are you losing it? They have counselors at the Bureau if you need to talk to somebody."

I laughed; embarrassed that she caught me in the midst

of my desperation. In times when I had nothing, I often sent my mind out on field trips, in an attempt to focus my thoughts. The thought of him harming someone I loved tore me up inside, and desperate times called for those desperate measures, even if it made me look like a lunatic in front of my girlfriend. "Yes, you should be worried, and yes, I am losing it," I confessed. "We have to find Calder soon."

Crystal hugged me, then pulled my head onto her chest and patted it. "We will, sweetie. I promise we will."

One minute, I was thinking about a homicidal maniac, and in the next, my thoughts were completely captured by her beautiful breasts, where my face now rested as she stroked my hair. I am a man, after all, and beautiful breasts make everything all right, if only for a while.

Chapter 50

For days, Calder spent all his time obsessing about Kroh, imagining his murder in various ways. He decided that his plan had to meet four conditions. First, he had to lure Kroh to a location where he could incapacitate and take him safely. If that step failed, there would be no others.

The second part of the plan was to allow enough time that Kroh would suffer and suffer greatly. That part was vital to Calder, because he felt Kroh had caused him much pain. It was the easiest part of the plan because he already had the perfect venue to carry it out, the Posner farm just northwest of Indy. It was remote, far away from the nearest neighbor, and a perfect safe haven for the punishment he had to deliver.

The third part of his plan would be the most satisfying of all: *Kroh will die.* All the deaths that came before were merely means to an end, and Calder very much doubted he would ever kill again, since there would be no need. He would deal with the president, but he had other ways to make little Johnny suffer without resorting to an attempted assassination that would likely get him killed by the men in black.

The fourth part of the plan was another deal breaker. He had to be able to get away safely. He felt he deserved to live happily off his millions, to spend the rest of his days as a wealthy, free man. His dream of dreams was to have his children by his side.

Calder was in his element; planning was what he did best. Every phase of his grand scheme had plans within plans, steps upon steps, goals and mini-goals, scenarios within scenarios. Also, every aspect of what he was about to do was furnished with at least three contingency plans, in the event that things went south. The only part of the overall plan that vexed him was the first stage. Everything else, he could control. He had a place he could torture Kroh and killing him was a given. He would have to be careful, but getting away would ultimately be a snap. He just needed to find a way to lure Kroh to a location where he could safely take him without alerting his friends or the authorities.

On the third day, while watching *Jeopardy* and finishing his cup of microwave macaroni and cheese, he thought of something he hoped would work. His humble dinner brought back fond memories of little Jeremy sitting at the dinner table, laughing when Calder stole a bite of his pasta. That tender moment started a tradition of food theft at the dinner table, and Jeremy even ate his broccoli, if it could be pilfered from his dad's plate. Even as he smiled, the pain of their separation hurt him deeply, but those thoughts of his family brought on an idea, one with great potential.

For the rest of the evening, Calder thought of nothing else. "If I can pull this off, it will be perfect," he told himself, "and I will!"

* * *

Calder parked his car in a wooded area not far from his ex-in-laws' home, and then made his way through the trees and weeds that bordered the back of their property. As he crouched there in his camouflage clothes and watched the house, about a football field's distance away, a grasshopper landed on his knee. He caught it before it hopped away and held it by its hind legs. He studied it for a moment, then took it in his other hand and squashed it. He wiped the bug guts off his gloved hand on the grass beside him. *You will die no better, Special Agent Kroh,* he thought with a sickeningly proud smile, then returned his full attention to the task at hand.

At two thirty, he saw Arthur and Beth get in their brand-new Cadillac CTS-V and leave. His thoughts traveled back to the time when he wanted to buy a new Honda, but his father-in-law scolded, "You've got to buy American, boy. No daughter of mine is going to be seen riding around in a foreign car." At the time, he wanted to smack Arthur right across the face, but like a good little son-in-law, he settled on a Chevy SUV.

Calder knew Lacy and Jeremy would be picked up from gymnastics by their grandfather at three, so that gave him plenty of time. As soon as the car was out of sight, he sprinted across the back yard and entered the house through a back door he knew they always left unlocked, like the naïve, uppity, out-of-touch idiots they were. As he shut the door, he heard a sound behind him, the paws of a quickly approaching golden retriever. Calder had never liked Caesar, and the dog certainly didn't like him, so the deep, menacing growl was one Calder knew all too well.

Calder smiled at the animal in the doorway, then slowly raised his silenced semiautomatic and shot Caesar right above his right eye. A single yelp escaped the animal's mouth before he fell dead on the floor in a furry heap. The thought of Arthur finding his beloved pet lying in the growing pool of blood made Calder smile. "Good riddance, you fucking son-of-a-bitch!" he said as he stepped over Caesar.

He made his way through the house and stopped at the liquor cabinet to grab Arthur's favorite scotch. He sat in a chair that allowed him a perfect view of the long driveway and poured himself a drink. He downed it quickly and turned when he heard someone coming down the stairs, the maid, Angie. She let out a scream when she saw Calder sitting by the window, a man she'd always felt uneasy around.

"Get the fuck down here! Move!" he screamed, pointing the gun at her.

"Pease don't kill me!" Angie pleaded, hesitating to move.

"Shut up, bitch!"

Calder walked her into the family room, dragging one of the heavy dining room chairs with him. He forced her to sit down and zip-tied her to the chair, then taped her mouth shut, so she could not alert the unsuspecting family to her presence. Once she was secure, he moved tree more dining room chairs into the family room.

He went back into the front room and again took his

Die by Proxy

place by the window. He was pouring his next drink when he spotted the white Cadillac coming up the drive. The thought of administering the same fate to Arthur that he had administered to the dog put another grin on his face, but he quickly reminded himself of the plan. *Not yet, old man, not yet. I still need you to take care of Lacy and Jeremy a while longer. Soon though. Sooner than you think.*

When his kids and former in-laws entered the house, Jeremy bolted up the stairs. "I need to get my DS," he said, not even looking back.

As soon as her brother reached the top of the stairs, Lacy spotted her father standing in the corner, pointing a gun at them, and she literally jumped. "Daddy?" she said, her voice trembling.

"What the hell are you doing here, Don?" Arthur growled. "I'm calling the police."

When Arthur moved to make the call, Calder fired his gun into the ceiling, and his father-in-law stopped in his tracks. "Do as I say, old man, or, God as my witness, I'll shoot you where you stand." There was a finality in his voice that told Arthur he wasn't lying. "Into the family room...now!"

Arthur put his hand around his wife's waist and held Lacy close as they did what they were told. When they entered the family room, the first thing he noticed was Angie, strapped to one of the dining room chairs. Next to her were two more chairs.

"Arthur, you and Beth take a seat. Please don't make me shoot you."

Arthur and Beth reluctantly sat in the chairs.

"Lacy, I want you to zip-tie your grandparents like I did Angie."

"No! What the hell is the matter with you, Dad?"

"Do as I say, or so help me, I'll..." Calder put the muzzle of the gun next to Beth's temple. "Do it now!"

Lacy reluctantly did as she was told, trying very hard not to cry.

At that point, Jeremy walked into the room. "Hey, what's going on?" he asked, seemingly excited. "Hi, Dad."

"We're playing a game, little man. Here, put your headphones on and watch some videos. When it's your turn, I'll call you." It was quick thinking on Calder's part, and Jeremy seemed to accept it.

Once Jeremy was pacified, Calder turned to Lacy. "I'm going to the kitchen for just a moment. Please do not try anything, or I might be forced to do something neither of us wants. Understand?"

She nodded.

He turned and moved toward the kitchen.

Lacy watched as he leaned down to get something in the doorway to the kitchen. A moment later, he dragged the lifeless Caesar into the family room by his collar. Lacy's hand lifted to her mouth, and she let out a shrill scream. Strangely enough, that was the point when Lacy was truly done with her father. Even with all the evidence against him, her hope of her dad being innocent was on her mind, right up to the moment she saw him as a heartless man who would put a bullet in a helpless animal.

Calder dropped the dog on the light brown, plush carpet, right at Arthur's feet.

"Don, you are a monster!" Arthur screamed, with tears running down his face.

Jeremy was now completely confused by his feelings for his father. "Daddy, why?"

"Monster!" Arthur screamed again.

Jeremy ran to his sister and hugged her tight. She put her arm around him and tried to comfort him the best she could.

Calder poured himself another drink. "Arthur, this is some really good scotch. I would give you some, but...well, no." Then, after the initial shock of presenting the body of the family pet wore off just a little, Calder turned to Lacy. "Honey, I need you to do something for me. If you do exactly as I tell you, no one will get hurt, and I will be on my way."

* * *

At six o'clock, I was getting ready to leave the Indianapolis field office, but my phone rang with a call from a number I did not recognize. Knowing that we had asked the public to call with any information, coupled with the fact that I'd given

Die by Proxy

my card to several people lately, I knew it was best to answer it. "Hello?" I said.

"Agent Kroh?"

"Yes. Who's this?"

"This is Lacy, Lacy Calder."

"Oh, hi, Lacy. Is everything all right?"

"Yeah. I'm just... I was wondering if it'd be all right if we talk sometime. I didn't know who else to call. See, my grandparents are great, but when you told me about losing your parents, I knew you would know what to do and what to say. This is so hard to deal with."

"I'm glad to talk to you anytime, Lacy. I'm leaving work right now. Can I drop by in a little while?"

"Sure. I told Grandpa I planned to call you, and he said it was fine. I think he kind of trusts you. Thanks, Agent Kroh."

"You can just call me Kroh, Lacy. How is Jeremy doing?"

"Probably better than me," she said, then gave a weak laugh. "You know how kids are."

"Yeah, I know, but remember what I said. You're a strong young lady. Anyway, I'll see you in a few."

Chapter 51

After Lacy hung up the phone, Calder gave his daughter a hug, but it was clearly an embrace she didn't want, and she certainly made no effort to return the affection. In fact, the look of revulsion on the young girl's face made it obvious that her father made her skin crawl. Not only that, but his gun felt cold on her back.

"You did good, baby," Calder said. "I know you don't understand what's happening, but you soon will. Remember, if you do exactly as I tell you, no one will get hurt."

"But you already hurt Mom...and Caesar," she cried.

"Now, now. Some things have to be done. Like I said, you'll understand it all sooner or later. Let's go back with the rest of the family, shall we?"

In the family room, Arthur and Beth sat in their highback mahogany dining chairs, with their hands zip-tied behind them. Jeremy just watched TV, as Calder ordered him to do. He was wearing headphones because Calder thought it best for him not to hear what was going on. It was clear that Jeremy's attention was not on the TV, though, as he glanced back every time he thought his dad was not looking.

"Let the children go, Donald. They've done nothing wrong." Beth pleaded.

"Shut up, old woman."

At that point, Jeremy looked up to see what made his daddy growl at his grandma, but when his dad pointed toward the TV, he went back to pretending to watch the silly cartoon sponge talking to an overgrown starfish.

"Donald, you're sick. You need help," Arthur said.

Calder backhanded Arthur hard with the barrel of the gun, causing everyone to jump. Finally, realizing something bad was really happening, Jeremy began to cry, but when Calder walked over to comfort his son, the boy again ran to his sister.

"Leave him alone," Lacy said, glaring at her father.

Calder pulled out a roll of duct tape and applied it to his in-law's mouths so he wouldn't have to listen to them anymore. They had never really accepted him, but the loathing was mutual. "I should just shoot you both and take the children right now," he whispered into Arthur's ear. "Your time's coming, you old geezer. Your time's coming, but if you play nice, I might let you watch me kill your bitch wife before I put an end to you."

Arthur struggled and protested against the duct tape, drawing another jack-o-lantern smile across Calder's face.

Calder looked around the room and saw the hate in everyone's eyes, but his son was only wearing a look of confusion.

"Daddy, why?" Jeremy asked; a question that went unanswered.

"When Kroh gets here," Calder said to the terrified Lacy, "I want you to go to the front door and invite him in. Remember, if you warn him in any way, if you let him know I'm here, I'll shoot Grandma first. That's a promise. You saw what happened to the doggie when he didn't cooperate."

A short while later, the doorbell rang, and Calder nodded to Lacy. She gave Jeremy a little hug, and then slowly got up to answer the door.

"Remember what Daddy told you now," Calder said as she left the room. He then pushed the barrel of the gun against her grandmother's head, just to emphasize the point, and the old woman's eyes filled with tears.

Lacy paused for a moment, nodded, and continued to the front door.

When the door opened, I couldn't help but think of how well the pretty young lady was keeping it together under all the pain she had to be suffering. "Hey, Lacy. Are you okay?"

I asked straightaway, when I noticed a strange look in her eyes. I expected to see a deep sadness there, but I saw nothing; it was as if she had somehow shut off her emotions altogether.

"As well as can be expected, I guess," she answered. "Grandma and Grandpa are in the family room. Follow me."

I followed her to the family room, and my eyes grew wide with shock. "What the hell's going on?"

Calder stood up from behind Beth and aimed his gun straight at my chest. "Welcome, Agent Kroh. I'm so glad you could join us for this little family reunion."

I started to move toward him but stopped when Calder placed the barrel of the gun against the grandmother's temple.

"Careful, Kroh. I certainly don't want to mess up this lovely carpet with pieces of Grandma's brain."

The scene was surreal, and I took it all in slow motion, doing all I could to determine some sort of escape that would bring no harm to the innocents. There were Arthur and Beth, with duct tape over their mouths and clearly tied to the wooden chairs. I looked behind him and saw the maid, also bound and taped, and the family dog was dead, with a bullet hole in its head. *Fuck!* I thought.

My mind was racing. I could see that Calder was out of control, and I wasn't sure the others, including his children, were safe from his wrath. "Your problem is with me, Calder. Leave them out of it," I finally said.

"If you do exactly what I say, I promise that no harm will come to them."

"Well, it seems you have the upper hand in this little game you're playing, so tell me what you want me to do."

"First things first. Lacy, we're going to fasten your brother to the leg of your grandmother's chair," he said, handing her three zip-ties. "Put one around each wrist, just tight enough so he can't get loose. Then put his arms around the leg of the chair and zip-tie his wrists together."

Lacy looked at me, and I nodded.

"Don't look at him! When I tell you to do something, young lady, just do it. Goddamn it, you're worse than your stubborn mother!" Calder screamed.

It pained me to see the fear in the children's eyes, especially Jeremy's. His innocence was taking another major hit in less than a month's time. First, he lost his mother, and now, the man who was once everything to him was threatening to harm his sister and grandparents.

Lacy walked Jeremy over to Beth's chair and gently told him to get on his knees and place his arms behind the legs of the chair. She sobbed as she placed the zip-tie on his thin wrists.

"Thank you, Lacy. Now, take these zip-ties, and tie Agent Kroh's wrists together behind his back, just like you did with Jeremy. You can make his as tight as you want."

"I'm sorry, Kroh," Lacy said, with tears running down her face as I reluctantly turned around to allow it.

"Just do as he says, and everything will be all right."

"Don't feel sorry for him, Lacy. He's the cause of everything bad that has happened in our lives. If it weren't for him, we would still be a happy family. Agent Kroh took that away from us, so he deserves to die," Calder said before he walked up and kicked me in the stomach, knocking me against the wall.

I had just enough time to tighten my stomach muscles so the blow didn't hurt as much as it normally would have, but the hardwood trim on the wall did a number on me when my head slammed against it, and I slid to the floor, a little groggy.

"And you said I could never be a field agent." He laughed. "I've accomplished things you can only dream of, and I dangled carrots that led you and the Federal Bureau of Idiots wherever I desired. I can be anyone I want to be. I have multiple IDs, and I've learned to change my appearance so I can walk right past you without the slightest recognition. Did you even know I was watching when those old men shamed you in basketball at that park?"

My mind suddenly jolted back to Pulaski Park in Anderson. *He was the man with the limp? Shit!*

"Did you feel it, Kroh? Every death that happened by my hand was you by proxy. Did your famous gut instinct tell you that?"

"Bullshit! You killed them because you're a sick son-of-a-bitch," I spat, "and a rebellious coward, pouting because you didn't get your way."

Ignoring the insult, he continued, "One after another, as their lives drained from their bodies, I saw only you. Each death brought me closer to you. Face it, Kroh, I have controlled you like a puppet, pulling this string and that to bring you right here, to this moment."

"Do you even know how sick that sounds, Calder? You're a fucking maniac," I said, not bothering to mind my language for the sake of the children, since I was sure they'd heard worse already from their biological father.

Calder seemed to experience some involuntary second of thought but just as quickly pushed it away. "Each death was necessary to right the wrong that was brought upon my family."

"What about the president's grandchild and the three innocent computer techs?"

"John could have stopped this from the beginning, but he didn't. Did he think of my family? No! He only cared for his image. Fuck him!" he said with a growl. "As far as the computer techs, fuck them too!"

"What about the mother of your children?"

"Fuck her most of all! In fact, that was what she was doing when I offed her, fucking someone else after she dumped our kids off with these two," he said, pointing at Beth and Arthur. "She abandoned me when I needed her the most, then jumped into another man's arms. She deserved to die, just as you do. Once I remove you from this world, I will disappear. I have more money than I'll ever need and a whole lifetime to spend it, living as anyone I can conjure up."

"I have to admit that you've accomplished a lot since you lost your mind...seven molesters, three innocent computer techs, a would-be kidnapper, a Russian mobster, your wife, and the man who made her happy. That makes what, a baker's dozen, thirteen of them? Truly, that's a legacy that any psychopath should be proud of. Tell me, though, Calder, if they were all deaths by proxy and you only wanted me, what are these four doing here? You have me, so let them go."

"Just to be clear, I am ten times the man Reynolds was. My wife was just a whore. As for letting people go, I am in control here, not you!"

"Okay, but why not just take me and leave them here? They're your children, for God's sake!"

"Shut up!"

"What happened to you, Calder? You were a good agent and father once."

"I'm still a good father, Goddamn it! Look at all I've done for them."

"I don't think they see it that way. Look at them. They're afraid of you," I said, words that seemed to strike a nerve as he looked at his wide-eyed, sobbing son and daughter. "What would *your* father say about this, about what you've become?"

At that point, all the anger that had welled up inside Lacy seemed to reach its boiling point, and she launched herself at her father, screaming and scratching. "You killed Mom, you bastard! You killed my mother!"

He backhanded her hard, knocking her to the floor, but she just held her face and refused to cry. Furious, he reached down and grabbed her by the wrist and dragged her to grandpa's chair. "Put your arms around the leg. Do it now, Goddamn it!" he barked. He zip-tied her tight and looked at her with hate in his eyes. "Maybe none of you deserve to live, but first, I need to take care of you, Kroh."

As he started toward me, Arthur stretched out his legs and tripped him. Calder grunted and stumbled down on all fours, his face a picture of rage. He grabbed the gun, turned, and pushed himself up to his feet, then rushed in Arthur's direction.

I knew I had to do something quickly, if the old man was going to be spared and the children were going to be saved from losing someone else in their young lives. I charged at him, and Calder barely registered that I was moving toward him before I drove my shoulder into the small of his back. I landed on top of him and heard him exhale forcefully. I scrambled to get up, with my hands still tied behind my back, doing all I could to incapacitate the monster before he hurt anyone else.

Calder wildly scrambled to look for his gun, then suddenly went statue still, his eyes wide. "Lacy?" he said, aghast.

Lacy had freed herself, and was now holding the gun on her father. With a bruise blossoming on her right cheek and tears pouring from her eyes, she stood before him, trembling with grief and anger.

I quickly worked my butt through my arms, followed by my legs. As soon as I could move more freely, I stepped toward her. "Lacy, honey, give me the gun."

"No! You'll just send him to court, and they'll say he's crazy and let him out in a month or something. He deserves to die for killing Mom and Brad and all those other people."

"Lacy, you don't want to do this."

"No, you don't understand. I said some mean things to Mom before I left for the weekend. Because of Dad, I never had a chance to say I was sorry."

"Lacy, sweetheart, please give me the gun," Calder said, reaching toward her.

"Shut up!" she screamed as she fired a shot into the ceiling. "You killed Mom, so just shut up!" Again, she leveled the gun at Calder, and again he stepped back, his eyes even wider than before.

"Lacy, please listen to me. This isn't the right way. You don't want to do this. Please give me the gun." I slowly moved toward her and carefully reached out and put my hands on hers, then slowly took the gun away.

"But I... I couldn't say I was sorry, and I loved her, and..." She collapsed to the floor, sobbing uncontrollably.

Calder lunged forward in an instant, trying to grab the weapon from me, but I twisted just in time to catch him on the chin with a hard elbow. That startled him, and he went down hard.

"Hold it right there, Calder!" someone yelled, and I was thrilled to see Zee and Vernon bursting into the room, while two other FBI agents came in from the rear entrance. "You so much as blink, I'll splatter your ugly mug all over the damn wall," Zee said. "I figure I owe you that anyway, you sick son-of-a-bitch."

I handed Zee Calder's gun, then reached down to help Lacy to her feet. I put my zip-tied arms over her head and hugged her tightly. After she calmed down a little, I gave her one more little hug, and then lifted my arms over her head. "Care to cut me loose?" I said with a smile.

"Sure," Lacy said, smiling as she took a pair of wire cutters from her pocket. She gave me another quick hug after she freed me, and then she made quick work of letting the rest of her family go.

Vernon grabbed the remaining zip-ties in Calder's back pocket and used one to secure his hands behind his back. He then pulled Calder up by the zip-tie, causing him to scream in pain. As Zee and Vernon led Calder from the room, he did not look at his children, but the anger in his eyes threatened to kill me where I stood. They quickly ushered him out of the house and into the car.

Once everyone was released, the family shared a group hug, and I sat on the couch watching while Zee checked out the knot growing on back of my head.

A little while later, Arthur walked up to me, a bit confused. "One thing I don't understand. Why did Lacy have wire cutters? That's not the kind of thing most girls carry around, you know."

"I slipped them to her as I came into the house."

Arthur thought for a second. "How did you know to bring them?"

Lacy walked up as Arthur asked the question, and she was clearly feeling better. "I told him to, Grandpa."

"Do you remember the last time I was here, when Lacy walked me out to the car?" I asked.

Arthur sat down on the couch next to me and nodded. "Yeah, why?"

"Well, I told her that if she ever needed me and her dad was listening, she should say, 'This is so hard to deal with.' That was her signal, to let me know her dad was here. The wire cutters were really just a lucky guess. He's used zip-ties before. Anyway, you should be very proud of her, Arthur. I know I am," I said, smiling at them both.

Arthur grabbed his granddaughter and hugged her close. "I've always been proud of her."

"Sorry about the hole in the ceiling, Grandpa," she said, looking a little worried.

"It was well worth it. Your dad just about shit himself." He started to laugh, and soon we were laughing with him.

Once everyone was okay and the crime scene detectives were there, Lacy walked me to my car again, obviously still a little shaken.

"I meant what I said back there. I'm very proud of you, Lacy. I really believe that if you didn't handle yourself that way, we'd all be dead. I think the bravest thing you did, though, was not shooting your dad."

"Yeah, thanks for stopping me. I really wanted to kill him right then," she said, frowning.

"I know, but it's better this way," I comforted her with a smile, and a hug. "Also, I know your mother knew you didn't mean those nasty words you spoke to her before you left. Mothers know these things, and she forgave you the moment it happened. That's what moms do, because they love us. That love she had for you, and you for her, will last forever. If there is life after we leave this Earth, I'm sure she is looking down on you and is so very proud. I only regret that your father ruined what remains of your childhood, forced you to grow up too fast. Yours and Jeremy's lives will be different now. The things you used to see as important will seem silly now, but it's really how you react to all these changes that will define you. Just embrace your life the way it is now, and you'll be stronger for it, for what you've been through. A wise person once said that what doesn't kill us makes us stronger."

"Hmm. So, my dad literally made me stronger then, huh?" she said with a smirk.

"I guess so," I answered. "I have to go now, but remember that you have my number, and you can call me anytime, even just to talk. Hopefully, we won't need signal words anymore."

I gave her one last hug, waved to Jeremy and his grandparents, then climbed in my car, relieved that Calder was in custody. I could have gone to confront him then, but I really didn't have the stomach for it. *Tomorrow will be soon enough,* I told myself as I pulled away.

Chapter 52

Later that evening, as I sat on Crystal's couch listening to Sinatra wail, "New York, New York..." I received a call I wasn't expecting.

"First of all, good job, Agent Kroh," Director Santiago said. "Of course, I didn't expect anything less, coming from you."

"Thank you, sir."

"Is this line secure?"

"Yes, sir."

"Good. I have someone here who would like to talk to you."

"Oh?" I said, at a loss. The director was not a man of many words. Not only that, but he was insanely busy, someone who typically said his piece in a hurry then moved on to the next thing. This time, he was handing the phone to someone on his end, so we could have a conversation.

After a bit of static and commotion, I heard a familiar voice: "Agent Kroh, this is John Burns. I want to thank you for your service to this country and for capturing the man who would have seen my grandson killed."

"I was just doing my job, Mr. President."

"Like I told your friend Marty, bullshit! You and your team not only captured an insane madman, but you also saved my grandbaby. Your modesty is admirable, Kroh, but it certainly isn't necessary."

"Thank you. I will pass this along to my team."

"I would like to ask you a favor."

"Anything, Mr. President."

"I would like you to be there when I see Calder. Can you do that for me?"

"It would be my pleasure, sir."

"Thank you again, Agent Kroh. I owe you a big one. I'm going to hand the phone back to Director Santiago now. Just keep doing what you're doing, and this nation will be better for it."

"Yes, sir!"

The director finished up with me quickly after that, and all I could do was sit there, dumbfounded and smiling from ear to ear like a goof, basking in the glory of presidential kudos. I couldn't wait to pass along the president's high praise. I thought about calling Marty to book a flight to DC for me, but figured I'd be told when to appear; besides, I knew he'd just rub it in that I didn't get a bitchin' cellphone like he did. Not only that, but I couldn't help but wonder why the POTUS wanted me there when he spoke to Calder. Something in my gut told me there was more to the story than Calder being walked away from his in-laws and children in a zip-tie.

I walked into the Indy field office feeling good. Calder had been transferred there the night before, and I wondered if he was still there. I also couldn't stop thinking about the president's odd request. *What does that mean? I mean, won't his Secret Service be with him? Surely, he isn't just scared.*

The office seemed extra busy, with everyone scurrying around like dizzied mice. I knocked on Supervisory Special Agent in Charge Chuck Harris's door, and when he invited me in, I was surprised to see that he already had noteworthy company, namely Director Santiago and President Burns himself. I had assumed Calder would be transferred to DC for the meeting, but now I knew I was wrong.

President Burns stood, and as I shook his hand, he pulled me in for a hug. I was a little taken aback by the show of emotions from the most powerful man in the world, but he had acted the same way with Marty. I knew the hug was really meant for my whole team, everyone who had contributed to finally catching Calder, and I made a mental note to pass the president's high praise along to all of them. "I still can't thank you enough, Agent Kroh."

"It was my pleasure, Mr. President, but it was a team effort."

"I know, and I have instructed the director to send my gratitude to all those involved."

"Sir, not to be forward, but along with my team, there were state and local law enforcement involved, all vital to Calder's apprehension. Can we make sure they are recognized?"

"Just give me a list, and I'll make sure they are included."

"Thank you, sir."

After a little small talk, we walked down the hallway, to a door flanked by two armed guards. As we entered, I noticed that the room had no windows and was obviously soundproof, and the security cameras in the room had obviously been disabled. In the middle of the room sat Calder, shackled to a chair that was bolted to the floor. When he noticed the president walking into the room, he looked away.

President Burns walked up to Calder and stared at him for a moment. "Un-cuff him," he said to the guards.

"That's not going to happen, sir," Director Santiago responded.

"Damn it, I said un-cuff this man now!" the president barked.

At that moment, I realized we were no longer in the room with President John Burns. The most powerful man in the world was now just an enraged grandpa, ready to rain hellfire and brimstone down on the man who dared to traumatize the baby he adored.

Director Santiago reluctantly nodded to the guards flanking Calder. They un-cuffed his hands and legs but remained close and at the ready, just in case the crazy man tried anything crazy.

Calder said nothing and purposely avoided eye contact with his old friend.

"Donald, stand up and face me."

Calder sighed and slowly stood but still would not look Burns in the eye.

"I don't know if I will ever understand how your life came

to this, Don, but I'm trying. My friends and family told me you were using me, even when we were children, but I did not believe them. I truly believed you were my friend. I know you think I abandoned you after your news conference during The Fingertip Killer case, but nothing can be farther from the truth. You screwed up, and my hands were tied. If you were in your right mind, you could see that what you have done is very wrong. You're sick, Donald. I have no idea what drove you to do the terrible things you've done, but I hope whatever God you worship will forgive you. I, however, cannot. You tried to kill my grandson, for God's sake. There will be no pardon for you in my heart."

Calder finally glared into the eyes of the president. "Fuck you and your grandson."

What happened next was a beautiful thing.

The president hit Calder square in the jaw, and not a man in the room moved a muscle to stop the assault. "That's for my grandson, you deranged bastard!"

After a second, the guards moved in to restrain Calder, but the president held up his hand. Calder lunged toward Burns, but the president was remarkably agile and swift, and he easily blocked the punch and hit Calder again, so hard he fell to the floor.

"I want you to know, Don, that I will do everything in my power to make sure you never taste freedom again." With that, the president resumed is professional demeanor, turned away from Calder, and walked toward the door.

Again, Calder lunged at him, but I caught him just under the chin with a violent clothesline worthy of the WWE and hurled him onto his back, so hard it knocked the wind out of him. "And that's for Zee, asshole!" I said, looking down at him.

Not too gently, and with one of them snickering under his breath, the guards pulled Calder to his feet.

"I-I'm going to get out of this, John," Calder threatened weakly, with blood oozing from a cut in his lip, "and when I do, I'm going to kill your whole family."

"No, Don. You will die in a cage, like the pathetic little animal you are," the president said before he walked through the door, followed by his security team, never looking back.

Before the director left the room, he looked at all of us sternly. "This never happened, gentlemen," he said. He then looked straight at me, smiled and said, "Right, Kroh?"

"I didn't see a thing, sir," I said with a grin.

Chapter 53

Calder's capture was the top story on every news channel, and our favorite reporter, Zach Tanner, was one of the first to offer his coverage. "For over two months," he said, "the world has been shaken by evil. What started as an apparent vigilante killing of child predators along Interstate 69 turned out to be nothing more than a psychopath on a killing spree. He killed seven child predators, three innocent computer techs, a man he employed to kidnap the president's grandchild, and, finally, he brutally murdered his ex-wife and her friend. Along with the thirteen dead, he also attempted to kill two federal agents. I can only imagine how many more would have died at his hand, if not for these brave men and women of law enforcement. We must wonder about the state of mind that would cause a person to venture down such a path of demented evil. Thankfully, two days ago, former Special Agent Donald Calder was captured and is in custody. Due to the diligent work of cooperating law enforcement agencies, the man once known as The Guardian of I-69 was brought to justice. Here to say a few words is Special Agent Benjamin Kroh."

I stepped to the mic and smiled at the crowd. "Everyone in law enforcement is glad to see this investigation come to an end. Calder, as a former agent of the Bureau, gave a black eye to everyone who wears a badge. Law enforcement agencies in Michigan, Indiana, Ohio, and DC worked together to bring this man to justice, and I am proud to work alongside so many people who are willing to sacrifice time with their loved ones to bring cases like this to their conclusions. Cooperation between these law enforcement agencies was vital to the apprehension of Donald Calder. I say to you all, thank you for a job well done. I thank you, and the world thanks you." Then, I stepped away from the mic, smiled my thanks to Mr. Tanner, and walked away.

* * *

At six thirty, Bradford, Vernon, Zee, Crystal, and I sat in my makeshift office at the Anderson PD. Marty joined us via the Smartboard. We were all smiles after watching my appearance on Channel 5.

Bradford reached into a paper sack and pulled out a bottle of whiskey. "You got 'em?" he asked, looking at Crystal.

"Sure do. Right here," she said, then set a stack of paper cups on his desk.

"Good. Then let's drink to a job well done."

He poured five exaggerated shots, and we each grabbed one. Meanwhile, Marty lifted a very expensive-looking goblet filled with what we presumed was a really nice wine.

Bradford raised his cup and said, "Even though I was not there when he was caught, I feel like we can all agree that it was me who solved the case...with a little help from you guys, of course."

Everyone laughed.

He continued, "Seriously, let's drink to all the people who worked night and day to bring this shit storm to a close."

We touched our cups together and drank to our success. We were six very happy people who had worked hard for two long months, and we were finally rewarded with a well-deserved victory. I looked around the room and wondered how I could be so lucky to have five good friends to share my life.

* * *

That evening, I just wanted to spend some time with Crystal. After having a late dinner at Famous Recipe, my new favorite chicken place, we relaxed on her sofa in front of the television.

"I just wish we could have caught him sooner."

"There is no way we could have known who he was or stopped any of the murders. You know that, right?"

"Yeah, I guess, but—"

"But nothing, Kroh. You did everything you could. Correction. *We* did everything *we* could, so stop beating yourself up."

I knew her words were true, but I couldn't stop thinking about Lacy and Jeremy. *If we had stopped Calder just a little sooner, their mother would be around to see them grow up.*

Crystal snuggled in close. "You know what this calls for, right?"

"No, what?"

"We-just-caught-the-bad-guy sex," she blurted, then promptly straddled my lap, pulled her shirt up over head, and sensually removed her bra. She pulled my face to hers for a wonderful kiss, and then moved her beautiful breasts into my face. "Right?" she asked again.

I couldn't possibly argue with that logic, so I simply answered, "Hey, when you're right, you're right."

I kissed her hard, not wanting to stop. The taste of her lips was everything I could have wished for in a million years. The lust quickly took control, and we both knew we were not going to make it to the bedroom. She moved on my lap, and not even the clothes that separated our bodies could stop the desire. We feverishly tore at our clothes and were soon naked to the world, lost in total desire. Our bodies knew exactly what to do and precisely when to do it. Suddenly, she arched herself toward me, and I pushed hard against her. It was as if a thousand years of lust and desire found that one moment in time to collide in an orgasmic explosion. Our bodies convulsed in sweet ecstasy.

It was a long time until I finally rolled over and just held her to me. Maybe it was the culmination of an intense case or it was just the right time and place, but it was amazing, and I told her so. "That was just... Wow," I said.

She looked into my eyes, conflict blazing in hers. "You know I love you, don't you, Kroh boy?"

"And I love you, Crystal," I said, hoping to settle the questions I saw in her eyes. I knew it was true, because since I met her, I had thought of no one else. I again kissed her hard, and a wonderful feeling of satisfaction and contentment washed over me.

Chapter 54

On Sunday, the Kroh compound was the site of a most beautiful get-together. Knowing summer was quickly coming to an end, we pulled out all the stops. The sizzling steaks, burgers, and hotdogs had drivers-by honking their appreciation of the aroma. Everyone was there, Noah and his family, Marty and Andrea, and Bradford and Lillie, along with Charlie, their grandson. Both my uncles managed to gather their children and grandkids as well. The barbecue was alive with celebration and togetherness, a happy occasion we'd long remember.

Little did I know that I was also in for another surprise. Ed Beckman and a lady friend, along with Archie Pembrook and his wife, pulled in the drive right as the lunch bell rang. I was overjoyed to see them and hurried to make all the proper introductions so everyone could get back to enjoying our wonderful day.

After some good conversation while we digested the feast, the children pushed me into the pool. I had my suspicions about who put them up to it, since I saw Crystal and Zee whispering to them just before it happened, but I really didn't mind at all. It was a warm day, and the water was refreshing. In fact, it wasn't long before everyone else joined us in the pool.

With her sons, grandchildren, and great-grandchildren all in one place, my grandma was beaming. It was a wonder she had time to do all she did to make the barbecue a success and still make sure her loved ones got all the love and hugs that were humanly possible. She left no one out, including me.

When Pops was free from grill duty, he talked and played with the great-grandchildren like he was a kid himself. I couldn't help but remember my younger days, when he did the same with me, and I almost envied the little ones. There were "A" grandparents and "B" grandparents, and it was plain to see that Grandma and Pops were the former, with a big plus sign behind it.

After an afternoon of swimming, basketball, and touch football with the kids, we were all ready for dinner. I was good at lunch and only ate a couple hamburgers, some potato salad, and tossed salad, but that was only because I wanted to save room for steak. Pops was a master on the grill, and when he pulled my twenty-ounce, bone-in ribeye off the grill, it was perfection. I had no idea what anyone else was eating, because as soon as that first bite hit my taste buds, I was suddenly alone in the universe.

Almost everyone had planned for a long weekend, so only my uncles and their families were in a hurry to leave. Since the girls prepared most of the feast, other than the meat that Pops insisted on handling, it was the job of the guys to clean up. After we finished, we relaxed on the deck. While the kids chased fireflies in the early evening, the adults enjoyed our favorite beverages and good conversation.

When no children were within earshot, I decided to let the gang in on a little secret. "You remember when I told you about the president calling me to be with him when he met with Calder?"

"Yeah," Bradford answered, wondering where I was going with it.

"Well, I did, and the president kicked the shit out of him."

"What!?" Pembrook asked.

"It was great. The pres just laid him out."

"No way! John Burns?" Bradford asked.

"I kid you not."

"What happened?" Vernon asked, literally on the edge of his seat, as they all were.

"Well, Burns told them to take the cuffs off Calder. The

director said, 'No way,' but the president argued, 'Damn it. Do it!'"

"So, they did?" Crystal asked.

"Oh yeah."

"Then what happened?" Zee asked.

"Burns told Calder to stand and face him. Calder wouldn't even look him in the eye as they stood toe to toe. The president talked about their past together, ending with the attempt on his grandson."

"And Calder just stood there the whole time, tight-lipped?" Noah asked.

"No. You know that asshole. He can't hold his tongue when he feels berated. He eventually flared up and told Burns, 'Fuck you and your grandson'. That was when the commander-in-chief gave him a presidential pop in the jaw."

"Way to go, Burns!" Noah said. "I know who has my vote next time."

"Are you serious, Kroh?" Vernon asked, impressed.

"If I'm lyin', I'm dyin'. Then the guards moved in to grab Calder, but Burns waved them off. Calder took a swing at the President, and Burns blocked it easily and hit him again, putting Calder down. Then, just like that, Burns straightened his tie, turned, and headed out the door."

"That is so cool," Crystal said, smiling.

"Yeah, I know, but that's not all."

"There's more?" they all seemed to ask at once.

"Oh yeah. As Burns was walking away, Calder screamed like a madman, jumped past the guards, and charged the president full bore."

"Holy shit! Did he get to him?" Pops asked.

"No, because I clotheslined him."

"What? No way!" Crystal offered.

"Yes way. Then I looked down at him and said, 'That's for Zee, asshole.'"

Zee hugged me. "Aw. My hero."

"There's just one thing."

"What?" Vernon asked.

"Promise you'll never breathe a word of this to anyone. It was done totally...off the record. Before he left the room, the director looked at me and said, 'This never happened.'" I then raised my hands, signaling that I was telling the absolute truth.

After a great day, and after I had their assurance that they would keep Calder's fate to themselves, we talked and laughed long into the night. *Am I a lucky guy or what?* I thought as I laid my head back on my chair, surrounded by my family and friends. It was a perfect day, and there, under the stars, I made a wish that we'd all enjoy many more perfect days to come.

Die by Proxy

PART FOUR

Epilogue

Chapter 55

Calder sat in his seven-by-twelve cell at ADX Florence, the federal supermax prison located in Fremont County, Colorado. He was completely alone. No one wanted anything to do with him, not even what remained of his family. It was hard for him to believe he had fallen so far in such a short time. Not so long ago, he was a respected supervisory special agent of the FBI, but now, he was serving three life sentences, without the possibility of parole. He was granted leniency for saving the children and sentenced for only the computer techs. *Without the possibility of parole? It may as well be 100 life sentences then.* He had almost no contact with the outside world, and that included no return letters from his children, to whom he'd written multiple times.

He looked around the cage that he already knew by heart. It was constructed mostly of poured concrete, and his bed, stool, and desk were designed so no inmate could use them for anything but their intended purposes. His only view to the outside world was a sliver of a window, constructed of reinforced, bulletproof glass, about four feet tall but only four inches wide, not a possible escape route at all. He was confined to his cell twenty-three hours a day, with one hour of exercise in a concrete pit, also designed so prisoners could catch a glimpse off the sky, that broad, open expanse that seemed to mock their freedom as the clouds billowed by. His cell had the added security of a vestibule. Three foot inside a solid steel door was a solid steel bar door, and that gave guards an extra layer of protection when dealing with the monsters they had to handle on a daily basis

During his first six months at Florence, Calder proved to be a model prisoner. For that, he was granted the use of a black and white television, though he was only treated to religious or educational programs. Mostly, he preferred to read; that was the only thing that kept him sane.

Something seemed different, as Chris, the guard who treated Calder with the least animosity, smiled when he brought one of his three hot meals for the day. "Calder, you got mail," Chris said, pushing the letter through the bars with his tray of olive drab goop that was supposed to be a meal. Truth be told, Chris didn't really have a problem with Calder. In fact, he believed the man did a great service killing those molesters. Not only that, but he didn't like the president that much anyway.

Calder sat on his bunk for a minute and stared at the envelope, in shock. Then, just as Chris turned to leave, Calder jumped up and moved toward the bars. He looked into the friendly guard's eyes as a tear threatened to escape his own. "Thanks, Chris," he said.

"Calder, the funny thing is that the letter was folded into one of those kids' games. You'll probably have to fold it back to read your message."

After Chris nodded and moved on, Calder returned to his bunk and stared at the envelope again, his first contact from the outside world since he arrived there, other than his lawyer, who visited as often as he could. Of course, the letter had already been opened and examined by prison personnel, checked for any foreign substances or undesirable content, but it didn't matter. Finally, someone was reaching out to him.

He didn't recognize the handwriting right away, and there was no return address. He hoped like hell it was not some crackpot looking to get his or her jollies by corresponding with a serial killer. He had seen it before, lonely ladies finding love with convicted criminals, their only contact those rare, awkward conjugal visits, fucking in state-funded trailers with guards right outside the door, like breeding livestock in a barn stall. *What kind of life would that be?* In his eyes, jailhouse romances were a joke, but he assured himself that he didn't have to worry about that, since the United States didn't allow conjugal visits with federal prisoners anyway.

The minutes passed as he continued to stare at the letter. Finally, his need for some kind of contact from the outside world overpowered his desire to prolong the anticipation. He slowly reached into the envelope and pulled document from within. He noticed that there were fold lines all over the letter. He briefly wondered why that came to his attention, but dismissed it, deciding that it was due to the rarity of the gift he'd been given.

He looked at the letter and noticed that it was not typed. The handwriting was beautiful, but it was jumbled. Then he remembered what Chris said: *"It was folded into one of those kids' games."* It took him a moment to remember how to fold it properly. He had made fortune tellers with Lacy long ago. Even though the memory was a sad one, he was too excited to dwell on the past. Once it was folded, he marveled at it for a moment.

He worked the game and started to read, in a barely audible whisper, "I need to thank you for keeping your promise. You have done much to remove a great weight from a loved one's load. I knew you were broken. I knew that when we first met. I just did not realize how badly. I hope you find peace in whatever life is yours to live. I am sorry to tell you that this is the last you will hear from me. Please do not try to try to contact me. Nevertheless, thank you, thank you, and thank you again. C."

He knew in an instant that Cassondra sent it, and he read it again and again. He desperately wished, more than ever before, that he could have gotten to know her better. Of all the people he knew in the world, she was the only one he truly wanted to see. The world accused him of not having a heart, but he knew he did, because in the short time he knew Cassondra, she had strummed the strings of it, leaving a warm and lasting impression on him. It was not sexual but, rather, a family closeness.

Of the few possessions he was allowed to keep in his cell, the letter from Cassondra, would become his most prized, and it became his ritual in short order to read it every day, just before the lights went out. Now, the paper she once touched was all Calder had to hang on to. If he held it close to his face, he could smell the faint scent of the perfume she wore.

The End

Made in the USA
Middletown, DE
06 May 2023